Blood Daughter

Flesh and Blood Trilogy Book Three

Dreda Say Mitchell

HODDER

First published in Great Britain in 2017 by Hodder & Stoughton
An Hachette UK company

1

Copyright © Mitchell and Joseph Ltd 2017

The right of Dreda Say Mitchell (Emma Joseph) and Anthony Mason
to be identified as the Authors of the Work has been asserted by them
in accordance with the Copyright, Designs and Patents Act 1988.

A CIP catalogue record for this title is available from the British Library

Paperback ISBN 978 1 473 62572 3
eBook ISBN 978 1 473 62571 6

Typeset in Rotis Serif by Hewer Text UK Ltd, Edinburgh
Printed and bound byClays Ltd, St Ives plc

Hodder & Stoughton policy is to use papers that are natural, renewable
and recyclable products and made from wood grown in sustainable
forests. The logging and manufacturing processes are expected to
conform to the environmental regulations of the country of origin.

Hodder & Stoughton Ltd
Carmelite House
50 Victoria Embankment
London EC4Y 0DZ

www.hodder.co.uk

To all of you who have got in contact over the years,
who kept me going and who spread the word. Bless you all!

Prologue

Dee banged a spoon on the table to get Tiff and Jen's attention before things got out of hand. She realised the noise had attracted the attention of the other diners and lowered her voice.

'You see the problem here? I call us together for a constructive discussion on our little issue and it's already turning into a Millwall match. What's the matter, Tiffany? Why do you need money in a hurry?'

Tiff shrugged and sank the rest of the wine in her glass before topping herself up. 'I don't.'

'Look, we're adults here, and we're sisters. We shouldn't have any secrets. If you don't need it, why are you asking me for a loan?'

Tiffany downed her drink in one and turned blazing eyes on Dee. 'Oh that's right. Wash my dirty panties in public, why don't you.'

Jen sat back in triumph. 'I might have guessed. She's living on tick. No wonder she wants to fleece the rest of us. It's to pay her bills off.'

Tiffany decided she'd done with her glass and reached for the bottle, but it was empty. She shouted at a waiter: 'Oi you – the one dressed like a penguin – another couple of these please. And no, I don't want to taste it first.'

A ripple of disquiet went through the restaurant but the Miller sisters were too engrossed in their squabble to take a blind bit of notice.

Jen was jeering now. 'Same ol' little sis. No different now than when she was a kid. Won't do any work, so she lifts money off others. What a ponce.'

'Won't work? I was a mechanic 24/7 when all your money was supplied by that Keystone car thief Nuts. Where is he these days . . .? Oh yeah, he upped and fucked off.' She wriggled her head provocatively. 'And left little Miss Iceberg.'

Seeing Jen was on the point of exploding, Dee slammed her palm in the air to halt the mudslinging. 'Tiff, enough of the bitch fest.' She turned her gaze to Jen. 'There's obviously something giving you the nark, so please enlighten me.'

Jen thumped her glass down. 'I'll tell you what the bovver is. Do you know what it's like raising two kids on your own on a place like The Devil? It's like wading through quick-setting diarrhoea up to your knees. All day. Every day. You're alright for money. Tiffany would be alright if she wasn't a greed hound. But I'm not alright. I don't see why we should split the money three ways. Mum should've taken my situation into account and put something extra aside for my girls. It's not about me, it's about my kids. You wanna know what my problem is? It's other kids calling my girls tramps in the playground. And Mum and you two could solve it in the blink of an eye but it never even crossed your minds.'

'I see.' Dee didn't mean to sound like a headmistress with a couple of naughty school kids but she knew she did. 'Well, all of our cards are on the table now. Got to say I'm very disappointed at your attitude . . .'

All the bitterness and resentment that Jen had stoppered up for years burst out like a cork from a bottle. 'It's alright for you, shacked up with your gangster of a husband. You're not even really part of our family anyway, are you?'

Tiffany nodded in a rare moment of agreement. 'That's true actually. You're not.'

At the other tables, diners looked in horror as Dee rose to her feet and then slapped Tiffany very hard across the face. Stunned for a moment, Tiff rolled back before she stood up in turn. 'Oh, you've done it now. You want some, do ya? If you want some, you've got it.'

She took a swing at Dee, who raised one arm to protect herself and punched Tiff in the face with the other. Tiffany fell back in front of a shocked couple who ran for cover when they saw Dee moving in for the kill. Bottles, plates and glasses were scattered on the floor. But so focused was Dee on Tiffany that she didn't notice that Jen wanted in as well. She only felt a wallop across the back of her head.

That was it! World War Three had been declared and Dee knew who the victor would be.

She staggered over to another table and asked the dumb-struck guy sitting there, 'Excuse me mate, do you mind if I borrow this?' Without waiting for his consent, she took the decanter of brandy from him and emptied the contents on the floor. She held it by the neck and turned menacingly back to her sisters. 'You want to sort this out East End style do ya? Alright, let's see what you two fake Mike Tysons have got.'

With grim relish she advanced on them.

PART 1: 2006
A MONTH AGO

'She began to wonder if she'd made a terrible mistake.'

One

'Call that justice . . .'

  'You twat – a rapist gets half that . . .'

  'She should be getting a medal mate, not a prison sentence . . .'

The memories of the angry shouts her daughters had directed at the judge as he sentenced her to five years for the manslaughter of her former husband, Stanley Miller, rang in Babs' head that Tuesday morning as she nervously waited outside the room where the parole board was meeting. She'd so desperately wanted to call out to Dee, Jen and Tiff that five years wasn't so bad. It could've been much worse. She could have got life for murder rather than a knock-down to manslaughter. And despite doing her 'I'm sorry Milord' spiel for the benefit of the jury, she was glad Stanley was dead. May the bastard rot in hell.

But the impact on her beloved family had been devastating. She would never forget the expression on her beloved Kieran's face as he sat in the back row of the gallery. Worn and bloodless like the very life had been drained away from him. Kieran Scott had been like a son to her, Babs having taken him under her wing during his troubled childhood on The Devil's Estate. People called him a thug, a psycho, a wrong'un, but Babs had never seen it. He would forever be her little Kieran.

As Jen's heartbreaking sobs filled the courtroom, Babs had taken one final look up at the gallery and nearly fallen backwards at the sight of the woman looking back at her with Stan's fox-like eyes. Florence fucking Miller. His wrong-side-of-the-blanket daughter with that posh Islington tart. Flo was scowling and furiously chewing gum under a platinum-blonde wig. It seemed no one had recognised her apart from Babs. Just as well. If her girls had clocked her, there might've been another killing. She'd had the brass balls to smirk and mouth 'Bitch' as Babs was taken down.

Babs had been dreading prison. She was afraid of sharing a cell with smackhead shoplifters, hard nut toughs and the type of dopey puss who brings a suitcase full of coke back from Spain and then wails she didn't know what was in it. But as she'd been led down the steps, she remembered that she'd been sharing The Devil's Estate with women like that for the past couple of decades. How much worse could the slammer be?

She'd soon found out . . .

Babs was slammed into her cell wall. She gazed, terrified, into the face of one of the scariest women she had ever seen in her life. And she'd seen a few.

Drying-out junkie Shazza Logan had been creating ever since she'd been shipped from A to C Wing a couple of days back. Word was, she'd threatened to stick her fork into another girl's neck in a row over brekkie one morning. And now she'd barged into Babs' cell looking to do some serious damage.

Babs had known this was going to happen sooner or later. Violence was a way of life within the walls of HMP Shithole. She'd kept her head down and stayed well clear of trouble. That had been the advice given to her the first day here by the kangas. Kangaroo was the nickname the girls gave the prison officers. Why they were called that, Babs didn't know. Her mind was dizzy with all she had to learn about being a jailbird.

Her nerves were cracking up because it wasn't so easy to get a when-you-want-it supply of her steady pills.

'Where's my fucking lippy Miller?' Shazza snarled, spit frothing like a ruptured spot.

Like Babs would ever nab something that had touched this nutter's scabby skin, much less her mouth. God knows what she'd pick up.

'How the heck would I know?' Babs knew about standing up for herself, but normal rules didn't apply behind bars. Bullies might back down on the outside but in here they were more likely to go ape. So she knew she shouldn't but couldn't resist adding, 'What do you need lipstick for anyway? Ain't like you're going out raving tonight, is it?'

By way of reply, Shazza socked Babs in the gut, making her double over in pain. She almost collapsed, but made herself stand steadfast. The biggest way to become a target in here was to show weakness. The pain was crippling, but she couldn't allow herself to fall.

'Where is it? You wanna ask around, Saggy Tits? No one mixes it with me. Not if they wanna keep their head facing the right way.'

Breath ragged, Babs stared directly into her attacker's tight, mean eyes. 'Know what I think? You ain't come in here looking for no war paint.'

Shazza shoved her face so close Babs could smell the hooch that was illegally brewed in many a cell come lights-out. How anyone could stomach that stuff she would never know. It was rank, plain and simple, more likely to strip your stomach lining than give you a buzz.

'What you mouthing off about?'

'Since you landed on the wing I ain't never seen you wearing no lippy. The way I hear it you're a bit of a bitch ... Oops, I mean a butch.' Babs played it all innocent although the

slip-up was deliberate. She added, 'Nothing wrong with that. One of my daughters is one too.'

Shazza's face spread into a nasty smile that really did make her look like a lunatic. 'Palm me a tenner and we'll say no more about it.'

'A tenner? Cheap at half the price. Let's see what I've got squirrelled away under my mattress.'

Looney Tune let her go and stood back in triumph. Babs pushed off the wall, the muscles in her back and tummy aching. She moved towards her bunk but kept her head turned slightly to keep an eye on C Wing's newest nut job.

'Get a move on. This ain't a boozer on Saturday night,' Shazza growled, folding her arms.

Babs made her move. She turned on a sixpence and threw a punch into her attacker's face. Shazza barely stumbled. Oops! Babs' terror really kicked in.

'Oh dear Miller. It seems this is bash-a-granny week.'

Shazza launched herself forwards, grabbed Babs' hair and dragged her towards the cell door. Babs lashed out all the way but her blows had little effect. When they reached the door, Mad Bird used a trainer to edge it open. She seized Babs' hand and tried to shove it in the doorway. Realising what she was about, Babs began fighting back with all her might. The classic punishment for stealing from another inmate was to have your fingers broken. But this was wrong; she hadn't pinched anything.

'You better let me go,' Babs yelled, her last-ditch attempt to save herself.

'Or what?' Shazza growled back, 'you gonna go blubbing to the kangas?'

They both knew that she wouldn't. No one went running to the POs. If you did you were marked as a grass and that was the end. Babs started flagging as her hand was pulled closer *and closer to the doorway. With triumph Shazza flattened her fingers on the doorframe. Grabbed the cell door . . .*

The door was shoved back violently by one of the screws, propelling Babs and her attacker away. Thank fuck for that, Babs sighed mentally. She couldn't remember the name of the prison officer, but she was big, pure muscle and had a face that looked like badly mixed concrete.

Without a word she kicked the door shut and took out her retractable baton, snapping it to full length with a loud click. Babs cringed. She'd heard all about officers who liked to take the law into their own hands.

'Miss—' Babs started but never finished because the kanga advanced on Shazza and cracked her over the head. Taken by surprise, C Wing's wildest crashed to the floor. Babs covered her mouth in horror as the officer dished out the battering of a lifetime. Less than a minute later, big mouth Shazza was a silent, bloody mess.

Babs shrank back when the officer turned her attention to her. I'm for it now. She steeled herself for the attack. But it never came. Instead, the officer smiled.

'I'm Mrs Reagan. I run C Wing.' She snapped her baton back together. 'Mister Scott sends his regards. Any problems Babs, you come to me.'

'Miller.' The insistent voice of the kanga next to her drew Babs back to the present.

She missed Mrs Reagan watching her back but was pleased to have been shipped out of that hellhole to an open prison two weeks earlier. In HMP Hillsworth things were plenty different. The tabloids had dubbed it 'Her Majesty's Hilton' and the papers had a point. The regime was more light touch in this spanking new, privately run prison. There were discreet bars on the window and though she was under lock and key she had a good-sized cell all to herself. The ladies called their cells houses because they had their own TVs, radio, mini bathroom, a bedside unit and a desk that doubled up as a dressing table.

'They're ready for you,' the officer said.

Right, here goes! Babs squared her shoulders and entered the room where the parole – or 'jam roll' as it was called inside – board waited for her. She was about to smile, but then thought better of it; it wouldn't do to look like she was having the time of her life. She sat straight in the seat she was directed to but her hands couldn't seem to keep still. Her gaze darted fretfully between the two men and single woman in front of her, making her feel like she was back before a jury. The next half an hour sped past as she answered their questions in a daze:

'I've taken loads of courses and got my Level 3 certificate in English. Plus I'm working outside, on day release, in the memorial gardens.'

'In the prison before this one I saw the shrin— I mean the psych lady, Pam, every week to talk out my problems, especially about my obsession with keeping everything spic and span and tidy all the time.'

Babs shuddered, remembering how the filth of the previous prison had tipped her and her manic need for order over the edge. She'd tried her best to keep her cell clean, but the dirt and dust just seemed to breed and the cockroaches that crawled on her at night . . . She'd ended up spending a month on the funny farm ward that first year. Of course her girls were none the wiser; she'd been too ashamed to let on. The prison had got her into a support group for inmates with something called OCD. That first meeting had nearly blown her mind; some of the other girls' stories made her own problem look like a stroll in the park. She'd never heard the like. One woman had to chant to ten over and over, every time she got stressed out.

The whole group had choked up when she'd finally spilled her guts to explain that her problem had started with someone spitting on her in the street and the loss of her first child. Talking had done her the world of good. She wasn't cured but the need to be in control wasn't nearly as bad.

Babs answered the next question quickly. 'I keep a diary of any of the risk factors associated with my crime so I know when I might need a helping hand.' One of the other ladies on the Wing had told her to say 'risk factors' as many times as she could because jam roll boards liked it.

It was the woman who asked the final question, the only question that really mattered. Babs answered in a clear and firm voice.

'I deeply regret, to the bottom of my heart, what I did to Stanley Miller.'

If I had my time again I'd do it all over again.

'He didn't deserve to die like that.'

Nah, I should've stabbed a stake right through the fucker's cold-blooded heart.

When the meeting finally came to an end Babs felt wrung out. She prayed hard that she'd done enough to secure an early release. She missed her family so much. And it was thinking about her daughters that made her reach a momentous decision. It was time to have a sit-down with them to tell them the news she'd been holding back for the past three years.

She turned to the prison officer and said, 'I wanna see the Number One.'

TWO

'Alright you wankers! Let's roll!'

The bulldozer lurched forward, picking up speed as it careered towards the wrought iron gates set in thick concrete walls of the security depot. The joint they were crashing had no signs to show what kind of business it was. But Kieran Scott, known to his makeshift crew only as 'the Boss', knew full well what went on in there. It was a private vault, the kind used by dodgy people who wanted to keep their property away from authority's prying eyes.

Kieran was perched on top of the JCB, dressed in black overalls, gloves and a crash helmet like the rest of his gang. Four other men held on for dear life while the driver stuck his foot down on the pedal. It didn't seem possible that even a vehicle of that size could take down the gates, but the guy who'd organised the raid had done his sums and promised Kieran that if they were hit at the right angle and at the right speed, they'd cave in.

But of course that guy wasn't there. It was Kieran taking all the risk.

They struck the gates, which squealed and tore but the fuckers wouldn't open. Kieran soon sussed out why. At the last moment, the prick at the wheel had braced for impact and eased his foot off the gas. And that meant there wasn't enough power when they collided. What a ponce!

Seething, Kieran grabbed him by the scruff of his neck and screamed, 'You yellow-bellied cunt!' That was the problem with the world these days – you couldn't get the staff, even for a robbery.

In disgust, he yanked the driver out and took over the controls, throwing the grinding gears into reverse and backing up. He looked up and down the industrial estate. Time mattered. Would it be five, ten minutes before the law turned up?

With no time to waste, when he'd got enough of a run up, he threw the gear stick forward and jammed his foot onto the accelerator. The walls of the depot loomed in front of him and the gates looked even hardier than they had before, but he didn't falter. He forced the pedal right down to the floor. Struck the gates again. The metal creased, buckled and bent while the tracks on the bulldozer furiously ground the concrete.

Kieran howled, 'Come on you fucker! Come on!'

As if obeying his command, the gates began to break open and the vehicle squeezed and lurched through the gap, throwing one of his boys off as they went through.

In the courtyard beyond, he headed for the shutters at the vehicle delivery point. They were partly open and two security guys were sitting on the parapet, staring in disbelief as he came storming through. They ran for their lives when Kieran ploughed the bulldozer's massive shovel into the gap and then lifted it upwards. The shutters sprang and rolled as they were torn from their fittings.

His gang jumped off and ran into the unit, shouting and waving sawn-offs. The boys went to key points so they could keep the place covered. They knew exactly where they were. One of the gang headed to the security office to stop the alarms being set off and they knew exactly where that was too. Kieran himself ran to the manager's office, a route he knew like the back of his hand from the model of the premises safely tucked away at his club. Inside, a middle-aged man in a suit and tie was sitting at his desk with his chops wrapped around a sandwich. Kieran pointed the shotgun at him. 'I want vault 25a opened and I want it opened now. Don't fuck about.'

The guy didn't move. He sat like a statue as all the colour drained out of his face. Kieran pointed his gun at the ceiling and let off one barrel. The office shook with deafening thunder and bits of ceiling and light bulb scattered down. He waited a few seconds for effect before pulling the trigger again. Another roar and more debris. The office looked as if the builders were in. After he'd loaded two more shells, Kieran walked around and pressed the hot barrels into the bloke's ear. 'I don't know what kind of money you're on mate but I bet it's not enough to get your head blown off for.'

The manager whimpered. 'I can't get you into the vaults. There's a time delay.'

Kieran was confident. 'You're a liar. There's no time delay.' He knew everything about this place. He took the sandwich out of the guy's hand, opened it up and showed it him. 'You see that tomato? That's the colour your head's going to be in a few seconds if you don't get me down there. You know I mean it bruv.'

As if he'd put his hand into a plug socket, the manager sprang up and led Kieran down a corridor. He pressed numbers on a keypad and went down a flight of stairs. At the bottom were steel security doors. Another number and they were inside, walking past rows and rows of deposit boxes. But Kieran wasn't interested in them. He was on strict instructions only to take what was in vault 25a. The bloke who'd organised the raid had warned him, 'Don't touch nuthin else. You might upset the wrong sort of people. Know what I mean?'

When he first walked into 25a, clutching his sports bag, Kieran found what seemed to be army surplus crates. They were covered in dust and looked like they'd been there for ever. He pulled a jemmy out of his overalls and used it to prise open one of the boxes. Kieran knew what he'd find but he still stood stunned when he saw the contents. Like a little kid with a present on Christmas Day, he ran his fingertips over a gold bar and whispered, 'Look at that – they're real.'

Kieran ran back upstairs to find chaos. Someone had managed to trigger the alarms and there were so many red lights flashing, you would have thought there was a rave going on. The metal walls were vibrating to howling sirens and the security guards were emerging from their hiding places to see if it was safe to take the gang on. One of his boys ran up to him. 'Time's short boss, the law'll be here in a mo.'

For a few moments Kieran Scott hesitated. He hadn't expected there to be so much gold to move and he was on a split second schedule. 'Get some pallet trucks and back our van up to the shutters – then get downstairs to the vault.'

Kieran fired two more blasts of his gun to warn off the guards and then ran back down to the strong room. He told the manager, 'Right, help me shift these crates upstairs. You look like you could use the exercise.'

But when they came back up to ground level, clutching the first of the crates, there were pallet trucks nearby but no sign of the gang. Nor was the van parked outside. The premises seemed empty. Kieran ran over to the shutters. He could hear police sirens even over the alarms in the unit.

His crew were gone. The wankers had run for it. The only vehicle he had left to make his escape was the bulldozer and he knew he wouldn't be able to outrun the cops on that.

He'd blown it. He felt like a lottery winner who'd put his winning ticket in the washing machine.

Firing off random shots, he grabbed the manager by the lapel and shouted in fury, 'Are you having a tea break or something? Get back in the vault and bring the rest of the crates upstairs!'

They carried on dragging the gold up the stairs. Their arms strained under the weight but they pressed on, piling the crates up until the pallet trucks could take no more. Then Kieran wheeled them over to the shutters. He put his haul in the bulldozer's massive shovel. He had about half of the gear but went back to get the rest. His arms were nearly numb when he dragged the trucks back for the second time. When he'd finished, the crates were piled up in the shovel. He climbed into the driver's seat. He took one gold bar out and gave it to the manager who was covered in sweat and dust. 'Here you are mate, get yourself a drink for your trouble.'

Kieran turned the vehicle round to see the first police car coming in through the gates. They parked sideways to stop him. The cops yelled at him to halt but he lurched the bulldozer forward, scattering the cars as he went. One was pushed through the gates and he went over the bonnet of a second, trying to follow the first one in. There was a whiff of fuel as the crushed engine began to ignite and then an orange flash in his rear view mirror as it exploded in flames.

Kieran carried on up the industrial estate's perimeter road. He did a hard right and rolled over the security fence and upwards into the muddy field beyond. Behind, a police van that had attempted to follow was hopelessly stuck in the mud, yawing with its wheels spinning.

The bulldozer rolled on at a steady twenty miles an hour, its tracks taking out hedges and fences and anything else that stood in its way. Of course a helicopter would be up shortly but Kieran was confident there was still time to pull this off. He had no choice now.

As the bulldozer rolled on, he saw exactly what he was looking for. He changed direction and made his way over to the farmhouse.

Kieran parked up outside and put a couple of new shells in his shotgun but there was no need to knock on the door; a stout farmer's wife had emerged to find out what the hell was going on.

He was cheerful. 'Hello there love. Sorry to disturb you but I see you've got a van parked on the drive. Do you mind if I borrow it?'

Three

'Twenty pound fifty please,' Jennifer Miller informed the customer as she sat behind the checkout at the supermarket in Bow.

'Do you have a reward card?' *No.*

'Are you collecting school vouchers?' *No.*

'Do you have a million going spare so I can get outta my crap life?' No answer to that because she didn't ask, but so wished she could.

Jen straightened and winced. Only an hour and a bit of her afternoon shift had gone by and already her back was murder. But she wasn't about to bitch and moan about it; this job was her one steady lifeline to the readies she needed to keep clothes on her girls' backs and food in their bellies. The wages weren't anything to brag about but it was better than taking a handout from the social, like some single mums she could've named on The Devil's Estate down the road in Mile End. No way did she want Courtney and Little Bea thinking that you got paid to sit on your jacksie all day.

'Jen,' a voice whispered in her ear. She'd been so stuck in her thoughts that she hadn't heard one of the other women come up to her. 'I've gotta take over your till. Her Upstairs wants a word.'

Her Upstairs was the store manager, Mrs Howard, known behind her back as Attila the Glum. Jen had never met such a sour individual in all her born days. Attila ruled her employees like she'd been an executioner in a past life.

'What does she want?' Jen griped as she passed the change to her customer.

'Heaven knows.' The other woman's voice lowered. 'But I tell you what, her face looked like it could give thunder a run for its money.'

Jen worried her bottom lip as she got up. She couldn't afford to get into Dreary Drawers' bad books. The word in the locker room was the supermarket might have to lay off some workers: a rival company had set up down the road and was pulling in the punters with bargain basement goodies.

As soon as she walked into the main office and saw the tight expression on her manager's face she knew something was badly wrong. She moved quickly to stand in front of the desk. 'You wanted to see me?'

Mrs Howard looked her up and down and her vicious, thin-wormy lips began wiggling at each end. She did not invite Jen to sit down.

'Jennifer,' she started, pronouncing the name as Je-neath-her, in that fake la-di-da voice she used to lord it over her supermarket kingdom. It was bogus alright; everyone knew she'd grown up in the back end of Canning Town. 'Can you remind me what my job is?'

Jen's face creased in confusion. 'You what?' was on the tip of her tongue, but she sucked it back, knowing she should be more respectful to the boss. 'Have I done something wrong?'

The other woman drew herself tall. 'Let me put this another way – do I look like your personal secretary?'

Jen felt herself shrinking with embarrassment, finally sussing what had Attila flapping her feathers. 'I'm really sorry if my girls' school's been on the phone again.'

That school must be calling her the boomerang mum because she'd been up there so many times.

The older woman squinted and leaned slightly forward. 'If there's one more instance of me having to answer one of your personal calls I'll have no choice but to issue you with a formal warning.'

Jen's heart started hammering away, although she was tempted to tell the curdled-faced witch she wouldn't need to answer her calls if she was allowed her mobile on the shop floor. But she held her tongue. Bloody hell, if the company did decide to start firing people, anyone with a warning would be first out the door. She couldn't afford to lose this job. It was at times like this that she really missed her mum. She would've been round to Babs' in a flash for advice. A wave of sadness washed over her as she pictured her poor mum banged up in the slammer.

Jen turned her attention back to her immediate problem. 'I'm really sorry. It won't happen again.' She said it slowly and with feeling. 'Did the school want me to come now?'

'I don't think I mentioned a school.'

Jen's head jerked back in utter surprise. 'If it weren't the school who was trying to reach me?' Worry was etched clearly on her face. God, what if something had happened to her mum?

Attila's lips twisted into a malicious, gotcha grin. 'The police.'

'When I get my hands on her . . .' Jen fumed as she swung furiously into Bow Road Police Station.

The only other time Jen had been in a cop shop was back in '93 when Tiffany had been nicked in West End Central. Jen knew the police had come a long way with what people called 'community relations', but she would never forgot what she saw one of them do to her brother-in-law's bar manager at the Alley Club in Soho. Not a pretty sight. She'd kept her distance ever since and warned her girls not to look 'em in the eye.

A woman with standout breasts and bum was having a row with the cop at reception. Her body jiggled as she said, 'I'm not leaving until you put up one of them posters with my Arnold's beautiful face on it.'

The officer, an old timer who looked like he wanted to click his standard issue black boots three times to be transported somewhere else, smacked his lips in irritation. 'I'm sorry madam, but that's not the type of service we provide.'

Jen was gobsmacked. What kind of nick couldn't be bothered to help someone find their loved one?

The woman wailed, 'But he hasn't had his tea. He always comes home for his tea.'

The officer leaned forward, the lines round his mouth sagging. 'I suggest that you make your own poster.' Heartless bastard. 'That's what most people do when their pet goes missing.'

Pet? Some might've laughed on hearing that, but not Jen. The poor woman looked like she was having her heart pulled out. She felt sorry that the woman's dog or cat had gone walkabout, but she had her own urgent business to get sorted. Very urgent indeed.

As the dejected woman wandered off, Jen swiftly took her place. 'I got a message from a Detective Johnson that my daughter, Courtney Miller, has been arrested. What's she supposed to have done?' After Nuts had left she'd changed her last name back to Miller and when it became clear her ex wasn't interested in playing daddy to his girls she'd changed their names too.

He consulted the admission book in front of him. Then he peered back at her. 'If you take a seat, I'll let Detective Johnson know you're here.'

She was frustrated that she still didn't know what Courtney was up for, but she parked herself in one of the hard chairs. She didn't have long to wait before the detective turned out. He was much younger than Jen was expecting and would have been easy on the eye if he wasn't looking at her with a sharp expression, as if trying to decide whether she was a good mum or not.

She got to her feet and braced herself for the worst. 'So, what's she done?'

'I think it's best if I take you through so we can talk about this with Courtney.'

As Jen walked beside him, she rattled off, 'You do know she's underage? Only thirteen. I hope you haven't been giving her the third degree without one of them appropriate adults there.' She'd learned that that was what the plod had to do from *The Bill*.

They entered a long, narrow corridor. 'She wouldn't tell us her age but her school uniform was a bit of a clue.'

So, she had a sarky 'tec on her case, which Jen didn't appreciate one bit. But she bit her tongue; she couldn't afford to throw her weight around if she needed to sweet talk him out of charging Courtney. The idea of her kid having a criminal record made her sick to her stomach.

She played it nice and friendly. 'Of course officer. Whatever's happened, I'm sure it's a misunderstanding we can soon clear up.'

He merely lifted his eyebrow as he opened a door. Inside the room sat her eldest with a female detective opposite her. Jen let out a weary sigh. She couldn't pinpoint where she'd gone wrong but Courtney had never been the same after her Nanna Babs had been sent down. That first year of Babs' stretch her poor girl had gone into meltdown, waking up most nights screaming her head off. Jen hadn't known what to do other than hug her tight and comfort her as best she could. The real nightmare had started when Courtney had gone to big school. The once gentle girl had turned into a brawler, slugging it out with any other girl who looked at her the wrong way and mouthing off at the teachers. At first Jen had been defensive and thought it was the school's fault. So she pulled her out of that school and found another. And then another. Until she reluctantly had to admit the problem was her kid.

Jen kept her beady eye on her sullen daughter. Although Courtney still wore her school uniform all the thick eye make-up made her look like a cross between Lady Gaga and a Marilyn Manson fan.

'What the hell do you look like? Going out are you?' Jen got a scowl for her trouble and lost her temper. 'Why aren't you in school?'

Courtney huffed and rolled her eyes. Eyes that were replicas of her dad's. Funny, but it was Nuts' piercing baby blues that had first attracted her. Other than that, her daughter was her image through and through, with light blonde-brown hair and a pretty face distorted by thick eyeliner and cherry-black lipstick.

'I forgot.'

Jen never hit her girls, but she was itching to flex the back of her hand. She reached out to grab her lippy daughter, but Detective Johnson's 'Mrs Miller' stopped her, reminding her where they were. Her hand dropped into her lap.

She turned to him. 'Alright, what's she done?'

'Shoplifting I'm afraid.'

Tea leafing? Her kid? Jen couldn't catch her breath. OK, all the kids did it. Her sister Tiffany had made a career out of it at Courtney's age. But her own kid?

'Where did this happen?'

'In Roman Road Market. She pinched a pair of trainers from a stall and ran for it, but she was caught by a couple of the market guys.'

Courtney sneered, 'They were a right manky pair anyway. I only did it for a laugh. There's no law against wanting to have a laugh, is there?'

Jen blew her stack. 'You like a laugh do ya? I'll give you a laugh later, don't you worry.'

As Jen reached for her, Courtney dived out of her chair and yelled, 'That'll be a first. I wouldn't be having to swipe stuff if you had money! All my mates are decked out in the latest clobber while I'm dressed like a fucking homeless. You never buy me anything new. NEVER.'

The last word left her mouth like a bullet, echoing around the room. Jen's face flushed hot and red with shame. Embarrassed that her daughter would air their dirty laundry in front of strangers but also because Courtney was right. There wasn't much money these days to splash out on something special. Whose was the shame really? Courtney? Or her broke mum?

'Sit. Down. Now.' Jen was not in the mood to take any more backchat and Courtney knew it.

Once her daughter was grudgingly back in her seat Jen turned to the detective. 'You don't need to make a federal case out of it. She was only mucking about. She knows she's done wrong and she won't do it again.' Her gaze drilled into her thirteen-year-old. 'Don't you?'

Courtney sneered. 'Yeah, I know it was wrong.'

'She's only a kid. She won't do it again.'

Courtney repeated, 'No, I won't do it again.' Jen gave her the eye; she was sure the little miss had muttered under breath, 'I'll go up West next time.' But she left it alone; she just wanted to get out of there as soon as.

Detective Johnson leaned forward. 'Fortunately, the stall-holder appears to know your mother, a Babs Miller, so he said he wouldn't be pressing any charges.' He coughed nervously. 'He said that one Miller behind bars was enough anyway.'

Him and his colleague shared a meaningful look. Jen knew what that meant – they were well aware who her notorious mother was.

The female officer proceeded to give Courtney a bollocking that was meant to frighten her back onto the straight and narrow, but from the contemptuous look on her face she might as well have been talking Russian. The officer did scare Jen when she finished with, 'Next time, we'll have to get social services involved.'

Jen was horrified. No way in hell was the SS snooping around her business. Everyone on the estate would know and start whispering about her being a no-good mother. One way or the other Courtney was going to step back in line.

The female copper surprised Jen by asking, 'Do you mind if we have a quiet word outside?'

Jen didn't like the sound of that. A cop wanting 'a word' was never a good look, but she followed the other woman into the corridor all the same. The officer got straight into it. 'I don't like having to set social services on any parent, but I wouldn't be doing my job if I didn't make you aware how it might end up if your daughter doesn't pull her socks up.' Her voice was soft and surprisingly sympathetic. 'Have you thought about getting her a counsellor?'

Jen stiffened. An outsider sticking her beak into her family business was not how things were done on The Devil. She shook her head. 'No need for none of that. I'll straighten out my girl with my own counselling skills, thank you very much.'

The detective's voice lowered. 'I had a bit of trouble with my boy a few years back. I talked to him till my face was a new shade of blue, but he wouldn't listen. In the end I got him this brilliant counsellor. I don't know what she did but within months he was back to the kid I gave birth to.'

Jen mulled it over. Just the thought of her baby girl going off the rails like her younger sister Tiff made her want to weep. Her mum had gone through hell with Tiffany, who'd only stopped her nonsense after being chucked in a cell and getting a break from a judge. She'd move heaven and earth to ensure that her kid didn't go the same way. Maybe she should take a helping hand, even if it was being offered by a copper.

She held the other woman's gaze. 'Alright, give me her contact details.' But she added with obstinate determination, 'I'm not saying I'll use her mind.'

Ten minutes later, Jen faced Courtney outside.

She took a couple of much needed deep breaths before saying, 'This has got to stop. Do you hear me?' Courtney threw her a surly snap of her eyes but nodded. Jen carried on, her voice gentler this time. 'What's the matter hun?'

Her eldest crossed her arms defiantly. 'I'm sick of us having no money.' And with that she stalked off in a strop, but Jen couldn't help but notice how her shoulders were slightly slumped.

Jen motored after her, at her wits' end. It wasn't her fault; she didn't have any spare cash to flash around. Maybe she should give this counsellor a bell . . . No. She pressed her lips stubbornly together. Tomorrow she'd be able to speak to the best counsellor she knew – her mum.

Four

Tiffany was buzzing, still high on speed and booze, as she rolled into her gaff after an all-nighter.

Her bubble burst when she clapped eyes on the pile of mail that greeted her. Shit was finally catching up with her. She hesitated before picking it up and staggering into her bedroom, where she opened the wardrobe. It was bulging with top-of-the-range designer gear – Armani, McCartney, Kors, Posen. It had the lot, some still unworn. Even the hangers were designer. There were two shelves for her growing collection of bling, individually stored in compartments, and an exclusive, very naughty range of sex toys she got from a ladies only sex shop in Hoxton. And in the bottom were neat rows of expensive trainers, sandals and flats; Tiff had never been and would never be a heels girl.

In the corner was a stash of envelopes – some opened, some not – and abandoned letters. She threw the ones in her hand onto the rest. The mini mountain of papers collapsed and spilled out onto the luxuriant blue carpet.

'Fuck this,' she swore. She knew as soon as she touched them she'd be confronted with what she'd been refusing to deal with for ages.

Tiff was tempted to leave them on the floor and turn her back, but she didn't. She knelt down, started to gather them up and, like a tongue that could not stop touching a rotting tooth, she couldn't help herself. She opened one of the letters.

We hope you are enjoying the Deluxe Dolby Vision DVD player we shipped to you in January. The agreement was to pay £30 each month. Your third payment is now overdue . . .

Tiffany opened one of today's letters.

Our records show that a balance of £357.51 remains overdue on your account . . .

And another

We have been most patient, but you have failed to respond to three previous notices about non-payment of your rent . . .

She crushed it up and hurled it with violent frustration across the room. How the hell had she managed to get into this mess in the first place?

Three years ago every dream she'd ever had had been right in front of her. She'd kept one step ahead of everyone else, manipulated the situation around Dee's stolen car and pocketed a cool fifty G. Finally she could put a hefty down payment on the one-bed flat in a plush, private block that had once been a sugar factory in Bow. Instead, that much lolly had turned her head and made her think big. A building where people had once sweated their guts out to pack sugar hadn't been grand enough for her. No, Tiffany Miller, one time tearaway number one on The Devil's Estate, decided to lease a fuck-off duplex within kissing distance of Canary Wharf. The building was all that The Devil would never be – spanking new, with huge French windows that reflected the London skyline and river. Now come on, Tiff thought, who wouldn't move heaven and earth to live here?

She'd never forget the day she moved in. She'd stood in the middle of the sitting room – no, den – and gazed around in wonder. The dreams of girls like her didn't usually come true, but she'd done it. Gotten outta The Devil. She wasn't one to dwell on the fact she'd traded up by ripping off her nearest and dearest. What mattered in this life was going places. Any way you could.

Back then Tiff still had plenty to play with so she'd kitted the place out to the hilt with state-of-the-art equipment, including a 70 inch plasma screen mounted on the wall, remote control curtains and a speaker system in every room. Something had triggered inside her, like comfort eating, and Spend, Spend, Spend became her triple-barrelled surname. Anything she wanted, Tiff got. Even when her bank balance went into the red she didn't stop. The debts piled up and she still couldn't put the brakes on the madness.

Instead of dealing with the demands she slung them in the wardrobe and slammed the door. What the eye doesn't see the head doesn't have to deal with. But when they started coming thick and fast she took out other loans so Peter could pay Paul.

Tiff shrugged off her troubles. She went into the all-mod-cons kitchen and put a glass under the water dispenser in the fridge-freezer that she still owed money on. Instead of water a stream of ice cool lager filled up the glass. Yeah, this was the life. She knocked her drink back in the den, her feet up on the partially paid for leather recliner next to the unopened box containing her new DVD player.

Her mobile went off.

'Yeah?' she answered, her eyes drooping as the night before caught up with her.

'Tiffany Miller?'

Sleep vanished in an instant as a chilly sensation slithered down her backbone. There was something about the man's voice that put her on edge. She kicked her feet off the sofa and lowered them to the polished wooden floor. She decided to play her usual little trick to throw someone off the scent.

'Tiffany?' she asked in a bewildered voice, the accent of the Polish girl she'd been doing the duvet tango with last year. 'No Tiff-fanny here. You have wrong number—'

He cut her off with a humourless laugh. 'The old Johnny foreigner voice scam. I've heard it all before.'

She sighed, knowing she was caught bang to rights. 'Which one are you then?' she asked in her normal voice. 'The land-lord's agent? I've already explained to the fella who works with you that my bank's got their numbers the wrong way round. The money will be in by the weekend '

'That's the trouble with people like you. The numbers are always the wrong way round, ain't they?'

For the first time she clocked that he had a pure bred East End accent. And it was rough. She swallowed hard. 'Yeah, look, mate, I ain't got the foggiest who you are but if you tell me what the problem is, perhaps I can help.'

She didn't even need to ask if it was about money. It was always about money now.

'Problem?' the man went on, sarcasm dripping like blood off a knife. 'I'll tell you what the problem is love. You borrowed five hundred off Jimmy down the Moon and he wants it back. With interest obviously, he's not a charity.'

Who the hell was Jimmy? And where the hell was the Moon? What five hundred nicker? Tiffany had so many Jimmys on the go now, she'd lost track. She'd performed a juggling act with her debts, paying off one credit card by getting another one, borrowing money from one Jimmy to pay another Jimmy. She'd been down the Citizens Advice Bureau to get help with rearranging and consolidating. But now the walls were starting to close in.

'Yeah, look, tell him I'm a bit short at the mo but I'll defo sort him out when my dosh goes in at the end of the month.'

Her caller wasn't happy. 'No, no, no sweetheart, you're a bit confused. He don't want it at the end of this month, he wants it at the beginning of last month, you understand? Otherwise he's asked me to pop round in person and pick it up. Or goods to the value of. Plus a couple of slaps by way of a penalty payment. Obviously, I'm a nice guy and I don't wanna get into that. I've persuaded Jimmy that you'll go down The Bad Moon by the end of the week and pay up. That's right, ain't it?'

Tiff's heart pounded, as she suddenly realised which debtor was on the blower. Fobbing off the banks and the stores was easy. Menacing lowlives she'd taken a sub from on the never-never, not so much. And these lowlives were a duo called Tommo and Errol. She'd asked around about where she could get a bit of cash in double time. Her old stomping ground The Bad Moon in Shadwell had been mentioned. She'd gone up there in a flash and asked the barman for a white wine spritzer with bitters, which was the code for the loan of a grand, no questions asked. He'd passed it over, told her the debt was owed to 'Jimmy' although she already knew Tommo and Errol ran the operation, and warned she'd need to keep up the payments or the next spritzer she ordered would be mixed with her innards. She'd never been back because she'd never made any repayments. Why oh why had she gone to The Bad Moon? Nothing good ever came out of that boozer.

'There's no need to get all Wile E Coyote on me bruv. You'll have your dosh as soon as—'

His snarl slashed over her. 'The arrangement is you pay up on time, not when you feel like it. You don't wait till after you've munched on one of them dollies you bring home. You like your birds, don't you Tiff-fanny fancier?'

The blood drained out of her face, leaving her pale and shaking. 'Are you spying on me?' That scared her silly. Her gaze darted around nervously.

'Jimmy wants his cash. The full amount. If he don't get it, things will turn nasty. Very nasty indeed.' He rang off.

When Tiffany put her phone back in her pocket, her hand was trembling. She always thought something would turn up and now it finally had. Men threatening to come round and give her a kicking, never mind the court cases and bailiffs. As she got to her feet in a blind panic, the flat echoed to a furious hammering.

Tiffany folded back on the recliner. She was done for. And there was no escape route. The hammering came again, but this time with a voice that got her breathing easy again.

'Tiffany, are you in there?'

She wiped her hand across her sweating forehead and opened the door. The young man in the neighbouring flat was usually smartly dressed but today he was decked out in T-shirt and black jeans.

'What's up?' She played it cool although she was still almost wetting herself from that phone call.

He handed over a letter. 'I found this on my mat when I got in. The postman must've popped it in by accident.' He leaned on the doorframe and switched on the charm. 'I've just got back from New York. Maybe I'll book you a first class seat up beside me next time I go.'

Tiff rolled her eyes in mock annoyance. They always played this game – him hitting on her and her giving him a knock back. When he'd tried it on for the first time, she'd let it be known loud and clear that he was missing the essential equipment that made her go gaga.

She stepped forward and laid her palms softly against his chest. Then playfully shoved him back. 'Knob off Tarquin.'

They both laughed. 'The name's Mike, as you well know,' he informed her. 'Got a little prezzie for you.' He handed her a small plastic bag with some blue pills in. Despite working in the City he was also her main supplier of speed.

'Cheers babe.' Her hand closed around the bag.

Once she was back inside her drum she turned her attention to the letter. Bloody hell, as if she needed another one. But she calmed down when she saw who it was from.

A V.O. from her mum. It must've been hanging around in lover boy's place for a week because it was a visiting order for tomorrow. A slow smile spread across her face. If Tommo and Errol came looking for her she'd be in the one place they'd never find her – behind bars.

Five

'Blimey O'Reilly, mate. What have you got hidden in here – a dead body?'

One of the guys loading Kieran's furniture into a huge storage warehouse was in a jovial mood as he huffed with the weight of the sofa.

Kieran wasn't, but he pretended to be. 'Yeah – one of the reasons I killed the wife was coz the bitch wouldn't go on a diet. Stuffed her in the sofa.'

'Like a bit of meat on the bone myself,' chuckled the other man.

'Yeah,' added the first mover as his shoulders shook.

If both men only knew what was inside the sofa they wouldn't be creasing up. Kieran knew he'd had a lucky escape during the robbery. Now he was nervy that his luck might not hold. He'd driven the van to a yard he owned in the burbs before stowing the gold away in some old furniture for a few nights. Now he'd brought the stuff to a storage unit off the M25. The guy who'd organised the raid had promised him it would only have to be there for a couple of days while he sorted out somewhere more secure. But there was no sign where that was going to be. Kieran didn't like it. It was sloppy and he didn't like sloppy.

One of the storage guys asked him, 'Moving house then?'

'Maybe.'

Kieran gazed at the bloke suspiciously. Innocent question? Or were these boys primed to ask that sort of thing and then report back to the higher-ups if they heard anything iffy? He looked around. There was CCTV everywhere. He pulled his baseball cap down lower over his eyes. He was taking a hell of a chance here.

The man kept it zipped after that and the two guys carried on loading and unloading. If the flimsy sofa or armchair came apart and tipped gold out all over the joint, he would be sunk. Kieran even thought about offering to do the work himself but he knew how odd that would appear. Instead, he lit a B&H and winced every time something was roughly handled or bashed about. He walked away ten paces. There was nothing he could do now except keep his fingers crossed.

He went into red alert mode when he heard a helicopter flying low and slow overhead. He peered hard trying to see if it had police markings down the side. He checked out the surroundings again and this time clocked a car parked awkwardly with no sign of a driver or passengers. It was quite possible the cops were tailing him already and knew he had the loot. Perhaps they were biding their time to see who he contacted and where he went before moving in.

The bastards.

'Alright mate? We're done.'

Kieran turned back. The container was sealed up and a forklift truck moved in to shift it to the warehouse. The helicopter disappeared over the horizon and a woman appeared, got into the parked car and drove off. Another risk taken and another risk he'd got away with.

When he started in the underworld, the top Cockney crim who'd helped him get started, and who was always 'the guvnor' to him, gave him a piece of advice. 'Tell me mate – are you lucky? Do you win raffles and that? Do tasty birds bump into your motor by accident and then say yes when you ask them out? Do you get dealt flushes in card games? Because let me tell you something – you need to be a bit lucky in this line of business. And brave. Fortune favours the brave.'

Kieran Scott had already proved he was lucky and brave. Since he was little he'd been eager to show the world he was more than the smelly, neglected kid who'd grown up on The Devil. He'd charged through life on a one-way high-speed train to get to the top. He'd carved out a fearsome slice of the underworld years back, and although there would be major ructions if people took liberties, he still hadn't managed to break into the real elite. You had to have done something daring, risky, off-the-scale legendary to earn a place in that club. To become the type of bad boy that people whispered about for donkey's years.

The big boys would have to deal with him now, whether they liked it or not. Just thinking about his accomplishments made him puff out his chest with pride. If that bitch of a mum of his was still on this earth he'd smother her slag face right in it. She used to scream at him, her gin flavoured spit hitting him left, right and centre, roaring at him that he was a good-for-nothing heading for the rubbish heap. Then she'd viciously turn the knife by yelling at him that the only reason he'd come into this world was because the abortionist had ripped her off with cough syrup instead of the meds she'd given a whole month's wages for. Kieran gritted his teeth. 'Well, here I am bitch, alive and kicking, about to prove how wrong you were.'

Behind the bluster he acknowledged he had to be careful about going around playing the big geezer. As soon as his name was in the frame for the job there'd be some just waiting to work him over. That was his most pressing concern.

But he had the gold and they didn't.

He was smart too. He knew sooner or later your luck always runs out. That was why, after years as one of London's second-tier villains, he'd invested his winnings in legitimate businesses and property while cutting down on the dodgy stuff. If anyone else had asked him to do a job as risky as this one, he'd have turned them down flat. But this wasn't anyone else. This was his underworld mentor, one of London's premier guys, the one who'd given him his first leg up; and he'd promised the gig was too good to turn down.

'I'm telling you Kieran, this is a big one. It's a private vault and I know the place inside out. The gear I want is in a strong room there and I can build you a model of the place and send you straight to it. I'll take care of all the paperwork afterwards and then cut you in.'

'I dunno guvnor. That's not really my thing anymore.'

'Not your thing? Are you nuts? We're talking millions here mate. And the place is so dodgy, they probably won't even call the law.'

When Kieran had said nothing, his mentor had continued, 'I'll tell you what mate, I'll come up to that club of yours and we can have a game of snooker and a snifter and I'll do you a little presentation. It's too good an opportunity to miss – I'd do it myself but that would give the game away.'

After their meeting, he'd agreed to put a team together and do the job.

When his container was loaded, he went into the office and collected his receipt using fake ID. He drove off in the empty van, cruising around for a while to make sure he wasn't being followed before pulling into a layby to make a call to the guvnor. He simply said, 'Job done.'

'Good boy. Any problems?'

Kieran didn't want to admit his crew had run out on him. It

made him sound like an amateur. In a way he was glad. He didn't owe the rats anything now.

'No. It was sweet.'

'Is the stuff stowed away?'

'Yeah.'

'Alright then, leave it with me and I'll be in touch in a few days about moving it on.'

'A few days? How long's a few days? We need to get this gear in a secure bunker somewhere asap. You know what I mean?'

He'd struck the wrong note. There was a long silence before the guvnor said, 'No, I don't know what you mean. I told you a high value job like this takes a bit of sorting out. Leave it with me and I'll tip you the wink. Now go up your club, down a couple and stop worrying. Alright?'

Kieran got the needle; he was being treated like a gofer. 'Well, how about this then – I drop by your place and you put me in the picture?'

This time the delay on the other end was so long that Kieran thought the line had gone dead. When he came back on, the guvnor's voice was raw with contempt. 'There's no picture to put you in. I told you from the start. Your role's just to get in there and swipe the stuff. It's up to me to sort out everything else. Disposing of a consignment like this is big boy's games and, with the greatest of respect mate, it's a bit above your pay grade, you understand? I mean, what's the matter, don't you trust me? Eh? I'm disappointed in you; I've always regarded you as a mate. I'm very, very disappointed.'

The line went properly dead.

Kieran sat back and stared out of the window. Of course he trusted the guvnor. This was still a bit rich though, him being treated like a bookie's runner. And then he remembered something else. The wise words he'd been given on his first job.

'Never forget, you can't trust no one in this game. Everyone's on the make and on the take. Anyone can have your trousers down in this line of work.'

Wise words indeed.

And they'd come from the guvnor.

Six

''Ere John, have you seen this?' Dee Black yelled at her husband, who was in the kitchen.

Her dark eyes were glued to the late news on TV in the lounge of their large Essex house. She was leaning back on a sofa with an automatic footrest, wearing black leggings, a baggy T-shirt and Kors wedge sandals that showcased her black painted toenails. A box of luxury chocolates sat in her lap. 'There's been a massive blag near London. The cheeky beggers rammed a bulldozer through the gates of a depot and then escaped across country on motorbikes – can you believe that!'

She was a true crime addict and loved to see a gang using the route one method for nicking things: in and out, no mucking around. The initial reports on the telly had only mentioned that a sum of money had been stolen. Later, rumours circulated that the heist involved substantial takings but the police weren't saying what was nicked. Now, a reporter standing at some distance from the smashed in gates said the law had confirmed what had really gone on. 'Fucking hell! They've only made off with a load of gold bullion!'

When she got no response Dee popped another choccie in her mouth, punched the remote for the digi box to record the news and headed towards the kitchen. Her husband was making one of those health juices she had him on. She had him under a healthy lifestyle cosh, which included him taking up the two Js - jogging and juicing. He was fifty-three to her thirty-four and though the age difference hadn't been that noticeable over the years, lately Dee thought he'd looked a bit ragged around the edges. She'd put him on a strict regime to get the pink back in his cheeks. Mind you, she'd caught him bang to rights the other day with a Big Mac, fries and strawberry shake smeared across his chops as he hid in his motor in the garage. Dee had gone ballistic and, with her finger jabbed in his startled face, had read him the riot act.

She entered the large kitchen but it was empty. She called, 'John! Where the bloody hell are you?'

She wandered back into the hallway and briefly stopped in front of the large, framed picture of her cat, Banshee. Her poor babe had cocked up her whiskers a good year now and Dee hadn't had the heart to replace her. Banshee had been a right madam when she wanted to be, especially when it came to sharing Dee with John, but she'd loved that cat with her whole heart. She sighed as she gazed at the fluffy puss in a tiny tiara and large pink bow. She might be long gone, but would never be forgotten.

Then Dee's ears pricked up. She was sure she could hear John talking to someone. As far as she knew they didn't have any visitors and their boy Nicky - her other pride and joy - was away at university. She followed John's voice and found him whispering on his mobile in the snooker and bar room.

'John, who you rabbiting away with?'

Startled, he twisted around so fast that if it hadn't been for the bar propping him up he'd have fallen flat on his face. After he'd righted himself he coughed dramatically and spoke loudly into the phone. 'Yeah mate ... right you are. I'll have my people onto it as soon as.' Then he ended the call and said to Dee, 'You alright doll?'

John might be knocking on, with his bald head, slight paunch and life-battered face, but Dee's heart always gave a tiny hiccup of pleasure as she looked at him. She was reminded of when they'd met, all those years ago when he was the owner of the Alley Club in Soho. It might not have been love at first sight on her part but it hadn't taken her long to realise he was the best thing to ever happen to her. He'd been a leading light of London's underworld back then but that was all behind him now; he'd given up the life and gone legit.

And that's what had Dee worried. Sure, John still had mates in that world but he kept his fingernails and cash clean these days, so why was he hiding next to the black-and-white photo of Henry Cooper and Muhammad Ali's legendary '63 heavy-weight fight? With blood streaming from his eye the British boxer stood near a very young Muhammad Ali, who lay dazed on the ropes.

It was a strange thing what you noticed about people when you moved in with them. What Dee had clocked about John when he was still a known Face was that he liked to deal with serious business in private, right next to that photo. So why was he standing there now when he hadn't been a paid-up member of that violent world for a good many years?

With determined steps she reached him and asked again, 'Who were you talking to?'

The sudden red that stained his cheeks made her fears grow. He laid his mobile on the bar and fobbed her off with, 'No one really. Just one of the lads from the golfing club.'

She wasn't buying it and the knowing expression on her face told him so. She slapped her fists against her hips. 'If you're wetting your toe back in that *business* I'll have your balls for brekkie tomorrow morning.'

He shook his head impatiently and scoffed, 'As if!' He leaned forward, kissed her on the lips, cupped her bum in his large hands and jerked her towards him. His breath tickled her neck as he crooned in her ear, 'Know where I do fancy wetting my big toe—?'

He got no further as she laid her palms firmly against his chest and pushed indignantly out of his embrace. If he thought he could soft soap her with a touch up he had another think coming. She stabbed her finger at him and warned, 'I mean it John, if those size elevens of yours are on the wonky path—'

He threw his hands in the air. 'Alright, you've got me bang to rights.' Dee felt her breath hitch with alarm. He continued, 'I was organising a surprise slap-up dinner on a cruise down the Thames for your birthday next month. Satisfied? Now it ain't much of a surprise anymore. That's why I come in here, weren't it, so you wouldn't hear me making the arrangements.'

Dee's face fell. She felt like a royal wanker. And then it lit up. Nothing made her squeal more than one of John's B-day surprises. Last year he'd taken her for a fortnight to Spain to visit Uncle Frank, the man who had taken John under his wing when he was a nipper running wild in Bethnal Green. Now her suspicions had wrecked this year's one.

She caressed his arm. 'Aww, sorry babes. I just worry that you might miss being one of the big boys and go and do something stupid.'

'No chance. The way I hear it it's full of crazies now.' His eyes twinkled. 'Why would I go back into business, I don't need it now, do I?'

A rush of love and affection choked her up. She gave him a lingering kiss on the mouth and now it was her turn to feel up his behind.

After the kiss was finished he asked, 'Did you want me for something?'

'There's only been an Ocean's Eleven involving gold bars.' She led him back into the lounge and hit the replay button so he could see the news report. In silence they both watched the footage of the taped-off bulldozer and its police guards outside the farmhouse where it had been dumped. She was so wrapped up in the unfolding drama that she didn't hear him slip over to the drinks cabinet and help himself to a stiff one.

Dee turned to him. 'What's that amount of yellow gonna be worth then?'

John thought for a long time before he sighed, 'In the case of the boys who stole that loot, I'd say . . . absolutely fuck all.'

'How do you figure that out?'

John walked around to his armchair and sat down, nursing his drink. 'To get shot of a consignment like that, you need to know the right people who can get it smelted down, turned back into bars, stamped up and sold on. There's only about a half dozen top Faces around who can do that and those tea leaves don't know 'em.'

Dee didn't get it. 'How do you know they don't?'

'Coz I do know them and, if they were involved, I'd have heard about it. You can't keep something like that secret. Word always leaks out. Nope, I'm afraid those numbskulls are gonna be stuck with their crates of golden goodies.' He chuckled to himself. 'Although I suppose their old ladies might get a nice pair of 24 carat earrings out of it.' He sipped his drink. 'They might be able to use the gold as collateral in a drugs deal although even that's doubtful. The law will be tearing the country apart on the hunt for them. Anyone with a brain won't want nuthin to do with them. I admire their front of course but facts have to be faced – the mob who did that job are a bunch of idiots.'

'What the hell's that you're drinking?' Dee's gaze zeroed in on his glass.

John looked sheepishly at it. 'Oh, you know, just a Diet Coke . . .'

Dee sniffed. 'Smells like a half gallon of brandy from where I'm sitting. What's the matter with ya? The quack says you won't be collecting the old age pension if you don't change your diet and get some exercise, and you're sitting there necking booze?'

John sipped his 'diet cola' before mumbling, 'Old age pension? Well, that's hardly worth hanging around for nowadays, is it?'

'Your one is. Go and throw the booze down the sink and do yourself a juice, one of those green ones with spinach.'

John looked relieved when his mobile went off. He checked the number, took the call and began laughing. 'Alright mate? Yeah . . . I've just been watching it on the news. What a bunch of amateurs. Nah . . . they won't have known it was there. I'll tell you bruv, if there's one thing harder than stealing bullion, it's getting rid of it afterwards . . . I know! That's what I just told the missus. I mean seriously, no one's gonna touch that are they . . .?'

He walked over to Dee and gave her his glass of brandy and Coke. He held his hand over the phone and told her, 'I'm off to the gym to have a few turns on my exercise bike. Happy now?'

'Who's on the blower?'

John shrugged. 'Just a mate, that's all. Blimey, coming to something when a bloke can't take a call from a mate . . .' The tone of his voice changed. 'Someone was telling me they saw Nicky in London the other day having a whale of a time with a real lively crowd.'

'Well that someone must be on crack coz you know Nicky's in Sheffield doing us proud at university.'

'That's what I told 'em.'

As he turned to leave Dee shouted, 'Oi,' and pointed at him. 'And lay off the sauce.'

*   *   *

Dee knocked back John's brandy as her thoughts turned to
Nicky. Fancy her having a boy at university. She loved their
adopted son to bits. He hadn't really taken to school, but after
Babs had been sentenced he'd surprised her by putting his
head down during his GCSEs and getting some good grades.
Now he was studying Media Studies, whatever that was.

On an impulse she got her mobile out and gave him a ring.
'Nicky baby?'

'You alright Mum?'

She could barely hear him – Rihanna's 'Unfaithful' was
playing loudly in the background. 'You at a rave or something?' Although she didn't want him to have a life that was
all work and no play she hoped he weren't taking the piss.
That college course was setting her and John back a pound or
two in fees and the like.

'Nah, just in the student bar with a few mates, chillin' after
a late night lecture about how the media can manipulate the
public . . .'

A delighted smile made Dee's face glow as she listened to
him chatting away, although she didn't fully understand what
he was talking about. But that's what he was meant to be
doing at uni – becoming a smart arse.

'Look Mum,' he said hurriedly, 'Got to run. Love ya. And Dad.'

And before she could utter another word he cut the call. Her
fingers tightened around the phone. Who would've thought
that small boy her and John had rescued from his nan's flea-
infested home after his dad's death – which she didn't allow
herself to think about – would turn into such a boffin. Nicky
had done the family proud and as far as Dee was concerned he
could do no wrong.

Nicky threw his mobile on the bed and smiled at his girlfriend,
Angel.

'Was that your mother?' she asked him.

He blushed slightly. He didn't want Angel thinking he was a mummy's boy. 'Yeah, she just wanted to catch up with me.'

She turned her eyes to him and he caught his breath. Those baby blues of hers did him every time. They'd caught his attention that fateful night he was out raving. She was as sexy as hell but it was her eyes that drew him, large and wide and glittering with fun and life. And naughties.

'You're going to have to tell her the truth sooner or later,' she said quietly as she caught his hand. Her thumb felt like a gentle kiss as it caressed his palm.

'Let's make that later. Much later.' His own eyes glinted with mischief as he pushed her back on the bed.

She let out a squeal of pure pleasure as he got down and dirty on top of her. Nicky had played the field hard, but this woman was something special. Unlike a lot of his previous ladies she made him laugh and knew how to push his have-a-good-time button. And she never talked about forever after. In fact, he was the one who was starting to think of forever after with his beautiful Angel.

Seven

The following Wednesday, a jubilant but nervous Babs was escorted down the corridor by a prison officer. She couldn't believe she'd managed to wangle a private visit with her daughters. She'd given the governor some BS about being on the verge of self-harming if she didn't see her girls. Babs hadn't held out much hope of it working, but the Number One had been sympathetic and caved in.

She snapped smartly out of her thoughts when she heard jeering. Ahead in the corridor stood three fearsome inmates. It didn't take her long to suss who was Queen Bitch. She was a large woman with hair shaved at the sides and spiked in the middle and tats popping all over her body. She was what Babs thought most prisoners would look like when she'd entered the system.

'I see new meat has arrived,' tattoo woman said in a sarky, sweet voice with no smile.

'Fuck off Benson,' the officer ordered.

'Woo-hoo,' the women all chorused nastily back.

Benson wasn't letting up. 'She your new girlfriend Miss?'

The officer was not amused. 'I've told you to do one.'

'Whatever,' Benson sneered.

The group swaggered towards them, their hard gazes fixed on Babs all the way, sending chills through her. That Benson looked like a right animal.

'I'll be seeing you Babsie,' Benson called in a sing-song tone as they moved past.

She knows my name. Babs swallowed deeply. She didn't need any aggro in here. So far Kieran hadn't sent a new guardian angel to protect her. If it hadn't been for the fearsome Mrs Regan watching her back under Kieran's say-so in HMP Shithole, Babs wasn't sure how she'd have made it through. Babs knew how to give as good as she got, but in here brawling was no holds barred.

'Who's that?' Babs asked, desperately trying not to show how much she was bricking it.

They'd reached the empty visiting room. The kanga answered, 'That's Paula Benson, aka Knox Benson. They call her Knox because she can knock someone out in two blows. Stay well clear of that one. She's nothing but trouble.'

Jen's feet were murder by the time she neared the prison. The tip of her left wedge pinched the corn on her big toe. Half a bloody hour it had taken her to walk the two miles from the railway station. She'd wanted to take a cab but she didn't have the cash to spare on a luxury like that. Dee and Tiffany had both offered to give her a lift but then Jen felt she had to offer them petrol money and she hated it when they said, 'Oh, don't worry about it, save your pennies for yourself and the girls.'

She couldn't handle their pity or being poor. It's another knock back every day when you've got no dosh. And what made it worse? Her sisters were always flush. No stomping a couple of miles for those two; they'd both be turning up in their motors. Dee in that fuck-off convertible, Tiff in her hot hatch. Good for them, of course, but it just rubbed her nose in it how badly she was doing, busting a gut bringing up two kids on a dump like The Devil's Estate.

Jen was limping by the time she saw her sisters waiting outside the gate. Dee was a knockout, as per usual, the white, lacy tunic over her leggings showing off the richness of her brown skin. She was blinged out in large hooped gold earrings, twisted chain and Blahnik mirrored heels. Her weave was done up all Beyoncé flyaway girl style. Tiff's jet black hair was held back in a Croydon facelift – a stretched-up ponytail that pulled on the skin of her face – and she wore designer skinny jeans and ballet pumps. Tiffany might've moved on from her teara-way youth but the strapline on her T-shirt still hinted at her days of being a bad girl – 'My Chemical Romance'. She was also sporting a nose ring these days.

Jen became very self conscious of her off-the-peg dress and yonks old jean jacket. Her sisters wore oversized shades while her eyes were red-lined from sleepless nights.

'Wotcha Jen. Like the dress.' That was Tiffany.

'You're looking good girl,' added Dee.

She took a deep breath. She knew they were both lying out of their rear ends; she looked like a chavette and she knew it. 'Yeah. Whatever. Are we doing this or what?'

While Tiff passed over her V.O. to the officer at the recep-tion, Dee whispered, 'How's my two princesses? Do they need any help with anything?'

God give me strength. Jen clenched her teeth in extreme aggravation. She knew that Dee loved her girls to death and was a bang-up aunt, but she hated it, loathed it when her half-sister made her feel like she couldn't take care of her own kids. This was how it always was. Jen refused any help from her sisters for her sake but she didn't feel able to refuse it for her Courtney and Little Bea. At the same time, she was too proud to say yes and too poor to say no so they all kept up the fiction that the money they gave her was a loan, although they knew that Jen would never be able to pay it back. Sometimes Jen hoped that a wealthy and handsome prince would sweep her off her feet and allow her to tell her sisters where they could stuff their cash. But she was old enough to know princes only existed in fairy tales. And if they did exist they wouldn't be caught dead near The Devil.

'That's nice of you Dee. Later eh?'

Mercifully, it was her big sister's turn to show her V.O. After Jen was done they put their valuables and forbidden items, such as mobile phones, in private lockers in the Visitors' Centre. As per usual, Dee started making noise about having to leave her mobile behind.

'Give it a rest will ya,' Jen snapped. Her head was throbbing like crazy.

Dee gave her a killer look that would've stopped most people in their tracks. 'Something wriggling round the hairs of your va-jay-jay? You've got a right cob on you.'

Jen's shoulders sagged slightly. 'Sorry. I'm just dead on my feet is all.'

Dee's face creased with concern. 'You want me to look after the girls for you? I can take 'em shopping up West.'

Again with the help! 'No ta,' she let out evenly. 'I thought we were here to visit Mum, my kids can manage thanks.'

Then she marched back over to the reception in case her mouth got her into some serious shit with Dee; her half-sister wasn't a woman to cross. Jen joined the line for security. As the person ahead of her went through a high-pitched screech sounded from the metal detector.

'For crying out loud,' Jen mumbled, her patience wearing thin. What could the problem be now? Someone's tongue stud? It turned out to be much more serious than that – a mobile phone. The offender was dragged off shouting the odds to anyone with an ear that they'd forgotten to put it in a locker. Yeah, likely story.

Ten minutes later, Jen and her sisters were shepherded into a small room. Even Jen had to laugh when she discovered that they had a private room to meet their mum. It seemed what they'd read about this open prison being cushy was true.

Their mum was already waiting for them and her face lit up when she saw them. 'Come here,' she announced, her voice cracking, opening her arms wide. After she'd given each a tight hug they settled down. 'How are the girls? Courtney doing alright?'

Jen couldn't understand why her mum always asked after her eldest more than Little Bea. Babs hadn't seen her grandkids since she'd gone down. She refused, resolute that she didn't want them seeing their Nanna Babs locked up.

Jen hesitated before saying, 'Oh, they're good.' But she couldn't help adding, 'Well, you know, as good as girls of that age can be. There's always gonna be a few wrinkles to iron out as they grow up . . .'

Babs stared knowingly at her three daughters. 'I know exactly how many wrinkles you need to iron out of girls of that age or indeed any other. Been there myself. But they're happy?'

Jen hesitated again. 'Yeah, they're alright.' She didn't want to burden her mum with how Courtney was getting out of hand. There'd be time enough for that when Babs finally got out, sooner if she wangled parole. Then Jen had to put up with Tiffany and Dee telling their mum about their latest well-funded adventures. Dee and John had been to Istanbul for a long weekend while Tiffany was planning on getting a new car, something a bit 'sportier'. Jen listened in resentful silence until the subject was changed to their mum's new home.

'I've no complaints here ladies. You wanna see my room – some on The Devil would likely wanna trade places with me. Far less argy-bargy in this joint. Although there are one or two . . . or three who think they're Top Dog.'

Dee cut in, 'Get the Number One to sort their arses out.'

Babs shook her head. 'It don't work like that in here. People who tell tales end up with a snitch badge on their lapel and no one wants that.' She covered Dee's hand. 'I'm alright love. Keeping my head down just like I did before.' She pulled her hand back, no doubt remembering the rule about no physical contact. 'They've sorted me a lovely job to prepare me for life on the outside. I've started working at a memorial garden a couple of miles away. Don't know how that's supposed to prepare me for a new career. Not much call for gardeners in Mile End. Still, better than playing table tennis with the other girls. I'm a bit crap at that.'

Tiffany was excited. 'So, come on Mum – what did the jam roll board say?'

'It's gonna be a while before I hear which way it will swing, but I've done a proper portion of my time and have got an unblemished record, so it should be a done deal.'

Jen seethed silently. Babs could've told her this on the phone. She loved seeing her mum, but the truth was she didn't have the type of spare dough needed to come up here just to hear her mum natter bloody away about her new career clipping roses in a friggin' park. She stared up at the watermarked ceiling and wondered what she could have spent the train fare on instead.

She'd had enough of this run around. Her chair screeched as she stood up. 'Well, this has been fun Mum but I've gotta get back. I had to switch to the evening shift to make up my hours.' Tiff and Dee got to their feet as well.

Their mum sat up too, her face looking very solemn between them. 'There's something else I need to discuss with you.' Suddenly her face brightened into a smile as broad as Mile End Road. 'My boat's come in and I intend to spread the love around. Now sit yourselves back down and cop an ear on. I think you'll like what you're about to hear . . .'

Eight

Babs felt like the cat with the cream when her daughters parked themselves round the table again. She wanted to rub her hands in glee; they were going to be chuffed to bits at her news. What person in their right head wouldn't be? She'd used the cover of the parole to mask the real reason for this family sit-down, as her news needed to be managed face to face. She loved her girls but they were so different. Dee had a big personality, big heart, but also a big temper. Tiff was sharp, but – Babs hated to admit it – she could be a sly one at times; you couldn't always turn your back on her. And Jen ... sadness tugged at Babs' heart. Her Jennifer was too soft-hearted for her own good. Look how that dickhead of an ex-husband had treated her before Jen had finally given him his marching orders. The poor love looked like life wasn't worth living anymore. What would it do to Jen if she ever discovered her and Courtney's secret? Just thinking it made Babs' tummy knot up.

She set a huge smile on her face. 'I've got some cracking news ladies. As chance would have it I've come into posses-sion of some property.'

'Whatcha mean, property?' Tiff interrupted, her face full of doubt.

'Like a caravan?' Jen added.

'Me? In a camper van?' Dee wrinkled her nose in distaste and kissed her teeth. 'Not in this life or the next.'

Babs held her hands up. Once she had their full attention again she continued. 'It's a couple of houses. In London.'

'Where in London?' Tiffany had her sly look on.

'That don't matter.' She didn't want to answer any awkward questions about how the houses had ended up in her possession. 'And I tell you why it don't – I've decided to shift 'em and split the money equally between my three lovely daughters to do with as they wish. With a bit of luck and the right buyer, they should fetch nearly a million apiece. Now then, what about that?'

There was a stunned silence. Tiffany rubbed her hands as she rocked back in her seat. 'Fucking hell! That's . . .' her eyes roved around as she did the sums in her head, 'two-thirds of a mill each. Fucking fantastic. When's my share coming?'

Jen and Dee didn't utter a word, which worried Babs again. They should be jumping all over the gaff like her youngest, but they both looked like someone had stolen their winning lottery ticket. They're probably in shock, Babs decided, just like she was when she found out about the houses.

'Ease up girl,' she answered eager beaver Tiff. 'The places need freshening up so I'm having them done over first. Probably stick 'em on the market later this year, I'd imagine.'

That wiped the happy-clappy expression right off Tiff's face. 'Later this year? That's stupid, that is. Get one of them estate agents round there pronto and let's cash in.'

Babs sighed inside. Typical Tiffany. 'If they're done up first, we can get the best price for them. Best price means more money and you do want maximum wonga . . .'

'Yeah, but . . .'

Babs cut across her and turned to the other two. 'Don't you agree girls?'

Dee raised her hands in disbelief. 'I'm sorry Mum but where did you get two million quid's worth of bricks and mortar from? That don't make no sense.'

Babs was ready for this. She was the only person left alive who knew where the houses came from. The real owner, her late ex-husband Stanley Miller – God rot his soul – had signed them over to her in the '70s as part of a scam he was running. She hadn't realised at the time. Of course in those days, two, run-down Georgian houses in the East End were virtually worthless, which probably explained why he forgot about them when he fled to Spain. When he returned, twenty-odd years later, they were worth a fair bit of poke and he'd run another scam to get his greedy mitts back on them. Him and that evil bitch Florence – the bastard in more than one sense of the term. It was only when Babs was on trial for kill-ing Stan that her brief had found out that legally the houses were hers.

He was a good stick that lawyer. He'd advised her that it was a good idea to let sleeping dogs lie until the authorities weren't interested in her anymore. Let the management company run them in the meantime. Now it was three years on and Babs was looking at parole, she decided it was safe to sell them and provide for her children. It had never occurred to her to keep the money for herself. She was a mum first and fore-most. Of course, only Jen really needed the money, the other two were alright. But even so.

'All you need to know is that they're mine—'

'You haven't gone and got yourself involved with some crooked deal while you're in here, have ya?'

Babs pursed her lips, hurt to her core. 'You know I'm not really a crim. You know why I'm in here—'

Dee covered her hand quickly, looking ashamed. 'Babs, I'm sorry.' Her eldest never called her mum, out of respect to the woman who had brought her up. It was something that would hurt her heart for ever. 'You know I didn't mean that. It's just I've been so worried about what's been happening to you inside . . .'

Babs squeezed her hand. 'I know hun.' There was a closeness between her and the daughter she hadn't brought up. Maybe they had this special bond because they knew how fragile relationships could be and that you should never take anything for granted.

But she was more concerned about Jen, who just didn't look right.

'You're very quiet – you're OK about this?'

Jen looked like she'd been slapped rather than had twothirds of a million quid stuffed in her handbag for nothing. 'Yeah. Sure.'

Babs didn't understand. 'I thought you'd be over the moon? It's a lot of money. You could really change your life with it.'

Jen remained deadpan. 'I am thrilled. It's great.'

Tiffany sneered. 'If she don't want her share, I'll have it.'

Her sister turned on her in fury. 'What do you want money for anyway? You're always flashing your latest buys around, you cocky cow; you don't need any more fucking cash.'

Tiffany tore into her. 'Where we're from, *darlin'*, you can never have too much loose change sloshing around. You know what I mean?'

'Girls.' Babs' stern voice stopped any further verbal in its tracks. She was alarmed. The honest truth was, she'd been expecting the girls to show some gratitude. Come on, for fuck's sake, it wasn't every day that a bundle landed in your lap. She began to wonder if there was something else going on.

She leaned in and stared at each deeply, in turn. 'Is there a problem between you two I need to be told about?' Jen and Tiff were very different from each other and every now and again rubbed each other up the wrong way. But above all else, they were loyal to each other. They were sisters. Flesh and blood always came first.

Dee broke in, asking, 'These houses – they're not anything to do with Stan are they?'

Now it was Babs' turn to get the right hump. She'd already decided that there was only so many details the girls needed to know about those houses and Stan wasn't one of them. 'You're not listening, are ya? I've told you, where they come from doesn't concern you.'

'Because if they are,' Dee carried on, as if her mum hadn't spoken, 'shouldn't Stan's other daughter be getting a share out? What was her name? Fleur? Florence?'

The mention of *that girl* was a red rag to the rest of the family. It was Tiffany who shouted, 'Fuck off – she ain't getting a slice. What's the matter with ya?'

Dee bared her teeth. 'What's the matter with me? I'm only saying if those houses are anything to do with Stan then maybe it's right and proper the other kid should be cut in. I ain't got no love for the girl, but I know what it's like being the kid on the outside . . .'

'Oh Dee.' Babs slumped slightly. She still carried around a ton of guilt about not being there for her beautiful Desiree as a child.

But Dee wouldn't let her butt in. 'It ain't the girl's fault she was born on the wrong side of the blanket. Those houses are something to do with your guy, aren't they Babs? He was the property man. I ain't weeping no tears for that cunt – he got what was coming to him – but that ain't his girl's fault. If I'm right, it's only decent to cut this Florence-Fleur into the loop.'

'Decent?' Tiffany sneered. 'Alright, we'll give her the door knockers and the garden sheds. How's that sound?'

Babs should've known that Dee would suss this had something to do with Stanley. But every time that bastard came into their lives, there was trouble. Even from the grave he was casting his evil spell. Babs made the decision to lie. 'You don't need to worry about any knockers. May I remind you that slag was Stan's wing-girl for his last scam, so she wouldn't be in for anything, even if they were his houses. Which they're not, OK? And I'd thank you for not calling your ol' mum a liar.'

Dee was off on one now. 'So these drums fell off a Christmas tree did they?'

'They belonged to your Granddad George. The papers were found recently by one of my cousins in a shoebox her mum had in the attic.' Babs rattled away with her desperate lie, crossing her fingers under the table. 'My dad was a canny man and always kept a bit squirrelled away. Poor soul started to lose his marbles towards the end, probably forgot all about 'em.'

Dee wasn't convinced but she eased back in her seat. 'OK. In that case, you shouldn't be giving us dick. If Granddad George left them to you, they're yours. Keep the money and pamper yourself when you come out. God knows you deserve it after what you've been through. We don't need it anyway.'

This was too much for Tiffany and Jen. They turned on their sister in fury. Tiff cried, 'Don't need it? Of course we fucking need it.'

Jen joined in the battle. 'It's alright for you, shacked up with your retired gangster. I've got kids to think about!'

Dee folded her arms in disgust. 'You're a right pair you two. Your mum offers you a load of money and you can't even say thanks very much – never mind tell her to keep the cash, move off that crap estate and enjoy her winnings. What a couple of right selfish freeloaders you are.'

In the silence that followed, the three women glared at each other.

Babs looked on in stunned horror. This was the last thing she'd expected. How had good news turned so bad? She was suddenly in a hurry to get this over with.

In a mum's voice she cut the meeting short. 'I've made my decision and it's final. I've asked a friend of mine to do the refurbishment and as soon as that's finished, we'll put them on the market. Hopefully I'll be out among the living by then and I can oversee all the paperwork. Alright? Dee, I've left a key for you at my brief's, just in case.'

Tiffany mumbled under her breath, 'Waste of time, flog 'em now . . .'

Babs had had enough. She hissed, 'You keep a civil tongue in your mouth, my girl, and do as you're told.' She was fed up to the back teeth of her daughters. 'That's it then. You can go.'

They filed out of the room in silence. Babs threw her hands up in despair as she heard them start to go at each other again in the corridor. She wasn't sure what she'd expected when she passed on the good news but it wasn't this.

The shouting got louder.

Babs began to wonder if she'd made a terrible mistake.

Nine

The first thing Flo Miller did when she opened the door to her grandfather's house was dump the black bin liners containing her clothes and possessions in the hallway. Her granddad, respectfully known as The Commander as a nod to his days in the Navy, lived in an elegant villa in trendy Notting Hill. It looked like something out of a fairy tale, a stunning white building with large windows looking out on the world from each of its four floors. Of course, he had an equally magnificent residence in the country, and another place in New York, but this house seemed to be where he most enjoyed kicking up his heels.

She rang the silver ship's bell that was hanging in the hallway. It had HMS Grenada engraved on it – the last ship he'd commanded. She always rang it out of habit when she visited.

'Back again Florence?' he called from the drawing room.

Just hearing his voice made her feel calmer. 'Mummy's thrown me out. Again. I was hoping I could have my room here for a while?'

Flo's features softened with love when she found her maternal granddad sitting at a fancy table with a pile of matchsticks, some glue and the model he was making of the HMS *Victory*. He was dressed in his usual rig of patent leather shoes, grey slacks, an expensive woollen jacket with a ship's crest on its pocket and a green and red silk cravat around his neck. His face was lined but impish and only his waves of snowy white hair showed his real age. He'd obviously been a bit of a dandy in his younger days. He'd been making a model of the HMS *Victory* out of matchsticks as far back as Flo could remember. He was crazy about ships. He was also an avid collector of mementoes from ports around the world and his house looked like a pocket British Museum. On one wall was an antelope head from Kenya. Flo hung her Chloe red suede handbag on one of its horns.

He didn't look up from his work. 'Oh dear, had another set-to with her?'

Flo wasn't in the mood to talk about it, but The Commander was the only person she wouldn't be rude to. 'You could say that.'

The Commander stuck a matchstick to the *Victory*'s mast. 'Yes, well, she's always been a difficult woman, your mother.'

'I prefer to describe her as a complete bitch personally.'

They'd always had a rubbish relationship. Her mother was always putting that stuff she painted – which she had the nerve to call art – before her daughter. And though she'd never come out and say it Flo was a reminder of the time in her life when a Cockney geezer had pulled the wool over her toff eyes, got her down the aisle and in bed on a bogus marriage certificate. But Flo didn't give a flying bollocks what anyone said – Stanley Miller had been the best dad in the world.

The Commander grinned when he finally looked up. 'Well, all I can say is that when your poor old granddad passes on to the great shipyard in the sky, he's put a little something to one side so you can buy a place of your own and forget all about your mother.'

Flo walked over and kissed him on his forehead. He squeezed her arm. But she was hoping she wouldn't need to wait for a legacy. She already owned property that had been stolen from her by the Miller family. And she was determined to get it back.

'Am I alright to crash here for a week or two while I get myself sorted out?'

'Of course my dear, although I'm surprised you don't want to stay with one of your wealthy gentlemen friends rather than your grumpy old granddad.'

Flo put a mock hurt look on her face. 'Wealthy gentlemen friends? Are you calling me a tart Commander?'

He chuckled. 'You make it sound as if I disapprove. The ability to attract wealthy gentlemen is a very useful talent for a young woman.'

That was what Flo loved about him. There was no side to him and no lectures. He knew she liked living her life 'the Flo way' and unlike her mum he smiled at her adventures instead of screaming that she'd end up like her no-good, cheating father.

'I'll take my stuff up to my usual room then.'

The Commander peered at her over his glasses. 'Ah, I'm afraid you can't have that room, I've let it to someone.'

Flo was outraged. That was her room. And she was confused too. No one came to The Commander's house apart from a long procession of prostitutes. Others would have condemned him for it but Flo took the view that for a bloke in his seventies, it showed admirable stamina. Flo's mother, Clare, was banned from the house after calling him a dirty old man when she met a lady of the night on the villa's steps one morning. The Commander didn't get on with Clare anyway and Flo thought it was a shared hatred of her mother that had brought them together in the first place.

'Who have you let my room to?'

'Well, it's not really your room m'dear, is it? Anyway, I didn't let it, she sort of moved in.'

'And who is this freeloader?'

'Her name's Jezebel. She's upstairs at the moment having a nap. Poor soul, I think she's tired.'

I bet, Flo thought maliciously. Jezebel? Obviously some tart who'd decided to take advantage of The Commander's good nature. She left the room without a word, marched upstairs to her old room and threw the door open. 'Alright, Miss Jezebel, you've had your bit of fun . . .'

But the only living thing there was a cat with purplish fur lying on the bed. Nor was there any sign that the room had a tenant or that it had even been touched since her last visit. So where was Jezebel?

The cat yawned and stretched its legs before it realised there was an intruder. For a moment, it tilted its head sideways and looked at Flo with cutting green eyes. When Flo made no effort to leave, the animal arched its back, wagged its tail, bared its teeth and began to hiss at her like a witch.

Flo went back downstairs. 'You let my room to a cat?'

'Yes, that's right – Jezebel.' He looked shamefaced. 'But as I say I didn't really let it, she just turned up here one morning, liked the look of your room and moved in.'

'A cat?' she threw back incredulously.

'I understand how you feel, but Jezebel is a Persian Blue, there's no arguing with them. They're very highly strung and liable to get hysterical if crossed.' He touched his cheek, which had a few small scabs on it. 'And they've got very sharp claws. It's not their fault. The Persian Blue is a bit inbred you see. We had one as the ship's cat on a destroyer I commanded. A couple of weeks after she boarded, there were no rodents for miles. Even the toughest sailors would avoid her when she was in a bad mood. And seafarers don't scare easily.'

Flo marched off again. 'We'll see about that . . .'

Having had her nap disturbed, Jezebel was grooming herself, licking her backside on the bed. She seemed shocked when, despite the warning she'd been given, Flo came back into the room. With contempt the cat turned her backside towards Flo and resumed her cleaning routine.

Flo held the door open for the unwanted guest and pointed at the landing. 'Alright *Jez*, I'm a bit inbred too and I don't like being crossed neither. Now move your arse or your fur's gonna end up as the lining on a pair of ladies' mitts.'

Flo couldn't help slipping into the East End lingo she'd learned at Stanley Miller's knee. Despite being educated at exclusive schools, when she got really rattled she became her dad's daughter. For some reason she could never understand, her ability to switch from upmarket to downtown seemed to frighten people. She used this to her advantage whenever she could.

When the cat ignored her, Flo made her move and grabbed the squatter by the scruff of its neck. The cat's paws flew in a blur of purple, forcing Flo's grip to loosen. She had four bloody nicks on her wrist. Jezebel looked up to see if Flo had got the message.

She had. But as she left, nursing her wound, Flo pointed her finger and warned, 'This ain't over. You bet your last tin of Whiskas on it.'

Flo went back downstairs to get her bag. Without looking up from the *Victory*, The Commander whispered, 'I told you not to argue with her.'

Flo flounced out with her bag. She went into the room next to Jezebel's and made a lot of noise unpacking just so her new neighbour got the message that the fight was still on. Then she sat on the bed and rummaged in her bag until she found what she wanted – a small, creased black-and-white photo of her dad, which she carried everywhere. It was him back in the '70s, wearing a safari suit, sitting like he was Lord of the Manor in the office of the modelling agency he'd once run.

The anger she felt towards the Millers filled her with poisonous thoughts. Her precious, kind-hearted father had rescued an
unmarried, pregnant Babs from shame. And how had she shown
her gratitude? With a stake through his heart. The bitch! Five
bloody years, that's all that pathetic judge had given her for
taking Stan's life. And now they wanted to keep his houses all
to themselves? She wasn't going to let that happen.

Flo would've got on to avenging her dad sooner, but after
Stanley's death she'd gone over the edge, including dipping a
finger or two into her mum's purse. 'I refuse to have a thief
living here. What are the neighbours going to say?' her mum
had finally declared.

Who gave two fucks about the neighbours? Since when did
they get a say in her life? OK, she was the first to admit she'd
taken a few liberties with her mum's gold card, especially that
first class, all-inclusive deal to the Bahamas. Her mother
shipped her off, minus credit cards and her allowance, to her
Uncle Max in New York. But she'd never lost the grief over her
father's death. It was like a knife carving away at her every
second of every day. And the only way she could deal with it
was to get off her face on booze and drugs. In the end she'd
made such a proper nuisance of herself her uncle and his stick
thin wife had thrown up their hands in despair and shipped
her back.

She'd never forgiven Babs Miller for thieving Stan's property out from under his nose and she was working on a number
of schemes to get it back. It involved working various wealthy
gentlemen. As Flo knew only too well, men were a lot easier
to push around than Persian Blues.

She looked at the photo and vowed, 'I'm gonna get them
tea-leafing cunts, Dad. Babs Miller will regret the day her
miserable life started.'

Ten

'I swear to God, I'll have his fucking knackers off!' Dee stormed as she parked up outside her house.

As if the drive home from Her Majesty's Hilton wasn't bad enough, she flew into another rage when she spotted that fucking car in the driveway. She held it back well but Dee hated seeing Babs behind bars. The mother she'd only got to know as an adult was so precious to her. Their relationship had got off to a very rocky start but as soon as Dee had twigged why her mum had been forced to give her away her heart went out to her. It couldn't have been easy for her back when there was so much shit thrown at white women who had birthed brown babies.

That's why she was so mad at her sisters. Babs had been through some heartbreaking struggles and now they wanted to pile up more crap at her door. After the meeting with their mum, the gloves really came off between them. Things had got said. The kind of things that take a lot of smoothing over later. But, as far as she was concerned, it was Jen and Tiff who would have to do the smoothing. Her ladyship Jen was an ungrateful moo who'd sulked when her mum had flashed the cash, while cocksure Tiffany was a selfish money grabber who couldn't even be arsed to hide her red-eyed greed.

So her journey home had turned into one long road rage. Dee had cut people up, flashed her lights and blown her horn at anyone who'd paused at junctions or dawdled when the lamps turned green. She'd even threatened to clump a bloke who was a bit slow getting over a zebra crossing.

She'd calmed down as soon as her house came into view. She'd fallen in love with the place the first time she'd clapped eyes on it. It was a monster of a home. Six bedrooms, three en suite, a gym and pool, a cinema room that she called The Hollywood, combined snooker and bar and a roomy lounge to die for. On the open market it would've cost John a packet and a half, but it had ended up in his hands as part payment for a debt. Dee felt she could really call this place her own, and she was particular about who came calling. Seeing the knocked-up motor outside made a tidal wave of rage rise up. That car only meant one thing – trouble.

'What the fuck?' she fumed as she slammed into the house. She slung her bag and shades on a side table. She heard voices coming from the kitchen so she made a beeline for it. Sitting at the brekkie bar was John and that fuck-off merchant Tom. Just seeing him put her on edge. Tom was years younger than her old man, but Dee was terrified their bond would drive John back into the underworld. Her hubby didn't think she knew anything about Tom, but she knew alright. She'd made it her business to find out. And there was another reason she didn't want the git putting in an appearance, which she'd keep tucked away for ever.

'Hello bird,' John greeted her. Dee squinted slightly; she knew her man and he looked jumpy. 'You remember Tom, don't you?'

Dee ignored the question and the git. 'Babes, can I bend your ear for a moment please? In private?'

John got up. 'Excuse me a minute mate.'

Tom waved his words off. 'No problem.' His gaze drifted to Dee. 'If I had a lady like your missus I'd use any excuse to be alone with her every minute of the day.'

Dee itched to throw something at the smarmy shit face, but marched off instead with John following her.

As soon as they were inside the lounge Dee kicked the door shut. 'What the hell is *he* doing here?'

'What, Tom?' John stared at her puzzled.

'I don't see any other plonker in our home. What does he want?'

John strolled past the large tropical fish tank at the back of the room and poured himself a sizeable Scotch. 'The fella's just dropped round for a cuppa. What's got your G-string in a twist?'

Dee marched over and snatched the glass from him. 'You promised you'd start a health kick. You ain't getting any younger.' She tipped the drink into the aquarium. The fish went into a frenzy swimming towards the brown liquid, their mouths gulping convulsively. 'I thought I told you, in no uncertain terms, that I don't want that creep round here no more?'

John threw his hands in the air. 'I don't get what your problem is—'

'*My* problem?' Her eyebrows flew to her hairline.

'Yeah, *your* problem. The geezer's always a proper gent and all you can do is gripe and grouse at him.'

Gripe and grouse? She resisted the urge to grab her block-head of an old man by the scruff of his Armani shirt. 'I've said I don't want him round here.'

'Yeah, I hear you loud and clear, as I'm sure do the neighbours. But you know what darlin', you didn't say why.'

Dee's face heated up. She twisted away from John, went over to the drinks cabinet and poured herself some Prosecco from the chiller. She gulped down a mouthful, trying to figure out what to say. 'He's as dodgy as a gilt-covered turd, that's why.'

John chuckled. 'Dodgy used to be my middle name but you don't mind me being around here, do you?'

Dee strode impatiently up to her husband. 'But that's the thing, babes, you ain't dodgy no more. You're respectable now, a pillar of the community. I can feel in my bones that that numb nuts is trying to get you involved in some Mickey Mouse venture.' She put her arms around his neck, her glass settling against his skin. She kissed John sweetly on the lips and whispered, 'Tell him to sod off and find some other bird's hubby to cosy up to.'

John got the needle and shook out of her embrace. 'He's not a villain. He's a builder, a bloody top one at that. He came up the hard way, just like me and he's done alright by hisself, making a pile along the way. He's just popped over to see if I want to sign up for a pro-am golf match for a local children's charity. That's what he does. He's a nice bloke.'

Dee threw the glass across the room. It shattered into tiny pieces as it hit the wall. Her chest heaved with anger. 'Get. Him. Out.'

Without a word John left the room. Dee's hands clawed in the air, ready to drag Tom out of the house herself. She was stopped from taking action when she heard laughter and the front door opening.

'Alright Tom,' she heard John say, 'sign me up for the golf. The quack says I could use the exercise anyway.'

'The quack needs an eye test coz you look as fit as a fiddle to me mate.' Dee rolled her eyes. The smooth talking fake-up artist.

'Gimme a bell about the golf.'

The front door closed. Dee went over to the window and lifted part of the curtain out of the way so she could spy on him as he left. He got into that disgraceful motor of his – fancy running around in a rust bucket like that – and, maybe realising she was watching him, looked up and caught her eye. He sent her a slow, slow smile. Dee kissed her teeth with contempt as she let the curtain drop.

Successful builder, my rear end.

John came back in and this time when he helped himself to a bevvy she didn't object. 'Satisfied?'

'There's something about Tom that don't add up.'

John let out a long puff of exasperation, plonked down in his armchair and picked up the newspaper. 'Whatever.'

'I'm warning you, if you get mixed up in any badness again, you're out. You can move in with Tom and drive around in his half-car picking up knackered tarts.'

John pursed his lips. 'I haven't been involved in the life for years. It's a young man's game anyway. Now then – how's your mum up at the Hilton?'

Dee was glad of the change of subject and got nice and cosy on her leopard-print chaise longue as she told him Babs' news. Her blood pressure skyrocketed again when she reported Jen and Tiffany's reaction. John read his paper and did that bloke's thing of listening without really listening. He obviously couldn't care less and merely grunted 'that's good' or 'that's bad' when she let him have a space to do so.

'I mean, really John, can you believe them two? Not a word of thanks passed their lips. Two million quid between the three of us and they can't even say ta very much? They're a right pair . . .'

John's ears seemed to prick up. 'A couple of mill? What are these properties then? Period places? With attics, basements, that kind of thing?' He paused for thought as he placed the paper in his lap. 'And who's doing them up for your mum? Babs should've asked me to get that sorted. I know loads of people who'll do a really tasty job and it won't cost a penny – I've got guys who owe me.'

'I don't care about any refurbishment. She shouldn't be giving nish away. She's had a hard life and ended up doing serious bird for killing a monster. She should be enjoying her just reward, not handing it over – especially to those two.'

John lost interest, opening his paper again. 'Yeah . . .'

Dee decided to go and ring a friend who would actually listen to what she was saying. She got herself a coffee and went to sit in the conservatory to have a good natter about her no-good sisters. But as she made herself comfy, alarm came over her. John wasn't thinking of– Dee flew back into the lounge. John was on the phone but rang off when she blustered in.

She pointed a long fingernail at him. 'You'd better get one thing straight mate – no way is your lousy chum Tom doing any work on my mum's houses. Is that clear?'

'Where are these houses?' he asked, avoiding her question.

'She wouldn't say. Says she inherited them from her dad. But she told me to pick up a set of keys from her solicitor for safe keeping.'

'Umm.' John tucked into his Scotch for a few seconds then said, 'I can always find out where they are. I've got a mate who's a dab hand at finding info on the land registry.'

Dee thought for a bit. It was betraying her mum's wishes, but still . . . 'Alright. Get him to put his snout about.' She squinted. 'Don't try no nifty shit behind my back, getting that twat Tom to do the building work. Although we both know that isn't his main business.'

John looked innocent. 'I don't know what you're chatting about.'

She shook her head. 'When will you learn that I wasn't born under a knows-nothing bush. I know who Tom really is.'

She watched with satisfied glee as panic spread across his lying face. 'And I know that his name ain't Tom, it's Kieran.'

Eleven

To say that Jen was pissed off as she emerged from a heaving Mile End tube was the understatement of the century. First off, she couldn't believe that her mum had a pile tucked away and had kept schtum about it all these years. Mum had always seen Jen as the sensible daughter and confided in her. OK, maybe Babs had held back about their dad all those years, but seeing what a total conniving crook Stanley Miller had turned out to be, she could forgive her that. Jen felt the same about talking to her girls about Nuts, their dad. But owning not one, but two fuck-off houses in London that were worth a mint and not letting on was something Jen didn't think she was going to come to terms with for a long time.

And if that wasn't enough, Mum thought that the money should be divvied up equally between the three of them. As if! Dee was living it large in that mansion Essex way, courtesy of tying the knot with former gangland hard man John Black. What did she need more dosh for? Probably to splash out on – yet again! – another deluxe Caribbean cruise or a fleet of new motors. Her half-sister did like her cars, as Jen remembered from that awful business three years ago. And if their mum thought a portion should go to Nicky . . . well, Jen liked the kid well enough, but let's face it he was only Dee and

John's adopted son; he wasn't really family at all. Plus, as John and Dee's only child he was in line to inherit the lot when they cocked their toes up; the kid didn't need a helping hand from someone else.

But what really stuck in her craw was Tiffany. Her one-time yobbo sister had landed on her feet like a *Big Issue* seller with a jackpot lottery ticket and ended up in some swanky block in Canary Wharf. Tiff had claimed that it was the council who'd set her up there, but Jen had asked around and the word was it was all privately owned. How her sister had got the rent she would never know, but at the end of the day that wasn't what mattered. Tiff had managed to get off The Devil's Estate and was living it right up. The only responsibility she had was to herself, unlike Jen.

She felt the weight of the world on her shoulders as she entered The Devil. There was a crowd near the flashing lights of a fire engine, no doubt due to some kids having a laugh and calling 999 to say someone was stuck in a lift. Sometimes she hated this place. She ignored the fuss and kept moving. The council had decided to do up a few blocks on the estate after years of neglect, so part of The Devil looked like a building site with buildings covered in scaffolding and tarpaulin. Of course, sod's law, Jen's wasn't one of the ones being done up. There had been a right have-a-go from some of Jen's louder mouthed neighbours, but the council were adamant – they didn't have the cash to do any more work.

Jen had kept herself well back from the row. She was a single mum with two growing girls who needed clothes on their backs and bread on the table. Her mum's windfall should be split five ways, not three, to take account of Courtney and Little Bea. That was only fair; anyone with a working brain in their head could see that. She'd worked her fingers to the bone and needed more of a leg up than her sisters.

She arrived at the lift in her block and realised that it was out of order – again. As she trudged up the stairs, guilt ate into her. She told herself she should be grateful. Two-thirds of a mill would cover a lot of bills. But her life-long problem was her soft heart. No way would Tiffany lose sleep in her position; she'd come out fighting for more money if she had kids. Whatever she got was still going to be a pretty penny. But even a pretty penny didn't go far these days. How could they not see that? Why was she always taken for a mug?

As she reached her front door her mobile went off. Probably some new customer wanting her to do their ironing, which she took in to make ends meet. It didn't improve her mood, making her feel more hard done by than ever.

But she plastered on her best voice; she couldn't afford to turn work away. 'Jennifer Miller.'

'I'm down The Knackered Swan. Fancy a snifter?'

Jen smiled hearing her best mate Bex's merry voice. She looked at the door. She should really go in, get the girls' tea on the go and a bit of shut-eye before doing the late shift tonight. But slaving away over the cooker was the last thing she fancied.

'I'll be there in ten.'

After she got her afternoon registration mark, Courtney wasted no time before doing a bunk. Five minutes later she was in the toilets of the nearby Nando's changing out of her uniform into a figure-hugging black T-shirt, mauve, mini ra-ra skirt and leopard-print flats. She topped it off with a pale blue stone necklace she'd palmed down The Roman a few weeks back, and knock-off D&G shades. The only slap she put on was some extreme black eye liner, lashings of mascara and bold blue eye shadow. The mags said it was all about the eyes these days.

Only one more thing to do . . . She pulled out the quart bottle of whisky she'd nabbed from the offy and slugged back two mouthfuls.

As soon as she hit the cool air on her way to The Devil, the booze turned the world nice and hazy. Her mum would do her nut if she sussed that she was on the sauce most days. The drink was the only thing that made her forget her and Nanna Babs' secret. It was the reason she didn't touch red lipstick; it reminded her of all that blood. Only bad girls did what she'd done, she told herself. Every day it was getting harder to live with. Sometimes she just wanted to tell someone the truth, but her nan had warned her to keep her gob shut. Nanna had said if she told a soul Nanna would get into trouble. And she didn't want more aggro coming to Nanna Babs' door; she was already banged up for pity's sake. Suddenly tears lined the bottoms of her eyes. She missed Babs so much.

'Court,' someone yelled as she walked onto The Devil.

She quickly sucked the tears back as she saw her friend Natasha on a bench near the chemists, smoking a fag. As usual there was a crowd of local lads hanging around her. Tash wasn't a stunner but she put enough skin on display to give the boys on The Devil ideas. Courtney liked hanging around with her. She was a few years older at fifteen and knew how to have a good time.

As soon as she reached her the other girl handed her a ciggy and Courtney puffed away. She thought smoking was disgusting but did it because she wanted to come across as all grown up.

'I thought you'd never get here,' Tash said. She turned her gaze to the boys and batted her lashes. 'But these gentlemen were keeping me company.'

One of the lads saw his opportunity and took it. 'So, you coming round to mine then?'

Tasha cocked her head to the side in a classy pose that Courtney often tried to perfect in the mirror. 'Maaaaybe,' the older girl strung out. Then she shoved her head back up straight. 'Nah. Me and my mate here have got real fellas to see.'

She grabbed Courtney's hand and they rushed away, giggling their heads off. Courtney's eyes darted apprehensively behind her sunglasses. She couldn't take the chance that any of her mum's mates might clock her. If that happened there would be murder when she got indoors. Her mum had made it crystal clear that she didn't want her daughter knocking round with the likes of Natasha Wood. *'She's going the same way as that mum of hers, mark my words, crooking her pinkie so men can sniff up her skirts. That girl is heading for trouble, if it hasn't found her already.'*

But that was her mum all over – always wanting to put a crimp on her. She loved her mum and had hated her dad when he knocked her about, but she didn't want to be like her, always mashed up and washed out. Tasha's mum was always turned out to the eyeballs, her make-up never out of place.

Anyway, after what had gone on with her and her nan she'd learned to take the good times when you could get them; you didn't know what was waiting for you round the corner.

Tash wasn't the only thing her mum had warned her to stay away from. She'd put her straight about the block of flats that they were now outside – Bridge House, aka The Devil's Playground. It was the newest building on the estate, a broad, six-floor block, built two years ago. The irony was it was built above the old underground car park the residents called Neverland, a place riddled with crime. Those in the know soon learned if you didn't want your car burned out, or ending up on a pile of bricks, you parked it elsewhere.

Soon after Babs had been sent down, the council had the brainwave of driving out the criminals in the shadows by bulldozing it flat and putting up a new block. But they'd got that spectacularly wrong. Soon a worse set of villains had taken over the top floor and created a whole new criminal empire.

Courtney swallowed nervously. The stories she'd heard about this place were enough to make her scarper home and hide under her duvet. Plus, her mum would be expecting her home in an hour. She didn't fancy her rearing up in her face again. So she asked tentatively, 'What are we doing here?'

Tash gazed at her. 'You ain't turning all scaredy cat on me?'

Courtney huffed, 'Course I ain't. What do I look like? A little kid or something?'

Tash arched her brow. 'Some mates of mine are having a little get together.' She linked her arms with Courtney's. 'Come on, it's gonna be a real giggle.'

Twelve

Jen perked up instantly when she heard Bex's raucous, nasal laughter as she walked into The Knackered Swan. That was her best mate all over; most times she was heard before seen. They had been bosom buddies since school days and had remained as tight as twins through their many ups and downs. The difference now was that Jen had been on a downer for too long whereas Bex had found herself a bloke who treated her like a queen. Just the thought of a fella making her his number one priority made Jen's heart squeeze.

The pub was packed. It had mostly shaken off its local nickname of The Knackered Swan – although Jen and Bex still liked to call it that. The longstanding landlord, Jacko, had handed it over to a young couple who'd put money and elbow grease into turning it into a boozer the estate could be proud of. Even some of those trendy types living on the other side of Mile End Road popped in every now and again.

Jen dropped a few hellos to neighbours and friends as she made a beeline for the bar, ordered a drink and then headed for Bex. She was sitting with a stunning, stylish woman Jen hadn't met before.

'You took your sweet time getting here,' Bex greeted Jen tartly.

Bex was a big girl who enjoyed pouring herself into too-tight clothes. Today was no different. Her jumper-tube dress, a throwback to the '90s, showcased her eye-grabbing boobs and muffin top. Her belly had been the cause of a lifelong addiction to crazy diets, and by the size of the drink in her glass, Jen decided she must be on the whisky one.

Jen didn't answer, gazing at the other woman. 'Who's your friend?'

'Naz. She's my Samuel's aunt.'

Jen's eyebrows shot up. Sam was Bex's only child, a year younger than Courtney. She loved that boy to death and, in Jen's opinion, let him get away with murder. She was trying to make up for a Turkish dad who had failed to tell Bex he already had a missus and a couple of young 'uns tucked up indoors. The wife had come after Bex with a baby oil bottle filled with acid, leaving the nasty scar on her left cheek, a reminder that nice girls don't always end up with nice blokes. Jen was surprised that her mate had anything to do with that bastard's family.

'A boy should know who his blood relatives are,' Naz said, as if reading her mind.

Jen had met Sam's dad a few times and he'd been a right ugly sort. But not his sister. Naz was a head turner with velvet brown eyes that could melt a man's heart and a curtain of thick black hair. She wore a navy box jacket over a plain white T-shirt and tight fitting jeans. On anyone else it would've looked everyday but on Naz, with her endless legs and long neck, it was a killer look.

'Well, that's good of you, I must say,' Jen said. 'My ex did a bunk years back and I haven't seen him or his people since, thank God.' She shivered just thinking about Nuts. How she'd let herself get hoodwinked by such a slime merchant she would never know.

Bex's eyes bulged incredulously as she looked at Jen's drink. 'What the fuck's that?'

'Orange juice,' Jen answered defiantly.

Bex scoffed. 'Are you having me on? Orange juice ain't been your drink of choice since we were in nursery.' Her laughter was wiped off her face as she whispered, 'You ain't put the kybosh on the booze have you? Become Saint Jennifer or something?'

Sudden heat rushed over Jen as embarrassment kicked in. Her purse was practically empty so the cheap juice was the only drink she could afford. She'd almost ordered a glass of tap water, but that would've been like broadcasting her money troubles to the world. She felt humiliated to tell Bex the truth. Ashamed. But she'd never been one to lie to her friend and she wasn't going to start now. 'Money's tight, that's all.' Her palms tightened around the glass, coldness seeping into her fingertips. 'It isn't right to spend dosh like a fish down the local when my girls need clothes.'

Bex's face fell. 'Why didn't you tell me you were hard up? I would've lent you the cash, no questions asked.'

Jen's hands slipped into her lap where they tightened into fists. Her bestie was turning into one of her interfering sisters. 'And that's why I kept my gob shut. I'm not a charity case.' Go to her mate on the scrounge? Not on her life.

With a huff Bex shoved back into her seat. 'You wanna contact that Nuts and make the tit pay through the nose for leaving you to struggle on your own–'

'No way,' Jen punched out. 'The best thing that arsehole ever did was sign those divorce papers. I don't know which dark, nasty stone he's slithered under and don't wanna know.' Just thinking about Nuts made her head ache and body hurt as if feeling the bruises his fists had left all over her.

With a determined expression, Bex stood up and declared, 'What you need, my girl, is a Scarlet O'Hara.' It was Jen's poison of choice. Southern Comfort mixed with cranberry juice and a shot of lime topped with ice.

'I've just said—'

Bex waved her words away like they were flies annoying her. 'This ain't charity. The best way of forgetting your troubles is to have a bevvy or two.' And without waiting for a response she headed for the bar.

'She's quite a woman,' Naz broke in softly.

Jen twisted to face her, having almost forgotten she was there. 'The best mate a girl could have. If it wasn't for Bex helping out with the girls over the years I don't know what I would've done.'

Naz shook her long, shimmering hair off her shoulders and crossed her long legs. 'I learned a long time ago that the best life for a woman is an independent one.'

'Oh yeah?' Jen announced sceptically. 'You sound like a woman who don't have any kids.'

Naz's smile lit up her face. 'Misha's twenty and Aydin is eighteen.'

Jen looked her up and down as if seeing her for the first time. 'Get outta here. You don't look old enough.'

Naz chuckled and added, with pride, 'Both of them are at university.' She shrugged. 'And I've done it more or less on my own.'

'How did you manage it?'

Naz's voice dropped. 'I took charge of my life and started my own business. Nothing big, just enough to make sure that my children would live a comfortable life.' She leaned across the table. 'I do hate seeing a good, honest mother struggling. You need money and I think I'm the person who can put plenty of it your way.'

Jen stared at her with open admiration. 'What type of business you into?'

Naz looked her square in the eye. 'Entertainment.'

'Like what? Music? The movies?' The woman looked the part, Jen decided, all gloss and glamour.

Naz placed her glass down carefully. 'Not quite. I entertain men.'

'How do you mean . . .?' Then Jen reared back, disgusted. 'You've got me dead wrong if you think I'm the type who puts it about for cash-in-hand.' She couldn't believe that Naz was a Tom. No wonder she appeared to be living in the lap of luxury. Selling her tail to dirty old codgers, that's how. And the fucking cheek of it, asking her to join her filthy club.

'You've got it all wrong.'

Eyes spitting fire, a furious Jen sneered, 'You just told me, point blank, that you entertain men. Where I come from that's got a name that's not very nice.'

'And that's the problem,' Naz observed quietly. 'Where me and you come from, women are told there are few options in life.' She settled back in her seat. 'I meet very rich, foreign businessmen who are away from home and just want a bit of company from a pretty lady for an evening. Nothing illegal or sordid about that. I worked with this other girl who went and got married, and good luck to her. But it means that I'm looking for another business partner.'

'Partner? I ain't got no money to put in—'

'I know that. It doesn't require an injection of cash. All it requires is your beautiful self.'

Jen dropped her head. 'I'm not beautiful and haven't got a clue how to chat up businessmen in fancy restaurants and play Lady Muckety-Muck.'

'Are you having a laugh? You're stunning.'

Jen bit her lip. Her mind moved a mile a minute. She did need extra cash. But meeting blokes . . .

She shook her head forcefully. 'Sorry, Naz, it ain't my type of thing.'

'Take this anyway, in case you change your mind.' Naz passed Jen her business card. She smiled as she lowered her voice. 'You're the type of woman wealthy, older guys would pay top dollar to meet.'

Thirteen

'Ere, have a little suck on that,' the man next to Courtney shouted at her, trying to compete with The Notorious B.I.G.'s 'Nasty Girl' blasting from the music system as he held out the half-gone spliff. He smacked his lips like he was getting ready to gobble her up as his greedy eyes ran up her clingy top. 'I've got a few other things you can suck on as well.' He laughed and winked. She didn't have a clue what that meant and from the rough look of him didn't want to know.

They were inside one of the corner flats on the top floor of The Devil's Playground. The sitting room looked more like a sleazy drug den with gear strewn on the battered coffee table and filthy floor. The place was crammed with guys, and she and Tash were the only girls, which made her very uneasy. Tash didn't seem to be having the same problem, busy getting all flirty-flirty with a couple of guys on the grubby sofa at the other end of the room. Courtney would've got up and left, but on top of the whisky she'd already downed she'd knocked back a large glass of voddy, which was making her head split and her vision blurred. She was so far gone she couldn't remember the geezer's name.

She took the spliff, wishing she hadn't as she started spluttering and coughing her guts out.

'Let me top you up.' The next thing she knew he'd swiped her glass and was back with a refill in seconds.

He got cosy next to her and she decided she didn't like the way he smelt. She wrinkled her nose as she took a deep swallow of her drink. The guy really needed to acquaint himself with some deodorant.

Before she knew it he was leaning right into her, pressing her back into the two-seater. If she had enough strength she would've pushed him off, but all of a sudden her limbs felt really heavy and her tongue thick in her mouth. Something was up; the booze had never made her feel like this before.

'Why don't you and me get comfy somewhere else?' His voice sounded distant. She couldn't understand why she was seeing three of him.

The glass slipped from her fingers, the spilt vodka adding to the dirt on the sofa. She desperately tried to move but couldn't. He picked her up as if she weighed nothing. She wanted to fight but her body was all floppy.

Now she was scared. Her hazy gaze flashed around the room until she landed on her mate. 'Tash,' which came out of her mouth as, 'Asss,' along with a dribble of spit.

But the multiple Tashes she saw only grinned back. 'Don't worry, you'll be alright and back out here in a jiffy.' At least that's what she thought her friend said, her mind was slipping in and out. She thought the others laughed as she was carried away into another room with a bedbug-ridden mattress on the floor. He dumped her on it. She wanted to wriggle away, but a powerful wave of sleep gripped her. Her eyes started drooping as she watched him undo his trousers. She was going to be sick. This couldn't be happening to her. Why wasn't her bestie doing anything to help her?

He got down next to her just as someone shouted in the sitting room, 'Where the fuck is she?'

She knew that voice.

Then she slipped into blackness as someone booted the door in.

John was in the garage, stuffing his face with a burger with all the trimmings, well away from Dee, when his mobile rang.

'Black? Is that you?'

The number on John's mobile had come up as unknown. Normally, John didn't answer unknown numbers but these weren't normal times. The voice on the other end seemed familiar, in the way of an old tune you could remember but couldn't place. 'Maybe – who's this?'

'We've got a problem.'

He coughed as the burger almost went down the wrong way. The blood leached from his face. No way . . . this couldn't be . . . He played dumb. 'Think you've got the wrong number bruv.'

The other man let out a half scoff, half laugh. 'Let's cast our minds back shall we. You were the one that recommended a private vault for my gold all those years ago. You set up an account there and did all the paperwork. I was promised my property would be totally safe. I recall you suggested Harry Houdini couldn't get in and steal it. Remember me now?'

John kept up the dumb routine. 'Nah, not really . . . Could you give me a bit of a clue here?'

The caller's voice became harsh. 'You crafty little weasel. You're the only other person who knew about it. Is that specific enough for you?'

John remained stunned. He hadn't seen this guy in years. Where the hell had he got his number from? The last time they'd met, no one apart from bankers had mobile phones.

He stalled. 'Course I remember ya. Long time no hear. How's tricks? You got something else you want stashed away? Coz if you have, I'm your man.'

John's phone nearly shook with the caller's fury. 'Do you not read the papers or watch the news Black? I've been robbed. Some Cockney yobbos broke into the vault and made off with my gold.'

'That's hard lines mate. Were you insured?'

'Are you trying to be funny? You recommended the place to me, so you're responsible for this. I'm warning you now, you'd better find out who stole it and get it back or I'll take matters into my own hands. And I might also start to suspect that you had something to do with the theft. Get my property back and get it back sharpish or there's going to be trouble.'

John was uneasy. 'Look mate, I'm a businessman not a detective . . .'

The angry caller cut him short. 'You think I lost my grip on reality as the years went by? Well, you're wrong my friend. Ask yourself how I got the gold in the first place. Then ask yourself how I got your phone number. Then ask yourself to what lengths a man in my position would go to get property of that value back. I'm putting you on notice my ol' Cockney china – find it and return it.'

The line went dead.

John put the mobile back in his pocket. Sweat popped out above his top lip. What a stroke of bad luck. He could just give the gold back . . . Nah, he shook his head. That wasn't going to happen. He thrived on this level of danger and always had. He'd heeded his wife's advice, kept his fingernails clean and only delved into business that was strictly legit for a number of years. But, truth be told, he'd missed the knife-edge life of the criminal underworld. It made him feel like a young guy again. There was no feeling like it. The rush. The adrenaline-pumping excitement. If Dee ever tumbled he was a goner for sure, but she wasn't going to find out, was she?

Organising a raid on the vault was the obvious way for him to get back into the game. On a social visit to one of the directors up there, he'd taken the chance to rummage through some yellowing manifests and found that vault 25a still contained the consignment of bullion. That was good. But even better was that no one up there had seen hide or hair of the owner for donkeys. This often happened. Villains would deposit their takings in a vault and then over the years, get killed, go on the run, get banged up or even forget where they'd left their gear. If, after all this time, the owner of the gold in 25a hadn't appeared, chances were good he never would. John didn't want anyone coming after him. But even if the bloke did turn up again, John was confident he wouldn't be armed and dangerous. He'd met the guy in a sauna and one thing had led to another, as they say. John should have been laughing. After all, he was John Black and the owner was a nobody. If the bloke had any muscle at his disposal, John would have known him, he knew all the big guys in London. But John remembered one thing about the geezer. He had, as they say, the cold blue eyes of a killer.

John couldn't do the raid himself as he was too well known. He'd flagged it up to Kieran instead and got himself a rock solid alibi. So, strictly speaking, it wasn't actually John who'd stolen the gold, was it?

Under his breath he whispered, 'Kieran had better watch out. That bloke sounds like trouble.'

Fourteen

Courtney woke up in the back seat of a car and started panicking straight away. It was parked round the back of The Devil, near the old cemetery.

'Get the fuck off me.' She lashed out at the man beside her and then wished she hadn't moved. Her tummy started rolling.

He grabbed her wrists as she fought as hard as her still foggy brain would allow.

'Knock it off Court.'

She stilled and looked at him with relief. 'Rockers.' She'd never been so pleased to see anyone in her life. 'Bloody hell, open the door.'

As soon as he did she chucked up in the gutter. Her body heaved until it hurt. He drew her gently back inside. Sixteen-year-old Dexter Ingram, nicknamed Rockers by his mates, was another entry on her mum's list of things to stay well clear of. She didn't understand what the problem was but there was bad blood between the Millers and the Ingrams. Surprisingly, it was her Nanna Babs who really flew off the handle anytime the Ingrams were mentioned. But she'd clicked with Rockers when they were at little school. It wasn't just that he was a beautiful boy, with a skin tone a similar shade to her Aunty Dee's and a gorgeous face. He was so kind hearted. They'd bonded years ago when she was seven and some flash Harry of a kid in the playground had smacked her and made her cry. He was the one boo-hooing after Rockers had finished with him, earning a two-day suspension. He'd gone at the kid so hard that some of the other children had said he'd been off his rocker, and the name Rockers had stuck. He'd been her secret good angel from that day.

His hands eased away as he checked her out. 'How you feeling?'

She shrugged and blinked a few times before answering, 'I'm alright. I'm a big girl.'

Anger covered his face. 'You're thirteen years old and if I hadn't busted up the party . . .'

She sent him a sheepish look. She didn't like to pee him off. Truth was she had a crush on him the size of Blackwall Tunnel. But she knew he didn't feel the same about her, probably because she was so much younger.

'Alright Daddy,' she let out playfully.

But he wasn't amused. 'How many times have I told you to steer clear of that place, eh? Most of the people who go there are off their nut—'

'I can take care of myself.' She loved him to bits but his finger wagging was getting on her nerves big time.

'Oh yeah?' He pushed his face close to hers. 'That's why I found you almost comatose. That dirty ole man you were with spiked your drink. He was going to have it away with you.'

'Nah.' She didn't want to believe him despite knowing full well the dangerous situation she'd ended up in. 'Tash wouldn't have let him cop a feel.'

'Are you for real? She was gonna let him cop more than a feel and you wanna know why?' She stared bug-eyed at him. 'You were her payment for money she took to buy drugs. That's the type of mate you have. Tash is trash and the sooner you get that through your thick skull the sooner you'll stop knocking around with the bitch.'

Courtney burst into tears at the sorry situation she'd allowed herself to get into. It hurt to think that her closest mate was no pal at all.

Rockers put his arms around her and hugged her tenderly. 'What's going on with you Court? Ain't nothing wrong with having a bevvy or two now and again, but you're hitting the bottle like Christmas is every day of the week.'

'I . . . I . . .' She so wanted to tell him the secret. Some days she felt the terrible thing was going to crush the life out of her. Courtney wanted to tell Rockers so bad . . . As she opened her mouth again her grandmother's words came back to haunt her: *'Whatever questions anyone asks, you've got to stick to our story. If you don't, things will get worse. Much worse.'*

She clamped her lips together. 'You can tell me,' he urged.

'No I can't,' she wanted desperately to scream back. Instead she asked, 'What were you doing up The Devil's Playground anyway?'

He pushed away from her. 'Never you mind.'

She'd heard that he'd jacked in school last summer and was running gear for some Face. But she didn't pursue it; he wanted to keep his secrets just as she wanted to keep hers.

'I need to get you home,' he said. 'Well as close to home as I can without your mum seeing me.'

Courtney looked down at herself. She was a right mess. 'Nah, if I come home like this my mum's gonna blow her top and want chapter and verse about what happened. Don't fancy that.'

'Can't take you to mine coz once my cousin Mel claps eyes on you she's gonna start playing up.'

Nanna Babs and his cousin Mel hated the very sight of each other. Courtney had been at Whitechapel Market with her mum one Saturday when they nearly collided with Rockers' cousin. Both women had blown up and would've come to blows if the guy on the fish stall hadn't pulled them apart.

'So where else can you go to get cleaned up?' he asked.

'I dunno.' Her face fell. 'My mum's gonna kill me.'

Tiff knew it wasn't going to be long before someone called the coppers. She was down The Roman but not as a punter; she'd got her own little 'stall' going, raiding her wardrobe as soon as she'd got back from visiting her mum. It was a hastily laid out blanket with her designer clothing looking like knock-down toot. She'd stuck on prices that probably wouldn't recover a tenth of what she'd paid. It was painful what she'd been reduced to but she needed the money or those two bully boys were going to do her.

Right, better get some fanny going! She launched into some OTT patter, careful not to look people in the eye so their gazes went to what she was selling not her. 'Everything is a steal! And I don't mean they've fallen off the back of a lorry neither. No, ladies and gents these are a steal coz I'm practically giving 'em away. Yeah, you heard right, giving 'em away. It's almost breaking my heart.' She placed her hands over her chest dramatically.

'Oi.' She looked across at the stallholder who'd shouted. 'You got a licence from the council?'

'Do you mean a licence to sell?' Coming out of her mouth it sounded like a James Bond movie. She shrugged him off; he wasn't the market police so he could get stuffed. 'I've got all my receipts.'

He sneered. 'Yeah, that's what all the crooks say. You can't just pitch up without a licence. It's illegal.'

'So is your face!' Tiff dismissed him, pleased to see a small crowd hovering. One woman pointed at a pair of shoes and asked, 'Are they real Blahnik?'

'Yeah, of course they are.'

'Are you sure?'

Tiffany drew breath. 'What do you want, Manolo himself to sign them for you? They're real, OK?'

The woman did a deal. Tiff started hustling more, her sharp talk drawing people to her wares. Someone said, 'This new is it?'

'As a baby's bum.'

The items started flying off and the cash rolling in. Tiff couldn't help chuckling at her good fortune. The money might not cover her whole debt but it was a start.

'Babe,' a flashy woman squealed to the man she was hanging off, 'get me those sunglasses. I always wanted a pair like that.'

Grinning for all she was worth – which wasn't much – Tiff looked at the man. The smile vanished in an instant when she clocked his face. Tommo, one of the nutters she owed. She didn't even think; she legged it leaving her prized goods behind. She could hear the bastard running after her. He might be faster but she knew all the nooks and crannies to duck into. Back alleys, side streets, a house being done up where the builders yelled at her. She finally managed to lose him as she entered the back of The Devil near the cemetery. She slumped against a wall puffing hard. That was a close one. There was no point going back to get her stuff; it would be long gone by now.

She dug her hands in her pockets and counted out her cash. Nearly two hundred quid. Not bad for fifteen minutes' work, but not enough to get Tommo and Co off her back. She shoved the cash away and started walking. She passed a car and then did a double take. She went back and peered inside. 'Why ain't you at school Court?' She looked at the young man with her – Stacey's nephew, Rockers.

Fifteen

Jen hammered her fist against her sister's door for the second time. What was taking her so long? Typical Tiff, always doing things in her own time.

'Is that you Jen?'

'No, it's a carol singer with a dodgy calendar.' For crying out loud, just open the feckin' door!

The sound of a lock pulled back and then another and yet another again. Where did Tiff think she was living? The Bank of flamin' England?

'So where's Court—?' Jen stopped, concerned, when she saw Tiff's face. 'What's up with ya? You look whiter than a movie star's teeth.'

'Forget about me.' She waved her sister's concerns away and led her towards the den. 'We need to talk about Courtney.'

Jen groaned inwardly. That's all she needed, more bovver. 'What's the little madam been up to now? And where is she?' Her daughter wasn't in the den when they entered.

Her mouth curled as she clocked the expensive gear spread all over the place. Well, well, well, look how the other half lives. She wasn't a bitter woman. She'd always been the good daughter, the good sister, the good mum. Always lived on the right side of the law, whereas Tiff had been a chancer at heart, riding her luck, ducking and diving. And look where it had got her – an Aladdin's Cave. And while Tiff was buying this, buying that, she didn't have her arse hanging out of her trousers like Jen felt most of the time. No one had to tell Jen nowadays she was looking more Dot Cotton than Kate Moss. Her skirt and top had seen better days and she had deep, dark circles under her tired eyes. Back in the day, Jen would've never let herself go in such a way. Looking the bizz had always been her thing. It wasn't fair. Life wasn't fair.

'Been on the rob again?' Jen couldn't help having a snide as she stared at the unopened DVD box.

Tiff sent her a pointed look. 'You know I ain't been part of that world for donkeys. My good fortune is down to hard work and clean living.'

Jen scoffed. 'What hard work's that then? You chucked in the job at the garage yonks back.'

Tiffany folded her arms. 'Your girl is in my bed fast asleep, looking like her world's about to end, and all you wanna do is give me the needle.'

Jen's cheeks stung with shaming heat. Tiff was right. She should stop getting in her face and find out what was up with Court. Tiff wandered off into the kitchen and came back with a couple of cans. She passed one to Jen as she sat down next to her.

'Did the school call you?' Jen's shoulders slumped with the weight of trying to bring up a teenage daughter. 'She's been playing up something chronic, giving me lip and not listening to a word I say. And the other day—' Her mouth snapped shut.

'Let me guess,' Tiff started knowingly, 'she got caught doing the five finger discount in some shop.'

Jen's mouth fell open. 'How do you know that? You psychic or something?'

'Come on Jen, you know the kind of stuff I got up to when I was a young'un. Tea leafing is one of the first rules in the

how to be an obnoxious teenager guide. We all do it.' A sly
grin spread on her face. 'And if I remember rightly you swiped
a thing or two from Woollies back in the day.'

Jen shifted uncomfortably. 'What did the school have to say
this time?'

'The only person who gave me a bell was Court. She just
wanted a bit of Aunty Tiff time.' That didn't go down well
with Jen. She didn't stop Tiff from seeing her girls, but she
put the brakes on Courtney coming to visit her. No way did
she want her daughter coming back home pissing and bitching about how much dosh Aunty Tiff had, while they had
sweet FA.

A serious expression settled on Tiff's face. 'Look, it ain't my
place to tell you how to bring up your girl,' *you got that right*,
'but there's something up with her. She looks like she's
hurting.'

Maybe it was because Tiff was younger than her but Jen
resented her baby sister giving her parenting classes. Like Tiff
knew anything about how to bring up kids. About responsibility. She spent her life gallivanting around doing what the hell
she damn well liked.

Tiff hitched her leg off the sofa. 'Why don't you send her
over to mine this weekend? If there's something bugging her
I'll find out what it is. I took on Dee's Nicky and won.'

The words twisted Jen's insides. Made her feel less than a
mum. 'No thanks. I can take care of my own kids.'

Her sister stared at her, baffled. 'Have you got a cob on or
something? Coz you know what? I don't need it. I'm only
trying to lend a helping hand here. I've got enough
problems.'

Jen could barely contain her anger. 'You don't look like
you've got any problems.'

'We've all got them love.'

Jen's eyes narrowed. 'Yeah, but problems are far easier to handle when you're living it large, don't you find?'

Tiff placed her drink on the table carefully. 'But you could be living it large too.' Her voice was barely above a whisper.

Jen frowned. 'How do you figure that out?'

Tiff shuffled closer. 'Mum's wasting time getting those houses done up. What she needs to do is put 'em on the market and get 'em sold, quick time.' Her eyes lit up. 'Then cha-ching! The readies start rolling in.'

Jen gazed at her closely. 'But that don't make no sense. If they're tarted up we'll get a whole heap more money.'

'Come on Jen,' Tiff coaxed. 'You need to get your hands on some quick cash—'

'But you don't. You're set up like the Queen of Canary Wharf here.' Jen studied her sister hard. What was going on here? But then Tiff had always been a greedy little mare.

'I think we should arrange to see Mum and make her see sense,' Tiff pressed on. 'She's already said she don't wanna cash in herself, so we should be the ones telling her what's what.'

Jen pushed out her chest slightly. 'I agree with you, we should see Mum about the houses.' Tiff couldn't help a knowing grin slipping out. It promptly vanished when Jen dropped her bombshell. 'But I'm gonna ask her to split it five ways.'

'You fucking what? She ain't got any other strays out there, like Dee?'

Jen set her face stubbornly. 'Course she hasn't—'

'So where's this number five coming from?'

Jen took in a deep punch of air. 'My Courtney and Bea should be getting their own cuts—'

Tiff didn't let her finish. 'Hold up a mo. Mum wants to leave something for her children, *not* her grandchildren.'

'Actually what she said was she wanted the girls to have cushy lives in the future.'

'And they will.' She stabbed her finger at Jen. 'From *your* share.'

Jen stretched her neck. 'Well, I don't see how it's right that I end up with the same share as you.' She ran her gaze sharply over her sister's designer pekpek shorts and leggings, her layered silver and gold chains. 'You're doing alright, plus you don't have the responsibility of kids.' She threw her arms out to emphasise the words spitting angrily from her mouth. 'You don't have a care in the world. Well, I do. I need that money and so do my children and that's why it's best that those houses get spruced up, sold on and divvied up five ways.' She cocked her head suspiciously at her baby sister. 'Why all the urgency to get your mitts in the cookie jar? What are you up to?'

Tiff gulped. 'Nuthin. I just think it's better all round – for the *three* of us,' she emphasised, which made Jen curl her lip, 'that we get those houses sold pronto. What if there's a property slump and we lose out?'

Jen folded her arms. 'You're up to something, aren't you? Trying to buy into a dodgy deal or something? That's what all your hard work usually involves.'

Tiff reared forward. 'Excuse me?'

Both women shot to their feet. Jen gazed at Tiff with scorn. 'None of this would've happened if you hadn't decided to believe our old man when he appeared like Dracula out of his coffin, claiming to be spreading the love. But, oh no, Tiffany Miller has to get her mum and sister to believe the shit he's spewing from his mouth. It's all about you, isn't it? It always is.'

Tiffany took a menacing step towards her sister. Her voice rose. 'You're getting fucking dangerously close to the line here.'

'I haven't said the half of it,' Jen ground out. 'You're the reason Dad got back into Mum's life.'

'No way—'

'Yes way. She saw through him straight away but you convinced her otherwise.'

Tiff scoffed loud and hard. 'Oh, and you didn't do your own bit of persuasion along the way?' Her lips twisted with disgust. 'That's your problem Jen, always playing Miss Little Innocent.' She slapped on a mimsy high-pitched voice. 'It weren't nuthin to do with me, I'm a good girl I am.'

'Mum? Aunty Tiff?' Courtney's startled voice called from the doorway but neither of them took a blind bit of notice.

Jen's face flamed nasty red. 'You're the reason our mother got banged up behind bars for five fucking years. I don't want my Courtney turning into you.'

Tiff reared back as if Jen had struck her in the face. 'That's charming that is. I take your daughter in when she's half off her face—'

'What do you mean?' With alarm, Jen turned to her daughter. She gasped. The only words to describe her girl were a right state. She was wearing her school uniform but her hair was a total mess and there were deep circles under her bloodshot eyes. If Courtney had been on the bottle she was going to swing for her. 'I'll deal with you later,' she snapped out and then snarled, 'Well if she's been on the lash we know who she learned that from. That's why I don't want her coming up here to see you. You're the type of bad influence my kid don't need.'

That stung. Really stung. People might be able to point at Tiff about many things, but not those girls, they were like daughters to her. She clenched her fists. 'Do you want some, sis? Eh? Do you want some? Don't think you're too grand to get a kicking.'

'I should've figured out sooner where my Courtney learned to give me lip and cuss me. I should've never let my kids anywhere near a piss poor human being like you.'

'You ungrateful bitch. I'm warning you, pack it in—'

Jen got right into her face. 'What? What you gonna do? Bring it fucking right on coz I'll take you down.'

They both trembled, chests rising, as they breathed angry air into each other's face. Neither was going to back off. It was Tiffany who finally took a half-step back as she shot her sister daggers.

She contemptuously flicked her fingertips twice against her shoulder giving Jen the brush-off. 'You know what I heard Nuts say to a mate once? There was more life in a blow-up doll than his own wife. Sad, sad, state of affairs babe.'

Jen spat in her face. Courtney gasped loudly as Tiffany staggered back, shock joining the spit on her skin.

Jen was deeply shocked too. It wasn't the first time she'd had a set-to with her sister – that's just how sisters got sometimes – but she'd never, ever dissed Tiff in such an awful manner before. But she wasn't sorry. Tiff had had that coming for years. Jen's hands screwed into fists by her side.

'You fucking better get out of my gaff now,' Tiff roared.

'I'm going, believe you me,' Jen yelled. 'You're greedy and the truth is Mum spoiled you rotten. Don't you ever bring your skank, lying self anywhere near me, my girls or my door again. I wash my hands of you.'

'Whatever,' Tiff answered silkily. 'But do you know what? You'll always be a loser. You never wanna take any chances do you? You never wanna get your hands dirty because you're too good for that!'

Jen marched over to her daughter, grabbed her, and a few seconds later violently slammed the door. She'd had plenty of ding-dongs with her sister in the past and they'd always kissed and made up. But not this time.

Things had been said and they couldn't be unsaid.

Sixteen

Next morning Babs knew there was trouble brewing as the women either side of her in the showers tripped over themselves to grab their towels and bolt. Water still cascading over her, she twisted around to find the other occupants fleeing for their lives too. And no wonder. Paula 'Knox' Benson and her two gorillas stood near the sinks, arms folded. Their menacing gazes were fixed on the single person left – Babs.

After her encounter with Knox in the corridor it hadn't taken her long to realise that she was Top Bitch in the prison. With her own eyes she'd seen the animal mete out a piece of hardcore punishment. Babs had been in the library flicking through a *Recipes For One* cookbook when hell had kicked off next to her. Knox and her toughs had bundled a terrified prisoner into a corner.

The cringing inmate had pleaded, with terror drenching her eyes, 'I'll have your Wholenut by tomorrow.'

Most people thought that cash and drugs were the most prized things smuggled into prison, but there was something else ranked up there as well – chocolate. The decent stuff was hard to come by so it was a prized luxury item.

Knox's nasty grin flashed two gold teeth either side of her mouth. She hadn't uttered a word, instead lashed out with her tattooed fists. A single left and a right knocked the other woman out cold. Babs got the message, loud and clear, why she was nicknamed Knox.

Babs' wet skin crawled. Oh, hell's bells; she didn't need the headache of any argy-bargy. Babs' number one rule of survival behind bars was simple – first sign of trouble, walk the other way.

She tried to do that now. 'I'll just be off so you can conduct your business without an audience.'

As she reached desperately to turn off the shower, Knox's voice stopped her cold. 'Did I give you fucking permission to move?' She turned to one of her thugs. 'Did I?'

The thug snarled, 'No, you didn't.'

The other thug added, 'You wanna teach her a lesson so she knows who's really running this joint.'

Babs shrank back into the chill concrete wall as the other woman's steely gaze settled on her once again. 'I think you're right girls.'

'Now hold up a minute,' Babs sputtered.

'Shut. It,' Queen Bitch growled.

They started advancing on Babs, who started pleading for her life. 'If it's money you want, I can get that. Or choccie. I can get my hands on a tin of Roses. You won't be wanting Wholenut after you've tasted hazelnut whirl.' They carried on coming. 'Whatever you think I've done, I know we can get it sorted out.' They reached the edge of the shower. 'Please, I've got bloody grandkids.'

Knox reached over her and turned the shower off. That's when Babs saw she was holding something tight in her other hand. Oh fuck, I'm gonna get battered like a scrambled egg. She slid down the wall until she was a damp, petrified huddle on the floor. They stood around her, looking down at her with the bloodthirsty gazes of playground bullies.

'I've got a message for you.' Knox crouched down beside her.

Babs prayed like she'd never prayed in her life. The other woman's hand started to move towards her. Babs wanted to squeeze her eyes tight but for some reason she couldn't look away. She was transfixed. Here it fucking comes. Babs silently cursed her ex for getting her into this mess. She waited for the other woman's legendary one-two knockout blows to fall.

But they never came. Instead, Knox opened her large hand and Babs gagged. Sitting pretty in the woman's palm was a small dead pigeon. Its belly was slit and its broken neck cocked to the side.

Knox said, 'I've got a little prezzie for you.' Babs had never heard of anyone being beaten to death with a dead pigeon but she supposed there was a first time for everything.

But instead of duffing her over, Knox twisted her fingers into the animal's grisly insides. Babs thought she was going to heave as the squidgy sound of guts being shifted filled the air. Knox pulled something out.

Babs went slack-jawed when she saw what she held. A tiny mobile phone.

'This is yours,' Queen Bitch informed her.

'You what?' Babs stared at the phone as if it were a hand grenade with the pin pulled out. Mobiles were strictly forbidden and anyone caught with one would find the full force of the prison establishment coming down on them like a ton of bricks. And that's when Babs remembered all about dead pigeons and prisons. They were lobbed over the wall with all manner of illegal things inside their swollen tummies.

'Kieran says hello.'

The penny dropped. Kieran had organised for her to have a mobile. She'd loved that boy to bits since the first time she'd met him back in '72. Her heart had broken for him because he'd been like a feral animal; a smelly, dirty, hungry thing, running wild on The Devil. That mum of his should've been shot for leaving him in such a state. There was an unbreakable bond between them. He was the son she'd never had. There was one thing that squeezed her heart with sadness though – the path he'd decided to take as an adult. She'd wanted him to be respectable, upstanding, like any mother would wish for her child, but he'd chosen to make the underworld his profession. It hurt her to do it, but that's why she kept Kieran away from her girls. Babs didn't want her daughters to be part of that world, even though she knew that Dee had already been involved in it through her husband. Thank God Dee and John had turned their backs on that life.

Knowing Kieran was connected she shouldn't have been surprised when he lined up the hard-faced kanga, Mrs Reagan, in her last prison to watch her back. She didn't know how she knew her and hadn't asked; but she was eternally grateful that someone was looking out for her. And just as well because those first few months behind bars had been the hardest. She'd wanted to cry herself to sleep most nights, she missed her family so badly. But he'd never done anything as nutty as smuggling a phone in before.

'You're to keep it in a safe place,' the other woman continued. 'Only use it when it's a priority. Got it?'

Babs took the phone. 'Thanks.' Then she got pissed off. 'So what's with trying to give me a flippin' heart attack?'

Knox leaned in, much closer this time, making her fear grow again. 'Couldn't have the others thinking me and you are tit buddies, now could we.' She stood up. 'Kieran says any problems, you come to me.' She closed one hand into a fist and punched it twice into her other palm. Babs swallowed. If this woman was protecting her she was going to be fine.

They turned and left the still shaking Babs. She stared at the phone in her hand. She was playing with fire. If the kangas twigged, she was done for and would have a couple of years added to her sentence. Screw it! Now she could call her girls and hear their sweet voices anytime she liked.

The mobile pinged, startling her. Her eyes darted around in fear that someone had heard, but no one came inside. Babs quickly gazed down at the screen.

A text.

She opened it and her face creased into a huge smile.

Gonna take you for a slap up Chinese up west when you get out.

Luv you, my second mum.

K

Bless him. Tears stung her eyes.

Seventeen

'Good evening Mr Scott, glad you could join us this evening.'

The Lock's doorman, dressed in the classic rig and top hat of his profession, hurried down the club's steps to open his car.

'Evening James. How's things?'

'Never been better sir.' James hurried back up the steps to open the club's doors. 'Enjoy your time tonight sir.'

Kieran lapped it up; he loved all this. The boy who'd reeked of neglect, running wild round The Devil back in the day, had done good.

He swaggered through the lobby where the receptionists and discreetly placed bouncers kept out undesirables like the mutt's nuts. They all chorused, 'Good evening Mr Scott.'

He'd got his hands on the club through John Black. In the days of the previous owner the ground floor of the former warehouse in Wapping had been a smoky snooker hall frequented by local likely lads and petty criminals. The place had a proper name but no one knew what it was. Everyone called it The Lock In as it served drinks to those in the know, after hours. John had got the place for a song. In his early days, Kieran had mentioned to his underworld mentor that he was looking for a place to use as a club. John thought he was clever unloading The Lock In on the young whippersnapper for twice the price he'd purchased it for. But Kieran bought it anyway. It was ideal for him.

Unfortunately for John, he sold around about the time London money was moving eastwards and the docks went from knackered to prime locations. John didn't make many mistakes but this was one of them. Kieran sometimes wondered if John had ever forgiven him for it.

Kieran had had a very clear idea what he wanted to do with The Lock In. He loved the old Hollywood high society movies he'd watched as a nipper with Babs, so he set out to stamp that style on his new club. He went to a great deal of time and trouble to make it work. He struck lucky when an old 1930s East End cinema closed down and he was able to buy all the art deco fittings for a knock-down price. He turned the various floors into restaurants, bars, a snooker room (a proper one this time), a cigar place and function rooms. He handpicked the staff to make sure they fitted in with his idea of what kind of club it was meant to be and didn't scrimp on paying top dollar wages. He considered changing the name of the place to something chi-chi but decided in the end to just lob the 'In' off and call it The Lock.

There was just one type of person Kieran wanted in his place – the stinking rich. He charged outrageous membership fees to ensure that only those with poke in their pocket came through the door. For a couple of months after it opened it looked like Kieran's dream was going to sink without a trace. Sometimes the only punters in the bijou bar were Kieran and John Black. One night, John patted him on the back and said, 'Never mind mate. We all make mistakes.'

But then word began to spread. There was nowhere else like it in the East End and some of the loaded brigade who lived in the riverfront developments, business people from down Canary Wharf way and the City itself, began to join. Finally, even the West End elite were applying. It was Kieran alone who decided who was going to become a member and who wasn't. There was to be no riff-raff, no B-list celebs and absolutely and definitely no criminals (apart from those he invited to the snooker room on the top floor).

Crime was his business but The Lock was his dream and his passion. It was also so that if the law wanted to raid the top floor office from which he actually ran his rackets, they'd have to tread on the toes of a lot of very powerful customers on the way up. And Kieran was confident they weren't going to do that.

He turned his mind to business and made his way to the snooker room where John was going to meet him. The room was filled with blokes he trusted. He took off his jacket and got into a hundred quid match with a Face from across the river.

The door opened and John come in. Kieran turned to look at the various other players. They got the message, put their cues on the tables and left. When they were alone, Kieran nodded at his visitor. 'Alright mate. Do you fancy a game? '

'Well, we're in a snooker room. It makes sense, don't it?'

Kieran gave a joyless smile. 'Yeah. I suppose it does.' He took the frame from under the table. 'Do you want to break?'

John pulled a face. 'Seeing as I'm the number one in our relationship, that makes sense too, don't you think?'

Kieran nodded. 'I've never suggested otherwise mate.'

John broke, clipped the reds and brought the white back up to their end of the table where it rested against the baulk. Kieran tapped the table in appreciation. 'Nice shot mate.'

For a few minutes, they played on in silence, the only noise the click of the balls as John ran up a score. Kieran knew he was wound up. He was always on his game when he was wound up. He decided to miss a sitter to get the conversation going. 'Whoops . . .'

John teed a shot. 'That's right mate – whoops. We seem to have a problem you and me and I ain't talking about the game either.'

Kieran shrugged. 'I ain't got a problem. I just want to know where the gold's going, that's all.'

John sank another. 'And I've already said we're in a need-to-know-basis business you don't need to know. I shouldn't really have to tell you that, should I?'

Kieran took a deep breath and tried to be reasonable. 'OK. And what happens if you fall under a bus? Where would that leave me then? With my finger up my rear end and no proceeds.'

John looked up in anger. 'Why? Has anyone suggested that I might be falling under a bus?'

'We're in the kind of business where people fall under buses a lot, accidently or otherwise. Anyway, you know what they say at funeral services? Man that is born of woman hath but a short time to live, he's cut down like the grass in the spring – or something like that anyway. We can all pop off anytime. Did I tell you about my next door neighbour? Fit as a fiddle and only thirty-nine – snuffed it in the night – just like that, he was gone.'

John was unimpressed. 'Sad story but you still don't need to know where the gold's gonna be stashed. If you're worried about me pegging out, buy some life insurance on my behalf. I'll be looking after the gold. That's final.' He walked around the table to finish the frame.

Without warning, John began smiling. 'Do you remember how we met mate?'

Kieran smiled too, his much more wistful. 'There's no need to go over the past Guv, I've never said I don't owe you. Of course I do.'

John was chuckling now. 'How you came running in that pub in Mile End with that stolen car radio under your arm, chased by them two coppers that were looking to take you outside for a hiding? How old was you then, eh? Fourteen?'

'Thirteen.'

'The plods grabbed you by the hair and started to drag you out and you said to them – *Alright officers, it's a fair cop.* And I was having a drink with some of the gang, so I shouted at 'em to leave you alone coz you was working for me. Do you remember that? I thought to myself then, "I like the look of that lad. He knows how to handle himself when he's in a bit of trouble." And do you remember how, after the law let you go on my account, I told you to chuck the radio away. How tea leafing from motors is for kids and if you wanted to get into some grown up business, I might be able to put a little work your way ...'

Kieran was silent. John sighed and went on. 'Of course, that was a long time ago. But if you look back over the years, I've never let you down, have I? I've always played straight with you like I've always played straight with everyone else. It's a failing of mine, playing straight, and I have to admit it's cost me over the years but that's how I like to roll.' John's voice rose. 'And now you're whining like a thirteen-year-old kid because I wanna play this game my way? What's the matter with you?'

Kieran was shamed. 'Look boss, I'm not saying—'

John cut him short. He spread out his arms and said, 'Come here.'

Kieran came over and John gave him a hug and a pat on the back. 'I'm not telling you where the gold's going. And, I repeat, that's final. OK?'

Kieran pulled himself out of John's embrace and looked at the floor for a moment before nodding and saying, 'Fair enough – you're the big Guvnor, I know that.'

John got back on with the game. The final black ball was a long shot and John spent a few moments studying it and chalking his cue. He sent the white down the table where it clipped the black into a pocket to clear the table. 'Pot black, my friend.'

Eighteen

Tiff shrugged off the cold of Friday morning as she walked into the 'Piggy Bank' store on Whitechapel High Street, knowing that if she didn't get her hands on a grand pretty lively she was dead meat. She'd been looking over her shoulder since that animal had called demanding his dough back and she'd given him the slip down The Roman. Tiff knew that once the money lenders gave her the cash she wouldn't be able to pay off much, but at least she'd have got that Tommo and Errol off her back.

The loan shop was done up like a mini bank with a few counters containing leaflets, a plastic teller window and two screened-off areas for privacy. It even had a little play area with nailed-down toys for kids. Tiff scoffed. So people can sell their kids as well?

She wasn't scoffing as she headed towards the teller, a blonde woman.

'Just one moment,' the woman said, her head down.

Tiffany gazed at her in horror. She knew that voice. Oh shit! One of the reasons she'd come down Whitechapel way and not done her business in Mile End was so she wouldn't see anyone she knew here. The shame of people seeing her with her hand out begging for money. And of all people . . .

Tiff did an about turn, but she was too late. 'Tiffany? Tiff?'

She cursed under her breath, and turned back. She stared into Stacey's Ingram's gorgeous face. The Ingrams and Millers had bad blood between them but that hadn't stopped the girls becoming secret, best mates in school. Of course the shit hit the fan when they were found out. Babs had given Tiff a stiff talking to, but things hadn't gone so well for Stacey. Just thinking back to that awful time made Tiff's head and heart hurt. Stacey still resembled a small doll, with her fine white-blonde hair. Back in the day she'd been delicate too, but the horrors she'd been through had knocked that out of her. She didn't look hardened, but there was something in those pretty eyes of hers that said she'd seen too much of life. Way too much.

Tiffany stepped back to the counter. 'Alright Stace. Didn't know you'd become a head and shoulders in a loan joint.'

Stacey self-consciously tugged down the end of her long sleeves where Tiff knew the old tracks of her past drug habit were hidden. 'I got myself sorted out. Mum getting attacked three years ago really shook me up. I knew if I didn't sort my sh—' Realising she was on the job, she cut the word off. 'I got myself into rehab or I would have ended up six feet under.' Her face covered over with pain. 'Then Mum had a stroke . . .'

Tiff had heard that Mel Ingram had never really recovered from the beating someone had doled out to her. There was no love lost between her and the woman she saw as a witch starting with a 'b', but she didn't like to see Stacey looking cut up like this. Even though they hadn't been tight since school days the other woman still had a hold over her. The plain truth was that Tiff had been bang in love with her best friend and hadn't even figured it out until it was too late. When they'd drifted apart she'd been heartbroken.

'I heard that you're doing alright for yourself,' Stacey said, perking up. 'Got a nice gaff near Canary Wharf. I'm right glad for ya. You've come a long way since we used to knock around in the cemetery.'

Tiff's face heated up. Her former best friend wouldn't be so proud if she knew the wheeling and dealing Tiff had done to get it all. And then gone and fucking blown it. Her embarrassment deepened when she realised that the person she was going to have to beg for a handout thought she was living the good life. Shit. She couldn't do this.

'Well, nice seeing you 'n all.' Then she was on that exit like she'd robbed the place blind.

She hadn't taken three steps into the street when she felt a small hand grip her arm. With a huff she turned, but closed her mouth when she saw that Stacey had a pack of ciggy's in the other hand.

She let go. 'It's nearly my break time.' She held the pack of Silk Cut out to her. Tiff's gaze roamed fretfully over her. Bloody hell, she was still so achingly beautiful.

'Why not.' She pulled a fag out and followed her former bestie around the side of the building. Soon they were puffing away in an awkward silence. Stacey broke it by asking, 'You settled down then . . .?'

Tiff spluttered as the smoke caught in her throat. 'You know me. I'm Tiff from the cemetery. Not likely, is it?'

'Why not? You always talked about wanting to build your nest.'

Tiff wasn't one of these people who were still stuffed in the closet. Fuck what anyone else thought about her; she was what she was. Anyone who wanted to make noise about it could dick off. But there was something awkward about meeting your one-time bestie from school and having to say point blank that she liked girls. They'd probably think you were coming on to them. Mind you, in Stacey's case . . . Stop that!

'I'm one of them lesbians, ain't I.'

Stacey rolled her eyes. 'I know that. I've got ears you know and heard the whispers on The Devil. Plus you tried to snog me in the playground that time.'

The tips of Tiff's ears went red. 'I did not . . . That was only to shake things up coz the kids in the playground were so effing boring.'

They shared a smile. Stacey said, 'But being . . . what you are . . . that don't mean you can't have someone special at home.'

'I like being a one-woman show.' Tiff was almost too frightened to ask the question, but she pushed her courage forward. 'You got anyone?'

Stacey went so pale, Tiff thought she was going to faint. 'I went with so many fellas to keep my habit alive . . .' Her shoulders shook with the shiver that went through her. 'Truth is, I don't really like no one touching me, you know.' She drew in a deep breath. 'One day, maybe I'll meet someone, but for now, I'm happy to work and look after my mum and my cousin Dexter.'

Tiff was so appalled she was speechless. Of course she'd heard how Stacey was selling herself to anyone with a cock and a wallet, but hearing it from her mouth made her feel sick to her stomach. How could any man take a woman in the state Stacey had been in? They needed putting down, that's what.

'Sorry—'

But Stacey cut her off. 'Don't say it. It happened. I'm over it. Have moved on. So what did you want? Can't believe you need a loan?'

'Nah, nothing like that,' she shot out. 'My sister Jen, she's a bit hard up and wanted me to find out what she needed to do to get a loan on the side. She couldn't face coming down here herself. Pride and that.'

'She got any C.C.Js?' Seeing the confusion on Tiff's face she added, 'county court judgements. Or owe any companies money?'

'Yeah. Quite a few.'

Stacey shook her head. 'We won't be able to help her then. She'll be on our creditors' blacklist.' She shrugged. 'My hands are tied.'

Tiff dropped her fag and mashed it under her Nikes to conceal her face. What an all-time idiot you are! She should've figured out she'd be on some 'don't touch 'em with a barge pole' lists with the number of firms on her case. Just as well she hadn't asked Stacey; not only would she'd have ended up looking like a proper prat, she'd have done it in front of the first love of her life.

'I'd better be off then.'

Stacey took an urgent step towards her. 'I can still get Jen some leaflets—'

'Don't worry yourself. I'll be seeing ya.'

Tiff quickly strode away before Stacey could answer. Although it had been good to see Stacey had rejoined the human race, it had hurt as well. But what was going to hurt even more was if she didn't get the money for those pair of pricks. She'd be royally fucked. There was nothing else for it. She was going to have to tighten the thumb screws on her mum about getting those houses sold pronto.

Nineteen

'Mum?'

Jen didn't hear Courtney because she was so engrossed in watching *Celebrity Big Brother* from the night before. That Pete Burns had a right gob on him. Jen was standing at the ironing board. She took in other people's ironing at twenty-five quid a bag to help make ends meet. She'd been slogging through this mountain of clothes for what felt like eons and her arms were fit to drop off. Her darling eleven-year-old, whose given name was Sasha, but who everyone called Little Bea because she'd been her Nanna Babs' shadow, had her head stuck in a book. She was so proud that her baby enjoyed a good read. Although what she would've said if she'd known Little Bea had another book hidden behind it – one about serial killers of the twentieth century – was another story!

'Mum? Mum? You hear me?'

Finally Jen flicked her gaze away to find Courtney hovering in the doorway. 'Thought you were doing your homework. Maths ain't it?'

After they'd left Tiff's the other day and got home Jen had laid into her about the evils of booze. Courtney had politely said, 'Yes Mum' to all her warnings, but Jen wasn't sure she believed her. But what could she do? What could any single mum do? She'd told her under no circumstances was she to contact that ungrateful mare Aunty Tiff. Aunty my arse; if she had her way she'd scratch the Aunty part for eternity.

'Sorted ages ago,' Courtney answered, wearing a sweet expression that reminded Jen of the lovely girl she'd once been. 'Do you want me to help you?' Without waiting for an answer she got into eager beaver mode, picking up a pillowcase and folding it.

Jen threw her an arch look. What was her girl up to? She never helped with the ironing. In fact, truth be known, Courtney's mouth often turned down with disgust as she watched Jen work her fingers to the bone, her gaze on the iron as though it were some kind of reptile. Jen was humiliated that her kid witnessed her being a skivvy, but what could she do? They needed the extra money.

'Don't bother asking me if you can go running around with your mates outside. You know that's a no-no on school nights.'

Courtney's bottom lip pushed out into a sulky pout, which she abruptly sucked back in as if remembering she was trying to get into her mum's good graces. She became all wide-eyed and innocent again. 'Kelly's having a birthday party at her gaff at the weekend.'

'Which one's Kelly then?' She couldn't keep track of Courtney's friends. Girls these days: one minute they were all lovey-dovey, linking arms, the next fighting like cats and cats, and then kissy-kissy chums again.

Courtney's hands smoothed over the pillowcase. 'You know.' She peered shyly through her eyelashes. 'You met her and her mum at prize-giving up the school last year.'

Jen screwed up her face. 'Not the one with Death Wish tattooed on her arm?'

'I don't have any mates with—'

Realising her mum was pulling her leg Courtney pursed her lips. They stared at each other and suddenly broke into soft laughter. Something inside Jen's chest squeezed. She couldn't remember the last time she'd heard her little girl laugh. Courtney had always been so filled with laughter, unlike Little Bea who was more intense and serious. Jen would kill to have that child back again.

'The thing is,' Courtney resumed, 'it's a cocktail party—'

'A cocktail party? That sounds like an adult's bash, the type where there's plenty of alcohol.' As if sensing the tension, Little Bea looked up from her book, peered at them, then dismissed it all as she was pulled back to what she was reading.

Jen pulled out a shirt from the bag and laid it flat on the ironing board. 'Let me guess, you need a cocktail dress.'

Her daughter's face began to glow. 'I saw this killer dress down The Roman. Oh you should've seen it Mum. Dark blue, all shiny, backless with straps around the neck. Just like the one Rihanna wore in that video.'

Jen couldn't help smiling wistfully as she recalled the times she and Bex would go up West as teens and window shop on Bond Street. She'd wanted to be a fashion designer back then. Well look at you now, ironing other people's clothes.

'Rihanna's a woman and you're thirteen,' Jen snapped, the pain of her lost dreams almost suffocating her. She could've kicked herself when she saw the hurt look on Courtney's face. It wasn't her daughter's fault she'd given up her dreams for a man who turned out to have the morals of a back alley dog.

Courtney chucked the pillowcase down furiously. 'Mum, why do you have to be such a B.I.T.C.H?'

They had Little Bea's full attention now. Jen reared back. She was not putting up with that. Not in her own home. She raised her hand. 'You're big enough to talk to your mum like that, you're big enough to get this across your face.'

Her hand shook. What was she doing? She'd never raised her hand to either of her girls in her life. Bex's advice had been to clout her one and remind her who the mum in the family was. 'Spare the rod and spoil the child,' was how she'd put it. Like Bex took her own advice, Jen scoffed; that boy of hers always running rings round her. More like, 'Do as I say not as I do.' Belt her daughter? Nah, that wasn't her way. She'd never, *ever*, in a million years lay a hand on her kids. How could she after what their father had put her through? Her hand dropped to her side.

Courtney looked at the clothing scornfully. 'That's all you do Mum, is work, work, work. And you never have any fucking money—'

Jen moved towards her daughter. 'I've warned you and you better heed my words coz there's only one winner in this house. Me.'

Courtney's chest rose as she fought with her raging emotions, tears sprinkled in her eyes. 'You know what Mum? I. Hate. You. Really, really hate you. I wish you were banged up, not Nanna Babs.' She stormed from the room and slammed into her bedroom.

Jen couldn't have moved if she tried. She was frozen on the spot with shock. They'd had their rough patches but never had her girl said something as spiteful as wishing her gone. That she hated her. And the twisted expression on Courtney's face as she'd chucked the words at her . . . She hated to say it but Tiffany was right; there was something seriously up with Courtney. And if Jen was truthful her baby hadn't been right since her mum was sent to prison. Things had gone downhill when she told Courtney that Nanna Babs didn't want her to visit her. The poor girl had cried herself to sleep for a whole week. And the nightmares after that. Jen shivered, remembering Courtney's piercing screams.

Jen slumped down on a pile of clothes feeling defeated. Oh God, she was losing her little girl and there was sod all she could do about it. Then she remembered, maybe there was something she could do about it . . .

She knew it was late but she wouldn't be able to sleep tonight if she didn't make this call. On the table in the compact kitchen she rummaged in her bag for the piece of paper the female cop had written the counsellor's details on. She looked at the name – Sally Foxton. She hesitated and then took that great leap forward.

She was surprised that the phone line connected instead of going to voicemail.

'Sally here,' a cheerful, very London voice answered.

Jen coughed nervously. 'I would like to . . .' she fumbled around for the right words, 'to enquire about your counselling services for young kids.' She added, 'Sorry about calling so late.'

'No problem. First of all why don't you tell me who you are?'

'Oh yeah, of course. I'm Jennifer Miller and I'm looking for some help with my girl.'

'I'd be more than willing to do an initial consultation. My fees are eighty pounds an hour.'

Jen's heart sank. This woman was talking about serious dough, the type she didn't have. Feeling embarrassed she said, 'I'll call you back,' and cut the call. Where the heck was she going to get cash like that? Whoever said that money didn't matter had got that so very wrong.

Feeling defeated she shoved the paper back in her bag. A small business card caught her eye. She pulled it out and read Naz's details, the glamorous woman she'd met down The Knackered Swan with Bex.

She heard her silky tones: *'You're the type of woman wealthy, older guys would pay top dollar to meet.'*

Jen didn't want to do this but she had to help her daughter. She picked up her mobile and punched in Naz's number.

Twenty

'Babsie girl, my boys don't want to know me, nor do my daughters. Won't even let me see my grandbabies. What am I going to do when I get out of here next week?' Pearl Hennessy asked Babs on Monday then sniffed, the audible sound of snot making Babs wrinkle her nose.

Pearl was the old lag from the cell next door. She gave the impression of being a tiny, harmless, Jamaican lady in her sixties but she was a proper nuisance, her constant bitching and whining ensuring she had few friends in HMP Hilton. Babs would've joined their number, but she felt sorry for the old girl. Pearl always looked so lonely and stooped that Babs hadn't the heart to turn her away the first time she'd come looking for company. But she suspected there was much more to this woman than met the eye. And she was well made up that Pearl was being released soon.

Pearl leaned forward expectantly. 'I can get rid of any unwelcome visitors in here so you sleep better at night.' Her usually cloudy eyes cleared. She must've heard Babs tossing and turning because she had to ration the meagre number of Benzos the prison quack prescribed her. When Pearl got her teeth into a subject she was all exaggerated arm and hand movements that were very elegant and slow like she was trying to draw her listener in. 'You should've seen me in my day. They used to call me Madam Pearl. I'd be decked out in this lovely shawl my Great Aunt Agnes left me – she had the gift too – and massive, chunky, silver bracelets. I cast this demon out of this woman's house once. Well, it was a prefab really . . .'

Babs let her rabbit on, restraining herself from rolling her eyes. Pearl had claimed, to anyone who had an ear, that she could get rid of evil spirits by waving some stick around. As if! If only life were that simple.

Babs' ears were burning from the non-stop chatter, so she cut in, 'I sleep very well, thank you.'

The mobile phone under her mattress vibrated.

'What's that?' Pearl half jumped, wiggling her bum.

Babs scrambled around for a plausible answer. 'There's something wrong with the mattress. I keep telling the kangas but they just fob me off.'

Pearl gazed at her with a twinkle in her eye, the creases in her face folding as the muffled noise continued. 'You ain't got something naughty hidden under there? One of them vibrators with the bunny ears that—'

Babs gave her a killer look. 'Don't be bloody stupid. Like I know where to even shove it.'

The older woman cosied up to her. 'Coz if you have, I wouldn't mind having a go. I could do with a little buzz. Know what I mean, Babsie girl.'

Babs rippled with disgust. She'd never had a vibrator in her life, but she was sure you weren't meant to share them. She needed Pearl out now. But if an old timer found a friend she stuck to them like a conjoined twin.

Babs needed to find the right excuse to get her to sling her hook. 'I don't wanna put the frighteners on you or nuthin . . .' Pearl's eyes opened wide with concern, 'but Knox is paying me a visit soon . . .'

The older woman was near the door in record time. 'Be seeing you Babsie.' And was – mercifully – gone.

Babs wasted no time getting the mobile out. Tiff's number was on the screen. She'd warned her daughters to only call if there was an emergency. Something was going on. Flippin' hell, she hoped Tiff wasn't up to her old tricks again.

Babs returned the call and asked in a hush-hush voice, 'Love, is everything alright?'

'I'm gonna fucking well tear her head off if she even dares look my way,' Tiff stormed. 'I've washed my hands of her.'

Babs was almost struck dumb by the venom spilling from her daughter. She found her voice. 'Calm down hun, don't upset yourself.' The line filled with Tiff's sharp, rapid breaths. 'Now tell me what's gone on.'

'My ex-sister, that's what's gone on.'

'Jennifer?' That didn't sound like Jen. As gentle as a breeze on a summer's evening, that was her Jen. She frowned. 'Has something happened to her?'

'She's a greedy bitch who wants you to divide your houses so that her kids get a share.'

'But they are getting some through Jen's share.'

'That's what I told her, but she wouldn't have it.' Tiff's voice developed a bite. 'She's pure greed. Just coz I made a go of my life and managed to get off The Devil, she wants to diddle me outta my share.'

Babs sighed wearily. How had the generous offer she'd put on the table in front of her girls ended up such a Godawful mess? The tiredness she was feeling came strong through her words. 'But I explained to all of you that it's a three-way split.'

'And that weren't all,' Tiff marched on, 'she spat in my face.'

Babs sucked in her breath. 'Tiff, no.' Her hand covered her heart. 'What did you say to her? I can't even picture my Jen doing that.'

'See, that's the problem Mum, Jen's always the innocent one. The one who can do no wrong. Whereas me, I'm always seen as the troublemaker.'

Babs almost said, 'If the shoe fits . . .' but stopped herself. 'You know I love you both the same way—'

But Tiff was already blasting again. 'She's a conniving, money-grabbing, heartless, scrounging, despicable human being who wants everything handed to her and her kids on a platinum plate.'

'Now stop that.' Babs grew stern. 'You don't chat about your sister like that, you hear me. You keep words like that for those that deserve it, not your own flesh and blood.' She might be doing bird for manslaughter but she was still the mum in this family. Her daughter had the grace to keep quiet. 'Leave Jen to me. I'll get this sorted.'

Tiff spoke with a tremble in her voice, but laced with defiance. 'Well, it ain't fair.'

'What? Me putting Jen straight?'

'That you're bothering to get the houses done up. There's this course I wanna do. You're always going on at me to better myself. You know what these college fees are like now. It's gonna cost a cool nine large, but I don't have that type of dough.' Her voice dipped to an enticing pitch. 'If you sold the houses NOW . . .'

Not this again, for crying out loud. 'We've already been down that dead end street. You can do this course next year when the money's in from selling the houses, after they've been done up a treat.'

There was silence on the other end of the line. Then, 'You always think I'm out to scam you Mum.'

'No love.'

'Well, I'm pissed to the teeth with it. I need a helping hand and the plain truth is, you can't be bothered. Thanks a bunch.' And on that incensed note, Tiff ended the call.

The violence of their conversation drove Babs to slump on her bed. She clutched the phone, trying to figure out how everything had gone so wrong. All she wanted to do was give her children a leg up in life and all she was getting back was a load of grief. Maybe Tiff was right. Maybe she should get the houses on the market as soon as. And what about what Jen wanted? Maybe she should be giving a cut to Little Bea and Courtney. Especially Courtney. And poor Jen had had such a hard life . . . No. Babs shook herself out of it. What she was doing was right and fair. If Tiff and Jen couldn't deal with that then that was their lookout.

Although she decided to stick to her guns, the idea of her two girls falling out with each other was tearing her up. She'd more or less brought up her daughters single handed and she wasn't about to let them both piss their family ties down the toilet.

With determination Babs punched another number into the mobile. 'Dee, it's Mum. Your sisters are going at it like two ferrets in a sack. I need you to get round there and put a stop to it.'

After she'd explained the situation, her eldest concluded, 'You should give the lot away to some cats' shelter. That'll show the ungrateful pair what it's like.'

'Leave it out. I couldn't do that in a million years. All I need you to do is to arrange a family sit-down and lay the law down.' Her voice ended in a painful hitch.

'Babs, you alright?'

She wiped a finger against the tear that dropped from her eye. 'I should be doing this on the outside. What a complete fuck-up I've made of my life.'

'Don't cry. Babs don't,' Dee said softly. Then steel entered her tone. 'Leave it to me. I'll knock their heads together and get them to see sense.'

They chit-chatted for a minute longer and then said their goodbyes. And it was just as well. An unusually flustered Knox rushed into her cell.

'The kangaroo squad are coming. They're having a spin.'

An unannounced search of cells. Both women looked at the mobile phone in Babs' hand.

Twenty-One

John let out a low whistle of appreciation as Dee slowed the four by four outside number 9 and 10 Bancroft Square in Mile End.

'Bloody hell,' he said, 'where did your old lady get the kind of poke to buy places like these? We ain't talking beer money here.'

Dee unbuckled her seat belt and closed her eyes for a few seconds. Her stomach was playing up. No doubt about it, if she couldn't shift it she was going to have to pay the doctor a visit.

'You alright love?'

John's concerned voice made her reopen her eyes. She sent him a weak smile. 'Yeah. Just a touch tired is all.' She deliberately turned her smile into something more brilliant. She didn't need a worried John on her hands. She gazed at the houses and frowned. 'Babs used to clean these houses. I know because we had Courtney's tenth birthday bash at number ten. I've never set foot inside the other. I don't get it. Why would she be cleaning houses that she owned?'

'We've all got our secrets.' Typical John. His life in the underworld had taught him that you only needed to know as much as you needed to know. Dee couldn't shake the feeling that there was something about these houses that Babs wasn't sharing. Oh well, she wasn't going to find out what it was sitting in their motor worrying about it.

She reached for the door. 'Come on then, let's go see what Babs' Aladdin's Cave looks like.'

John had insisted she take him on a tour of her mum's properties. She hadn't been keen at first, but he kept going on about her being the eldest and needing to be Babs' eyes on the builders. Only after he had told her a few cautionary tales about the shortcuts builders took did she relent.

She was surprised that the first thing John did was inspect the overflowing skip outside.

'What are you doing? If they're off the clock they won't be hiding in there.'

John shifted through the skip. 'Just making sure that they aren't chucking out anything that they shouldn't.'

'Oi,' a man screamed from number 9, 'what the bloody hell do you think you're doing? Sod off.'

They both looked up to find a man with a ruddy face and little hair glaring at them.

'Watch your mouth,' John growled. 'No one talks to John Black's wife like that. You know who am I and if you don't you should.'

Dee placed a restraining hand on his arm. 'It's alright.' She looked back up at the man. 'I'm Mrs Miller's daughter. We've come to inspect the houses.'

His face turning white, the man disappeared from the window. Dee and John walked up the stone steps and by the time they got to the plain black door the man was there to greet them.

'I didn't know it was you, Mr Black.' With a trembling hand he shook John's fist. 'I'm the foreman. The name's Freddy Baxter but most people call me Shorty.' Dee could see why. The guy couldn't be more than five-four with a small head, tiny hands and beady little brown eyes that would have given a teddy bear's face the finishing touch. He led them into a long hallway that Dee couldn't help staring at in wonder. Black and white tiles adorned the floor, nicely setting off the cream walls, and there was fancy plasterwork on the ceiling. A staircase, covered in light green carpet, led to the upper floors.

Shorty puffed his chest out slightly as he caught Dee still giving the place the once-over and with a pleased as punch voice informed John, 'I can see that the missus likes our work. Me and the boys have been working day and night to get the place up to scratch, so there isn't much more left to do. Even found the parts to fix up the original radiators.' He lowered his voice. 'Mind you, the way I hear it, back in the day both places generated their own heat.'

Both John and Dee looked at him puzzled. He persisted, 'Know what I mean, nudge-nudge, wink-wink.'

Dee finally said, 'What are you going on about?'

Seeing their baffled faces he pulled himself straight again. 'There's an old biddy that's lived in the square for fifty years. She claims that both of them used to be one big knocking shop, back in the '70s. Claims a lot of high kickers used to frequent it.'

Dee's mouth tipped open. 'You're having a laugh.'

With a twinkle in his eye John teased, 'Maybe that's why your mum won't spill the beans how she got them. Trying to cover up her scandalous secret life as Madam Miller.'

She elbowed him in the side. 'Stop talking stupid. My mum connected to a cat house? That'd be like the Queen Mum running a gambling school at Buck Palace.'

John turned back to the foreman. 'We're just gonna have a bit of a nose around, so we won't keep you.'

Dee oohhed and ahhed as they checked out the downstairs. She had grown up in an East End house with Aunty Cleo but it was nothing like this. There were fireplaces everywhere, including one with a large surround and mirror in one of the reception rooms. She couldn't imagine in a million years that this place had ever been a brothel and said as much.

'Back in the '70s,' John told her as they made their way upstairs, 'you couldn't have paid this trendy, latte lot who are moving in to live in Mile End. Or any other part of the East End for that matter. These houses looked like Hitler had just finished with them. A lot were bombed in the Blitz. No one wanted to live here, least of all the people who ended up here.'

'How do you know so much about it?' Dee asked as they entered a large room with no furniture in it. 'Knocking around here after the war were you?'

She could've bitten her tongue off when she caught the strained expression on John's face. There were nineteen years between them and lately he'd got very touchy about his age. He'd started wearing leather jackets, like the one he had on today, and sunglasses like he was the same age as their son. She was waiting for the day he'd come roaring home on a motorbike. God forbid.

Dee smoothed things over by grabbing his hand so they could continue their tour. When they got to the next floor, her tummy started going into meltdown again. She tried to ignore it at first, but when she felt her belly turn over she looked at John and said, 'Fuck, I need to find a Ladies, like now.'

Startled, he stared at her, looking green himself. 'You going to chunder?'

'Right on your effing shoes if you don't find me the khazi.'

They made it just in time to a tiny toilet the size of a broom cupboard. Dee refused to have John present as she threw up. Afterwards she held on to the wall, her skin hot and clammy. She couldn't understand what was going on. She wasn't the type of person who got sick.

'Dee? Dee?' John called out. He banged on the door. 'You ain't gone and collapsed on me?'

'If I had, you pillock, I wouldn't be speaking to you, would I?' Her voice was ragged. She felt like death had come calling. She splashed some water on her face and slapped her Tom Ford shades on. She might be feeling terrible, but that didn't mean the rest of the world had to see her looking like it. She shook her hair back before she opened the door. Poor John's face was pale with concern.

'I'm fine babes,' she reassured him with a feeble smile. 'Tell you what, why don't you check things over with mister builder downstairs and I'll make myself nice and comfy in the motor until you're ready to go.'

'You sure love?' That surprised her. She'd have staked her life that John would've wanted to take her straight home. Then again they were here, so might as well make sure everything was ship shape.

Once she was in the car, Dee leaned back with a sigh.

She couldn't put it off any longer – she was going to have to pay the doctor a visit.

It didn't sit well with John that he'd left his wife in their motor on her own when she wasn't feeling the full ticket, but he still had business to take care of. And it was better that she wasn't around to see him do it. The one thing he didn't need was a barrage of questions.

He found Shorty and two younger men at the kitchen table all nursing a cuppa that he was sure wasn't only the PG variety. He could smell malt whisky in the air.

Shorty scrambled guiltily out of his seat. 'Me and the lads here were just taking five.'

John smiled, nice and easy. 'No problem bruv. Just wanted to ask you a question.'

He moved to the hall so Shorty's workmates couldn't overhear.

'My missus' mum assures us that these houses are four-storey properties, so is there a basement or cellar?'

The other man let out a long sigh of relief, clearly happy that he wasn't going to be dragged over the coals about the tea situation. 'Yeah, they've both got basements, which Mrs Miller's brief wants us to convert into self-contained flats. The basement links up with a coal bunker under the front reception room.'

John raised an eyebrow. 'A coal bunker?'

'Yeah. A lot of these older houses have them.' Shorty's face scrunched up. 'Is there a problem?'

'You could say that. I need the keys.' He stretched out his palm, menace glittering in his eyes.

'You what?'

'You and the fellas are off the job.'

Twenty-Two

Babs stood like a soldier on parade outside her cell. She was quaking so much she thought her bones were going to crumble. All of the women on the wing were positioned just like her as the POs did a thorough sweep of everyone's cell. She knew the routine well from the other prison. The kangas would go in looking for contraband – drugs, illegal drink, homemade brews, weapons and mobile phones. If they found that mobile not only would she be busted but she'd probably lose her shot at parole as well. Why, oh why, had she taken that phone?

Well there was no point crying a river now.

Two officers came out of Pearl's cell and walked to her.

'You got anything in there we need to know about Miller?' Mrs Bradley was a scary piece of shit. A Yorkshire woman you would never dream of calling a lass. Built like a box, she had eyes so dark and deep Babs often felt like making the sign of the cross after gazing into them.

'No Miss.'

Bradley huffed. 'In you go.' All the searches were conducted in the prisoner's presence to counter any accusations of planting evidence.

Babs managed to stop shaking as she stood just inside the door watching them tear apart the cell, her little home from home. Flippin' hell she couldn't take her eyes off the mattress. But, thank God, they didn't start there.

They checked under her small table.

Behind the toilet.

Back of the pipes.

Light fitting.

Window bars.

Toiletries.

Finally they turned to her bed. Babs stopped breathing for a few seconds.

Bradley turned to face Babs and squinted. 'Miller, are you positive there's nowt you want to share with me?'

Her heart started beating like a drum machine was lodged in her chest. 'No Miss.'

The other woman's lip curled. She took a stride to the mattress and yanked it off.

Babs froze. The only thing visible was the iron frame of the bed. Bradley and her colleague got busy checking every inch of the frame: the sides, the legs. They even lifted it up. All clean.

Bradley's face was an angry shade of beetroot. Babs couldn't help saying, 'Is that all Miss?'

Before the other woman could answer there was the sound of a loo being flushed a few cells down and all hell broke loose. Babs had been in prison long enough to know what the sound of the toilet meant – someone had been trying to flush drugs down the bog. The two officers flew out of the cell to join a group of kangas struggling on the landing floor with one of the younger inmates.

A scarlet-faced Bradley turned to the rest of them and cracked, 'Right, ladies, time to get back into your des reses.'

Babs quickly closed her cell door. She almost collapsed against the wall. She pulled down the front of her jogging bottoms and, grimacing, pulled the tiny mobile out of her vagina. The mattress was no longer a good stash hole – nor was the other hole she'd just used. Babs knew exactly where to hide it. During the search she'd noticed that the officers had gone through her toiletries, including her stick deodorant, but they had only lifted the lid. Unknown to them there was only a tiny bit of deodorant left, leaving a space underneath where a small mobile could be hidden. She moved towards the deodorant as her cell door opened.

Babs jumped, shoving the phone behind her back. She breathed easier when she saw that it was Knox.

'They didn't find it then?' she asked.

'Would I be standing here now if they had?' Babs paused as her brain went into overdrive and something dawned on her. 'Bradley knew it was here. She made a real song and dance of turning over the mattress.'

The other woman's face turned ugly; not a pretty sight. 'You saying I snitched?'

'Course not. But only me, you and your two shadows knew anything about it.'

Knox slammed her fist into the wall. It started bleeding but she took no notice. 'If it was one of those two numbskulls, I'll batter 'em.'

One of London's former premier gangsters, Frank McGuire, known to one and all as Uncle Frank, took a swing with a ten iron. His ball flew straight into a bunker on the tenth.

Uncle Frank's grey hair and wrinkles were those of a man in his sixties – well, that was the age he claimed to be, but most in the know knew it was probably a decade on top of that – but his body was still thick set from the workouts he did most mornings. Even when he was sitting in the front room of his Spanish villa watching British TV on satellite, he was pulling dumbbells to keep himself in shape. But his face was leathery and aged from the sun; despite all the years he'd spent on the Costas, he was still English enough to refuse to use sun cream.

On the course, he wore the same designer jackets, slacks and golf shoes that pros dress up in, to show he had the money, but he added a tatty Union Jack baseball cap to remind everyone that he didn't care about that fashion crap. Uncle Frank needed everyone to know that was he was his own man and a man's man at that.

Frank bit his lip as he squinted into the distance where the golf ball had landed. He'd fucked up but his fellow players didn't seem to think so.

'Nice shot Frank but I think your clubs are letting you down.'

'Lovely swing mate but I think there's something wrong with this course, they don't look after it properly. We should find another one.'

In fact, the course was the best in Southern Spain because Uncle Frank only used the best but he was grateful to the other players. They showed him respect and he was big on respect.

He peered at the two suited ladies next to him who acted as his constant bodyguards. 'Make a note ladies – I need a new set of clubs.'

One nodded. A golf buggy appeared in the distance and made its way towards them. On board was one of the club's staff, an attractive young man. He pulled up next to them and said, 'Uncle Frank!'

'Yes Pablo, what's up?'

'There's a gentleman who would like a word with you.'

'A gentleman? What's his name then?'

Pablo smiled but couldn't help. 'He wouldn't say. But he said he was sure you would want to speak to him. He seemed very firm about that.'

'A guy with no name? Who is it then? Clint Eastwood?' He turned to his friends. 'Carry on fellas, I'll be back shortly.'

He climbed into the buggy, his female minders riding on the back, and Pablo drove him back to the clubhouse. In a corner of the luxurious bar, a man was waiting for him. Frank McGuire went stock-still. He'd never done a runner in his life but seeing who was waiting for him made him almost break that rule. His tension must've radiated off him because his ladies took a threatening step ahead.

'It's alright me lovelies,' he said though he knew nothing could be alright if this ghost from his past had put in an appearance. 'Get yourselves something fruity to drink.' He knew they'd be parked not too far away in case he needed them.

As Frank approached the bar, memories of his misspent youth flashed before him. '63 when that fight had kicked off in the basement brothel off Commercial Street. '66, during that terrible winter, when he'd slashed that cocksure geezer's face to ribbons with his razor. He gulped as he recalled the one, terrible incident he tried never to think about.

He swept it savagely from his mind. His visitor turned his laser blue eyes on him.

'I thought you were long away from the life,' he said by way of a greeting. They both knew which life he was talking about; London's murky underworld of a bygone era.

'Still a Bacardi man?' Instead of waiting for an answer the man ordered his poison of choice.

Frank took a seat as a neat was put in front of him. He picked up his glass, but didn't drink. 'Truth be told I thought you was dead or something. One minute you were there, the next you were gone.'

'A wise person knows when to call it a day. I had personal obligations that were more of a priority.'

Frank's visitor sipped his drink, which Frank knew wouldn't contain any booze. His old mucker had never touched the stuff. He'd always remained clear-headed, which was what made him so scary. Back in the day when the man beside him lost it, he really lost it and, unlike most blokes who would blame it on downing a spirit or two, violence had been part of his DNA.

'I take it you haven't come all the way here to top up your tan?' Frank continued.

The man downed his drink in one and then gave Frank his full attention. 'I'm assuming what happens back home reaches your ear?' Frank nodded tersely. 'So you'd have heard about the bullion job?'

Frank didn't wait to hear the rest; he shook his head, lowered his voice and bit out, 'If you're the face behind that job you need to get up and walk away. I don't want nuthin—'

'That gold has got my name on it.' Frank couldn't help his mouth tipping open with surprise. 'My property. My legacy. Names are being mentioned but there are too many for me to wade through. And I don't want my face back in that world.' The guy leaned close to his ear. 'My understanding is that you're still a man with considerable influence back in London.'

Frank let out a sarcastic scoff. 'You seen the kinda life I'm living here? Sun, sea, sangria and sex ain't just happening on the beach, you get me? Why would I trade that for sticking my beak in business that don't concern me?'

'Because of John Black.'

'You what?' Frank growled low and nasty like a dog ready to attack.

Seeing his posture change, his female heavies stormed to their feet and started moving towards him. He waved them back, but instead of retreating to their seats they settled at the other end of the bar primed and ready. Uncle Frank had a thick skin, but one of the things he was touchy about was John.

'You saying John pulled this blag?'

'No. What I'm saying is that when the gold came into my possession John had the resources to help me put it away safe. So he's the only other person who knew where it was . . .'

'Plus the guys who worked there. Could be an inside job. And over the years there must've been loads of security guards, so one of them could be in the frame. Nah, John's retired, has a killer missus and is taking it quiet.'

'One of the names that keeps reaching my ear is a yob connected to him called Kieran Scott. It's rather strange that John is associated with this chap Kieran and John is the one who helped me put the gold there.'

Put that way, Frank thought, John wasn't coming up smelling of roses. He took a long gulp of his white rum to wet his suddenly dry mouth.

'I'm not saying for sure John's involved,' the man next to him kept on, 'but I need a man who commands respect who can find out.' He sweetened the pill. 'If you were to get my gold back there will be a substantial reward for your trouble. Very substantial. If I was to offer you only 10% of it as a finder's fee that would come to several million pounds. All you have to do is pass word back to Black and Scott that my property's covered by you and I'm sure they'll see reason and return it. Imagine how many times you could have sex not on the beach with that type of money.'

He scrawled a mobile number on a napkin and stood up. 'Now if you'll excuse me, I have to catch a flight back to England. Please call me when you've come to a decision.' He gave Uncle Frank a last penetrating look. 'Don't forget me and you go back to a time John Black knows nothing about.'

Uncle Frank studied the phone number. He would've said this was a wind-up, except that those in the know knew the man who'd just left wasn't the type you mucked around with;

at least not back in the day. He took out his mobile with the intention of calling John, but instead held it in his hand for a long time before switching it off and putting it back in his pocket. He folded the napkin and put it away before taking a buggy back to the golf game.

Uncle Frank won the round of golf. In fact he hadn't but his fellow players decided it would be wise to juggle the results around a little to make it look as if he had. He took his party back to the clubhouse for tequila and tapas by way of a celebration. At one point he got up to go for a whizz and locked himself in a cubicle. He took out his mobile and the napkin.

'Uncle Frank here. Listen, I'm coming back to Ol' Blighty in a few days' time. Why don't you and me discuss your little problem further?'

Twenty-Three

Dee let out a little hiccup of giddy surprise when John pushed her up against the wall in the hallway as soon as they got back from visiting her mum's houses. He leaned his body softly into hers wearing a wicked, wicked smile.

Dee chuckled and beamed back. She adored it when he was feeling frisky. 'My handsome soldier looking for a bit of action while he's on parade?' She wiggled her body, making him groan.

Their sex life had taken a bit of a hit in the last few months because John had been unusually busy. Dee had got the nark about it, but had kept her grumbles to herself. Then she'd gone and done something really stupid . . . but she wasn't going to think about that. Not now she was back in the secure, loving embrace of her other half again.

'You ain't feeling rough again or anything?' he asked, stilling his body.

She reached down and placed her hand over his eager knob. 'That feel sick to you?'

John leaned down. Dee pushed up. They met in a powerful kiss. After that they got into it quickly with Dee's Calvin Klein hipsters off in a flash and John's trousers yanked down. She wrapped her legs around his waist and arched as he hit her G-spot. Oh yeah, that was the way to make her chill and shrill.

Suddenly John abruptly froze inside her. His head jerked to the side.

'What's up?'

Slowly he eased out and away from her and her legs dropped to the ground. 'John–?' she started, but he shushed her with a finger over her lips. 'There's someone in the house. Upstairs.'

Dee didn't argue with him. John's past life had given him a sixth sense when something wasn't right, just like when her beloved car had been nicked from their driveway. Dee quietly fixed her clothes as John disappeared into the main room. He came back with an automatic in his hand.

'Stay here,' he whispered.

Dee grabbed his arm. 'You're not going up there on your own, no way.'

She quickly stuffed her hand behind the large photo of Banshee and felt for the taser John had given her years ago, which was taped to the back. She always kept it there for these types of emergencies. He opened his mouth to argue with her, but the stubborn set of her face told him straight that he was wasting his time. They made their way up the darkened staircase, Dee behind John. They reached the wide landing and started to check all the rooms. No one was there.

Dee felt a sense of relief until a tapping sound came from above, where they had made an office and den for Nicky. Shooter and taser at the ready, they both took the smaller staircase to the room upstairs. The light inside shone beneath the closed door. The tapping sound came again as they neared the room. Then it stopped and footsteps sounded inside. John looked at Dee. He mouthed 'three' and began the count. On three he booted the door, gun drawn. They couldn't see anyone inside. It was Dee who felt the presence near the wall behind them. She didn't hang around and pounced. She pressed the taser to the intruder's neck. He screamed in pain and toppled over onto his back.

A grim-faced Dee and John stood over him.

She growled, 'You'd better be able to explain in two seconds flat what you're doing here Nicky.'

'I'm asking you again, why aren't you at uni?' Dee winced as Nicky pressed the frozen pack of peas over the scorched mark left from her taser. Nicky was the last person on this earth she'd ever hurt, but she was pissed that he was home.

'One of your dad's mates said he saw you slinking around the village, knocking booze back like it was going out of business,' she continued. 'But I says, no way José, my boy's got his head down in that big library at the uni reading one of them books that's a thousand pages.'

He gazed sheepishly at her. Her boy had been a total cutie when he was little; now his good looks were going to make women do cartwheels. His golden hair shone and highlighted the small scar near his right eye, courtesy of an accident as a child.

Before he could answer John said from the doorway, 'Give the kid a rest love. Chat to him tomorrow.'

'Tomorrow?' She swung around and gave him the look. 'He's back here like an alley cat and you want me to give him a break. Un-bloody-believable.'

But she could see that her husband was only going to stick his oar in so she stood up, pointed a stern finger at her son and said, 'Don't think you're off the hook young man.'

Her mobile trilled. Impatiently she pulled it out. She pursed her lips when she recognised the number.

'Whatcha want Tiff?'

'I need a word.'

'Yeah, whatever.' Then she remembered what Babs had asked her to do. 'Actually, I need to have a word with you as well. I'll send a text later telling you where and when we'll meet.'

She clicked off and turned back to her son. 'Let me tell you where I think you're going if you keep this up. To the knacker's yard, skid row, bookie street and losers' avenue.'

Before he could answer the doorbell went. 'Who the fuck ...?' They weren't expecting any visitors and, more importantly, she wasn't in the mood. She kept her eyes on her son. 'That's the final word on this Nicky.'

She moved to the window and looked down. There was a car on the drive and two men in suits at the door. She'd never seen them before in her life. Dee opened the window and shouted down, 'Whatcha want?'

One shouted up, 'We're the police.'

'Oi, Knox wants to see ya,' announced one of Queen Bitch's bully girls from Babs' doorway.

For crying out loud. Babs was tempted to roll her eyes heavenward. She was eternally grateful to Kieran for making sure someone was looking out for her, but did he have to pick someone who was such a nutter? Babs didn't like associating with Paula Benson and she certainly didn't like being at her beck and call. But she didn't show her irritation because she was still scared shitless of the violent bird.

Babs dutifully put her flip-flops on. 'What's she want then?'

The other woman said not a word and turned, so Babs followed. Her face scrunched up as she realised that they were headed for the kitchen.

'Why are we going in there?' But her perplexed question was never answered.

The kitchen work duty was inside rustling up dinner. One caught Knox's girl's eyes and nodded to the back. They ended up by a pile of large boxes shoved against a wall. But when the other woman pushed them out of the way, Babs realised it wasn't a wall but a door. When they went through Babs was gobsmacked to see they were in the chapel.

It was the most beautiful part of the prison. It was all wooden beams, arches and panels and gorgeous stained glass windows. Their colours made Babs long for the sun outside and feel a desperate need to be home with her family.

As she moved further in she realised that Knox and her other thug were standing in front of someone she couldn't see. Whatever was going on it was no prayer meeting. Babs went slack-jawed with shock when she saw that the person they were looking down on was Pearl Hennessy, her next door cellie. The old timer looked like she'd been crying for a week solid and the brown skin on her face was tinged with grey. Pearl didn't look great at the best of times, but she appeared a right state now.

Scandalised, Babs marched forward. ''Ere, what the effing hell's bells is going on?'

Pearl just sniffed, leaving Knox to do the explaining. 'Your so-called mate here is the person who grassed you up to the kangas.'

Babs' brows knitted in a wiggle of confusion. 'Don't be daft. Pearl didn't even know I had it. I told you that the only folk in the know were you and your two darling girls here.'

The other woman's face turned murderous. 'If you think anyone close to me would even cough in a kanga's direction without my say-so, you're living in another universe,' she spat. 'No, the person with the loose lips is her.' She stabbed an accusing finger at Pearl who sniffed again. 'Go on, fucking ask her. That's why I brought her here, to confess her sins. That's what my old priest used to do with me and my brothers when we were young – except my big bruv, he was always too quick to grab. And believe me we needed it after the things we saw that slapper of a mother of ours get up to.'

Babs had never even associated Knox with having a mum, much less having been dragged up as a church-going Catholic. But that's what being banged up did to you; you only ever thought of the women in here as having a prison family.

She turned her shaky gaze onto her friend. 'Pearl—?'

'I'm real sorry Babsie.' Pearl's voice was listless as she hung her head in shame.

The stab of betrayal left her feeling sick to the tips of her toes. 'But I don't understand.'

'Effing well look at her, you dozy, treacherous cow,' Knox growled.

Pearl levelled her bloodshot eyes on Babs. 'That day I was in your cell it went off under your mattress. We had a giggle about it being ... well, you know what.' She sniffed loudly. 'Course I knew what it was.'

Babs got mad. 'How. Could. You.'

Pearl swallowed. 'Bradley said if I ever heard or saw anything to drop a little whisper in her ear and she'd personally write to my eldest daughter to say what a good woman I am. You know I'm getting out in a couple of days.' Tears gathered in her eyes. 'I ain't seen my kids or grandkids for ever such a long time—'

Knox furiously cut in, 'That's because you dumped them all in a home so you could go gallivanting off with your new fancy man as you played your mystic Madam Pearl routine.' She made a nasty sound at the back of her throat. 'Well, Madam Pearl should've thought about keeping her kids.'

Pearl's face crumbled. 'I was stupid and young. As soon as I saw the error of my ways I came and got them out of there.' Her shoulders shook. 'But they never saw me the same way again.'

Knox huffed loudly in disgust. Babs inhaled wildly when she produced a homemade blade. 'It's time for this loose-lipped cunt to pay the piper.' She raised her eyes heavenwards. 'May God and all his angels and saints forgive me.'

Babs wasn't sure what horrified her the most – Knox showing reverence and respect at being in God's house or the shank wickedly ready for action in her hand. 'Bloody hell, you're not gonna do her in?'

'Snitches need stitches,' one of the other women said gleefully.

With deadly intent Knox approached the old woman. 'I'm gonna carve you from ear to mouth on both sides of your face.' Pearl began crying openly. 'Then everyone's gonna know that you're the kind of woman who speaks from both sides of her mouth.'

Babs couldn't stand this any longer. 'I'm not having this. Stop it now.'

Knox turned on her. 'Helloooo! I don't take orders from no one.'

Babs stretched her neck. 'Not even from our mutual friend on the outside?'

A muscle twitched in the other woman's cheek. Babs hated to admit it, forever thinking of Kieran as that cute, needy lad she had saved, but truth was he was a force to be reckoned with.

'You cross me that means you cross him,' she added in a hard, I'm-gonna-get-my-way tone.

Both women stared at each other, their gazes clashing. Babs had no doubt she would get the upper hand; not many people wanted to go to battle with Kieran Scott. Well, not if you wanted to live to tell the tale.

But she had spent enough years in the slammer to know that the best way to do your time was forming good relationships with others, and shoving Kieran into Knox's face had the potential to make her lose her crew's respect. Queen Bitch might back off now but she would hold a grudge against Babs as long as she remained in here.

So she sweetened Knox up with a blinding smile. 'You're a top bird and top dog and I'm gonna make it my personal mission to let our friend on the out know how much you went outta your way for me.' She winked. 'I'll make sure he sends you an extra special little drink while you're in here.'

It did the trick because Paula Benson swaggered over to Babs, back to being queen of HMP castle. 'No problem Babs. What you gonna do with blabber mouth there?'

'I'll make sure she'll never think of grassing anyone up again.'

Knox turned an evil eye on the still snivelling Pearl. 'I say you should still cut her, but I know that ain't your way.' She looked back to Babs. 'You've got five mins max before the kangas realise you ain't where you should be.' She clicked her fingers at her girls, but before she left she bent her knee and made the sign of the cross.

Pearl gazed pleadingly at Babs. 'I didn't mean it. I swear.'

Babs clipped out, 'Course you meant it, you old fool. You've been on this earth long enough to know that doing a wrong don't make a right.'

Pearl clutched Babs' hand tight. 'I haven't got long left in here, but I swear I'll do anything you ask. Anything.'

Babs looked her dead in the eyes. 'I know you will. That's why I want you do something special for me when you get out.'

Twenty-Four

Dee tossed her taser into the laundry basket while John dumped the pistol in Nicky's gym bag. He wasn't worried about the house being searched. He knew the law had no grounds for a warrant. He warned his son, 'Keep your gob shut.'

Then he came downstairs at a jaunty pace to find two plain clothes being kept firmly outside by Dee. She was looking daggers at them and then at him and then at them again. He gave her the nod that he'd sorted out the shooter.

'So gents, how can I help you?' John asked, all sunshine and smiles.

He recognised one of the cops from his days in the bizz. He was Detective Sergeant Borne then, although he'd probably been promoted by now. John remembered him as a by-the-book cop but a bit slow-witted. Just the sort of officer of the law he liked.

They introduced themselves. Borne was now a Detective Inspector. The other one, Crane, was a DS. Borne either didn't remember him or was pretending not to. 'Mr Black, we'd like to have a word with you please.'

'Of course, always delighted to help officers of the law. Is this about them travellers on our neighbour's land?'

Borne shook his head. 'No sir, we're part of the team investigating the theft of a consignment of bullion.' His gaze bore into John. 'Perhaps you read about it in the press? It's been quite widely reported.'

Sarky! John sometimes wondered if they included a special sarky course when they trained them up at Hendon.

John paid him back in kind. 'Bullion job? Bullion job? Nah, I don't think so . . . Oh yeah, I remember now; I saw it on the news.' He looked over at Dee. 'Do you remember love, you called me in from the bar to tell me all about it.' He turned back to the detective. 'Was it worth a lot of money then? They didn't say on the channel I was watching.'

Borne gave him a grim look. 'We don't have a final figure yet but it was quite a lot of money, yes.'

'That's very reprehensible I'm sure, but I don't see what it's got to do with me.'

'Just a few questions sir. So we can eliminate you from our enquiries.'

John checked his wife again. He winced slightly. No doubt about it, she was fizzing with fury. But it was difficult to tell if she was angry with the Bill for suspecting him or angry with him for being a suspect.

She spat, 'He ain't done nuthin. Why don't you piss off?'

John raised his hands to calm the situation. The last thing he needed was volcano Dee creating. Plus, he had to play the helpful citizen to put Starsky and Hutch here off the scent. 'Alright sweetheart, there's nuthin to worry about here, we'll soon sort this out. Gents, why don't you accompany us to our morning room and I'll answer any questions to your complete satisfaction. Dee, could you sort out some teas for these gentlemen?'

'Like fucking hell I will.' She kissed her teeth.

John didn't have the time to bring her around, so as soon as they entered the hallway he yelled up the stairs, 'Nicky. Come here.' His son appeared, a right strop on his face.

Nicky complained, 'I was doing a bit of work—'

'Ditch that for now son. Sort a pot of tea and biccies out for these boys, will ya?'

In the morning room, John couldn't have been more helpful although he'd tried and failed to get Dee to make herself scarce. She sat on her leopard-print chaise longue glowering at all three of them.

To the obvious first question, 'Where was I when the bullion job was done? Well, I dunno, do I? When did it happen?' When he was given a timeframe to provide an alibi for, John looked defensive. 'I dunno. I could have been anywhere.' He looked at Dee. 'Can you remember where I was?' She stayed silent. He scratched his head. 'I know I was out somewhere . . .'

The two cops had suddenly become very interested, as John had intended, so he could enjoy himself all the more when he told them. 'Hold up, I know where I was. I was at a committee meeting for ESCSA.'

'ESCSA?'

'The Essex Stray Cats Support Association – ESCSA. That's where I was.' He looked lovingly over at Dee. 'My missus is a real cat lover and after her Banshee was taken off to cat heaven she wanted us to show our support. Would have done it herself but it makes her upset, know what I mean?'

'Stray cats sir?'

John was confident now. 'Yeah, that's right.' He shook his head in sorrow. 'You wouldn't believe the number of strays around here living on the edge and needing help. Of course, I contribute financially but it's not enough is it? You've got to put some time in as well.'

John couldn't figure out from the expression on the other man's face whether he believed him, but it didn't matter, his alibi put him in the clear. 'I see sir, very commendable. Is there anyone who could confirm your whereabouts?'

John reeled off a list of various local worthies who'd been at the meeting. They included a justice of the peace, a vicar's wife, the sister of a wealthy landowner in the area and a fella with an OBE at the end of his name. It was a ball slammed in the back of the net moment.

Borne closed his notebook. 'They'll be happy to confirm your attendance at this meeting?'

'Course they will. Unless they were involved in the bullion job themselves.' He laughed and winked. 'To be honest, that vicar's wife looks a bit dodgy to me. You might wanna pop round and ask her a few pointed questions – have her floorboards up and see what occurs.'

Borne's face turned stony. 'You think this is funny Mister Black?'

John was sitting pretty. 'Anything else fellas?'

Borne did have something else. 'Alright John, I'll level with you. You know as well as I do that there are only a handful of guys in this country who could have pulled off a blag as cheeky as that one. And there's an even smaller number of guys who'd know how to clean the gold up, filter the yellow back into the system and turn it back into cash.'

'And?'

'You're one of that handful, aren't you? You're not telling me you haven't heard any rumours about who was behind this? I'll buy the idea you were looking after our furry friends when it happened but not that you haven't heard any whispers about who was behind it. Come on John – help us out – what have you heard?'

'Look officer, I weren't involved and I ain't heard any tales about who was. You see, I'm retired now and I don't wanna know. I don't care about the young pups these days but I'm guessing it was one of them. I'm out of the game. Check your intelligence reports – they'll tell you.'

Borne reached into his wallet and took out a card. 'If you do hear anything – anything – you'll give us a ring, yeah?'

John took the card while Dee eagerly showed the boys in blue out.

Her face was troubled when she came back. 'John, you better tell me the honest to God's truth, do you know anything about this job?'

He stared back at her as if she'd just landed on planet Earth. 'What do you take me for, eh? Even if I was back in the life, do you think I'd try to pull off a wanker's job like this?'

Her stare turned worried. 'We're alright babes, ain't we? We've got plenty of wang sloshing around?'

'If there's one thing I know how to do it's turn a penny into a pound.' God forgive me, he prayed, hoping that she never discovered the truth. He made his eyes sparkle. 'Now, if I remember, before the Bill came a-knocking we were gonna do some a-knocking of our own.'

Dee giggled as she sashayed towards him, forgetting all about the accusations she'd thrown at him. She hooked her pinkie in his belt and with a saucy wink led him up the stairs.

After John had left an unusually wiped out Dee in bed he made a call in the huge back garden.

'Lad, it's me. The plod have just been around . . .'

'Whatcha tell 'em?'

'That I know fuck all about the robbery, which is the truth. I weren't physically there. But they wanted to know if I'd heard any whispers about how it was going to be gotten rid of.'

Kieran paused on the other end of the line. 'John, you need to sort out a place–'

'I've found somewhere no one will stick their snout into, but I've got to get all my ducks in a row.'

'John–'

'Be patient laddie. All the best things come to those who wait.'

'I know fuck all about the robbery, which is the truth. I weren't physically there.'

Kieran mulled over what John said as he stood on the balcony of his plush pad in Chelsea. And he didn't like it. It was almost as if John was already covering his back if there was trouble.

'Trust no one in this business.'

He hung onto what John had told him years ago as his expression darkened.

Twenty-Five

Jen nearly bottled it when she reached the expensive Italian restaurant in Canary Wharf at seven. She was meeting Naz and two businessmen for a double date. She didn't think she could go through with it. Then she heard the teen counsellor, Sally Foxton's voice in her head:

'My fees are eighty pounds an hour.'

She could sort all Courtney's problems out; all she needed was money. Jen determinedly shoved all doubts from her mind. Naz had told her to look like a knockout and she was worried that she hadn't hit the mark. Self-consciously she pulled down the hem of the black number she wore, hoping that it didn't look like what it was – something she'd picked up down The Lane two years back from a guy who specialised in designer clobber that fell off the back of a lorry.

Right girl, here you go. She straightened her shoulders and tipped her head back and walked in with an outward confidence she was desperate to feel inside. She spotted Naz waiting for her by the low-lit bar. Jen felt like a total scrubber when she caught the classy long royal blue dress the other woman was decked out in. It had a plunging neckline and a cropped front that showcased her stunning legs and black stilettos. The handle of a sparkly evening bag was looped elegantly over her wrist while Jen held on to the pink clutch bag Tiff had bought her for her birthday.

Naz assessed her and beamed. 'Don't you look a right picture.'

Jen groaned. 'More like Frankenstein's bride.'

'Stop putting yourself down. It always makes a much better evening if we girls appear very different, show these guys that there's more than one type of English rose.'

To Jen's horror, Naz reached over, put her palms under her breasts and plumped them up.

'What the fuck you doing?' Embarrassed, Jen peered around to make sure no one was looking.

'If you've got it, flaunt it. Our guys don't want to think they're having an evening out with some bird from *Blue Peter*.'

'So, who are these fellas?'

Naz's face lit up. 'Kareem and Hari are from India. They own a very successful IT company. I've been out with Kareem a couple of times. A total sweetie and most importantly,' she whispered the rest gleefully in Jen's ear, 'he doesn't scrimp on chucking the wonga around.'

'So how much am I gonna clear tonight?'

Something about Naz's face changed but Jen couldn't put her finger on what. All the powder and paint Naz wore suddenly seemed like a mask; only her lush, brown eyes had any life in them. 'We'll get that all finalised later.'

Jen wouldn't be put off. 'I'll need to clear a good seventy.' Being greedy wasn't her style but getting a cab here hadn't come cheap.

Naz threw her a sly look. 'Oh, you'll be tucking a load more than that in your purse, if you play your cards right.' She ended on a wink.

Jen frowned. What did that mean? But before she could find out the other woman took her hand and led her into the dining area. Jen gazed around at the candle-lit room in wonder. How the other half lived. What must it be like to have this life on tap every day of the week?

A man in a black suit and bow tie greeted them with, 'This way ladies.'

Jen became confused as she realised he was taking them to the back of the room. 'Where we going?' she whispered.

Naz raised a perfectly plucked eyebrow at her. 'You didn't think we'd be eating with the riff-raff? I only go with men who take me out in style.'

Jen's excitement grew as they reached a door, which opened to reveal a stunning small room with a fireplace, crystal chandelier and a beautifully set table. Jen had never seen so much cutlery in her life.

Kareem and Hari got to their feet. They were in their late fifties, not lookers by any stretch of the imagination but their suits were definitely top drawer. Naz was right, these two had a lot of readies to flash around.

After Naz did a round of introductions, Hari took Jen's hand and dropped a soft kiss on the back of it. Her mouth shaped into an O. No one had ever done that to her before and she should take it as a compliment, but all she could think was he had enough hair on the back of his hand to make himself a toupee.

Naz spent much of the night chatting with Kareem, which left Jen with hairy hand Hari. She found it painfully awkward at first, so when the Dom Perignon started popping she knocked it back to loosen up. She was surprised that he kept his hands to himself and talked ever so swell in a cut glass voice. Half way through the dinner she was enjoying herself. It had been years since any man had paid her over-the-top compliments like Hari.

Your eyes remind me of the beautiful sky.

Your skin is soft as silk.

Your voice is a ray of sunshine.

Yeah, pure bollocks; Jen wasn't kidding herself. But, oh, what a chuffed feeling it gave her just to hear someone saying cracking things about her. Made her feel like a woman again. A real woman. Not the skivvy who ironed other people's clothes or swiped other people's reward cards at the supermarket.

After coffee and mints were served, Naz caught Jen's eye and suggested, 'Why don't you and I go powder our noses.'

Naz was all saucy as she pointed her French-manicured acrylics at both men. 'Now you two, don't go away.'

Once inside the ladies a triumphant Jen said, 'I can't believe I'm getting paid to sit with some geezer saying sweet nothings to me and knocking back Bolly like it's been supplied by Thames Water.'

Naz beamed back. 'I knew you were a natural as soon as I saw you. You're wasted on that estate you live on. You could be living it large like me.' Then the merriment in her drained away, her face and tone turning serious. 'Kareem said that Hari really likes you.'

Jen shrugged. 'He's an alright fella. Seems decent.'

Naz opened her bag and passed her an oncer, in crisp twenties. 'That's yours to keep for the night. If you want more come back to the table.'

Jen's hand folded around the cash. 'I don't ... I don't understand.'

Naz's gaze was as sharp as a blade. 'I think you do. There's a monkey going on top.'

Jen's confusion grew. Five hundred smackers? What for? Only when Naz laid two items near the sink did the penny drop. A condom and a tube of lubricant.

Naz looked dispassionately at the tube. 'That's to get your-self ready, if you need to. No bloke likes to feel he's having it away with a piece of sandpaper.'

Then she was gone. To say Jen was stunned was putting it mildly. And disgusted. Disgusted with her so-called new friend. She should've known it was all too good to be true. That drop-ping her knickers was part of the deal. To be fair to Naz she had helped out money-wise with Courtney. But five hundred nicker waited for her if she returned to the table. Temptation clawed away at her. But that's what prossies do. The thought of Hari on top of her made her skin crawl.

Five hundred quid . . .

No, take the hundred and never look back.

Jen straightened her shoulders and opened the door.

Less than thirty minutes later Jen winced and whimpered in pain as Hari fucked her.

'You're just a dirty whore,' he rasped like a maniac as he sweated and pumped away. His fingernails bit into her hips as he got his rocks off. Jen's face screwed up tight. This was much worse than she thought it would be, tons worse. She was almost prepared to tell him to fuck right off . . . but she needed that dough. The one bit of luck she did have was he was doing the dirty from behind, which meant she didn't have to look at his ug mug as he mauled her.

She had left the loo in the restaurant earlier with the best of intentions, marching with purpose towards the exit, but the promise of five hundred nicker had dogged her every step. The leccy and gas bill were due in a week's time and she could use a serious cash injection. When would she get another chance to earn money as quick and as easy as this? All you have to do is sleep with the guy. Squeeze your eyes tight, pretend he's Brad Pitt and it will be over in no time. Simple. And no one has to know. Plus, this would be a one-time thing only, so it wasn't like she was becoming a Tom or anything.

Jen had fought hard within herself until, as if by magic, her feet were backtracking to the Ladies. She'd grabbed the condom and lube and touched up her slap. Naz couldn't resist a triumphant grin when she got back to the table. Ten minutes later she was riding in a chauffeur-driven black Merc on her way to his hotel room. To give the guy his due he didn't pounce on her in the car. No, that had happened as soon as they entered his hotel room. He'd been all over her like a rash, slobbering over her cringing skin. Once her kit was off he'd made her kneel on the bed and he was off. Hadn't even bothered to properly get undressed. And the sweet, respectful Hari who'd so chivalrously kissed the back of her hand was gone, replaced by some raving nutter who kept calling her vile names. She knew there were some fellas who could only get their rocks off by degrading the women they went with, but in all honesty she'd never expected to be shagged by one. Even that cretin Nuts, who was as rough and ready as they came, had kept it all upbeat and clean in the bedroom department.

'You like it rough?' he grunted behind her and to emphasise his words he thrust very hard.

Jen had no idea what she was meant to say, but if agreeing with him made him shoot his load quicker she was all for that. Her fanny felt like it was cut to ribbons.

'Yeah, yeah,' she hurriedly agreed. 'Naughty birds like me like it any which way they can get it.'

'And hard.'

Fucking hell, was this man going to keep talking for England? 'Yeah, that too.' Jen's voice rose as pain laced through her.

Please let this be over soon. *Puhleeeeeze.*

'I'm a whore. A cunt. Like getting shafted all over the shop . . .' Jen kept up the filthy patter until, less than a minute later, his hairy hands gripped her hips tighter and he came, his breath hot and wheezing in her ear.

He collapsed onto the bed in a puffed-out heap. Jen was off it in a flash. She already had the five hundred in her bag, having made him pay up front.

'My dear, I do hope you'll excuse me calling you a whore,' a hard-breathing Hari said as she chucked on her clothes.

'Yeah, whatever.' Jen didn't even look over at him; she wanted out.

'Maybe I can tempt you to earn some more cash?' She looked up sharply to find him waving a wad of notes in the air. It had to be at least a grand. She was transfixed by the money.

Jen knew she should get out of there but, like the Devil was whispering in her ear, couldn't help asking, 'Oh yeah, what'll I have do?'

He rolled his fat flesh to the edge of the bed and pointed to a holdall. 'I always bring a friend along to spice up the party.'

Get out now! But she didn't; she walked over and opened the bag. Her breath caught as she gazed down at an assortment of vibrators. The dirty beggar was no doubt expecting her to put on a show diddling herself for his personal entertainment. Nah, that wasn't gonna be happening. The words on her lips, she staggered back when she saw he was kneeling on the bed with his pudgy bum in the air.

Breathlessly he told her, 'I like playing the whore as well.'

There was no mistake about what he was asking her to do. Bloody hell, I've got a right one here. Her fretful gaze strayed to the cash he'd laid on the bed. If she did this, she'd leave with nearly two large.

Jen took out a vibrator and held it in the air.

'Black and in the back,' she said in an authoritative voice

and then moved towards the bed. For the first time she smiled. She'd show him a good time where the sun didn't shine . . .

An hour later Jen was tempted to sag against the back of the lift as she made her way downstairs, but she didn't. She no longer felt dirty, but powerful. Alright, so she'd let some pot-bellied geezer have his end away with her, but she had more cash than she'd held in ages. And she could afford to get her kid some sessions to stop her going off the rails. What had Tiff called her . . . Oh yeah, a lonely, bitter cow that no one would want. Well, she'd show her smart-arsed sister.

Jen pulled out her mobile and called up Naz. As she walked into the night cold the call connected and Naz got straight to it. 'How did it go?'

'He got what he wanted, plus a bit extra with knobs on.'

Naz let out a low, throaty laugh. 'Told you you're a natural. I've got a couple of other clients—'

'Thing is Naz, as much as I thank you for the opportunity, I won't be doing it again.'

Jen punched off. This type of work was one up from being on the game and it just wasn't her style. Now she had a taste of the good life she wanted more and that meant making her mum understand that she and her girls were due more of a cut. Jen was done playing the good girl. In fact, she was going to take some of the lolly in her purse and get some new clobber. After she'd paid for Courtney's counselling sessions of course.

Twenty-Six

The next morning, Dee grabbed a snoring Nicky by the ankle and yanked him off the bed. He sat on the floor in his boxers, staring up at his mum with such a stupefied expression it looked like someone had smacked him with a dead fish. She slapped her fists onto her hips.

'What's going on?' He blinked rapidly trying to get fully awake. There was no doubt about it, his mum was on the warpath.

She stepped menacingly forward and loomed over him like a crow about to pick at her prey. 'I'll tell you what's up. It's gone eleven and if you think you're dossing about the place, you've got another think coming. I wanna know what you're doing back here.'

He gritted out, 'Because I hate it.'

That took her by surprise. 'Whatcha mean, you hate it? It ain't something you love or hate, it's something you just have to do to get on in life.'

He let out a huge puff of air as he picked up a T-shirt, shoved it on and got up. Then he plonked himself down on the bed, reached for his fags on the side table. He offered her one, which she took. They lit up at the same time.

'I'm waiting Nicky.'

He gazed back, his face coated with confusion, which made her feel bad about getting mad at him. In that moment she was reminded of the cute little boy she and John had taken into their home. He'd stolen her heart from the get-go. His dad Chris, who had been John's right hand man, had died. Yes that was the word that Dee always used to describe his passing. She wouldn't think of it as murder because then she'd have to think about the part she'd played in it all. But that was why she enfolded this young man in as much love as she could give. Guilt was such a nasty emotion, always clinging and needy, reminding her of the people she had sacrificed to get to the top. Most people thought that her husband was her weakness, the person she'd fight tooth and nail for. They were wrong. Her weak spot had always been kids and her boy was at the top of the list.

She couldn't help feel the pain she saw etched in his expression. 'Has one of them beardy lecturers been giving you a hard time?' Her voice grew fierce. 'Coz if they have I'll go up there and batter him with one of those fat books they've got you reading.'

He grinned, but she could see the wistfulness in it. 'University ain't for me. All that study gives me a proper headache. And I'm bored out of my box.'

'Have you had a word with your – what do ya call it? – form tutor?'

'Tutorial lecturer,' he said and then shook his head. 'Waste of time. She don't get me. Don't understand where I'm coming from.'

Dee's face scrunched in sympathy. Poor boy! His school hadn't understood that he was artistic when he did that graffiti on the wall of the headmaster's office. And the next school they'd paid top dollar to get him into hadn't got it when he whacked that kid with the hockey stick. Why didn't folk get that her darling lad was full of talent but just didn't like playing by the rules?

'And I've been thinking about my dad. You know, Chris,' he added.

Dee stiffened in shock. Christ Almighty! Do. Not. Panic. Nicky had rarely asked about his real mum and dad when he was a kid, seemingly happy with the story John and Dee had told him. That his mum had passed with cancer when he was a babe and that his dad had died in a tragic accident. The first was true, the other one not. If Nicky ever found out the truth about Chris . . .

She made her voice sound calm as she asked, 'What's brought this on, eh?'

He puffed on his ciggy. 'Dunno really.'

Dee laid her palm over her son's hand. 'You know your real dad was a good mate of John's and worked for him too. I knew Chris as well. A more upstanding bloke you would never meet. I didn't know your dear mum, but John did.' Dee ran her hand over Nicky's hair. 'And from what he says you get those killer looks from her.'

The old Nicky would've pushed his chest out with pride at that, but this new Nicky just sighed heavily. 'My dad never went to no posh college so why should I?' His gaze fired up. 'Remember when you got Tiff to sort me out?' She nodded. 'She used to take me to that garage she worked at under the arches in Bethnal Green and I got a flavour, an understanding, of what Chris's life must've been like growing up. The East End's in my blood Mum, it runs through my veins . . .'

'Are you saying you wanna become some kinda of ghetto rat, playing the Big I Am?' As much as she understood what her son was telling her, no way did she want him mixed up in that world. She'd given him everything but this would not do. See him end up like his blood father? An icy shiver shot through her just thinking about it.

He stubbed his smoke out. 'Most of the other kids talk different from me. I feel like an outsider. I've been asking myself, who am I really? Where am I from? Where am I going? Down the arches with Tiff I felt like I really belonged. I didn't have to strain to hear what the guys were saying – it was my lingo. My world.'

Despite the shockwaves going through her Dee couldn't help but sympathise. 'I know how you're feeling. I felt the same when I was your age, wanting to find out who my real parents were–'

'And if you hadn't,' he jumped in, 'you'd never have found Babs and Tiff and Jen.'

He was spot on. Dee had been such an angry and rebellious young woman, wanting to find her birth mother to punish her for dumping her as a baby. But that wasn't what happened. When Babs Miller had finally spilled her side of the story Dee had clung to her like she was her only lifeline in this world. That was the problem with digging up the past – it never turned out to be the way you thought it was. Nicky's past was no different. Except Dee knew he wasn't going to be clinging to her when he discovered the truth.

She needed to nip this in the bud. 'We've paid a bundle on schools and university to set you on the right path. That's what Chris would've wanted. He wasn't your usual type of Face, he had a working brain.' She tapped her temple. 'And he would've wanted you to use yours too. So I'm gonna brook no more nonsense from you. You're going back to uni.'

He didn't say yes, didn't say no as she kissed his cheek. Suddenly her nostrils flared. She sniffed. His clothes reeked of perfume and not that rubbish going for a fiver on a market stall, but a pricey one called Opium Oriental. Dee would know; she'd fallen in love with it the first time one of those checkout assistants at Harrods had sprayed her with a freebie sample. Its limited edition status made it pricey; only women with dosh to burn could afford that. She frowned. If Nicky had a girlfriend that was not a problem, but she thought all those students were on their uppers, so how did one splash out on something as expensive as this?

She looked deeply into his eyes. 'You ain't giving uni the push coz of some bint?'

He threw his head back and roared with laughter. 'Give over. As if!' Now he did puff out his chest. 'I'm a babe magnet, so it would be a crime to limit myself to just one.'

'Babe magnet,' she huffed. 'Who do you think you are? Leonardo Di Capricock?'

The tension in the room wafted away as they both chuckled. She didn't press the issue of going back to his media degree; time enough to work on him. Plus she'd get John to have a word. Idly she began picking up the rest of his strewn clothes. Each time the aroma of perfume greeted her. No matter how much he denied it she knew there was a woman involved somewhere. But she kept her thoughts to herself.

As she folded his jeans the smell of the perfume turned to an overwhelming stink and she started gagging.

Her son was off the bed in a flash. 'Mum? You alright?'

She couldn't help herself; she heaved her guts up right in the middle of his room.

'Dad,' Nicky yelled.

'Will you stop with the Mother Teresa routine,' Dee slammed out as she lay down on the bed, a damp flannel against her forehead.

After she'd been sick in Nicky's room a concerned John had swept her into his arms and carried her into their room. But then that was her John all over, always looking after her to the max. The silly sod had wanted to call their doctor, but she'd told him all she needed was a bit of a rest.

'I must've been overdoing things or eaten something rotten,' she continued, her voice quietening down.

'Like that green juice you keep pumping into me,' he answered in a sarky tone, although his features were anything but cocky. He looked ravaged, as if she was on her last legs.

'I'm alright.' She smoothed her palm over his and got some fresh air into her lungs.

'No you're not,' he insisted. 'You threw up when we went to your mum's houses. I'm not having it Dee. You, my girl, are taking a trip to the doctor's.'

Dee didn't bother arguing. When John got all man of the house there was no point. 'I'll go tomorrow. Satisfied?' Then she frowned. 'We've got a problem with Nicky. Says he's jacked in college.'

John cocked his head to the side. 'I told you that you were making a mistake pressurising him into going. That boy ain't built for books, he likes to use his hands. You should've let me sort him out a trade.'

'What? Like with your mate Kieran, the so-called builders' merchant?'

'Don't take the rise girl. There's no point trying to fit something round in a square box.'

She swiped off the flannel and threw it across the room. 'He gave me all this flim-flam about needing to find himself, but I know there's a woman involved.' She squinted, which was always a dangerous look on Dee. 'If some bird has pushed her double Ds in his face and derailed his chances—'

He placed a restraining palm on her shoulder. 'Calm down before you do yourself another mischief. I'll have a quiet word with him. Find out what's what.'

* * *

John found his son floating in the indoor pool at the back of the house. He eased down with a cigar and Scotch in one of the poolside recliners and allowed himself one minute of peace. It felt like forever since he'd had a bit of downtime. Funny thing, when he was younger he'd always thought that by this time he'd be kicking his feet up, not a care in the world. But life hadn't worked out like that.

'Nicky, a word if you please,' he called, deciding his moment of precious peace was up.

The water splashed as Nicky heaved himself out. As John gazed at the boy, who in his opinion looked like a wet Greek god, he couldn't help thinking that his old man would've been proud of him. John didn't often let his mind wander to Chris because it hurt so very much. Chris had been more than a lieutenant to him, he'd been like a brother. He'd had to do what he'd done, but it didn't make the pain of dealing with it any better.

Nicky picked up his half-drunk rum and pineapple cocktail and lay back. 'Has Mum asked you to give me the third degree?'

'She's only worried about you.'

'I ain't going back Dad,' Nicky said stubbornly.

'Between me and you son, I never wanted you to go from the off. I've never trusted a geezer who had his head stuck in a book too much, unless it's the accounts of his business. A man should know how to use his hands other than for turning a page, know what I mean?'

Nicky sipped his drink. 'That's what I told her. I ain't one of them poshos. No word of a lie Dad, there's this one, when he talks it's like he ain't even moving his lips. And then I can't make out what the eff he's going on about.'

A huge smile transformed John's face. 'I remember this one time, me and your old fella were in that club I used to own, The Alley, one Saturday night. There were a bunch of upmarket blokes in there. Anyroads, one of 'em, Toby

Farquhar La-di-da-da or something, made the mistake of handling your mum's aris.' Nicky was wrapped with wonder like he was a little kid hanging on a bedtime story. 'You should've seen her knock him flying. Cut his leering face to shreds with her rings.'

His tone became sombre. 'See, that's the thing about your mum, she had it tough when she was growing up. Sometimes the only way she could defend her honour was with her fists. She don't want that for you. Neither did your other dad.'

Silence sat uncomfortably between them at the mention of Chris. 'If you ever want to know about him,' John finally said, 'you come to me.'

'What was he like?' There was a slight hesitation in Nicky's voice.

Puffing on his cigar John started reminiscing about Nicky's blood father. For a good half hour he had his son creasing up with funny stories, his mouth and eyes going wide with amazement at their daring exploits.

'I wished I'd known him for longer,' Nicky said quietly when silence descended again. 'I can't even remember his face.' His voice shook at that simple statement.

'Don't matter. Where you have to remember him is in your heart. And talking of hearts, your mum has got it into her nut that some bird is at the root of why you want to say ta-ra to university.'

Nicky went straight into denial mode. 'No way. I—'

'You know what Chris said to me once: "I can always tell when my Nicky is telling a porkie. His voice goes high and he starts talking like the clappers".'

Nicky groaned, knowing the game was up. 'Her name's Angel.'

'And is she the reason you ain't going back?'

'Not really ... well kinda. I felt like a total wanker in uni, but she makes me feel ...' John noticed the poor lad's ears pinked over. 'Nice. Good. Makes me laugh.'

'Your mum might feel better if she knew more about this Angel. Why don't you bring her round for tea one night.' Seeing the sceptical expression on his son's face he added, 'Don't worry, I'll tell her to be on her best behaviour.'

There was no doubt about it, John decided, his boy looked like he was head over heels for the first time.

Twenty-Seven

Tiff couldn't believe her luck. The hottest girl in The Bow Bells was coming on to her with the force of a runaway train. Not bad for a Wednesday lunchtime. *Toot! Toot! You can get on my track any day of the week babe!* Tiff's usual type was short-cut blonde, but this one was all wavy long dark hair, sexily flicked over one shoulder.

'I've seen you at The 343,' hottie said, naming a club Tiff often went to up West, an exclusive lesbian hangout. She'd have to be blind to miss the blatant invitation in the woman's caramel eyes.

Tiff wasn't sure if she was in the mood for some lovin', but she certainly needed something to take her mind off her money troubles. She'd been lying low and looking over her shoulder trying to avoid serious damage.

'I'm not looking for no long thing.' Tiff made her position clear. This was one sexy Susie, but she wasn't the settling down type.

The woman smiled back as she dramatically flicked her hair off her shoulder, her shimmering, pink nails flashing. She leaned into Tiff, boobs first. 'Do I look like an everlasting type of girl, sweetie?'

Nuff said; they took it back to Tiff's drum across the road. She was in pure bliss as they got their kit off in record time and started snogging on her bed.

The woman suddenly crawled backwards, purring like a kitten. 'I've got a few toys with me. Let me get them. Why don't you shut your eyes for my surprise?'

Tiff was into that. She closed her eyes.

'You have been a naughty girl Tiffany,' growled a rough, male voice.

Her eyes slammed open to find two men standing in the doorway. One was black, the other white, but other than that they were almost the same. They were decked out in matching navy Hugo Boss suits and skinny, burgundy ties, polished, black ankle boots and snarls that slashed their mouths like scars. Tommo and Errol.

Tiffany snatched up the duvet over her naked body. 'What do you want?'

The woman from the bar materialised behind the men and said, 'Sorry about this darlin'. It's just business.' Then the bitch was gone.

Tiffany knew she'd been royally stitched up and would have to drum up some of that old Tiff street magic to tough her way out.

The men inched closer in unison like robots. Tommo said, 'It's always such a bummer coming looking for money.'

'And you owe us quite a bundle,' Errol chipped in, 'so where is it?'

'As far as I'm aware fellas, I still have another month to deliver the cash.' Tiff kept her voice nice and calm.

'You what?' they burst out together.

'That's what the fella behind the bar at The Bad Moon told me when he gave me the loan. It's him you wanna have a pow wow with. When I've got the readies I'll slap it into your eager hands.' She knew she was spouting utter bollocks, but it was worth a try.

Errol turned to his partner and mimicked her voice, 'When I've got the readies I'll slap it into your hands.'

'Oh she will, will she?' Tommo added with a strange wriggle of his head. He ripped the duvet back.

She quickly put her hands over her boobs and bush. 'I ain't scared of ya,' she threw out defiantly. And she wasn't. She'd been in plenty of scraps in her time including being hung out of a window. If Tweedle dick brain and Tweedle numb nuts thought she was bricking it they didn't know Tiffany Miller.

Tommo tutted at Errol. 'I hate it when they get like this.' He gave Tiff his full, menacing attention again as he started to undo his belt. 'You ever had a hard dick up that cunt of yours?'

'Bet she never has.'

Now she was scared. Shock shivered through her. No way. That wasn't going to happen. Tiffany inched back. 'I'm sure we can come to some arrangement.'

He undid his zip. 'I like this arrangement. We fuck you every which way till Sunday and then you still give us our money.'

Tiff sprang off the bed, but Errol caught her by the arm and chucked her back. She trembled as they stood over her. 'Please, don't do this.'

Her answer was Errol grabbing both her arms and pinning them to the bed. Tiff fought like a banshee, but she couldn't dislodge him. Tommo got his cock out. It was ugly. Looked like something the butcher would sling on the offal heap. He grabbed her kicking legs and shoved them apart. She cried out as he ground his hips against her.

'Never had a dyke pussy before,' he mocked her.

His mate sniggered. 'I heard they have canines. Rip your tackle right off ya, so better watch out.'

Tiff whimpered and sobbed, knowing there was no way to get out of this. She'd only ever been with a boy once when she was fourteen. She'd hated it then and knew she would hate it now. Just the thought made her want to puke.

The man moaned as he took his cock and started masturbating. Tiff was shaking like crazy; she couldn't believe this was happening to her. He groaned for God knows how long and then a sickening splash of wet hit her tummy. The shame of it almost made made her cry. But she stemmed the tide of tears. Not on her life would she give them the pleasure of seeing her blub.

There was a knock at the front door. He got off her and did himself up. He leered down at her. 'The next time, if you don't give us our dough, we'll take you somewhere where the geezers won't give a fuck whether your cunt's as sharp as that tongue of yours.'

'Give a fuck,' the other giggled, 'that's funny.'

The knock came again, more furious this time.

They left a trembling, shattered Tiffany on the bed. She heard the door open and close. She curled up into a ball and now allowed herself to cry. She'd really got herself into the shit this time. But where was she going to get the money to get out of it?

'Tiff?' Her head jerked up when she heard the soft voice.

'Stacey? What you doing here?' Snot ran from Tiff's nose. She grabbed the duvet to cover what the man had left on her body, but from the look in Stacey's kind eyes she knew she'd already figured it out.

Her former bestie marched in. 'What did those baboons do to you?'

'I owe 'em money. A lot.'

Stacey shook her head. 'Errol and Tommo are a right pair of proper nutters. The only reason they let me in was coz they knew my dad.' Mickey Ingram might be living it up in Portugal but people still remembered that his family were off limits.

'They were gonna rape me. I'm in trouble. Big trouble.'

Stacey's face grew sad as she took Tiff into her arms.

'I thought you were in a bit of a pickle,' Stacey said after Tiff had spilled her guts, 'that's why I popped around.'

They sat in the den, each nursing a glass of lemonade shandy topped with ice. Tiff wasn't sure how she felt about her former best mate being in her gaff, but she was glad she'd come around when she did. Who knows what might've happened if she hadn't started knocking at the door?

'But I don't get it,' she said slowly, 'how did you know those nutters were here?'

'I didn't. When you came to see me about the loan for Jen, I suspected that was pure bollocks, so I checked our blacklist and there your name was. I came around to see if you needed some help.'

Tiff's heartbeat sped up, seeing all her troubles solved. 'You mean you can get the dosh for me?'

Stacey put her glass down and shook her head sadly. 'No can do. It's against the company's policy. I'd give it to you from my own pocket. Trouble is I'm not packing that kinda cash.' She looked around the room. 'But I don't get it. You've got all this gear and rent this drum, so how come your pockets are bare?'

Tiff shrugged, humiliated that she was having to explain herself. Anyone else she'd have told to mind their own, but not Stacey, especially after she'd saved her from those goons. 'I got in over my head.' Seeing the other woman's raised eyebrows she stubbornly added, 'Ain't nuthin wrong with wanting a taste of the good life.'

Stacey sighed. 'Only it ain't the good life if you're up to your neck in debt to a couple of heavies who will fuck you over to get their dosh back. It seems to me that the number one question you need to be asking is how you're gonna get out of this muck-up?'

Tiff thought for a while. 'You know what they say, Stacey girl, where there's a will there's always a door marked exit.'

Twenty-Eight

'Courtney,' Jen cried as soon as she got in from the hairdressers.

She's already been in the sitting room and couldn't see her daughters anywhere. If Courtney had gone AWOL again she'd . . . Jen opened her girls' door to find Little Bea reading, as per usual, and her sister sitting cross-legged plugged into her CD player.

She pointed at Courtney. 'Right, get them earphones off. Me and you need to have a word.'

Little Bea put her book down and gazed at her mum in wonder. 'Cor Mum, I like your hair.'

Jen self-consciously puffed up the ends. As she'd promised herself, she'd used some of the money from Naz's job to give herself a little makeover. Nothing too much, just enough to make her stop feeling like a drab. It was a short-styled Keira Knightley do, dyed a plum red, spiked at the crown with longer layers combed sideways. She'd never had such a short crop before and at first she'd felt naked, but seeing the look of approval on Bea's face made her feel all modern.

'What did you say?'

She turned back to her other daughter. No comment about her hair. Oh, well! 'We need a word.'

Less than a minute later they were on the sofa together, Courtney slouched slightly back in her usual disrespectful pose.

'Tomorrow you're off to see a counsellor.'

'You what?' Jen pressed her lips together with satisfaction when that got Courtney sitting up. 'I ain't seeing no counsellor. There's nuthin wrong with me.'

Jen became stern. 'You will see her and that's final. I'll drop you off. Her name's Sally Foxton. She sounds nice.' Her voice softened. 'You need someone to talk to.'

Courtney shoved up in a huff and a few seconds later Jen heard her bedroom door slam. She didn't get up like she usually would. After what she'd put herself through to get this counsellor Courtney was going whether she liked it or not. And now she was finally sorting her girl out it was time for her to insist the houses got divvied up five ways.

John was about ten miles from home, the rain really coming down, when he clocked that the motor behind was following; well, that's how it looked to him. The other car was a tasty bit of kit, a black Merc with smoked glass windows. John set his mouth into a grim line. Whoever was tailing him was a prized plonker because by the time he got through with their high-end car it would only be fit for the knacker's yard.

John wanted to make sure that he had the right of it so he took his motor into a sharp turn down a country lane. His mood darkened as the car behind followed. He knew it could only be the owner of the gold, or someone he'd paid to tail him. John knew one thing – he was going to be very, very sorry.

He flicked his gaze down to the baseball bat tucked under his driver's seat for emergency situations. He brought the car to a skidding halt, picked up the bat and stormed out into the rain. Then he belted towards the Merc, which had shuddered to a stop.

He held the bat menacingly high as he confronted the occupant. 'Open the fucking door, or I'll smash this piece of crap to pieces.'

There was a click and the driver's door opened up. With a growl he shifted closer.

'Oh fuck,' he said as he saw the shooters the two women in the back were pointing at him.

The man in the driver's seat asked, 'Johnnie, is there a problem?'

There was only one person who called him Johnnie. He switched his gaze to look at Uncle Frank.

'I didn't know you were back in town, Uncle Frank. I would've rolled out the red carpet. It's a bit late to be calling.'

They were making their way to the bar and snooker room. John was a bit uneasy because it wasn't like Uncle Frank to not let him know when he was visiting. This man meant the world to him. They'd met when a young John had tried to pick the older man's pocket. Of course he didn't know that he was choosing the wrong mark; if anyone knew about scams it was Uncle Frank. He'd grabbed John by the shirt and given him a cuff around the head. Uncle Frank had seen that he was half starved and taken him to a basement brothel in Bethnal Green where the ladies had fussed over him. When John had found out who it was he'd tried to roll he'd been scared out of his bony wits. Uncle Frank was a living legend in The Green. He was a man who would give his last bob away but also one that you crossed at your peril.

He must've seen something special in John because when John fell out with his drunk of a father, and word reached Uncle Frank that he was sleeping in any dark doorway he could find, the older man had taken him in hand. Uncle Frank liked the ladies but had no wife, so they'd become a pair. Where you saw Frank McGuire you saw his ghost John. Everything he'd learned about the business he'd learned at this man's knee.

'It's never too late to catch up on my old mucker's news,' Uncle Frank answered as he wandered over to the black-and-white photo of the Henry Cooper and Muhammad Ali fight. 'I was there that night back in '63.'

The other man had told him the story many times but John played along. 'Oh yeah?'

'He was called Cassius Clay back in those days.' Frank became wistful at his memories. 'That was a night my lad. Packed it was. When Henry hits him with his famous left hook, which was called 'Enry's 'Ammer, and Clay goes down, you should've heard it, thought the bloody roof was gonna blow off.' He gave the photo one last look and then parked himself down comfortably on the leather chesterfield.

John turned to the bar. 'What can I get ya?'

Frank tapped his nose. 'Shouldn't really you know – doctor's orders. But seeing as it's you, I'll have a Bacardi. You remember how I like it, don't ya?'

John chuckled. 'What do I look like? Someone who lost their brain?'

Frank winked at him. 'So, what's happening in Johnnie Black's world? How's that wonderful Dee of yours doing?'

Dee and Uncle Frank had hit it off as soon as they'd clapped eyes on each other. The man was a notorious flirt and he'd tried it on with Dee that first time. She had played flirty-flirty right back.

'Good,' he answered simply as he fixed a drink for both of them. 'She's been a touch under the weather so she's having an early night, I won't wake her if you don't mind.'

'Wouldn't dream of it. And what about the kid? Nicky isn't it?'

John was hoping that Uncle Frank was going to get to the point quickly. He knew this wasn't a social call. Frank McGuire didn't do social. 'Yeah, he's good too. He was up at university but he didn't take to it so he's back home.'

'Sometimes the best place for the young uns is in the bosom of their family.'

There was a long silence before Uncle Frank casually asked, 'So, what's happening on the scene these days? Any new Faces on the block I should know about?'

John was equally casual. 'I wouldn't know bruv, I'm retired these days.'

His visitor nodded. 'Wise move. You've got to get out while you're ahead, haven't you?' His old eyes twinkled. 'You should move to Spain like me. Lovely weather, lovely beaches, lovely birds. You should get a place near me and then we could catch up more often.'

John was leaden. 'Yeah.'

There was another long silence. 'So, no gossip then?'

'No.'

Frank nodded again before adding with a glint and a grin, 'Oh, come off it John. Surely you've heard something about the gold job at that private vault – they made off with a couple hundredweight of the yellow stuff – lucky bastards!'

John's heart sank. 'Oh that, yeah. I read about it in the papers. Lucky bastards indeed.'

'You ain't heard who was behind it?'

John got up and poured himself another Scotch. His back was turned when he answered carefully, 'Not a peep. I bet my life it was some new boys on the block.' When he retook his seat, he realised Uncle Frank was giving him a long, cold stare, the same one he'd used on John as a kid when he'd put a foot out of place.

'Oh? Bet your life on it, would you Johnnie?'

John maintained eye contact. One of the first things he'd learned from this man was the way to tell if someone was trying to have one over. You looked them directly in the eye and if they looked away they were a wrong'un. John kept his stare steady and straight.

Uncle Frank wet his lips. 'You've got to admire their front pulling off a stunt like that. That takes some nerve. Good luck to them I say. But still, a bit cheeky, don't you think?'

'In what way?'

Frank shrugged. 'Well, not checking who the gold belonged to for starters or whether it was covered by someone. I mean, what a bunch of amateurs those boys must be! Those kind of details are basic . . .' He caught John's gaze again, 'as you know, of course.'

'And was it? Covered by someone?' John downed his Scotch, which left his throat burning in a way seasoned drinkers like him didn't often feel.

'As it happens it was – by me.' John tried desperately to keep the shock from showing. 'And I'm gonna make it my personal mission to find out who took it and get it back, ship shape and Bristol fashion.'

John knew he was being toyed with and decided to cut to the chase. 'Got any leads then?'

His mentor spread his mouth wide. John knew it was meant to be a smile but it looked like the mere stretching of the lips. 'A little dickie bird told me you might have had something to do with it.'

John was stony-faced. 'That's pure bollocks.'

The old gangster burst out laughing. 'I know! That's what I says to the little dickie bird! A pile of dog shit! Besides, I'm sure you've got a rock solid alibi for the job.' When he got no answer he went on, 'As it goes, another, more likely name's gone in the frame. A chancer by the name of Kieran Scott, some kind of jumped-up nightclub owner. Know him, do ya?'

John chose his words carefully. 'I've heard the name.'

'Do you reckon he could be my man?'

John furrowed his brows so it looked like he was thinking, which he was, but not about Uncle Frank's question. What a fucked-up mess the blag had turned into. 'Possibly. I have heard he was planning some kind of job to raise money for a drugs deal. Perhaps he got lucky up at that private vault. I'd say it was more than possible, I'd say it was quite likely. Very likely in fact. Can't think of anyone else who might have done it, and I know all the players.'

Frank gave him a sly grin. 'I know you do Johnnie, me lad. That's why I thought I'd drop in and pick your brains. You know what's going on, don't you? Anyway, I don't see any need for any unpleasantness here. I'll swing by and see this Kieran geezer, explain what's what and if the bullion turns up somewhere for me to collect, we need say no more about it.'

Frank got up. 'Nice to catch up and get your take on the take. We should go out for a jar some time and have a natter about the old days. Of course, if you hear anything more about this job, you'll be sure to let me know, won't you?' When he reached the door he turned back. 'Oh yeah, pass my love on to that gorgeous lady of yours.'

A few minutes later, John was alone, his mind moving a hundred miles a minute. He didn't feel bad about dropping Kieran in the brown stuff. The first rule of getting your finger-nails dirty was to look after number one.

He got up to stand in front of the boxing photo. He saluted Henry and Muhammad with his empty glass. 'Looks like Kieran was right. I can't be trusted after all.'

*   *   *

Chuck Berry's 'My Ding-A-Ling' started playing in Babs' dream that night. She rolled over restlessly; something wasn't right here. But she couldn't wake herself up. The song got louder and louder ... Babs pitched forward in her bed with the speed of a zombie rousing for a night's work. The music wasn't playing in her dream, it was bloody playing in her cell.

Shit! Fuck! It was the phone hidden in her deodorant. She must've forgotten to pop it on vibrate. If she wasn't in such a state she'd have smiled because she knew why Kieran had put that ringtone on it. The tune had been playing in the former washhouse on The Devil all those years ago, while she and Kieran happily folded bed sheets together and the other women of the estate sang along loudly. That was until his mum had appeared, creating a fuss. And because she had, it had been the day Kieran and Babs silently agreed that she'd become his second mum.

Babs rushed over to the bottle, scared that one of the kangas on night duty might have heard it. If she got busted that would be her parole gone. The deodorant was rocking with the vibrations like it was dancing.

With shaking hands she pulled it out, clicked on the call and whispered, 'Hold your horses a sec.'

She crept over to the cell door and listened. Waited for the sound of footsteps. When none came she let out a long sigh of pure relief.

'Who is it?' she asked quietly as soon as she got back to her bed.

'Tiff.'

Babs rolled her eyes. God give her strength. 'What the heck are you doing calling at this hour?' Her voice might be quiet, but it wasn't soft. She laced it with all the annoyance she was feeling.

'It's only eleven for fuck's sake.'

'This ain't the Ritz, you plank. Lights-out is at ten in here.' It had taken her ages to get used to when she was first banged up. Some nights she'd stare aimlessly at the ceiling because it was so hard to sleep. 'What couldn't wait until the morning?'

Her daughter paused. This was never a good sign. Finally Tiff answered, 'My bank account's a bit low, so I need to get my hands on some hard cash.'

Babs groaned. She should've guessed. No wonder Tiff had been on her like a ton of bricks about getting the houses on the market. 'You got yourself into a bit of bovver?'

'Course I ain't,' Tiff batted back quickly. 'I got laid off from the garage—'

'Oh, Tiff hun.' Babs' shoulders slumped. Her daughter had been such a tearaway in her youth that Babs had worried she'd end up doing serious bird or, God forbid, six feet under. But Tiff had turned it around, getting a steady piece of work in a garage under the arches in Bethnal Green.

'I'm sure I'll find another job in no time, it's just that I've got a few bills to pay and my cash is all tied up, know what I mean?'

'Is that why you've been going into one about selling the houses? You're not really wanting money to sign up on a course?'

Tiff sniffed. 'I've got my pride Mum.'

Babs felt so ashamed. Her girl had been crying out for help and she'd more or less told her to sod off. 'The problem is, love, I don't have any spare cash—'

'You must have a little tucked away,' Tiff pressed.

Babs smacked her lips irritably together. 'Oh yeah, let me look under my bunk, shall I? I've got a mint stashed away there.'

'Sorry Mum.'

The girl needs a helping hand and you're being sarky. Babs'
shoulders slumped even more. Abruptly she got to her feet as
an idea hit her. It wasn't something she would ordinarily do,
but Tiff was in a tight spot . . .

'There's a mate of mine who will dosh you up the cash. I'll
arrange a meeting for you in a couple of days.'

Twenty-Nine

'I'm telling Mum,' Little Bea whispered to her sister in the dead of the night. 'It's dangerous out there.'

Courtney was pulling on a mini dress her mate had lent her and a pair of heels another mate had filched from a shop down The Lane.

She confronted her sister as she struggled into a shoe. 'And you'd know all about it being a bit screwy out there from those books you keep reading.' She marched over to her wide-eyed sister. 'You blab to Mum and I'll have to blab about the books you're really reading, you get me?'

She stared meaningfully at the *Swallows and Amazons* hardback on the side table. They both knew what was really in there was the autobiography of a now-deceased East End gangster. Her baby sister couldn't get enough of this true crime stuff. They had a deal – Courtney would get the books for her from the library and in return Little Bea would stay schtum about Courtney's little adventures.

She stepped back and smiled. She loved her sister really and didn't want her to worry. 'I'm only going out for a couple of hours. I'll be back before Mum wakes up.'

Courtney had been sneaking out for the last year, going out and about in the wee hours when her mum thought she was tucked up in bed. She didn't even have to sneak out the window like some of her mates because she'd nicked her mum's keys once and got some dodgy geezer down Bridge House to cut a set. You wanted anything off the beaten track on The Devil, Bridge House was the place to be.

As Little Bea burrowed under the duvet, Courtney got her face on and then took a long, hard slug from the can of cider hidden in the wardrobe. She couldn't go to sleep most nights without being boozed up. It was the only thing that kept the nightmares at bay. She tiptoed into the passage. She didn't know why she was bothering to be quiet because an elephant could've wandered into their flat and Mum wouldn't have woken up, she was that knackered most nights.

Courtney opened the door and closed it behind her with a tiny click.

Courtney didn't need directions to the party. You could hear it for miles, somewhere far away on the Devil. There was a party most nights in one part or another of the estate; it was just a question of finding it and the noise was its own invitation. As soon as word spread there was an empty flat, kids would find it, tear down the metal sheeting the council hammered over the door and that was your venue for that night's rave. The kids would stick a big guy on the door to collect money to cover the sound system but, of course, it was bring your own drink and gear. These weren't charity events.

Some nights these parties were actually alright. But usually they ended in gang fights, punch-ups or, worse, a stabbing. It wasn't often the police turned up; mostly the neighbours decided they weren't getting fingered for calling the cops. Just occasionally, a van load would appear and get pelted with cans and bottles for their trouble. And the law weren't unwelcome sometimes. Getting chased across the estate by the boys in blue was a lot more fun when a gig turned dark. The worst end to one of these gigs was when a caretaker who took his job more seriously than most went down into the basement and switched the leccy off. When the lights went out and the music stopped that was when you were in danger of being attacked or robbed.

Courtney followed the noise round one of the blocks into the courtyard below. There was an open door on the top balcony, kids hanging around outside while beats were thundering inside. Some of the fallout from the party was already around her. One girl, unsteady on her feet, was being walked up and down, supported by her mate who was telling her, 'Chuck up babe, better out than in.'

A bottle from above crashed and splintered near Courtney's feet. The girl telling her friend to heave turned to her and said, 'I'd give this one a miss if I was you. It's getting a bit lairy up there.'

Courtney looked upwards. The girl was right, it was. But Courtney went on anyway for the same reason she always did. It was better than waking up from a cold, shivering nightmare. Besides, if her luck was in, Rockers might put in an appearance. He loved these kinds of gigs, preening around with his mates, playing the big shot.

On the door, the guy asked for a fiver.

Daylight robbery. These parties were usually only a couple of quid. 'I ain't got a fiver.'

'How much have you got?'

'Nuthin.' Sod him, after he'd tried to rob her she wasn't stumping up a penny.

He looked inside the flat. 'Alright, we need some more birds; it's getting a bit boysy in there.'

When Courtney's eyes adjusted to the light and her ears to the music, shouting and screaming, she saw kids propped against the walls cradling bottles, others stretched out on the floor or in small groups leering and sniggering. She nodded at some and ignored others. Everywhere smelt of leaf and stale booze. But there was no sign of Rockers or any of his crowd.

She felt a tug on her arm and looked around to find a boy much younger than the other partygoers. He was at the door-way to an empty bedroom. In one hand he was holding on to a small gas canister and in the other a bag of balloons. 'Do you wanna sniff?'

She crinkled her brow. 'Dunno. What is it?'

The kid seemed proud he knew and she didn't. 'It's NOS. You know, laughing gas. Like you get at the dentist.'

'And what's the point of that?'

The kid rolled his eyes like she was a proper thicko. 'Gives you a bit of a buzz, don't it? Whoosh – and off you go!'

Courtney was pissed off that there was no sign of Rockers. 'Nah, you're alright kiddo, I'll wait until I need me molars done.'

'You sure? As I know you, I can do you a special price.'

She didn't know him. Instead of answering, she looked around to see that trouble was starting already. Two boys were squaring up to each other.

'I got my mates downstairs!'

The other kid was tougher; he opened his palm and pushed it into his oppo's face. 'Well, go and fucking find 'em then!'

Courtney was thrown against the wall in the struggle that followed and fell to the floor as other boys piled in. When she managed to get to her feet, she found herself face to face with Rockers. He was laughing. 'Courtney. Alright beautiful.'

He had his arm around a girl's waist and Courtney was stunned to see it was Tash.

'Alright Court,' Tash greeted her smugly.

It was all Courtney could do not to smash her fake gob in. Of all the girls Rockers had to step out with, why did it have to be her? He knew what she'd tried to do the other day and still he went with her. It made her feel small, like the little girl she was.

Rockers eyed up the room and then turned to Tash. 'Gimme five babe; I've just got to say hi to a few guys. If I can get past the brawlers . . .' He stepped forward and began pushing the fighting kids out of the way. 'Excuse me boys! Big shot coming through! Make way!'

Courtney stared into Tash's malicious eyes. There was no pretence they'd ever be mates again. 'What the fuck you doing with him?'

'What do you mean – what the fuck?' the other girl preened. 'Me and *my guy* there are fucking, that's what the fucking fuck.' Her eyes were stone cold, her pupils dilated. 'I mean, face it girl, you didn't seriously think you and him? He's way out of your league.' She swayed for a moment before snarling, 'Where do you get a fucking drink in this crap hole?'

Then she threw her hands crazily into the air and started gyrating to the music. Man-grabbing bitch!

As the party swirled around her, Courtney felt an urgent need to blot it out, blot out Rockers and Tash, blot out this estate, blot out her terrible secret.

She walked back to the kid with the NOS. 'How much?'

He didn't seem sure. 'A couple of quid?'

'I ain't got a couple of quid.'

The boy was disgusted. 'Why you asking then?' But he made her an offer. 'Have you got 50p?'

'Nope.'

'How much have you got?' She had a handful of coppers. The boy looked, sighed and put them in his pocket. 'I'll get into trouble for this.' He took a balloon from his bag and attached it to the hose on his canister and she watched as it inflated. He handed it over. 'You're robbing me blind, you rip-off merchant.'

She carried her balloon into the hallway, held it to her lips and sucked the gas. It was like a half bottle of vodka and a couple of spliffs in one hazy hit. Then there was no party anymore, no Rockers and Tash, no Devil, no family and no deaths, past or future. She stumbled forward, steadying herself on partygoers and the walls until she reached the door and went out onto the balcony to find her way home.

Thirty

After her appointment at the doctor's on Thursday morning Dee drove home and sat in her convertible like she was paralysed. Even the discarded fries carton she'd seen on the garage floor when she arrived, evidence of John abandoning his health kick, didn't penetrate her shock. She gripped the steering wheel as the doctor's devastating news hit her over and over again. *Oh God, what am I going to tell John?*

Dee wasn't one to waste her life on tears, but she leaned her head against the dashboard and cried.

Babs hugged a tearful Pearl Hennessey tight. Her next door cellie was finally going home. Babs was surprised by her own tears; she hadn't realised how she'd taken to this old lag. Sure, she rolled her eyes when she chewed her ear off, which was a lot, but she'd mostly been a good mate. Apart from grassing up the mobile of course, but Babs understood the pull of family. It wasn't what she'd have done, but wanting to see your family was an important thing.

Pearl wiped a tear from her eye. 'Gonna miss you Babsie girl.'

She let out a heartfelt smile. 'Same here.' She leaned in close. 'You owe me, don't forget,' reminding her of what she'd asked her to do once she was out.

'It's at the top of my list. You won't be disappointed.'

Babs stepped back sadly. That was one of the contradictions of prison – you wanted your mates to be released but at the same time you didn't want to see them go because they were your prison family.

'Be seeing ya Babsie,' Pearl whispered.

Then she stepped out onto the landing where the other girls had all gathered to give her a rousing send-off. The girls started clapping as Pearl made her way to the metal stairs. Then they started singing the song they always did when one of them got out – Gloria Gaynor's 'I Will Survive'.

'I don't believe you John,' Dee muttered furiously at her mobile phone. She'd been trying to get him on the ol' dog for the last hour with no joy. In less than twenty minutes Nicky was bringing his latest steady, Angel, around to meet them over a slap-up lunch. And this girl better be an angel; only the best for her Nicky. John was meant to be here, but he'd gone into town to take care of some business and hadn't come back. She'd been on the blower so many times she'd lost count. Where was the Herbert? She'd give him what for when she got her hands on him.

Dee ran her gaze over her reflection in the large, heart-shaped mirror in her dressing room. She didn't want to go overboard on what she wore, or come across as mutton dressed as lamb, but she didn't want this Angel getting the impression that Nicky's old lady was some bun and flower-print skirt wearing, prim and proper suburban mum. Her teeth twisted into her bottom lip as she worried whether Nicky would approve of her get-up.

She wore a turquoise shift dress that looked simple but was made of luxury duchess silk that shifted with the lines of her body. She'd gone to the hairdressers to have her better-put-a-ring-on-it Beyoncé weave toned down to soft, fluffy curls. The one thing she wouldn't compromise on were her Choos – four-inch, cut out gold, suede heels.

Staring at herself reminded Dee that she hadn't told John what the doctor had said. Her gaze intensified as she raked it over her body. She knew she was going to have to tell him sooner or later . . . Later, much later.

The doorbell went off. Blimey, they were here.

Dee went downstairs and quickly inspected the dining room. She'd got in a catering company to put on a spread fit for royalty. Dishes upon dishes were laid out, most of which had names Dee couldn't even pronounce. A chilled bottle of Cristal was ready to pop on the sideboard.

A key turned in the lock and Dee hurried out to greet her son and his girlfriend. The front door opened and the pair strode in. Nicky looking very pleased with himself in a russet suit and open-necked shirt, his girlfriend on his arm. She clutched him tightly as if he were a valuable handbag. She was dressed in an LBD and expensive heels that showed off her figure so powerfully it left aftershocks; her long hair was both done up and hanging locks down her neck. Dee bet she had track extensions in it to give it extra bounce. A girl after her own heart.

And then Dee saw her face and was struck dumb. In fact, she thought she might have gone into shock.

'Alright Mum? This is Angel.' Leaving his girlfriend behind in the hallway he strode towards the stairs. 'Just got to pop to the can, it was a long journey and I'm dying for one, you get me?' He turned to his girl. 'Make yourself at home baby.'

He rushed up the stairs and the two women were left alone. Angel tilted her head back and gave Dee a long and knowing smile. Then she twitched her nose like a rabbit.

When Dee recovered herself she folded her arms. 'So, you're Angel are you?'

The young woman's accent made the Queen sound common. 'That's right. Angel by name, Angel by nature.'

Dee whispered, 'I don't wanna show my boy up, but later on me and you are gonna have words.'

Angel nodded. 'That's good because I'm hoping to have a word with you too.' Then she added archly, 'Shall I call you *Mum* this evening?'

Dee clenched her fists and hissed, 'You can if you're ready to leave here in a body bag.'

'Oh dear, that's a shame; Nicky promised me that you and I would get on like a house on fire. But if you prefer, I'll stick with calling you Dee.'

'You wouldn't believe what I'm gonna call you later.'

Nicky bounced back downstairs and came round to give his mum a hug. As he went past Angel, he grabbed a handful of her arse. She winced in disgust but by the time Nicky was facing her again, she was all smiles. But still she said, 'Don't do that Nicky; you'll embarrass your mother.'

'Embarrass my ol' mum? Impossible. She don't do embarrassment. Ain't that right Mum?'

Dee could barely contain herself. 'Yeah, that's right.' The words felt like sand in her mouth.

Poor Nicky didn't seem to have noticed the doom-laden atmosphere. He clapped his hands together. 'Right, what's for grub then? I'm starving. I hope it's proper food and not that catering company crap. Where's Dad by the way?' He took Angel by the hand and led her past Dee towards the dining room. As she went by, Angel gave Dee a knowing smirk.

Dee was left standing alone. She gasped under her breath. 'What the fuck?? What the fucking fuck??'

Because Nicky's girlfriend Angel wasn't really Angel at all. She was Flo Miller.

*   *   *

Nicky didn't notice that he was doing all the talking but then he usually did all the talking anyway. As Flo had noticed, he was a mouthy little sod. The two women faced each other over the table like a couple of boxers at a weigh-in. Both looked relieved when Nicky finally said, 'I need another Jimmy Riddle.'

Dee turned to him. 'Why don't you take your time babes.' She slapped a sweet grin on. 'Gives us two girls a little mum and Angel time.'

'Girls' talk, eh? That's cool. I'll powder me nose as well while I'm up there – and I ain't talking about me coke habit either.' He waited for a laugh but didn't get one. As he stood up, he gestured at Flo with his thumb. 'Classy bird, eh Mum?'

'Yeah, very classy.'

Nicky finally noticed that the evening wasn't going as warmly as he'd hoped and looked downcast. 'Alright then, I'll see you both in a long minute.'

When the door closed, Flo reached for her handbag. 'Do you mind if I smoke Dee?' She didn't wait for an answer but took a cigarette out of a packet of Marlboro Lights and lit it. She blew smoke over the table and tapped the ash into a Limoges saucer. 'Well, nice too see you again my dear. It's been a long time.'

'That's right, it has. When did we last cross swords? Must have been at that solicitor's office when you and your father Stan were trying to diddle my mum outta her houses.'

Flo shook her head. Her accent was changing like the leaves in autumn, going from BBC announcer to Cockney sports presenter at a rate of knots. 'Nah, that was the time when my dad was trying to stop your mum diddling him out of his two houses—'

Stunned, Dee said, 'His two houses? You've got that wrong bitch, those houses came to Babs from somewhere else.'

Flo laughed full and loud. 'Your dear ol' mum can't even tell you the truth. That's why he came back, to get his hands on the houses that witch robbed from him.' She scoffed, 'Like Babs Miller has got the brain or cash to invest in property.'

Dee was still for a moment, hearing the truth in her words. Hadn't she asked Babs whether they were once Stanley's and been told no? She shook her head; wherever those houses had started up they were now legally her mum's. 'Those belong to Babs fair and square. If your old man gave them to her then he's a grade A idiot.'

Flo bristled. 'Don't you talk about my dad like that. The last time I saw you was at your old girl's trial when she got away with murdering my old man by pretending it was manslaughter. Amazing what a good brief can persuade a dopey jury to believe, ain't it?'

Dee leaned forward. 'Alright Flo, let's cut the banter. What are you up to?'

The other woman gave her a wide-eyed innocent look. 'I dunno what you mean.'

'With Nicky you little bitch, you know full well what I mean.'

Flo giggled and cooed like a teenager. 'Oh that. Me and Nicky met and fell in lurrrvv! You know, in lurrrvv!' She scowled, blew smoke again and sneered, 'It's just like the movies. A real life Romeo and Juliet.'

Dee squinted. 'You're after the houses ain't you? It won't work. When I tell Nicky who you are and what you're up to, he'll drop you like the tuppenny tart you actually are.'

Flo shook her head. 'I don't think so. He won't believe you. You seem to be forgetting he's an eighteen-year-old boy and I ain't the usual Essex trailer trash that lads like him cop off with. I'll tell you, what I can do in the bedroom is nobody's business; I'm a veritable circus contortionist. You think he's giving that up for some shaggy dog story his ol' mum's gonna tell him? He's loved up ... *babes* ... and he ain't going nowhere. Face it Dee, there's gonna be a war for these houses and your son's gonna be on my side. Of course, if you were willing to be reasonable, I could tearfully tell him it's over and he can go out with a bird called Tracy from Basildon instead and everyone's happy. But that's up to you, of course.'

Dee rose to her feet. 'You're a piece of work aren't ya? Taking advantage of an innocent young guy for your own greedy, selfish ends. Pity my mum didn't do you over and all, along with your old man.'

Flo stood up in turn, resting her fists on the table. 'Oh that's a laugh; I'm getting a lecture on morals from a member of the Miller family. I hear you cut a few corners when you went after your hubby, darlin'. Didn't his fiancée fall off the love cart while you were driving it? So get off your fucking high horse sweetheart. We're birds of a feather, cut from the same cloth. Fight me if you like but don't look down your nose coz I ain't buying it.'

'Fucking get out!'

Flo chuckled nastily. 'Oh don't worry, I'm going.' She marched out of the room shouting, 'Nicky! Move your arse, we're leaving, I ain't staying here to be insulted by some gangster's moll.'

Dee followed and grabbed Flo by the hair. 'Oh no, you're going on your own, my son's staying put.'

Flo rammed her elbow back into Dee's ribs. 'I don't think so.'

The two women grappled and fell into the hallway, screaming, punching and kicking each other. Nicky came bombing down the stairs and pulled them apart. He turned to his mother and shouted, 'What the fuck have you done?'

Behind them, Flo called out to her outraged hostess, 'Think about it babes. I want my property back and I'll go toe to toe with you for it, any time, any place.'

Dee saw Nicky's horror when he realised that his girlfriend was walking out. He made to race off after her, shouting 'Angel! Angel!'

Dee grabbed him and twisted him around. 'Fuck her.'

His face was stained red with rage. 'What the effing hell's going on?'

She grabbed his shirt and jerked him close. 'That, you prat, is no angel, she's Flo Miller, Stanley Miller's bastard kid.'

She released him as she saw the news dawn on his face. Then he was back to being defiant. 'So what? I don't care. I like her.'

She thrust forward into his space as if hoping her words would slam into his brain. 'All she wants from you is to get close to me so she can get her hands on Babs' houses, which she's mistakenly got into her nut belonged to her dad and so belong to her.'

He scowled. 'If Stanley had anything to do with those houses then surely she deserves a cut.'

'What she deserves is a kicking she won't forget.'

He shook his head, thoroughly fed up. 'I'm outta here Mum.'

She roared after him, 'Nicky! Nicky!'

Dee heard Nicky's sports car engine rev up and then the two love birds tore off down the drive at high speed, wheels spinning.

Dee slammed the front door and went back to the dining room. She sat down, massaged her temples and tried to think. There was already war going on between three sisters and now a fourth had been added to the mix. And this one, she bet her life on it, was the most ruthless of them all. Dee was worried. Would Nicky see sense before Flo hurt him? She had no doubt that bitch would use him any which way to get her hands on those houses. But Dee wasn't going to give in. No fucking way.

When Dee stood up to get herself a proper drink, she winced with pain from one of the blows Flo had landed. The girl had quite a kick on her.

Ruthless and with quite a kick on her?

There was no doubt about it. She was Stanley Miller's daughter alright.

She dismissed Flo when she heard her mobile going in The Hollywood. She found it near the popcorn maker, but the ringing had already stopped. It pinged with a text.

Have you put ur sisters straight?!?! B

Dee groaned. She'd forgotten all about organising a sit-down with her sisters. She'd told Tiff but not Jen. She'd been feeling so unwell it had clean gone out of her head. She texted back.

It's all in hand.

Thirty-One

'I've just popped the kettle on. Fancy a brew?' Maggie Sparks asked Babs in the office at the memorial gardens.

Mags' family-run business had the contract to keep the memorial garden in tip-top condition with loving care and respect. She was a similar age to Babs and had grown up in London before moving out this way, so they got on like a house on fire, although Babs thought she had busybody tendencies.

Babs took off her gardening gloves and plonked herself down in a chair. One of the responsibilities of the open prison was to find inmates jobs to get them ready to face the world again. Babs was gobsmacked to find that some of the women didn't take up the option. I mean, who wouldn't wanna get out for a couple of days a week? It was Pearl Hennessy who gave her the lowdown that some found it too agonising to be on the out for any length of time without doing a runner. The urge to be with family was so strong. Babs had similar feelings, but scarper? No way. That would royally mess up her parole chances. In fact, she loved tending the plants and flowers because it reminded her of how she'd looked after her family. Another plus was despite gardening being a dirty job she no longer got those crazy urges to wash her hands manically. That support group had done her good. Babs knew she wasn't cured, but heck had she come a long way.

Mags popped a cuppa in front of Babs and groaned as she sat down. 'My corns have been playing up something terrible,' she uttered in her sing-song voice.

Babs sipped her tea. 'You wanna start wearing flip-flops like I do. Gives your feet breathing space.'

Mags shook her head. 'Nah, my Harold wouldn't want me to be seen around town like that. We've got an image to uphold.'

Mags had married up, to a man from a family with money and a few businesses well on the go. Most times, Mags looked like a woman modelling clothes from an old Kays' catalogue and talked in a la-di-da fashion. Only around Babs did she let her hair and speech down.

Mags squinted at Babs and cradled her mug. 'You know me Babs, I'm not one to poke my beak into other people's bizz,' like hell! 'and you know the prison's not allowed to say, but what exactly are you doing bird for?'

The tea nearly sputtered out of Babs' mouth. Crikey! It wasn't something she talked about. A few of the other girls had tried to worm it out of her but she stayed schtum. One of Babs' big rules was, you mind yours and I'll mind mine. Well, that's what she told herself, but in her heart she was scared that as soon as word got out she'd lose any friends that she'd made. Come on, who wanted to be mates with a convicted killer?

'Only my Harry,' Mags continued slowly, 'says you're in for . . .' she lowered her voice, eyes darting around as if checking that no one was earwigging, 'doing in your old man. He remembers the case from a few years back.'

Babs' mouth filled up with spit. That's how she got every time she remembered that rotten animal, wanting to gob a large one on the floor. She hated, *hated*, even thinking about Stan, much less the day he'd had the life snuffed mercifully out of him. It made her feel yucky. All those years she'd tried to be the best missus a man could have and what had he done in return – chucked a load of bollocks and shit right back in her face.

Instead she spat bitter words. 'That foul cunt deserved it.' Babs could've bit off her tongue. Whatcha go and say that for? Might as well wave ta-ra to this cushy job.

Mags' hands were shaking, her face bloodless, as she placed her cup on the desk. With a huff Babs spoke before the other woman could say anything. 'You don't have to worry, I'll be outta your hair by the end of today and then you can ask the prison to send someone else.' She looked away but her new friend's voice stopped her.

'I've got a brother doing time.' Babs' mouth fell slightly open as she turned back round. Mags' hands fretted in her lap. 'What were your mum and dad like?'

Babs smiled as she remembered Rosie and George Wilson. 'They were cracking. I was the apple of my dad's eye.' Her face clouded. 'We had a major falling out for a few years, but once we put that behind us we became a loving family again.'

The other woman looked sick. 'Wish I could say the same. You're brought up to love and respect your mum, but mine was rotten to the core. God, she used to belt us, Monday through to Sunday. None of us said a peep; you didn't back-chat then, didja? What happened behind closed doors stayed behind closed doors. Even when we got big, she'd take a swing at us.' She became paler, eyes staring ahead, unseeing. 'One of my brothers couldn't take it no more. I swear, one minute we were eating Sunday roast, she's going on and on and on . . . next thing he picks up the carving knife . . .' Her mouth moved like a fish, no more words able to come out of it.

Babs quickly went over and put her arms around the grieving woman. 'He got life Babs,' she cried. 'They wouldn't take all the heartache and punishment into consideration. A really good man helped us, giving us money for a good lawyer, but it didn't help.' She eased out of Babs' arms. 'That's why I do this work with the prison. I know people have done wrong, but I don't want them to do any wrong again, so I give them a chance to sort themselves out.'

Babs was touched by her story and vowed never to call her a busybody again. That was the thing; you never quite knew the ins and outs of someone's life. Just like people didn't really know what had happened that day with her, Stan and Courtney.

Mags smiled shakily, took out a pretty hanky from her bag and mopped her eyes. 'So you don't need to worry girl, I understand. If you say your old man was a toerag, that's what he was.' A sudden, mischievous smile spread across her face. 'I got those choccies you love in.'

Babs groaned with utter pleasure. Chocolate. The only way to get any decent choccie inside was to owe someone and she wasn't about to do that.

Ten minutes later, Babs was humming 'Dancing Queen' happily away to herself, potting some gorgeous roses, when she noticed a hoodie character in the park. Nothing wrong with anyone being there but whoever it was was making a beeline for her. If they were out to mug her they were going to be sadly disappointed. Mind you, if they wouldn't take no for an answer she could do some serious damage with her trowel.

She stood, clenching her mini shovel by her side as the figure got closer and closer.

When they reached her, she held the trowel up and growled, 'What do you want?'

The person flipped the hood down. 'You planning to plant me one here as well?'

Astonishment took over. 'What the effing hell are you doing here Jen?'

*　　*　　*

Babs grabbed her daughter by the arm and pulled her behind a tree. 'You better have a bloody good explanation. If the big house finds out that could be my parole down the pan.'

Jen tutted as she tugged her arm back. 'What, like having a mobile phone stashed in your cell ain't already doing that.' Babs gazed at her guiltily. 'You never did say who got the phone for you.'

'Never you mind that.' Her eyes suddenly grew wide. 'It ain't Courtney . . .?'

Jen cut her off. 'That little madam has been over-stepping the mark once too often these days. But don't worry, I'm sorting her out.'

Babs couldn't quite meet her daughter's gaze. 'She's a teenager. All those hormones make 'em moody.'

Jen shook her head. 'Nah, I think it's more than that. I think she's hiding something bad from me.'

Oh heck, Babs thought. She'd made her grandchild swear not to breathe a word about their secret. If Jennifer ever found out . . . 'Probably some lad she fancies.'

Jen compressed her lips. 'If it is, it had better not be that Dexter Ingram.'

Courtney had a soft spot for Melanie Ingram's young cousin. Dexter, or Rockers as his friends called him, was a real cutie, with good manners, but there was no way him and Courtney could ever become an item with the bad blood between the families.

'Jen, whatever you want, you need to state your business quickly because I can't be seen talking to people. You know the set-up.'

'Mum, I know I've said it before, but you need to give my girls a share of those houses.'

Babs rolled her eyes, thoroughly fed up with this muck-around. 'No. That's not how it's gonna be. If I cut your kids in then I'll have to provide for Dee's Nicky too. And what if Tiff has some nippers in the future, they won't get a share coz they weren't around when the dosh was being dished out.'

Jen huffed. 'As if! *They* don't have kids—'

'Well, that's where you're wrong. There's a couple of girls inside who are of that persuasion and they have children. Why can't you just—'

Babs' heart lurched when she noticed that Mags was coming out of the office accompanied by a man in shades. She desperately pleaded with Jen, 'You've gotta get out of here. That's the woman who runs the place. If she sees you I'm in the shit up to my eyeballs. And that fella she's with could be checking up on me.'

Jen maintained, 'This ain't finished Mum; not by a long shot.' But as she tugged her hood back up, Mags called out Babs' name, making them both freeze.

Babs muttered, 'I'm done for now.' She warned her daughter, 'We'll have to make up some Mickey Mouse story. Let me do all the talking.'

As soon as Mags and the man reached her Babs spurted, 'This lady was just looking for . . .' until she realised who the man was.

Kieran.

Babs immediately said, 'I don't know this fella.'

Mags' face crinkled into a sunny smile. 'Of course you do.' To Babs' astonishment, she leaned up and kissed him on the cheek. 'He did me a favour many years ago.'

It didn't take Babs long to figure out what that favour had been. Kieran had been the 'good man' she'd spoken of earlier who had given her money to get a decent lawyer for her brother. How like Kieran to help someone who had been standing trial for murdering the mother who had abused him as a child. Kieran had once been in that position himself. Thank God Kieran had never gone the way of Mags' brother.

'So, when this darling lad asked me to do a favour in turn,' Mags gazed adoringly up at him, 'what could I do?'

As she walked merrily back off to the office, Babs asked Kieran, 'You got her to sort out this job for me?'

He smiled cheekily at her. 'Anything for you Babs.'

Jen chimed in, none too pleased, 'Are you the one who got her hooked up to T-Mobile in her cell?'

Kieran held his hand out. 'You must be Jennifer.' Tiff and Jen had been too young to remember Kieran when he was living on The Devil. And when he'd moved away Babs had decided to keep it that way. As much as she wanted her girls to know the young boy she'd helped raise, she didn't want them anywhere near his badlands lifestyle.

But Jen only had eyes for Kieran. 'How do the two of you know each other?'

'We go back yonks,' Babs filled in. 'Kieran used to live on the estate when you and Tiff were still nippers.'

Jen continued to eye him up. 'Well, you must've done well for yourself,' her gaze slid to her mother, 'because there's some of us still stuck on that shithole coz their family won't help them out.'

'Jen . . .' Babs warned tightly.

'Nice meeting you. I'm off.' Anger coloured her features again. 'But it's not fair Mum, not fair at all.' She strode off, Babs keeping her mouth tightly zipped. What was the point in arguing? Jen was never going to see it from her point of view.

Instead she launched herself at Kieran, wrapping him in a big, warm hug. 'My old eyes can't get enough of you.' And it was true. In times of trouble, if she ever needed him, her boy was always there for her. The only time she'd kept him well away was when Stan had turned up again.

'What are you doing here?' Babs asked.

'I'm not stopping long but I just wanted to see me ol' mum.'

They walked back to Mags' office, arms linked together.

Fifteen minutes later Kieran pushed his foot to the pedal of his flash motor when he saw Jen up ahead in the distance, almost at the train station. She stopped when he pulled up alongside her.

He activated the automatic lock on the passenger door and it sprang open. 'Jump in, I'll give you a lift.'

Jen wavered before taking him up on his offer. She flipped the mirror down and touched up her lippy. He punched the CD player and *Frank Sinatra Live* filled the car with 'My Way'.

As he took off, he asked, 'So how's your sister Dee and her husband John getting on?'

Thirty-Two

'My goodness me, what's happened to you?' Flo's granddad asked, raising his head from *Navy Weekly* and staring at her. Strangely he didn't look shocked at her appearance.

Still in a strop after her battle with Dee, Flo hung her handbag over the beak of a stuffed flamingo. She examined her face in the stylish art deco mirror. 'I don't know what you mean; I've had a lovely day.'

'Your dress is torn and you've got bruises and scratches on your arms.'

'Oh that. I slipped on some ice.'

'It's summer my dear.' He sighed heavily and added, 'You've been fighting again haven't you? It's not often I wish you took after your mother but I'll say this for her, at least she doesn't get involved in any fisticuffs.'

Flo was still checking the damage to her face. 'Mummy hasn't got the bottle, that's why.'

The Commander was pained. 'And I wish you wouldn't use vulgar expressions like *bottle* either or I might start to think the money spent on your education was wasted.'

'Yes, sorry about that, I'm afraid I've been in Essex.'

'Essex? Ah, that would explain it. Your young gentleman comes from the area?'

'That's right.'

The Commander put his magazine down. He was curious. 'Who exactly is this young chap then?'

Flo was finger combing her hair. 'His name's Nicky Black. His father is John Black, a retired East End gangster, and his mother Dee fancies herself as a bit of a scrapper. But I'm afraid she picked on the wrong opponent this time.'

'East End gangsters? Are you going around with people like that because of your father?'

Flo's fingers stilled in her hair. It was the one thing that they couldn't agree about – Stanley Miller. The Commander might not like his daughter but he strongly disapproved of the man who had hoodwinked her into a bigamous marriage. She tightened her lips, not willing to get into it tonight.

Instead her granddad said, his tone conciliatory, 'The Blacks from Essex? That must be interesting for you.'

Flo smirked, enjoying the way it twisted her lips in the mirror. 'It certainly will be for them. His mum's only going to push Nicky further into my arms.' She shook her hair back. 'Right, I'm off for a bath. Do you want a sherry before I go?'

'Yes please. Oh and Flo, keep the noise down upstairs. I'm afraid you're not the only householder who's been in the wars today.'

Flo was disgusted. 'Not Jezebel again?'

The Commander shrugged. 'Yes, I'm afraid the tom from over the back came snooping around and as you can imagine that was a red rag to our Persian Blue.'

'That tom's about twice Jezebel's size. Did she win?'

The Commander hitched his brows high. 'Of course she won, she always wins. The tom scarpered with a flea in his ear and half the fur on his tail missing.'

Flo was impressed. 'Good for her. I'm starting to warm to that cat actually. I'm going up to have a long soak.'

Just as she reached the door he informed her, 'If your Nicky needs a place to rest his head he's welcome here anytime.'

With a smile she walked over to him and kissed him gently on the forehead. 'I love you Granddad.'

Courtney was surprised the first time she saw her counsellor, Sally Foxton. Instead of being a dead ringer for one of her deadbeat teachers as she'd presumed, she was youngish and had three silver studs in each ear and a gold one in her nose. And she was expecting to meet in her a boring office but they were in a quiet corner in a burger bar. And she said she liked to be called Foxy, which Courtney thought was kinda cool, but she didn't let on. Instead she slouched back in her seat with her lip curled.

'So what do you fancy Courtney?' Foxy asked.

'What do you mean?' she shot back suspiciously.

'Food. Do you want some fries? A burger? I like the cheeseburger myself. And they do a mean apple pie.'

Courtney couldn't believe her ears. This woman wanted to buy her some nosh. She thought the counselling sessions would be this woman chucking loads and loads of questions at her while she told her to piss right off. But at the same time it felt like she was offering her a poisoned apple. 'Nuthin. I don't want nuthin,' she answered stubbornly.

'Well, I'm going to have a chicken burger with large fries and a cuppa.'

For the next twenty minutes Foxy got stuck into her grub and talked endlessly about the day she'd had. Courtney's mouth started watering, she couldn't help eying the meal. In the end she got Foxy to order her some nuggets and a milkshake. And that's what they did for the first session, just ate and chatted about Sally's new motor, her dog Bagsie and her love of junk food.

*   *   *

Jen was a bag of nerves as she anxiously waited for Courtney to come out of her first counselling session. There weren't many times in her life when her mouth fell open, but finding Sally Foxton waiting for them outside a burger joint instead of a bona fide office had been one of them. She'd nearly grasped her daughter by the shoulders and swiftly marched her away. A burger bar for Christ's sake! It had taken the counsellor a full five minutes to soothe her feathers and allow the session to go ahead. That hadn't stopped her nail-biting worry as she waited. But at the end of the day, what alternative did she have? Things with Courtney couldn't go on the way they were. Call it mother's intuition, Jen knew that if something didn't change something serious was going to happen. She could feel it deep in her bones.

She jumped out of her glum thoughts as the passenger door opened and Courtney got into the car.

'How did it go, hun?' Jen searched her daughter's face as if trying to see an immediate change in Courtney's behaviour. She slumped back slightly with disappointment when the only thing she saw was the same old same old sullen teenage girl expression. Jen mentally ticked herself off for expecting the counsellor to be some kind of miracle worker. Getting through to Courtney was going to take time.

'Alright,' her child mumbled back.

'So,' Jen drew out the word, 'is there anything you want to tell me about?'

'Foxy says—'

'Who the heck is Foxy?'

Courtney's voice filled with life. 'It's what everyone calls her. You know, coz her surname is Foxton.' Jen pressed her lips together with disapproval. Foxy indeed! Her daughter continued. 'She says that what we discuss is between her and me.'

'Oh she did, did she? Maybe I need to remind her who's paying for the sessions?'

As soon as she saw the angry, vulnerable trembling of Courtney's chin she wished she'd kept her mouth well and truly shut. On impulse Jen pulled her eldest into her arms and hugged her tight. 'I'm dead proud of you. No mum could ask for a better daughter.'

'Mr Scott? We've got Environmental Health here,' The Lock's receptionist informed Kieran.

He felt a prickle on the back of his neck as if his hair there was really standing up. If his visitors were Environmental Health he was Prince Harry. He paid a regular backhander to the health inspector to turn a blind eye and, more importantly, not to come calling. Environmental Health often paid evening calls because that was when the type of premises they kept their eye on opened. But in his gut, he knew that something was off here. He didn't know what was going on but he couldn't take the chance that the mysterious owner of the gold wasn't already on his case. And a secret part of him still didn't trust the man who had shown him the criminal ropes – John.

'They're insisting they need to speak to you during the inspection or they're going to issue a notice and shut the place down immediately,' she finished.

If there was any shutting down to do Kieran would be the one doing it.

He played it nice and easy. 'Find the duty manager, tell him to pretend to be me and show these inspectors around the kitchen. I'll take care of the rest.' She didn't ask any questions. Number one rule about working at the club was never to question Mister Scott.

He went to the filing cabinet he used as a makeshift ward-robe and changed into a pair of black trousers and a white shirt. After checking the CCTV to make sure no one was hanging around outside his office or on the stairs, he went down to the staff changing room on the ground floor. He put on one of the blue jackets that the porters used and went into the kitchen, picking up a crate of vegetables as he went so he could look busy. He spotted both inspectors straight away, together with his manager, a Yorkshire man doing a very, very bad impression of a Cockney club owner. 'Right, d'you wanna look in the freezer then? I dunno what this is abaht, you people were only here last munf. I mean, leave it aht, I've got a bizness to run 'ere, you know what I mean?'

The manager caught sight of Kieran as he pretended to rifle through the veg but he gave nothing away. In the meantime, Kieran studied the two visitors. One was a middle-aged woman in glasses who seemed to have a stick up her rear end. The other was a pudgy bloke with a combover. The Jackal he wasn't. They were both wearing official ID badges but Kieran knew you could get them run off at any print shop.

But the guy certainly had a whiny voice as he explained, 'Please don't tell us how often to inspect these premises Mr Scott. We come when we like and as often as we like. Now, when was this freezer last cleaned? It looks a bit grubby.'

The fake Kieran complained, 'Oh blimey bruv, are you pulling me plonker? You could eat your fackin' dinner off that floor and no mistake.'

The real Kieran smiled to himself. He watched as the two inspectors were escorted around the kitchen, making notes on their clipboards.

Perhaps, Kieran decided, he'd been wrong. The business he was in could make you a bit paranoid. But on the other hand . . . It was time to find out.

When his two visitors asked to see the bins outside, Kieran stepped in and told his pretend me, 'Shall I do that Mr Scott?

I know you're a very busy man and you don't want to be rummaging around in your nice suit.'

After some hesitation, his manager agreed. 'Yeah, sure, if you wanna. You do that.'

Kieran led the two inspectors into the alley that ran down the side of the building. He checked the line of the guy's suit but could see no sign of a firearm. He couldn't see anything in the woman's clothes either. She was carrying a handbag, which could contain a shooter, but Kieran decided neither of these two looked like they were in the whacking business.

The three of them stood in front of the green bins. The combover job asked him, 'Is all the organic waste bagged before being put in these bins?'

Kieran didn't know. So he was told to open them up. When he'd climbed the steps and done it and turned back, the woman was about ten paces away, keeping watch on the alley. The guy was standing with a pistol in his hand. Kieran bit his lip. He knew he should have patted them down. At times like these, it was important to take precautions. He was smirking. 'Kieran Scott? You nearly had us going there. I knew the geezer who was posing as you wasn't legit but I never thought you'd have the brass to make an appearance disguised as a kitchen porter. Clever.'

Kieran raised his hands and came down the steps, stooping slightly. 'I don't know who you are but you've got the wrong end of the stick.'

Kieran was baffled. If they were there to kill him, why hadn't they done it yet? Professional murderers tended not to get into small talk. If only because that might give the victim an opportunity to fight back. He also knew that in a situation like this you would only get one chance to kybosh the opposition and if you didn't take it, you were dead.

'No Kieran, it's you who's got the wrong end of the stick and I'm here to put your head straight . . .'

He tapped the side of his balding head with the barrel of his gun. It was Kieran's chance. And he took it. He rushed forward at the pistol, grabbed the guy's gun hand in one fist and screwed a punch into the man's face with the other. Kieran could feel the bone buckle and splinter while he fell to the ground. He turned quickly to see the woman running away up the alley before delivering one kick after another to his victim's ribs. The heel of Kieran's shoe ground into the guy's hand until the gun fell away from his already swelling fingers.

Mr Comb Over was gurgling. 'I'm only here . . . to deliver you a message . . . not shoot anyone . . .'

Kieran shook him violently by the lapels. 'Who sent you? Was it John?'

'John . . .?'

Kieran looked up to see the woman and two more men coming back down the alley. He picked up the guy's gun and dropped it in his pocket before delivering one final kick and heading for The Lock's side door, which he bolted from the inside. Taking the stairs two at a time, he ran to his office and opened the windows. There was a clear view of the alley but everyone had gone. In the distance a powerful car was accelerating away.

Bastards! Whoever thought they could come on his manor and take him on was wrong. He picked up the phone and got his manager. 'Double security. Anyone who comes in gets searched. And then searched again, got it?'

He put the phone down without waiting for a response. Kieran realised he should have asked the guy what the message was. But he didn't need to hear it coming from the bloke's mouth to know what it probably was.

'Where's the gold?'

He gave John a ring on his second mobile phone. As soon as it clicked on he said, 'Do you want to keep the merchandise all for yourself?' He didn't have time to beat around the bush.

'Whatcha going on about?'

'Let's just say I had a couple of callers who don't have membership.'

'What? And you think it was me?'

Kieran ran his free hand roughly through his hair. 'Well was it?'

'Don't be fucking stupid. What would be the point of me doing that? You're the one with the stuff.'

'Look—'

John urgently cut him off. 'Uncle Frank and his mate have obviously sussed that you did it. It's just as well you called.' He paused. 'I've found a secure place for our pot of magic.'

Thirty-Three

Around eight in the evening a cab dropped Jen on The Highway at St Katharine Docks. The majestic Tower of London and brightly lit Tower Bridge loomed in the background. As she stared at the marina and the busy restaurants it was hard to believe this part of London had almost been bombed to oblivion during the war or that a generation ago some people were ashamed to admit that they came from the area.

Jen looked away from the restaurants and started to walk towards the collection of flashy yachts, excitement growing with her every step. She'd never been on a boat before, despite living a stone's throw from the Regent's Canal. A man who passed her gave her an appreciative once-over and she grinned, knowing she looked the part. She'd used some of the cash she'd got from Naz to splash out on new clobber. She was wearing a roomy, above-the-knee knit dress layered over metallic leggings and black ankle boots. A leopard-print jacket kept the cold out. Her clothes screamed money but she'd got the lot for under two hundred from her guy down The Roman who specialised in a bit of knock-off every now and again. It might come from the back end of a lorry but it made Jen feel like the bizz. She hadn't felt like this in a month of Sundays.

When she reached the yacht she was pleased to see him waiting for her on the deck. She gave her full-on smile. 'You're a bit keen,' she told him saucily.

'Some other bloke's gonna snap you up if I take my eyes off you,' Kieran threw back.

That made Jen roar with laughter. That's what she liked about this man, he had the potential to bring the fun back into her life. This was the first time she'd seen him since he'd given her a lift back from the memorial gardens a few days ago. He hadn't beaten about the bush, more or less asking her out on a date after five minutes in his car. Jen hadn't been sure at first; it was clear the bloke lived on the shady side of the street and she'd already experienced a life of misery with one of those, thank you very much. But her mother had known him most of his life, which was a big plus; it said a lot about the type of man he was. Why Babs hadn't introduced him long ago she couldn't figure out. But since he was so close to her mum, Jen had another reason for wanting to cosy up to him.

He got her on board and downstairs to a cabin that made Jen's eyes nearly pop. Luxury, wood-panelled walls interspersed with the occasional porthole peeping out on the soothing water and a pyramid chandelier above a table set for two. On opposite walls, facing each other, were brilliant white leather sofas. She couldn't fault him, he'd certainly pulled out all the stops.

'This yours then?'

He grinned at her. 'Let's just say that you won't need to worry about the rozzers turning up during your pudding.'

That made her laugh out loud again. Oh, she liked this man very much indeed. As he gallantly helped her off with her coat she couldn't help gazing around again. To have the money to live like this must be something. To take her children on a Mediterranean cruise would be a dream come true. Her determination to get what was rightfully owed her girls kicked in.

Halfway through their meal she asked, 'So, you used to live on The Devil?'

Kieran had already finished his meal and was leaning back enjoying a whisky. 'Born and bred. Moved there when it was newly built. All full of promise it was back then.' He knocked his drink back. 'It weren't called The Devil in those days. For the folk who moved there it was paradise.'

Jen scoffed at that. 'I can't imagine that. That place has always been trouble.'

Kieran looked at her intently as he swivelled his drink around his glass. 'That's what the pointy heads want you to believe; that us lot who live on places like that are scum.' Jen was mesmerised as he closed his eyes, lost in the past. When he reopened them they glittered with fire that made Jen almost catch her breath. 'That's what your mum taught me. Never, ever let anyone boot you to the kerb, that's what she told me. You always hold your head up straight and look life in the eye.'

Jen looked *him* in the eye. 'Sounds like you and Mum are close.'

Instead of answering he eased out of his seat. Jen's heart started thumping as he pulled her out of the chair. He wrapped an arm around her waist and held her close. He leaned in to her ear. 'It ain't your mum I wanna be close to at the mo, you get me?'

A thrill went down Jen as his lips kissed the side of her neck. This was nothing like the mauling at the hands of that pot-bellied businessman. Kieran was so gentle, so caring, like she was the most precious thing in his life. Years back Jen would've fallen into this and not thought of anything else, but she wasn't the same dumb, innocent woman she'd once been. Sure, she loved what he was doing to her, but Kieran was her way of getting to her mum. Making Babs see sense.

Jen pulled away and then recklessly swept her arms across the table sending dishes, food, glasses flying onto the wooden floor. With a hot gleam in her eye she turned back to a stunned-looking Kieran.

'What's the matter?' she almost taunted him. 'I thought you wanted to get close.' She leaned back on the table and hitched up her dress. She could've almost laughed at the gobsmacked expression on his face when, after she'd seductively rolled down her leggings, he clocked she wasn't wearing knickers underneath. A minute later he was screwing her like she was the dish of the day.

Although Jen was thoroughly enjoying herself she didn't forget what she was really about. As soon as he came she panted in his ear, 'I need you to ask Mum something for me . . .'

'What?' His voice was breathless and slightly dazed, his body still shaking with the aftershocks of sex.

Jen pushed at his shoulders so that she could make eye contact. 'My greedy sisters are trying to cut my kids out of their inheritance. I don't know if Babs told you about the two houses she owns, but it's only right that my girls get what's due to them. Will you have a word in her ear? Make her see sense? Babs thinks the world of you, she's bound to listen.'

The muscles of her fanny squeezed around his cock, milking him dry. Kieran groaned as she smiled up at him.

Jen couldn't help whistling as she floated into her flat. She'd had such a smashing night out. She'd forgotten what it was like to be with a fella – no, a gentleman – who knew how to treat a woman like a lady. Wined and dined, that's what she'd been tonight. Plus Kieran had said that he'd talk to Mum about cutting Courtney and Little Bea into the houses.

Seventeen-year-old Sonia from next door was with the girls in the sitting room. She watched Courtney and Little Bea when

Jen needed her to and, bless her young heart, she wouldn't take a penny. They were all glued to a video of an episode of *The Apprentice*, which Jen hadn't got around to watching yet. Courtney and Sonia were glued to the screen as one of the contestants did something really, really naff. Little Bea had half an eye on it, the rest of her attention on the book in her hand.

'Alright Mum.' Poor Little Bea's voice sounded so sleepy and her eyes were drooping.

Courtney didn't smile and used her hair to cover her face like a veil, but Jen knew her daughter was watching her alright.

After Sonia had gone Jen tucked up her daughters in bed. She pulled the blankets securely around Courtney's chin. 'So, did you enjoy speaking with your counsellor?'

Courtney's huff turned into a full-blown yawn. 'You already asked me that earlier. It was nuthin special.'

Jen didn't take the bait. 'Well, it won't be long before you're seeing Sally again.'

'Foxy,' Courtney corrected, 'she likes being called Foxy.'

Jen smiled; so her girl had been taking notice in this first session.

She hoped hard that this counselling would work. If it didn't she didn't know what she would do . . .

At two in the morning Jen was startled awake by screaming. She rushed out of bed and belted into her girls' room. Courtney was huddled in a corner of her bed with tears streaming down her eyes. Her face . . . Jen felt like weeping herself. Courtney's face was devoid of blood and her eyes sunken into her head. Her baby sister was right beside her, stroking her arm soothingly and whispering, 'It's gonna be alright. Gonna be alright.' But her little face told another story. She looked like the worst day of her life had arrived.

When Jen reached Courtney, her daughter flung herself into her arms. Tears burst from Jen's eyes, but she made no sound. She clutched her child tight. This was breaking her heart. She didn't know what was going on. And that's when she prayed like never before; that Foxy would be able to cure her darling daughter.

Thirty-Four

The storage place closed at six. John had arranged to meet Kieran there at half five on Monday evening to transfer the gold to John's care and ship it to its new hiding place. Kieran arrived early and parked up next to a motorbike on the forecourt. He got out to stretch his legs, then leaned against his car and smoked a B&H. It was a matter of trust. And the truth was he didn't trust John anymore. Perhaps he never had. It was nothing personal against his old mate. But the underworld is just like any other business: it's all about the money. He wouldn't expect John to turn the situation to his advantage, but you could never tell. He'd heard about many a deal done between friends that had ended in betrayal. His mouth twisted as he imagined Dee egging on her old man to do the dirty. He knew how much Dee hated him. John was pretending that he hadn't told Dee about the gold but that wasn't believable either.

At half five a large anonymous van made its way up the slip road with three men in the front. Two were heavies and sitting in the middle was John. The van swung round and then backed up to the shutters. The men climbed out and Kieran sauntered over. John was full of the joys of life. 'Alright mate?'

'Yeah, good.'

John put his hand on Kieran's shoulder. 'Good boy. Let's get in the office, do the paperwork and get the stuff loaded up.

Sooner we get this done, the sooner I can get the ball rolling and the sooner you can get your share.' Share? It was his fucking gold. 'I hope you're not planning on following me to my destination. Don't forget, the folk I'm dealing with don't want all their secrets out in the open.'

Kieran let out through gritted teeth, 'But it's my gold.'

'I know that and I'd feel the same in your situation. But you've been around long enough to know how it goes.'

Kieran gestured at the Mini with his thumb. 'I couldn't follow a push bike in that anyway.'

The second hand furniture was loaded up in the van and the doors closed. John added a large padlock to make sure nothing fell out. Kieran looked around. There seemed to be no sign that John had brought any other vehicles to act as outriders but Kieran guessed they'd be joining him on the motorway. He sat back against his Mini. It was John who took the wheel this time. He leaned out of the window. 'I'll be in touch.'

Kieran watched the van go down the slip road towards the motorway. When it was out of sight, he opened the boot of the Mini and took out a crash helmet. He climbed on the motorbike next to the car and set off in pursuit. If John really figured he was going to let him waltz off with his loot without knowing where it was being taken he was living in La-La Land. He soon caught up with the van, which had been joined by an SUV just behind. Kieran hung back about half a mile so he was in sight but keeping a low profile.

John didn't seem to know where he was going. He was doing a steady fifty in the slow lane. From time to time, he left the motorway at an exit and then doubled back in the other direction but he didn't seem to realise he was being followed. Finally he left the M25 and headed down the A12 towards the Blackwall Tunnel. At the Hackney turn-off the SUV left the little convoy and was replaced at the Mile End one by another. Kieran expected John to turn before the Tunnel – south of the river wasn't really his thing – but the van went through. Kieran stayed well back until they reached the other side. But at the A2 junction, John came back round again and began heading northwards back towards the Tunnel, still at the same steady fifty.

'What's he playing at . . .?'

As they approached the northbound entrance and the three lanes narrowed to two, there were a number of cars between Kieran and John's van so he was out of sight. As the traffic slowed to a crawl, Kieran watched the van disappear, heading for the East End. Then he heard a squealing of brakes and the thumping and crashing of metal. Right at the entrance to the tunnel, two cars had crashed into each other. Alarmed, Kieran weaved between the halted vehicles and tried to pass but the knackered old saloons were at right angles to one another, blocking the road. There was no way through. The two drivers got out, both shaking their heads and looking at the damage. One shrugged his shoulders at Kieran. 'Sorry mate, I lost control of the steering wheel.'

The other one swore. 'Looks like they're closing the Tunnel . . .'

In front of them, red lights were flashing and a gate was coming down to block traffic.

Kieran jumped off his bike and stepped around the men. Shit.

John, his van and Kieran's gold were long gone.

On the other side of the tunnel, a grinning John took the first turning into Poplar and parked. As expected, his mobile rang. It was Kieran. He ignored the call. Then it rang again and it wasn't Kieran this time, so he took it.

'We crashed the cars and stopped the traffic,' said one of the guys he'd paid to make things happen in the Tunnel. 'The geezer on the bike couldn't get through and he's long gone. He drove up the ramp, came down the other side and headed south.'

'Probably going to Dartford or Rotherhithe then. Fat lot of good that'll do him. Have you had any trouble with the law?'

'Nah, the cars got towed out of the way by the Tunnel boys but they still haven't reopened it yet. I'm afraid them ol' bangers are totalled. Hell of a queue here; it's going back miles.'

John laughed. He knew all about queues at the Blackwall but this one was for a good cause. What a prat Kieran was. Fancy thinking that John Black of all people wouldn't realise he might be followed. 'Alright boys, a job well done and you can go and pick up your lifts home. I'll settle up with you for the cars anon.'

Satisfied, John set off northwards, taking back roads and still checking his rear view mirror to make sure Kieran hadn't pulled a fast one. When he was happy, John made his way to his destination. In a smart Georgian Square in Mile End, a builders van was waiting for him. When John arrived, the builders moved so he could park up outside Babs' houses.

John hadn't been back since he fired his mother-in-law's builders and brought in his own crew but he'd kept in close touch with them by phone. When he arrived, the owner of the firm who'd done the work was waiting for him by the front door. He was an old friend of John's who went by the name of Chunks and he was totally reliable. Chunks opened the door for him and they went inside the back reception room. Chunks bent down and pulled up the carpet in the far right corner. Underneath was a trap door which opened to steps down to a spanking new basement. Chunks showed off his team's handiwork. 'There you go John. Most of the work had already been done by that lot who were here before. We sorted out a nice spot in the old coal bunker.'

The flight of stairs led down to a room that seemed wider and longer than the house itself. Chunks put on a series of lights as they walked down. The floor was concrete and the walls were built of reinforced steel, which made it look like a bank vault. John inspected his builders' work. 'Are you sure you haven't damaged the foundations or anything? I don't want the floors above coming down on my little hidey hole.'

'I'm a builder mate. I know how to build.'

John nodded. He felt the walls. They were solid. 'OK. I've brought some furniture with me so if anyone comes in here they won't suspect I might have other uses for this place in the future.'

Chunks laughed. 'You've spent a lot of money on this basement to store second hand furniture.'

They went back upstairs and used their guys to move the heavy furniture down into the underground room under cover of the darkening evening.

'Answer the fucking phone you bastard.'

John always seemed to be doing a flit these days. What the bloody hell was he playing at? Even when Dee had explained about that slag Flo getting her hooks into Nicky, John had only mumbled, appearing preoccupied. She was starting to become best mates with his friggin' voicemail. She took a couple of deep breaths to steady her nerves. She couldn't afford to be blowing her stack anymore. Which reminded her, she still needed to tell her husband what the doctor had told her. Dee knew she couldn't keep putting it off.

She heard the roar of a high-powered motorbike in the distance. It drew closer and she realised it was accelerating up the driveway. With a scattering of gravel the bike pulled up outside and the engine was cut, leaving silence again.

Dee hurried to the window to see who the hell was coming to her house at this time of night. She was scared it might be the cops with bad news about John. Or maybe he had finally bought that bike she'd been dreading as his way of trying to hang onto his youth, like the leather jacket and sunglasses. Her mate Tania's other half had gone through something similar, partying at raves and dying his hair so much it was the mangy, brown-red colour of a tabby that had been slumming it on the street for too long. I'll soon shake him outta his midlife crisis by the scruff of his neck!

But when she opened the window, she saw it was a biker in a black crash helmet, not the same build as her John. A chill ran deep inside her. He was a dead ringer for a hit man. He climbed off the bike, walked up and rang the bell. It wasn't often Dee shook with fear but she did now. Cautiously she headed towards the front door, but stopped short and yelled, 'What do you want?'

The guy shouted but his voice was muffled under the crash helmet. 'I've got a message about John.'

Dee didn't stop to think. She threw the door open. 'What?' But when the visitor took his helmet off, she gasped, 'Kieran? I thought I told you never to come near me or my husband again!'

Kieran sighed, 'Yeah, you did. And that's probably right, given the lie of the land, but the thing is babe—'

'Who do you think you are, calling me *babe*! Now piss off or I'll tell John you've been round here harassing me.'

Kieran looked at her with wolfish eyes. 'Yeah, sure you will. The thing is Dee, I've been trying to do a bit of business with John but I suspect he's trying to have me over. His mobile keeps going to voicemail. Of course he thinks, because he's higher up the food chain than me, I'll have to take it. And in normal circumstances he'd be right. But these aren't normal circumstances and I've got a couple of cards up my sleeve that he don't know about, but you do. What I need is for you to have a quiet word and tell him he needs to play fair with me. Now then, what about that? You tell him. Because otherwise the cards might slip outta my sleeve.'

Dee went eyeball to eyeball with him. 'Are you threatening me?'

He stared back at her but it was a long time before he said, 'I'm not a good loser Dee. Good loser is just another way of saying loser as far as I'm concerned and I'll do whatever I need to do. You can understand that. You're not a good loser either, are you? No one who gets on in life is. Now then, are you having a word with John or not?'

She folded her arms. 'You disappoint me Kieran, you really do. You seriously think you can come round here on that lawnmower and tell me what's it like? Me of all people? Now get on your bike and wheelie off. I'm going to be generous and pretend you never came round. But I won't pretend the next time and you know what I'm like when I'm not pretending. I go to the max. Now fuck off.'

Kieran nodded. 'You've been warned.'

'Yes. And so have you.'

Kieran opened the engine up and disappeared into the night.

When John walked through the front door, Dee didn't know whether to hug or slap him silly. But when she saw him looking drawn with a deathly pallor, she went for the hug option.

Her voice was gentle but chiding as if a lost cat had appeared. 'Where the hell have you been? I was worried sick. What are you playing at?'

She got no answer and he was stiff in her arms. When she let him go, he stood looking at her with searching eyes.

'John?'

It was a long time before he answered. 'Yeah . . .' He walked down the hall, scanning the coat rack and staircase as if he was examining the place with a view to buying it. 'What you been up to?'

She followed him into the front room where he was picking things up and looking at them. Now he was less like a house buyer and more like a detective interviewing a suspect. He stopped and stared at her.

Dee was rattled. She knew that stare. It was a look he gave people when they'd tried to double cross him. Why he was aiming it at her she didn't know. 'What have I been up to? I was ringing you on the hour, every hour to see where you were. Why didn't you take your phone with you?'

John ignored her, strolled to the drinks cabinet, took out a bottle of Scotch and poured himself a long one. He seemed lost in thought and not at all worried that she would fly off the handle at him having a snifter. 'Yeah . . .'

What's with all the yeahing, Dee thought, puzzled. It was like he kept repeating it because something more important was on his mind. Whatever it was, he didn't look like a happy bunny.

She followed him into the kitchen where he began casting his eyes around again. What was he looking for? Dee began to wonder if he'd had some kind of turn and whether she should call an ambulance. 'John babes, sit down and rest for a moment. It doesn't matter where you've been as long as you're home safely.'

She took his arm but he shook it off with such force she stumbled back. She was stunned. What the hell was going on? John eased down at the table, scowling, his half-gone drink in one hand. Then he tapped his forehead as if he'd just remembered something. 'By the way, has Kieran been in touch with you? Only I noticed some motorbike tyre marks in the driveway.'

Dee kept her cool even though inside she felt like a freight train had just run over her. If that fuck artist Kieran had said one word to her beautiful John she'd put him down with her own hands. 'Kieran? Why would he get in touch with me? He knows what I think about him. And so do you.'

John sipped his drink and nodded. 'So he hasn't popped around while I've been out?'

Dee was shaken but she gave no hint. How could he possibly know about that? She played a straight bat. She was good at it. 'Nah. He might come around to see you but he wouldn't come around to see me. He knows better than that.'

Dee made herself pop on a bright smile and strode towards the cupboards. 'I've got those frankfurters in a tin you like. I'll rustle you up some with scrambled eggs and toast. You must be famished.' When she turned, his unsettling gaze was still fixed on her.

'Thing is, you've never actually explained what it is about Kieran you don't like. Or how you knew his real name was Kieran not Tom . . .'

She got defensive. 'You wanna be asking yourself that question. Why introduce him to me using a bogus name?'

'Coz I knew as soon as you clocked who he was you'd think I was back in the life again. So come on, Dee, what's your problem with him? He's just a bloke. No better or worse than anyone else. So what is it? What gets your goat?'

Dee walked over to her husband. She folded her arms. 'Some people don't like sugar in their tea. Some people don't like flying. I don't like the fella, end of.'

They stared at each other warily, just like the time they'd met in his club all those years ago. John gave her one last, intense look before he quit the room to answer a phone call.

After he was gone her tummy went into orbit and she just managed to get to the sink before she threw up.

John didn't go up to bed with his wife. He sat in the dark in the bar and tried to figure out why Dee hadn't told him that Kieran had paid a visit. As soon as he'd got out of his car he'd noticed the marks of a motorbike in the gravel. He only knew one bloke with a motorbike who'd been on his tail. Kieran had come over to find out what he'd done with the gold. So why wouldn't Dee tell him? He'd married his first wife when he was seventeen because she wouldn't sleep with him and his second because he'd been pissed out of his skull and realised it was a mistake the following week. But Dee ... It was like he'd been waiting for her all his life. Most people seeing them for the first time thought they were a mismatched pair, not realising that underneath they were cut from the same East End cloth. And at heart that meant two simple things – have lots of money and a family to call your own. He hadn't been able to give her kids because something in him just wasn't joined up right; that's why his first wife had divorced him. But it never mattered to his Dee. Having Nicky was enough for her.

John's mobile rang. Kieran's name came up. This time he took his call.

'Where is it John?'

'Somewhere safe.' John's voice was as dead as he felt inside.

Kieran hissed, 'If you're trying to fuck me over–'

'Look, you know how it works – the fewer people who know the better.'

'I ain't just people John, there wouldn't be no goodies if it weren't for me.'

'Things have changed with those heavies turning up at yours. If Uncle Frank has sussed it was you, he can be a very persuasive man, and if he catches up with you, you might spill where it is. Now me . . . He doesn't know I'm involved for sure. And if he tries it on I'm the one person who knows how to keep him well back.'

Silence. Then, 'I don't like it.'

'I'll come over to the club tomorrow and we can sort things out, mano a mano.'

After the call was ended a very tired John entered his bedroom and made love to his wife tenderly and sweetly.

Thirty-Five

Bright and breezy the next morning John's builders in 9 Bancroft Square were having a laugh and a few glasses of gin when the knocker on the front door went twice.

'Best look lively fellas,' the foreman, Chunks, warned as he got to his feet, 'wouldn't want the gaffer to think we're taking the mickey.' Which they were of course, stretching the job out to get a few more pounds in their pockets. But Chunks knew they needed to be careful because they were dealing with John Black.

While his crew scrambled to get their tools he opened the door. He gazed puzzled at the very old lady standing on the doorstep. She wore a green headscarf, a gypsy-style mauve, fringed shawl over her black coat and had loads of silver bracelets dangling on her wrists. Very strange indeed.

'Can I help you love?' He spoke slowly and loudly as if she were deaf.

Her brown face crinkled up at him. 'This Babs' place?'

He frowned. 'Who?' Poor dear was probably suffering from dementia and had wandered out of her home, now lost and confused. Mind you, those eyes of hers looked razor sharp.

'Babs Miller,' she clarified.

The penny dropped. 'Oh, Mrs Miller. That's Mister Black's missus' mum.' His voice grew louder and slower. 'Sorry to say but none of 'em are here.'

'I know that son,' she chirped cheerily. 'Babs just wanted me to pop over and do something.'

Chunks turned a bit hostile. 'How do I know that you're not telling me a funny one?' John Black had warned him not to let another living soul into the houses.

Her smile became crooked. 'Do I look like one of the Great Train Robbers?' She took out a mobile phone from her large handbag. 'Babsie says if you want a word with her, I'm to ring her up.'

He stared at the phone. He didn't really have time for this. Anyway, what harm could the little old duffer do? He opened the door wide. Her bracelets jangled as she stepped inside.

'I don't know what you're looking for,' he added, bemused, 'the place is more or less cleared out.'

She smiled sweetly at him and patted her bag. 'No need to worry. I've got everything I need here.'

Without another word she proceeded slowly up the stairs. He looked after her, his confusion deepening. Maybe he should phone Mister Black. As he pulled his mobile out the woman turned around, her eyes twinkling.

'I wouldn't wanna tell Babs that you'd been drinking on the job. I always find it wise to pop a mint in my mouth after a hard slug. And I'll need to do the whole house.' With a smart compression of her lips she resumed her journey up the stairs.

Pearl Hennessey wheezed as she waited to hear the man speaking on the phone. When all she heard was silence she smiled and stopped the pretend wheezing act. She only did it so people thought she was harmless and felt sorry for her. If they knew the type of life she'd lived when she was young they would think again. Babs had warned her if she received any trouble to think on her feet. Pearl hadn't been in the criminal life for this many years without learning a trick or three.

The first room she reached was a bedroom with a large, cast iron fireplace. She took out a bundle of long sage leaves wrapped tight together from her bag. She lit the end with a lighter and waved it around until the fire had gone out and only plumes of smoke wafted in the air. Pearl had agreed to do this for Babs and in return she wouldn't allow that gorilla Knox to cut her from ear to ear. She'd been more than happy to oblige, having helped many people exorcise the evil in their lives. Shame she'd never been able to do the same to her own.

She began the smudging cleansing ritual, waving the smoking sage stick through the air as she chanted aloud, 'Cast out the evil that Stanley Miller left . . .'

She was going to make the same powerful chant over every inch of this house and the one next door.

Tiff stood outside the door of the posh flat in Chelsea Harbour, still having trouble believing that her mum knew the notorious Kieran Scott. How did a woman on the right side of the law know one of the bad boys in town? She'd tried to squeeze it out of her mum, but Babs had stayed schtum. Tiff knew Kieran Scott by name, but had never met him; although she knew loads about how he'd risen in the East End badlands. That was the one of the beauties of her time as a mechanic; as the motors came in they brought in the latest street gossip and Kieran Scott had been a hot topic of conversation. E tabs had been his start-up game until he got enough cash to invest in clubs across the capital. Getting control of the bouncers on the doors was the same as getting a nice cut of the drugs trade. Maybe, just maybe, she could squeeze him for a touch more than the money she owed those cunts.

Tiff shivered, getting the funny feeling she was being watched. She lifted her head and saw a camera in the corner of the ceiling turned her way. Its red light gazed at her with the ferocity of an eye. Unnerved, Tiff turned back to the door. As she raised her hand to knock the lock clicked open. Only when she got inside did she realise that the door was made of reinforced steel. This was a man who wasn't taking any chances.

'In here,' he called. Tiff was surprised at how soft his voice sounded. She'd been expecting something rough and raw like many of the lowlifes she'd grown up with on The Devil.

She walked into a huge lounge that had her whistling in appreciation. It was in-your-face flash to the max and reeked of money. Leather sofa, black coffee table, mounted plasma telly. The man himself sat in a cream high-back chair near the floor to ceiling window which led to a balcony with stunning views over Chelsea Harbour. There was a small table next to him with a glass part-way filled with drink and he held a book loosely in his hands. A gangster who spent his time reading; she hadn't met one of them before.

Tiff's appreciation of the room extended into a smile as she gazed at him. 'Look like you've just had the place done up.'

'You could say that.' A man of few words. She could live with that.

No point beating about the bush. 'The thing is Kieran—'

'It's Mister Scott.'

That threw Tiff. She'd assumed because he knew her mum this was all going to be child's play. Ask him for the cash, he stumps up and she pisses off. Her eyebrows wrinkled together. 'I thought you were a mate of my mum's.'

He took a slug of his drink. 'I am. Have been for a very long time.' He placed the book on the table. 'Remember you as a nipper. The only way your poor mum could get you to stop screaming the place down was to shove a sweetie ciggy in your gob.'

Her face heated up. This man was bent on putting her down, no doubt about it. Why he was doing it, she didn't know, but she needed to get past it if she was going to leave with the cash. So she did a little trick she'd learned years back – ignored what he'd said. And that's when she noticed the photo in the small, loveheart frame on the table near the book. She would swear it was a black-and-white snap of him and her mum. It was a strange photo of him as a small boy with a plaster over one lens of his glasses and her mum with an arm over his shoulder. They were both grinning like hell. What made it odd was that they were standing next to a basket full of washing.

Catching her looking at it, he laid the picture face down on the table. But it was too late. Tiff had already sussed that he had a very close relationship with her mum indeed. That's why he'd mounted it in a loveheart frame. Everyone had a weakness and his was Babs.

So she played her newfound knowledge to the hilt. 'I'm ever so grateful that Mum – Babs – said you'd sort me out . . .'

'That's where you're wrong.'

Tiff had to bite her tongue to stop from lashing out at the arrogant ponce. 'But Mum said that you'd see me straight.' She flashed her eyes innocently at him. 'I don't know what I'm gonna do if I don't get my mitts on that dosh.'

He widened his legs slightly and leaned forward. 'Babs is tickled pink that you managed to turn your life around. But me,' he pierced her with his steady stare, 'I don't think a leopard changes its spots that easily. And I've got the funny feeling you're gonna bring a wagonload more trouble to your mum, just like in the bad ol' days.'

Tiff had had enough. She eyed up the room scornfully. 'You're living the life, Mister Scott, and what I'm asking for is spare change. It ain't like you're gonna miss it.'

'How much are you after?'

'Three large.'

'The best way to ruin a good friendship is to lend a mate some dough. I could end up giving it to you and then watch as it comes back to bite me in the jacksie and ruin things between me and Babs.'

'That ain't gonna happen,' Tiff pleaded.

He pointed at the leather sofa. As she sat she noticed a gorgeous pink velvet clutch shoved down the side. Frowning, she held it up. 'I got my sister Jen the exact same one for her birthday last year.' She ended on a whisper, 'That's when I was still chatting to the cow.'

Kieran pursed his lips. 'You wanna talk about your situation or go on like you're on the Shopping Channel?'

She ditched the purse on the floor. She opened her mouth but he got there before her. 'This time, fuck stringing me along and tell me the truth.'

Tiff knew she didn't have much choice, so she started, 'I've kept my fingernails clean for years. The problem is, I got in a bit over my head, finance wise. Now these two Herberts . . .'

Five minutes later she finished with, 'And that's the honest to God's tale. I swear on my life.'

He considered her for a moment, then asked, 'You on good terms with your sister Dee?' She nodded back eagerly, not a clue why he was interested in her big sis.

He eased up and moved towards the wall, which she was gobsmacked to see him push back to reveal a drinks cabinet with glass shelves trimmed with gold.

'What's your poison?' For the first time he smiled at her. Not a bad looking fella. She might be into him if she wasn't into girls.

Satisfied, Tiff got nice and cosy in her seat. 'Voddy and Coke.'

When he handed her the glass he said, 'I'll give you the readies, with some on top. As for those two cretins, no need for you to sweat about them no more.'

Tiff saluted him with the glass. 'Thanks Mister Scott.'

He grinned. 'Of course you don't get nuthin for anything in this life. I'll need you to do something for me in return.'

The V&C spluttered out of Tiff's mouth.

After Babs' daughter had gone, Kieran drained his glass of brandy, walked past the clutch purse on the floor and over to the table near his armchair. He picked up the book he'd been reading. *Charlotte's Web*. He opened it up and read the hand-written dedication inside.

> Happy birthday my beautiful boy.
> Babs

She'd gifted it him on his tenth birthday. If it hadn't been for her he'd never have . . . Kieran abruptly froze the thought. Looking backwards wasn't going to help him deal with John Black. His mentor was holding out on him. Trying to diddle him out of the gold. Why else would John have given him the slip when he stashed it?

He put the book down and stared at the snap of him and Babs. Would she feel betrayed if she found out what he was up to? If she ever found out . . . He shuddered. But he couldn't keep the thought at bay. If the one person in the world he loved found out what he was doing, he'd end up crucified.

He turned away from the old photo and stepped out on the balcony. As he gazed down at the harbour he convinced himself that he wasn't betraying Babs at all. This was simply business.

Thirty-Six

Thomas Berry, aka Tommo, punched off his mobile and smiled triumphantly at his partner. 'That was the dyke bitch. She's ready to pay up.'

They'd been doling out some street justice to another unsatisfied customer when the call had come through. He hadn't answered it immediately, too hyped up on the sound of the cracking bones and screams as he broke the stupid berk's legs. When would people learn that if you delayed you were gonna have to pay double. He chuckled away to himself as they walked through the dark, deserted street.

Errol said, 'Probably the thought of seeing that wrinkled dick of yours pushed her to the edge.' He ended on a long sniff as he snorted some Special K up his nose.

Tommo didn't go in for drugs; a waste of time and hard-earned cash. 'You won't have a dick left the way you're going through the gear bruv.'

Errol let out a crazy, loud laugh. 'That ain't what the ladies say.'

'Yeah, well, the type of birds you go around pumping—' He finished on a harsh shriek of pain as something hard whacked into his calf. He tumbled over, his nose spewing blood as he slammed face first into the ground.

Shaken to the core, he raised his bloody face to see a large, shadowy figure aiming a sawn-off at his head. Next to him another figure shoved a hood over Errol's head. 'Think you've got the wrong geezers, fellas.'

The wheels of a vehicle screeched towards them. Without a word, the man holding the shooter took something out of his pocket and threw it on the ground next to Tommo. He knew the score so he quickly pulled the hood over his head, clenching his teeth in pain. He heard footsteps beside him and then behind him. A firm hand grabbed his ankle and started dragging him down the street.

A woman with plastic boobs and come hither mouth moved seductively to the tune being spun by the DJ – Gnarls Barkley's 'Crazy' – and deliberately got in Kieran's face as he made his way through The Lock.

She flashed her mascaraed-to-death eyelashes at him and planted her artificial strawberry creams nearly in his face. 'I thought me and you could take the floor by storm.'

I bet you did, bird, he thought. 'I don't think I remember your name on the membership roll.' The only way a woman of her stripe would be was if she had a rich hubby or sugar daddy bankrolling her.

She softened her voice to all lovey-dovey and Little Miss La-di-da, but he heard Essex in there, probably Romford. 'I hear you are a good mover Mister Scott. Know how to do the Hokey Cokey,' she said, seductively.

He had nothing against Essex folk; they just couldn't become members of his club.

As if on cue, one of his team came over. He grabbed the woman by her sunbed-tanned arm. Startled, she tried to wriggle free. 'Oi, what the heck you doing?' Deffo Romford.

'Right, darlin', it's time for you to take your business elsewhere.'

The bouncer dragged her away as she shouted, 'This is a free country. I can speak to who the heck I like.'

'See, that's where you're wrong,' Kieran heard him answer. 'This ain't a free country, it's Mister Scott's country and you, my girl, are being deported . . .'

Kieran smiled reassuringly at the few clubbers who had stopped to watch, but they soon lost interest and got back into their booze and the groove.

He quickened his steps; he had business to take care of. He headed for the top of the building and entered the large attic. He shifted the boxes at the end out of the way, revealing a keyhole. He inserted the key that he alone kept, and turned it. He slid part of the wall across, revealing another room in the attic next door: a building he also owned. It was in complete contrast to the luxury of his club. Bare walls, scarred wooden floor with flecks of blood ingrained in it and a window left wide open, just in case one of his visitors needed to learn a lesson the hard way – head first falling back down to earth.

Two of his crew stood by while he approached the two hooded knobheads shackled to the back wall. They were secured so that only their toes touched the ground. Kieran had inherited the room in its present condition, including the chains and shackles on the walls. Apparently the previous owner had been an S&M freak who got his rocks off with a bit of spanking and whipping. Kieran had got rid of most of the hardcore gear, except for the wicked-looking thick whip he took down off the wall. It uncoiled like a snake.

Time to get this show on the road. He nodded to his men, who stepped forward and whipped the hoods off. He was glad to see Errol Banks and Tommo Berry go slack-jawed when they clocked him.

Errol sputtered, 'Mister Sc . . .Scott—'

Kieran cut him off with a savage crack of the whip against the floor. He shook it out with relish. 'I hear it's possible to use

this on someone without slashing them to ribbons.' His steady
gaze pierced them. 'Never could master that meself.'

Tommo's body convulsed like he was shitting his pants. 'We
don't know what this is about Mister Scott, but it ain't true. We
ain't done nuthin.'

Kieran tutted and shook his head sadly. He inhaled through
his nose as he stepped closer, the whip wriggling by his side.
'What do you see on my face?'

Both men frowned. 'Er, what?' Errol slowly let out.

Kieran smiled brightly. 'Don't be shy fellas. What do you
see on my face?'

Tommo had a stab. 'Eyes. And very nice they are too.'

Kieran shook his head. 'You're getting warm though.'

Errol punched in, 'A nose.'

Kieran flicked the whip so its head slithered along the floor.
'I better put you out of your misery. A pair of ears. And the
way I *hear* it, you been collecting debts on my turf without my
say-so.'

Both men looked at each other. 'Now that's naughty,' he
added in a quiet, deadly voice. 'You know the rules. You wanna
take a piss in my pot, you ask my permission first. I mean
that's basic manners, innit.'

He cracked the whip so that it caught one of Errol's shirt
buttons and ripped it off. Back in the day Kieran had stepped
out with an older dominatrix who had shown him a thing or
two about handling a whip.

Errol cringed back. 'We're sorry Mister Scott, we'll take our
business elsewhere.'

Kieran carried on as if he hadn't spoken. 'Trying to get one
over me I can deal with, coz let's face it fellas, you're pond life.
Not worth my notice.' His tone hardened. 'But when word
reached me that you've taken to humiliating some poor Doris
who owed you dosh by threatening to rape her . . .'

Tommo couldn't help himself. He strained against his chains as he spat, 'That fucking minge muncher—'

With a fluid one-two flick of his wrist, Kieran slashed him across both cheeks, leaving him screaming in pain as blood trickled down his already damaged face. 'You really should learn how to respect women. Mind you, my old girl was a slag of the first order, who really should have had her legs sewn together so she'd stop popping kids out every nine months.' His eyes glazed over as a small smile turned up the corner of his mouth. 'Then I met a lady who showed me that birds are to be loved, cherished, pampered. You don't fucking go around threatening to stick it up them like they're a piece of meat from Spitalfields.'

Errol opened his mouth, but the shake of the whip made him snap it shut. Kieran carried on. 'The thing is fellas, going round doing shit like that makes folk think my turf is a homeland for nonces. And that can't be allowed to stand.'

'We're sorry Mister Scott,' both men threw out together.

Kieran paused for a second or two, then said, 'Maybe you are, maybe you ain't. Who knows? But I'm thinking to myself, this girl does owe these two morons some blunt and fair's fair, they should get their money back.' He shoved his free hand into his pocket and waved a bundle of hundreds in the air. 'A grand is what I hear, am I correct?'

Both men nodded quickly. Kieran let the whip drop and divided the cash up. Then he passed one wodge each to his men. 'You need to open those mouths of yours wide now,' he said, like he was offering a child its favourite treat.

Kieran's men shoved the notes into their mouths. He smiled, long and hard. 'Now eat up.'

He stood with his arms folded as they finally swallowed the money down. Errol looked like he was going to puke, so Kieran warned, 'You'll be using your mouth another way if there's

one speck of crap on my floor.' Errol nodded, his eyes
watering.

'Now you've got your money back, piss off outta here. And
don't let me hear another word about you taking liberties in
my manor.' He inched his head menacingly forward. 'Coz if I
hear tell you have, it won't be a whip I'll be coming after you
with.'

Without waiting for a response, he left the room. He
straightened his jacket and smiled. Now Tiffany Miller was his
to command.

Thirty-Seven

'Good evening Mister Black. Glad you could join us.'

All the receptionists at Kieran's club knew John, Kieran had made very sure of that. John appreciated the effort, but he didn't much care for this bowing and scraping. Then again, John was convinced that Kieran enjoyed rubbing his nose in the fact that he'd bought the premises from John for a knock-down fee, just before property went stellar in Wapping. John didn't resent the fact that the guy had made a killing. But he did think it was a bit saucy that Kieran hadn't even offered him a little drink by way of a thank you very much. Still. Not that it mattered of course.

He stepped forward but a hulking, great beast of a bloke appeared out of nowhere to halt him in his tracks. 'I need to search you sir.'

Was he for real? Then John remembered the trouble that had gone on here. So he gave himself up to be patted down.

The first man he'd spoken to said, 'Mister Scott has asked if you could wait for him in the bar.'

John walked off muttering, 'Wait for him in the bar? Who's he think he is? My fucking headmaster?'

He grew even more narked as he waited a good ten minutes with a Scotch in his hand until Kieran appeared. The other man got into it straight away. 'So, where is it?'

John shook his head. 'I've already told you it's on a need to know basis.'

Kieran bared his teeth. 'And I need to know.'

John sipped his drink coolly. 'Sorry mate, I can't tell you that – you understand. A mate of mine has got it secured.'

Kieran's nostrils flared, clearly pissed off. 'What do you mean, you can't tell me? It's my fucking . . .' he looked around to check no one was listening, 'gold. You're expecting me to leave it with persons unknown in a location unknown? I ain't stupid.'

'What do you want? A receipt? And you ain't handing it over to persons unknown.' His voice softened. 'You're handing it over to me. Your old mucker, unless of course you're saying you don't trust me?'

It seemed to John that it was a long time before Kieran responded. 'Course I trust you.' But the atmos was cooling. 'It's not really a question of trust, is it? You can't really expect me to hand my hard-earned product over and not know where it's gone. That's not realistic.'

John was enjoying this moment so much, he didn't notice the storm cones going up. He took the tone of the kindly uncle. 'Look son, you've done well for yourself and you're getting near the top of the tree, but no disrespect, you're not actually on the highest branches. As I've explained to you before, the kind of boys who deal with this kind of work don't like publicity. I know, I'm one of them. If the guys I'm using find out I've been dropping their names, they're not gonna be very happy. I wouldn't be. Let me take care of things for you. Of course, if you're not confident I'll see you right, you're welcome to make enquiries with someone else and I'll get it shifted there.'

He smiled at Kieran, who gave him a long stare before finally cheering up. 'No need for that.' He placed his arm around John's shoulders. 'I've got a tasty bottle of Macallan

Reserve Vintage Scotch behind the counter. We never did celebrate our little earner together.' He clicked his fingers and told the barman to fill them up.

They faced each other and clinked their glasses. 'To friendship,' John said.

'To friendship.'

Neither man was fooled.

Dee was pleasantly surprised when she walked into The Lock, unbeknownst to her just ten minutes after her husband. She'd always figured it would be the kind of boys' club where the only things on the menu were brawling, smoking and gambling. That's why she'd never given it the time of day. But when she read in one of the glossies that it was one of the top ten places in London for the elite, she remembered John was a member and asked him about it. He seemed a bit cagey. 'It's a nobs' club. You know, money from the City, that type of person. Total tossers.'

'So why did you join up then?'

John became even cagier. 'They've got a very good snooker room.'

She'd gazed at him pointedly. 'It's a long way to go for a game of pot black.'

'It's always a long way to go for anything decent.'

Then he changed the subject and he always changed the subject again when she suggested he take her up there. It was partly why she'd decided to book a table there for her meeting with Tiffany and Jen. Babs had asked her to sort out the dispute between her half-sisters and get them back in line and that's what she was going to do. Although, if she were being honest, Dee also wanted to know if it was more than snooker that made her hubby renew his membership each year. And she liked a bit of class and The Lock sounded like class. When she rang to book a table, she got the brush-off.

'I'm sorry madam but I can't take a booking unless you're a member.'

'My husband's the member.'

The receptionist cheered up. 'Oh in that case, you can always ask your husband to book a table for you.'

'I don't ask my old man to do nish for me darlin, I'm not that kind of wife.'

The receptionist remained cool. 'I'm afraid we can still only take a booking from the member.'

Dee decided to see if John's name made a difference. It often did with people and it did this time too. 'Oh, you're Mister Black's wife? In that case I think we can accommodate you. I know the owner likes to keep Mr Black happy.'

Dee was curious. 'Does he? And who is the owner if I may ask?'

'You can ask Mrs Black but I'm afraid I'm not at liberty to disclose that kind of information.'

Dee made a mental note to find out when she was up there. Back in the day she'd known who all the Faces were, but now John was out of the game she'd stopped sticking her snout into the life. In this instance it was plain, old-fashioned curiosity that had her wanting to find out. Better not be some Doris, or John was going to find himself well and truly in the crapper.

The place was class through and through; not your usual East End hangout at all. Dee fit right in with her Chanel LBD that showcased her glossy brown skin and snakeskin Laurent heels. The camel-coloured Chloé Paddington handbag and white-framed Jackie O shades topped off her look to perfection – well that's what she told herself.

The staff were only too eager to get into John Black's wife's good graces and she was escorted into a restaurant that was as flash as the main area. On the walls were large, framed black-and-white photos of old movie stars. Dee recognised Bette

Davis. Oh, she did love to watch Bette on screen playing the ultimate bitch who wasn't ashamed of her claws.

She was escorted to her table by the maître d' himself. There was no sign of Tiffany so Dee ordered the most expensive bottle of white vino on the menu and told the waiter to charge it to Mr Black's account. While he was pouring, she enquired, 'Is the owner in tonight?'

'I'm not sure madam.'

'Who is the owner as a matter of interest?'

Like all waiters, he was a good liar and answered, face expressionless, 'I'm afraid I don't know madam.'

Dee tasted the wine. Mmm, nice and fruity. 'Very good thank you.' She was even more curious to find out who owned The Lock and why he was so keen to keep her John happy. She drank her glass of white and looked at her watch. She'd told Tiffany to meet her at 7.30 sharp but the bint was already ten minutes late. How that girl ever managed to keep herself in the expensive lifestyle that she enjoyed flaunting was a mystery to Dee. She put the glass down and looked around at her fellow diners. John was right. The place was full of rich tossers. Her gaze drifted over to a connecting door into the neighbouring bar. She looked away and then back again with a start when she saw two men standing behind the stained glass. She slammed her drink down and crossed the floor to investigate.

It was John and Kieran.

They shook hands and gave each other a hug. Fizzing with fury at the sight of her husband meeting Kieran despite warning him not to do so, she stepped forward to enter but the waiter reappeared. 'Your guest has arrived madam.'

Dee peered with squinty eyes through the window but decided there would be time to sort him out later. As she went back to her table she asked the waiter more forcefully, 'Is the owner of this joint Kieran Scott?'

The hesitation was all Dee needed to know.

Her little bastard of an old man. No wonder he wouldn't bring her up here. And why was he willing to defy her when it came to meeting that little rat Kieran? She wasn't in the best of moods when she sat back down.

Tiffany was already at the table. Her sister hadn't made much of an effort, decked out in a white T-shirt with the strapline, 'I like my ladeez hot, horny n willing' across it, although Dee suspected it was designer. And that bloody nose ring of hers always got on Dee's nerves, big time. She didn't know why, but she wanted to yank it out.

'Alright babe? What did you bring us down nob city for? We should have met down the local. This place is a wanker's club.'

Dee drew breath. She knew this meeting was important so she wanted to keep it civil. 'Meeting down the boozer is what your grandparents do, not people like us. Anyway,' she eyed the Hermès bumbag Tiff had plonked on the table, 'I thought you liked nice things.'

'I do. I just don't like these snobs. And why have we have got a third place set for here? No one else is coming are they? I want to talk in private. Here, pour us a drink will ya?'

Dee studied the menu and kept her mouth zipped. Keeping her blood pressure down with Tiffany wasn't easy.

Her half-sister poured herself a large one and went on, 'Look babe, I ain't got time for dinner anyway, I gotta bounce, so let me cut to the chase. I need to borrow some wonga, quite a lot actually, and I need it in a hurry. I know you and John are good for it and I'll pay you back when we get the houses sold, which is something else I wanna chat to you about. The thing is—'

Tiff sprayed wine over the table in shock.

Dee looked up with satisfaction to see that her third guest had arrived. Jen. But she did a double take; it was a Jen she hardly recognised. Her sister now sported a super short hairstyle that was dyed sherry red, an A-line dress and a black-and-white duster jacket. Her slap was perfect, bringing out a healthy glow in her sister's skin she hadn't seen before. Jen walked with an elegance that put Dee in mind of those Miss World contestants on the telly. In her mind she heard Jen softly coo out, 'I'm Miss Devil's Estate. I want to save the world and help children.' Yeah right! She was happy that Jen looked a knockout, but that look didn't come cheap. Where had she got her hands on cash to tart herself up?

Dee's half-sisters greeted each other with glares. While Jen hung her jacket over the back of her chair, Tiff mouthed, 'What's she doing here?'

Dee raised her a warning finger to tell her to keep it well and truly shut. She raised it again when Tiffany leaned over and whispered, 'Are you sorting me out with a loan here or what?'

Dee stared at the other two in turn and then told them, 'Alright ladies, choose something to eat and then we need to get down to business. And Jen, don't choose the cheapest thing you can find. I'm paying, OK?'

While Jen looked both resentful and relieved, Tiff threw her menu on the table. 'I'm not hungry, and anyway, I've got an appointment somewhere else.'

Dee chose the prawns before warning her, 'Your backsides are gonna remain glued to those seats until we get things straightened out.'

'Get what straightened out?' Tiff countered brazenly.

Jen chose the house burger and trimmings, then Dee laid down the line. 'I'll tell you what needs straightening. It's you two and this business with our mum's properties. I can't believe what's happening. She calls us together and does us a massive favour out of the goodness of her heart and you pair of ungrateful gits can't even say thanks. Now, I hear you've at each others' throats like a couple of washer women over the share-out, while Babs is going spare in the slammer. Do you know what you two look like? Well, I'm putting the brakes on it now.'

Tiff looked all mock wide-eyed innocent. 'There ain't been no bust-up, has there sis?' She turned to Jen for support but didn't get any. Annoyed, she went on, 'I'm entitled to my opinion. I think we should sell up pronto and cash in on our winnings.'

Dee drummed her fingers on the table, tempted to knock their heads together. 'It's not our money; it's our mum's, which she's generously giving us.'

'And it's because I know it's her money that I want things sorted quickly. It would be dissing Mum to drag this out. She wants to see us spend the loot so let's do it as soon as.'

Jen finally snapped. 'Spend the loot? You don't seem to have any trouble spending loot as it is. I don't know what the hurry is.'

Tiff was clearly on the edge. 'I dunno what your problem is. You should want the dosh faster than me, save you walking round the gaff looking like a fucking homeless most of the time.'

Jen gave her a nasty smile. 'At least I've got my self respect.' Then she added pointedly, 'Perhaps you haven't? After all, it's a bit of a mystery how you can afford to spend like a drunk sailor.'

'Don't worry about my money treacle, you worry about yours.'

Dee banged a spoon on the table to get Tiff and Jen's attention before things got out of hand. Realising the noise had attracted the attention of the other diners, she lowered her voice. 'You see the problem here? I call us together for a constructive discussion and it's already turning into a Millwall match. What's the matter Tiffany? Why do you need Mum's money in a hurry?'

Tiff shrugged and sank the rest of the wine in her glass before topping herself up. 'I don't.'

'Look, we're adults and we're sisters, we shouldn't have any secrets. If you don't need the money, why are you asking me for a loan?'

Tiffany sank the glass in one and turned her blazing eyes on Dee. 'Oh that's right, wash my dirty panties in public.'

Jen sat back in triumph. 'I might have guessed. She's living on tick; no wonder she wants to fleece the rest of us. It's to pay her bills.'

Tiffany decided she'd done with her glass and reached for the bottle but it was empty. She shouted at a waiter. 'Oi you – the one dressed like a penguin – another couple of these please. And no, I don't want to taste it first.'

A ripple of disquiet went through the other diners but the sisters were too engrossed in their squabble to take a blind bit of notice.

Jen was jeering now. 'Same ol' little sis. No different now than when she was a kid. Won't do any work, so she lifts money off others. What a ponce.'

'Won't work? I was a mechanic 24/7 when all your money was supplied by that Keystone car thief Nuts. Where is he these days . . .? Oh yeah, he upped and fucked off.' She wriggled her head provocatively. 'And left little Miss Iceberg.'

Seeing Jen was on the point of exploding Dee slammed her palm in the air to halt the mud slinging. 'Tiff, enough of the bitch fest.' She turned her gaze to Jen. 'There's obviously something giving you the nark so please enlighten me.'

Jen thumped her glass down. 'I'll tell you what the bovver is. Do you know what it's like raising two kids on your own on a place like The Devil? It's like wading through quick-setting diarrhoea up to your knees. All day. Every day. You're alright for money. Tiffany would be alright if she wasn't a greed hound. But I'm not alright. I don't see why we should split the money three ways. Mum should have taken my situation into account and put something extra aside for my girls. It's not about me, it's about them. You wanna know what my problem is? It's other kids calling my girls tramps in the playground. And Mum and you two could solve it in the blink of an eye but it never even crossed your minds.'

'I see.' Dee didn't mean to sound like a headmistress with a couple of naughty school kids but she knew she did. 'Well, all of our cards are on the table now. Got to say I'm very disappointed at your attitude . . .'

All the bitterness and resentment that Jen had stoppered up for years burst out like a cork in a bottle. 'It's alright for you, shacked up with your gangster of a husband. You're not even part of our family really anyway, are you?'

Tiffany nodded in a rare moment of agreement. 'That's true actually. You're not.'

At the other tables, diners looked in horror as Dee rose to her feet and then slapped Tiffany very hard across the face. Stunned for a moment, Tiff rolled back before she stood up in turn. 'Oh, you've done it now. You want some, do ya? If you want some, you've got it.'

She took a swing at Dee who raised one arm to protect herself and punched Tiff in the face with the other. Tiffany fell back in front of a shocked couple who ran for cover when they saw Dee moving in for the kill. Bottles, plates and glasses were scattered on the floor. But so focused was Dee on Tiffany that she didn't notice that Jen wanted in as well. She only felt a wallop across the back of her head.

That was it! World War Three had been declared and Dee knew who the victor would be.

She staggered over to another table and asked the dumb-struck guy sitting there, 'Excuse me mate, do you mind if I borrow this?' Without waiting for his consent, she took the decanter of brandy from him and emptied the contents on the floor. She took it by the neck and turned menacingly back to her sisters. 'You want to sort this out East End style do ya? Alright, let's see what you two fake Mike Tysons have got.'

With relish she advanced on them.

As John and Kieran laughed together at the bar there was a noise in the restaurant that sounded like feeding time at the zoo. Kieran jumped off his stool and John followed. When they threw open the connecting doors they ran into chaos. Tables and chairs were overturned, terrified diners were flee-ing for cover and waiters were unsure whether to break the fight up or join in. John was horrified when he saw who the three women slogging it out were. 'What the fuck are they doing here?'

He pitched in and grabbed Dee round the waist, pulling her backwards out of the ruck. But as he did so, his grip seemed to loosen and he tumbled backwards before letting her go and steadying himself on a table. He shook his head as his legs folded under him and he sank to the floor as if he'd been punctured. For a moment it looked like he'd taken a hit. It was a few seconds before it became clear he'd collapsed.

Dee got down on her knees, crying, 'John! John!'

He looked up at her and said. 'Stop mithering, I'm alright.'

His eyelids flickered and he frowned. His head rolled to one side.

Dee looked at Kieran in terror and screamed, 'Don't just stand there, call an ambulance!'

Thirty-Eight

'What happened?' A scared out of her wits and angry Dee slammed the question at Kieran in the hospital corridor near John's room.

She didn't notice how she was trembling because her mind was back in The Lock watching her beloved husband falling. And falling. It was as if it was all happening in slo-mo. Then crash; he was on the floor. Thank God one of the other diners had been a doctor. She didn't remember who called the ambulance but it was there in a flash, taking her and John down to The Royal London Hospital in Whitechapel. She'd grimly held his limp, cold hand, tears streaming down her face as he lay still. Once they reached The London everything had speeded up in a blur with the staff rushing him into emergency. She'd kicked up a real storm when they refused to let her in. Someone restrained her – she didn't know who and didn't care – until she slumped forward in exhaustion and heartache.

'He'll be alright,' Tiff piped up as she sat in a seat, her hands curling and uncurling in her lap.

'Back home in no time,' Jen added, two seats down from Tiff.

Dee cut her eyes at them and then turned accusingly back to Kieran. 'What was my old man doing at the club with you?'

He let out a tired breath and shrugged. 'He gave me a tinkle to say he wanted a word—'

'Oh yeah.' She advanced, her face turning nasty. 'And what would my husband wanna be speaking to you for?'

Kieran stood his ground. 'That's between me and John.'

She got in his face and jabbed her finger at him. 'No, that's where you're wrong matey. It's between me and you.'

'Leave him alone,' Jen chucked out as she got to her feet. She marched over and possessively linked her arm in Kieran's. 'I know you're upset, but Kieran's not to blame.'

Dee wasn't listening. She took in their joined arms and sneered. 'Well, well, if it ain't Posh and Becks.' She looked them up and down with disdain. 'Don't think *Hello* will be after this photo. When did this little hook-up take place?'

Neither answered as Jen tightened her hold. At least Dee knew who was supplying Jen's new cash injection. She turned to Tiff. 'You know about this?'

Tiff shook her head sharply. 'How would I know? I ain't passed two words with Jen since she spat in my face when all her kid wanted was to see her kind-hearted aunt.'

Before any more cross words could be slung a voice rang out along the corridor, 'Mum? Mum? What's going on?'

Dee rushed forward and took a terrified Nicky into her arms. 'Your dad's just had a funny turn, that's all. The quacks are giving him the once-over and after that we'll be taking him home.' She said the words for herself as well because that's what she was desperately clinging onto.

A doctor emerged from John's room. 'Mrs Black, can I have a word?' Once she reached him the doctor said, 'We think he may have a problem with his heart.' She sucked in her breath. 'We're going to need to operate.'

'Can I see him?' Her voice quivered.

'Me too,' Kieran pumped out.

Dee snarled and informed the doctor, 'That one's not a blood relation. I don't want him anywhere near my John.'

Sensing the tension the doctor coughed nervously. 'He's awake, a tad groggy, but you can have five minutes with him.'

As she hurried Kieran called out, 'You need to ask him a question for me.'

'Piss. Off,' she growled without turning around.

She entered John's room and was horrified. Her knees went weak at the sight. John was laid up on a bed with every kind of drip, syringe and electrical lead hanging off his body. His eyes were closed and he was deathly pale. He looked dead already. Dee hurried over to his bedside, took his hand and squeezed it.

John's bloodshot, watery eyes flickered open. He squeezed her hand. 'I'm alright love, no need to look like I've already pegged out.'

'Oh babes.' She gave him a searing kiss on the lips and the gentlest of hugs.

She almost jumped when she felt his palm cup her tummy. She stared at him, shocked. 'Oh God John, how did you know?'

'I remember what my mum went through when she was carrying my younger brothers and sisters. I've been waiting for you to tell me.'

Her face was wary. 'John—'

'Come here,' he ordered. Cautiously she let him take her hand again. 'You think I'm gonna hit the roof because I know it ain't mine. We both know I'm firing blanks.'

'John—'

'Because it's Kieran's.'

Dee's face crumbled. The tears fell as she blurted out, 'It was one time. I don't even know how it happened.' Her voice grew strong. 'But I swear on my life I told him it was never going to happen again. That's why I didn't want him to come around no more. Not coz I was tempted but because every time I clocked him I felt so ashamed.' She lowered her eyes. 'So very ashamed.'

'I wasn't completely sure until Kieran came over to ours yesterday,' her head slammed up, eyes wide with disbelief, 'and you denied he'd been there.'

'I swear, John, I told him to sling his hook.'

He let go of her hand and placed it squarely on her belly. 'I don't care how this baby came into being, he's ours. Mine and yours.' Dee started crying openly. 'Anyone who says different will have me to deal with. Now you need to listen to me carefully and dry those eyes.'

She swiped her hands over her tears. 'I've got a confession to make as well.' He coughed but waved her back when she bent over him with concern. 'I couldn't help it love. I got back in the life. I missed it, so I—'

Dee knew whatever he'd done was bad. 'What did you do?'

'I had to . . .' his eyes started drooping. 'I . . . I . . .'

'John? John?'

The doctor said from the doorway, 'We gave him something to help him sleep.' She turned around. 'When he's awake we'll be taking him to the operating theatre.'

Dee gave her husband one final kiss on his forehead and left, wondering what John hadn't been able to tell her. But no matter, he could tell her everything after the operation. And then she was going to give him the bollocking of a lifetime.

Dee was greeted outside by a voice calling in a very posh accent, 'Nicky darling, darling.' She seethed as Flo flung her arms around her son and squeezed him tight.

Dee bellowed, 'You bring that two-faced bint in here while your dad's fighting for his life?' She lunged at Florence with both hands. Tiffany, Jen and Nicky tried to restrain her while

Kieran stood back. The shouting, screaming and fighting brought the doctor running out of John's room. 'Excuse me, this is a hospital not a venue for cage fighting. Now calm down before I call the police.'

Flo straightened herself up and led Nicky away, saying she was going to get him a coffee. Kieran decided he was taking Jen for a coffee too. Dee and Tiff were left standing alone.

Dee was still seething. 'If my John wasn't sick I'd tear that bitch apart. Just thinking of her with my boy is making my head spin.'

Tiff touched her arm. 'Go and get yourself a coffee as well. I'll join you in a bit. Just gotta make a phone call first.'

Thirty-Nine

In the hospital café the following lunchtime, the family occupied three tables in different corners. At one, Jen was asleep on Kieran's shoulder. Nicky and Flo were stretched out together napping on one another while Tiff sat with Dee. The doctors still wouldn't say how John's op had gone and none of the family was allowed to see him.

Tiff quietly asked, 'What's Stan's evil spawn doing going out with Nicky? She must be nearly twice his age. Cradle snatcher.'

Dee had a theory about that. 'He's an idiot just like most teenage boys. When my John's back to himself I'm gonna make it my personal business to put that bitch down. For good.'

Tiff tilted her head to the side with a knowing expression. 'She's worming her way into his life to try to get her cut of Mum's houses, ain't she?'

With a sigh Dee stood up. 'I can't think about none of that now. I'm off to check on John.'

Tiffany rested her head on the table and shut her eyes. She could barely keep them open. The previous night had been one long night.

'I'm going to get myself a latte darling.' She scoffed as she heard Flo's sugar-coated voice from across the room. 'Do you want one too?' Tiff tuned out Nicky's reply. All she wanted to do was to get a bit of kip. The next thing she knew, her shoulder was being shaken. She looked up and did a double take.

'Mum? What are doing here? You're meant to be in prison.'

Babs was stony faced. Next to her stood Mags Sparks. 'But you called me about John.'

Tiff still stared with disbelief. 'To keep you in the know. I didn't tell you to do a runner. Shit mum, the Bill will be after you.'

Babs gave Mags a meaningful look. 'They ain't none the wiser. They think I'm at Mags' working at the memorial gardens. I had to come down.' She scanned the room, her eyebrows lifting, taking in Jen and Kieran. They looked a bit chummy to her. Then she dismissed it, remembering how they'd met at the memorial gardens. 'Everyone gather round,' she called. 'I can't stop long.'

The broken family assembled at the table under Babs' beady eye. She looked at them all, one by one.

'What the fuck is going on with this family?' No one said anything. In fact no one wanted to meet her gaze.

Then Babs breathed a sigh of pure relief when she saw Dee entering the room. 'I came as soon as I heard hun.'

Dee's voice was toneless.

'John's dead.'

PART 2: 2006

'My family are at war.'

Forty

'That bastard killed my husband,' Dee yelled, the unbearable grief inside her clear for all to see.

Before Babs could deal with her shock at the tragic news, her eldest daughter jumped Kieran. They ended up on the floor with Dee lashing out madly.

'Get security,' the woman at the till shouted in panic as people in the canteen scattered.

'Mum, Mum, let him go!' Nicky frantically tried to yank her off Kieran, but she wouldn't stop. Kieran wasn't fighting back, instead using his arms to deflect her attack, protecting his eyes, which she seemed intent on scratching out.

Babs couldn't believe what she was seeing. And then things got worse; Jen joined in. To Babs' surprise she wasn't helping her sister but letting rip at her. She was slapping Dee's back, screaming, 'Get off him, you bitch.'

Dee turned on her. 'You're the bitch. A double-crossing bitch. My own sister going out with this piece of filth.'

'You what?' Babs' gaze slammed into the man she'd always thought of as a son. 'Is this true?' She didn't want it to be true. She loved him to bits but she didn't want her girls mixed up in his world.

'Enough,' she roared.

They all fell silent as she vented her rage. 'I dunno what's going on here but I'm disgusted to the core. John is dead.' Her voice choked. 'Dead. And all you lot are doing is fighting like ferrets in a sack.' Her mouth turned down. 'Shame on the lot of you.'

Flo chose that moment to flounce in. She stopped dead in her tracks when she spied Babs. Her lip curled as she spat, 'What are you doing here?'

Babs looked her up and down. 'I think you've pinched my line love. What are you doing anywhere near my family?'

Nicky pulled himself away from Dee. 'She's with me Nanna Babs.' Tears clouded his eyes. 'And I need her.' He gazed desperately at Flo, as the tears finally fell. 'My dad's checked out.' Flo rushed over and pulled him into a deep embrace, murmuring sweet words of comfort.

Babs' head was in such a spin she thought it was going to whirl clean off her shoulders. John was dead. Nicky was with Flo. Jen was with Kieran. Dee was claiming Kieran murdered her husband. How had her family come to this? Mags was looking on, her mouth slightly open, eyes wide as if she'd descended into hell.

Dee began wailing like a wounded animal. 'My John's dead. He's dead.' Her awful sobs tore through the air.

Babs turned to Tiffany. 'Get everyone outta here. Now.'

'Right you lot . . .' Tiff got on with the job.

Babs parked herself on the floor and took her devastated daughter into her arms. She rocked her just like she'd done the one and only time she'd held her as a baby. 'It's gonna be alright. Mum's here to take care of you.'

Babs stood silently by Dee's side as they looked down at John's still face in the hospital bed. Mags waited patiently outside. She had warned her that they needed to get their skates on before the prison authorities got suspicious. But Babs couldn't leave her beloved Desiree in this state. She'd been robbed of being her precious daughter's mum when she was young; she wasn't going to cut out on her now.

Dee ran her fingers lovingly down his cold cheek. 'I didn't think much of him when I first saw him,' she confided to Babs as she sucked the tears back. 'Truth be told I thought he was a bit of a short arse.' A ghost of a smile haunted her face. 'It didn't take me long to realise he was the best thing that ever happened to me. Anything I wanted he got it in a heartbeat. Even when I was ranting and raving at him.' She leaned down and tenderly kissed him on the lips, which brought the tears to Babs' eyes.

Dee turned and Babs got choked up at her ravaged expression. 'What am I going to do without him? He was my world.'

Babs took her into her arms. 'I know hun, I know.' She gazed at her with love, but determination too. 'But this is the way of life. We're here for a short time and John was one of those people who made the best of his time here.'

Suddenly Dee became angry again. 'I know Kieran did something to him.'

'That's not the Kieran I know. He's a bit urgent but he wouldn't do that.'

With wide-eyed shock Dee twisted out of her embrace. 'What? You know that sleaze ball?'

Babs took a deep breath. 'I more or less brought him up. Poor lad had the mum from hell. I know he's no angel, but hurt John?' She shook her head with conviction. 'No, not happening.'

'But John collapsed after seeing him.'

Babs moved forward and took Dee's ice-cold palms in her own. 'That boy was such a source of strength for me when you were born.' Dee stilled.

They rarely spoke of the time Babs hadn't been there for her because those harsh memories hurt so bad.

Babs' face turned wistful. 'I'll never forget when you were in the hospital and I thought I was gonna lose you. Kieran put his little hand in mine and asked if he could come to Mile End ozzie to see you. Do you know what he did when we got there?' Dee's mouth tightened. 'We were looking at you through the window in the premature baby unit and he puts his little hand against the window and says, "Keep fighting like Henry Cooper. Your mummy loves you little one". He could never hurt you because he's loved you since he first laid eyes on you.'

Dee snatched her hands away. 'I don't give a monkey's nuts about what went on in the past. I know he did something to John. Maybe he said something that put John on edge, but as far as I'm concerned John would still be here if he'd never gone to see that scumbag.'

The door opened and Mags popped her head in. 'Babs, we've gotta run. I've just had the slammer on the blower and had to tell them some flim-flam story.'

'I don't want you to get into any trouble. You need to go.' Dee teared up again. 'Cheers for coming. I needed you Mum.'

Babs nearly broke down. This was the first time Dee had called her Mum. How she had longed for this day. Mum was such a simple word, one most folks took for granted, but for Babs it was the greatest gift of all to hear her daughter finally call her that. The shame of it was the honour had come through such tragic events. They embraced once more before Babs reluctantly left her daughter looking down at the body of her dead husband.

She was surprised and none too pleased to find Kieran waiting in the corridor. He looked like he wanted to punch the wall. 'Babs, I never touched him—'

Her eyes flashed with hurt indignation. 'You've got a lot of accounting to do.'

'You don't own me Babs,' he bit out. His stare was stone cold as if she were one of his rivals and he was making a promise to flatten them. It shook her up; he'd never put her in her place like that before. It made Babs realise, with open-eyed clarity, what her beloved boy really was.

Then everything changed as he ran the tip of a finger gently down her cheek. 'You know I'd never do nuthin to hurt you. Nuthin. I'd rather slice out my own heart. I feel the same about Dee. And John took me under his wing and showed me the ropes when most wanted to boot me to the kerb. I loved him like a father.'

A worried Mags cut him off. 'Babs, I'm sorry lovey, but I think I've got us into a bit of a tricky situation.'

'What?'

The other woman waved her hands fretfully. 'I told the prison people I had to take you down the ozzie to get 'em off our backs. But they wanted to know what was wrong . . .' She bit her lip. 'I'm dead sorry.'

Babs could feel doom looming. 'What did you tell 'em?'

'That you'd broken your finger.'

Forty-One

Babs squeezed her eyes shut with vexation and disbelief. She hadn't thought this day could get any worse. It just had. She fixed her troubled gaze on Kieran, her face tight. 'There's only one thing we can do.'

He nodded grimly. 'I know. Let me find a place – somewhere to do it.' Babs gulped as he set off down the corridor.

'I'm real sorry Babs, this is all my fault,' Mags spluttered as she wrung her hands together.

Babs wasn't having someone else taking the blame for her shambles of a family. 'None of this is at your door. You done me a favour bringing me here. It's that bloody family of mine that are the real problem.' She shook her head sadly; she still couldn't believe what had gone on. 'They're falling apart and I feel helpless, like there's sod effing all I can do about it.'

'They do seem to be a lively bunch, I grant you that.' Mags' tone switched to stern mode, which was unlike her. 'But they're adults, not nippers crying in their nappies. If they can't live without you holding their hands, what does that make 'em? They need to learn to stand on the two feet God give 'em.'

Babs huffed. 'They wouldn't know their own two feet if they reared up and kicked them in the gob . . .'

'Ladies,' Kieran called, his head poking out of a room further down the corridor.

He beckoned them to shift themselves, so they hurried over. He shut the door on a small, white room filled with hospital supplies and equipment.

'I'm gonna dress your finger.' He pointed to a trolley where he'd laid out a bandage and pair of scissors. 'That way—'

'What are you chatting on about?' Babs interrupted, gazing at him like he was off his rocker.

He looked at her puzzled. 'We agreed that I need to wrap a bandage around your finger so that it looks like it's broken.'

She frowned. 'But I thought you understood *what* we had to do.'

His mouth worked wordlessly for a few seconds, then clamped shut as his face turned white. 'No way Babs . . .'

'You don't have a choice.' She stepped closer to him to emphasise the importance of what she needed him to do. 'As soon as I get back they'll have the prison quack on my finger like a dose of salts, and if it ain't broken . . . me and Mags will be for the high jump.'

Kieran wouldn't back down. 'No—'

She grabbed the front of his shirt and yanked him so close their faces were inches apart. 'We ain't got time to play "Here We Go Round the Mulberry Bush". You have to break my finger.'

Mags gasped. But Babs didn't have time for any more drama. 'We need to find something to do it with.'

Kieran let out a sigh of resignation. They began searching through cupboards, trolleys, shelves . . .

'Got it,' Kieran announced brandishing a small hammer, the type used to test knee reflexes. 'Mags, stuff the bandage in Babs' mouth; if anyone hears you screaming the ozzie down, we're sunk.'

Babs swallowed convulsively as she laid her ring finger on the counter by the sink. It seemed fitting because every last bit of trouble she'd ever had came back to the day she'd tied the knot with Stanley Miller. The sweat beaded on Kieran's forehead. He raised the hammer. Babs squeezed her eyes tight. And waited. And waited. Nothing happened. She snapped them open to find Kieran like the statue of a labourer, his hammer frozen in the air.

'I can't,' he gritted out.

It was Mags who stepped in. 'Boy, if you don't I'm gonna take that hammer and ram it . . .'

He slammed it down on Babs' finger. Her scream was an awful muffled sound behind the bandage. Hot and terrible pain sliced across her hand. Her eyes watered and her legs wobbled, making her sag against the counter.

'I'm sorry Babs,' Kieran said in an agonised voice showing that Babs wasn't the only one in pain.

He chucked the hammer down when Babs muttered, 'Take it out.' They looked at her baffled. She said it three times before they twigged that she wanted the bandage out of her mouth. Mags did it.

Babs stared at Kieran, the air hot and aching in her chest. 'You need . . .' she sucked back the pain, 'to do it again.'

'Are you going potty or something?'

'Look at my finger.' All three of them stared at it. It was red and slightly battered. 'It's not broken. You're gonna have to do it again. With a bit more welly this time.'

He wasn't happy, but there was no arguing as he picked up the hammer again. She didn't close her eyes, but held them steady. He raised the hammer and smashed it hard against her finger. There was the sound of a crack as pain exploded in Babs' hand and head. Kieran quickly took the bandage out of her mouth and held her close.

'Don't ever ask me to do something like that again.'

Mags checked her watch anxiously. 'Babs, you're already in serious bovver. We need to go.'

* * *

Mrs Field, the Number One, was giving Babs the eye and so was her poodle. When some of the other girls had told her that the Governor sometimes brought her dog to work she thought they were having a laugh. Now she could see they weren't. The poodle's black fur looked like it had just had a shampoo and set and all it needed to top off the look was a bright, pink bow tied round its neck. Its owner wasn't so fortunate with her looks, all angles and sharp bones with a colour that made her seem a few steps away from death.

Babs stood in front of the Governor after seeing the prison doc who had confirmed that her finger was indeed broken. She'd given Babs some painkillers and splinted it. Mrs Field looked at her through horned rim bifocals. 'The funny thing, Miller, is that according to the doctor the break in your finger is not consistent with it being shut in a garden shed door or any other door.'

Babs should've figured out that the one thing the prison quack would be an all-time expert on was fingers slammed in doors. It was the standard punishment doled out to anyone lifting stuff from someone else's cell.

Babs played the wide-eyed innocent. 'I don't know much about doctoring Miss, except having to nurse my girls' scrapes and grazes when they were little.'

'Well, you no longer need worry your head about shed doors. I'm revoking your outside work permit.'

That took Babs' breath away. 'You can't do that Miss.'

The poodle bared its teeth. Babs was tempted to do the same back.

'Is there any decision on my parole?' Maybe it wasn't the best time to be putting the Governor on the spot about it but she just wanted to get out of this place.

The Number One lifted her nose. 'I believe there are a

backlog of cases. When I know I will let you know. You may leave, Miller.'

What an HMP bitch. Babs turned grudgingly towards the door. Now she had no way of getting out of the prison. And she was worried. What she'd witnessed today at the hospital was bad.

She whispered fretfully under her breath, 'My family are at war.'

Forty-Two

A week later, shocked gasps and scandalised whispers greeted Dee as she walked into the church and people got an eyeful of what she was wearing to send her husband off. If they'd been expecting her decked out in doom- and gloom-laden black they didn't know Dee Black. She wore a stunning, shimmering scarlet Saint Laurent sequin evening dress and Valentino mile-high heels. John had loved that dress. His eyes would light up in delight and chest-puffing pride every time she stepped out in it. She looked heavenwards and hoped that her adored man was smiling down at her now.

She continued to move with dignity, spine ramrod straight. Inside she felt like she was choking. The day she had dreaded for so long had finally arrived. It was time to lay her John to rest. She was going to bury her husband the same way he'd lived his life – in style. Her legs trembled slightly as she reached him, laid out in a gold-plated coffin she'd got specially imported from New York. The scent of the wreaths of oriental lilies swam over her as she looked down at her much-loved man. He was dressed in his favourite, navy suit, a strawberry coloured hanky folded neatly in the top jacket pocket and, most importantly of all, a polished pair of his stacked heels. He was gone. Gone. Gone. She began to wail.

'I've got ya,' Tiffany said firmly as she wrapped an arm around her shoulder and Aunty Cleo, her foster mum, gently took her hand.

Both women had walked behind her as she entered the church. Gently they led her away and got her sat down on the front pew.

After she'd wiped her eyes Tiff whispered, 'Blinding turnout.'

Dee looked back over the packed church. 'Yeah, my John had a lot of friends.'

And a lot of enemies. And they'd all turned up. Half the mourners were Faces Dee didn't recognise but who'd played their part in her husband's long journey from scrawny street kid to retired crime lord. The other side of the law had put in an appearance as well. Greying and wrinkled ex-coppers who'd booked John in his younger days and others who he'd helped out with gambling debts or treats for the missus. There were some younger detectives who'd told the ushers that they'd come to pay their respects but who Dee would bet her life were really there to keep an eye on this villains' reunion and get some steers for their enquiries.

Dee turned back to Tiffany. 'If I was the law, I'd brick this building up during the service. The crime rate in town would drop by half. By the way,' she squeezed her sister's arm, 'I haven't said how much I appreciate you coming to stay with me since John closed his eyes. So I'm saying it now.'

Tiffany looked embarrassed before giving Dee a pat. 'I know we had words, but no way was I leaving my sister in the lurch.' She didn't add, 'unlike our other sister.' But then she didn't have to. 'Have you spoken to Jen?'

'I sent a message saying she was welcome, but on the strict understanding that it's just her and the kids – not *him*.' She couldn't bring herself to say Kieran's name. 'I ain't having him here. And anyway,' she looked around the church again, 'he wouldn't have the front.'

Tiffany nodded and hesitated before saying, 'No sign of Nicky either.'

Dee drew breath. 'Yeah. He's been on the piss most nights. I know he's hurting over John's death, but if he don't show he'll find himself in the ground next.' All the life seemed to suddenly drain from her. 'Can you believe it? My Nicky and that good-time tart Flo? Jen and that plastic gangster? Mum's right. What the hell is happening to this family? Mind you, she's done a San Quentin with the prison barring her from coming.' She squeezed Tiff's hand again. 'You're the only person I can rely on.'

Just then another ripple ran through the congregation as an older man joined the proceedings, accompanied by two very tall, stunning women. For the first time that day a big smile split Dee's face.

'Uncle Frank. I didn't know you were back in town.'

'Didn't John tell you I paid him a visit?' On uttering John's name his face became sombre. 'My Johnnie going before me? That ain't right. Tragic, Dee, really tragic. There's not many of us left from the old days now.'

She squeezed his arm, feeling his pain. 'Tiffany, this is Uncle Frank. He took John under his wing when he was a nipper.'

Uncle Frank smiled, then he seemed to remember something. 'By the way, I was wondering if I could have a quick word with you after the service?'

'OK – about anything in particular?'

He became vague. 'Oh nuthin, you know, just some loose ends I need to tie up. Is Kieran Scott coming to the service?'

Dee was becoming nervous. Uncle Frank didn't do small talk. This was business. 'He's barred so he'd have the nerve of the Devil to put in an appearance.'

'That's a shame. I was hoping to have a word with him. Still, I'll chat to you later. Nice to meet you Tiffany.'

He took a seat while Dee whispered. 'What's that about? I didn't even know he knew Kieran.'

The sound of footsteps coming down the aisle ran round the church. Dee turned and saw Nicky in an ill-fitting black suit hurrying along with . . . Dee nearly cursed loud and clear. Stan Miller's spawn of Beelzebub hung off him like a Top Shop accessory.

'Can you believe it?' Nicky spluttered when he reached her. 'Notting Hill tube was shut so we had to leg it to the next one. Have I missed anything?'

Dee was speechless. His hair was all over the shop and he stank of leaf. After the day was done she was going to sit him down and read the riot act. Nicky quickly took a pew, but when Flo went to follow Dee and the others all shuffled their bums so that there was no space for her.

Flo gave Dee a rude smile, blew Nicky a kiss and then flounced off to find a seat. Dee looked daggers at her and watched her go. But when she saw Flo had found a pew, she realised that her son and his so-called girlfriend weren't the only late arrivals. Sitting near the back with her two children was Jen. She was dressed in an elegant black suit. She nudged Tiffany who told her, 'At least she came and didn't bring that fake-up villain with her. That's something.'

For a brief moment, across the crowded church, Dee and Jen's eyes met. They held each other's gaze before looking away. She had to admit that her sister looked the bizz in her new short hairdo and pricey clobber, but there was a harshness in her expression Dee hadn't seen before.

The poor vicar wasn't used to this kind of crowd and seemed in a hurry to get the service over with. He knocked out a short speech, which included the phrases 'much-loved man' and 'someone who touched many people's lives' together with a few bible readings. Before the first hymn, to his obvious relief, he invited Aunty Cleo to say a few words. Apart from a slightly arched back, Cleo didn't look that much older than when she'd agreed to look after baby Dee. Dee knew that Cleo's tribute would cause ructions but she'd asked her to do it anyway. Aunty Cleo was a truth teller and she knew that John would have wanted the truth told at his funeral.

In front of the congregation Cleo got into her stride. 'We mustn't forget that John was also a sinful man who committed many terrible deeds. He was no stranger to thieving, violence, lying and all forms of law breaking.' At first there was some half-hearted laughter in the congregation who thought this was a rather off-colour joke. But as Cleo went on, there was mumbling, muttering and finally some jeering. But like a stand-up in a rough club, she took on the hecklers. 'And, of course, John was the proprietor of the Alley Club where drunkenness and lewd behaviour, fornication and adultery were not so much frowned on as encouraged.'

The crowd didn't like it but Dee gave Cleo nods of encouragement. John hadn't left any instructions but she knew how he felt about funeral speeches. After one, he'd whispered to her, 'You think they would have mentioned that the deceased was one of the biggest coke traffickers in Europe as well as talking about all that charity work he did. When I go don't varnish it for the punters. I can't stand all the lovable Cockney rogue stuff.' In fact, he hadn't seemed keen on the idea of a funeral at all. After one underworld interment, he'd said, 'When I go, put me in a sack and chuck me off Southend Pier. Funerals? Wakes? Waste of money – spend it on a month in the Caribbean instead.'

Aunty Cleo was finishing up. 'Of course, who are we to judge? We are all humble sinners in need of redemption.'

Dee gratefully squeezed her foster mum's hand as she sat down. But it seemed Cleo's unvarnished tribute had caused more trouble than Dee had bargained for. The vicar lifted his hands to indicate that everyone was to rise but as he did so, there was more murmuring and whispering and finally shouts behind them. She turned to see that Uncle Frank had gone to the rear of the church and was having words with someone. Other mourners nearby, who obviously didn't know who big Uncle Frank was, were telling him to pack it in.

Dee hurried along down the aisle. She couldn't see Kieran at first; he must have slunk in after the service started. Her view was blocked by Uncle Frank, but as she approached, she heard the two men exchanging words.

'I've been trying to get in touch with you Kieran but you seem to be keeping a very low profile at the moment. Funny that.'

'Not now Uncle Frank, it's a funeral.'

'I know why we're here mate – I know a coffin when I see one. I've seen plenty over the years. But there's no need for us to have words now. How about you and me book a time for a chat instead?'

'I've got nish to say to you.'

Dee steamed in. 'Kieran? What are you playing at? You're not welcome here. And Uncle Frank? I can't believe it, this is John's funeral. If you want to row, do it on your own time.'

Uncle Frank raised his hands. 'Sorry, you're right Dee, I'm being disrespectful.' He turned to Kieran. 'Get in touch mate. If you don't, I've got other ways of communicating with people, as you well know.'

Kieran was unimpressed. 'Leave it out granddad, your day's long past. You ain't got that kind of clout anymore. Stick to golf and keep yourself out of trouble.'

As Uncle Frank returned to his seat Dee shouted, 'Carry on Rev!'

The poor minister, who looked as if he wished he had a nice christening to go to, gestured at the organist and the opening bars of 'Abide With Me' kicked in. It was the only other steer John had given Dee. He'd told her he wanted that hymn because it reminded him of the Cup Final. When the singing started, Dee sat down next to Kieran. 'You need to give those legs of yours some exercise and stroll right outta here.'

Kieran was cradling a large bunch of red roses. He shrugged. 'I've come to pay my respects to my old compadre John Black. It's not up to you whether I come or not. You didn't own John. Nobody did, it was one of the things I liked about him. Now why don't you go back to your seat and start praising the Lord.'

'Get. Out.'

'I've got as much right to be here as anyone else. And anyway, I wanted a word with you.'

'You ain't getting one.'

Kieran scoffed. 'We'll see about that.'

Dee leaned into his face. 'What was that about?'

'What was what about?'

'You and Uncle Frank?'

Kieran shrugged again. 'Dunno. Poor old Frank McGuire's been in the Spanish sun too long. He's confused.'

Dee began to make her way to the front of the church as the organ and singing soared their way through the final verse. But as she went, a man she didn't recognise, who'd been lingering nearby, realised that Dee had failed to persuade the intruder to go and he took the law into his own hands. He grabbed Kieran by his lapels and dragged him to his feet, scattering his roses. Kieran broke his grip by forcing his hands up between the guy's arms and pushing outwards while, in the same move, kneeing him in the privates. As he fell forward, gasping for breath, Kieran elbowed him on the cheek before stamping on him several times as he slumped down between the pews. The final bars of the hymn faded away and the only sound in the church was the whimpering of the beaten man. Kieran picked his roses up one by one and resumed his seat.

In the distance, Dee heard one woman say to another, 'A punch-up at a funeral? That's so disrespectful.'

But the neighbour smiled sadly. 'Nah, it's what John would've wanted.'

Forty-Three

After the service, Dee and Tiffany set off for the graveyard at high speed to make sure they were the first to arrive. They scented trouble. It was clear Uncle Frank had a beef with Kieran and wasn't afraid to use a funeral to pursue it. Dee wanted to lay her husband to rest in peace.

As mourners appeared and headed for the grave, Dee and Tiffany warned them, 'Remember this is a burial, alright?'

Dee hoped against hope that Kieran would do the decent thing and give the actual burial a miss. But she knew her man. He would think the decent thing would be to turn up, especially now he'd been warned off. While she waited for the hearse, she noticed Nicky and Flo hanging around by a grave topped with a tall statue of an angel looking upwards, her hands clasped together in prayer. Nicky was choking back the tears and Flo was giving him a hug, being supportive. Credit to the girl, she might have been a chiseller but at least she was being human about it.

When the hearse arrived, Dee supervised the removal of the coffin and organised the pallbearers: five top villains and a disgraced former Flying Squad detective. The six men carried her husband's body to the graveside. Overhead a police helicopter was keeping watch on proceedings and there were press photographers on hand to snap celebs from the underworld. A

Merc parked up nearby and Kieran, still clutching his roses, got out. He was alone. There was no sign of Jen or the kids. He took up a spot near the back of the crowd.

Tiffany whispered, 'Shall I go and have a word with him Dee?'

'No, leave it alone. I know Kieran, he'll only blank ya and it'll just cause more bovver.'

Uncle Frank turned up in a Roller with his bodyguards. He pushed his way through the crowd to a prime spot by the grave, as befitted the man who had helped bring John up.

The vicar said a few words. Dee was heavy with relief when the burial came to an end. She choked up when grieving friends and relatives were invited to use a gold trowel to throw some earth onto the coffin. There seemed to be no trouble when Kieran stepped forward to join the queue. When his turn came, Kieran stepped up, took the trowel and threw earth in. But instead of stepping aside, he took the roses he'd brought with him and began chucking them, one at a time, into the grave.

This was too much for Uncle Frank. He shouted, 'Get a move on. Who do you think you are – fucking Morrissey?'

Kieran took no notice. There were quiet gasps that someone had the brass to ignore Uncle Frank in public and he himself decided he wasn't having it. Elbowing people out of the way, the ageing but still handy man pushed through and shoved Kieran aside. Kieran threw the rest of the roses into the grave, clenched his fist and levelled a punch at Frank who fell backwards into the vicar. Frank's bodyguards and associates piled in while a surprising number of the younger guys came forward to support Kieran. He picked up the gravedigger's shovel and swung it at his attackers. Some of the plain clothed cops stepped forward to intervene but when they realised how badly outnumbered they were, they thought better of it. A horrified Dee watched as her husband's send-off turned into a boozer brawl.

'Pack it in! I said, fucking pack it in!' she yelled. 'Excuse my language vicar – fucking pack it in!'

Dee had never shied away from a fight but as she tried to separate the warring groups, she found herself dodging fists and on the end of flying punches. A thin spray of liquid went across her face as she toppled over. She was lying on the ground and when she ran her finger across her wet cheek, she saw it was blood. Around her, mourners were fleeing the scene, criss-crossing tombstones in an effort to escape. Nearby she saw one man get hit, lose his footing on the earth and tumble into the open grave.

She gritted her teeth. Enough was enough. She ran over to the tomb with the twenty-foot angel standing over it. She struggled and monkeyed her way up the statue until her head was touching its white stone cheek. She had a commanding view of the battle below. She drew breath and bellowed, 'Show some fucking respect!' so loudly that her voice seemed to come from the heavens above.

In slow motion, the fighting below began to stop and men dusted off their suits and straightened their ties. The brawlers divided into small packs and moved off, swearing threats at each other. Several senior associates of Uncle Frank's warned Kieran that he was a dead man. In the end, only the gravediggers, Tiffany, Nicky and Flo were left. Uncle Frank helped her down from her perch on the statue. Seething, he took the grieving widow firmly by the arm and frogmarched her away. And it turned out that it wasn't to apologise.

'Listen Dee, I don't want to be unpleasant on today of all days but I'm afraid I've got a little problem. Shortly before Johnnie met his maker, he did a badness when he thieved some gold from a private vault that I had an interest in. I expect you heard about it?'

Dee shivered in horror. So that's what he'd been trying to tell her in the hospital.

'I had to do something drastic to secure your future.' She looked over at his grave. He'd promised. He'd fucking promised not to get involved again.

'Cobblers,' she said to Uncle Frank, 'He had eff all to do with that job; he had a cast iron alibi.'

Uncle Frank angled a hard stare at her. 'Yes, well, Johnnie was always very good at arranging cast iron alibis and obviously I'm not suggesting he took the stuff himself.' He gestured at the cemetery gates. 'He got that little scrote Kieran Scott to do it for him. Now then, as long as I get my gold back pronto, we can keep the whole temperature on this unfortunate business down to a reasonable level. Where did John hide my gear?'

'He didn't do it.'

Uncle Frank shook his head. 'Maybe your grief has made you a bit deaf so I'll try again. Where did Johnnie stash my gold?'

'I've got no idea where any fucking gold is. Even if John did take it, he wasn't gonna tell me, was he?'

Uncle Frank nodded in agreement. 'That's possible. Alright then, let me suggest this. You have a word with your little friend Kieran and tell him to put my property where I can find it and I might – only might mind – decide to overlook his very disrespectful behaviour at the graveside.'

Dee kissed her teeth dismissively. 'I don't have nuthin to do with Kieran. You've got this all arse over elbow. Ask around. John was out of the business.'

Uncle Frank put his arm around Dee's shoulder and squeezed. 'Look Dee, truth is I'm finding the gold on behalf of the man who it belonged to. He'll take down you, your kid, your mum, your sisters, your cat, Kieran and all his people to get what he wants.' He pinched her cheek. 'Put your thinking cap on and see if you can remember where Johnnie tucked away his winnings.'

Forty-Four

When they got back to the house Tiffany put a large drink down in front of Dee, a cocktail that was more Tequila than Slammer. 'You get that down ya babe. Chill out. I'm gonna pop down the chippie and get us some fish. You look like you could use some downtime after that circus.'

A shell-shocked Dee picked up her drink and sipped. With sadness she gazed down at the once beautiful dress that had been John's pride and joy. It was torn, sequins hanging off it, some of the scarlet covered in dusty flakes of white stone. Tiffany's fury was growing. 'What a disgraceful carry on. I can't believe it. Kieran's an animal.'

Dee looked upwards with a sad smile. 'Yeah, I know. And he's not the only one. John always said he wanted to go out fighting. If he's up there somewhere, he'll probably be pissing himself laughing. I wish to fuck I was.'

'Kieran's a pig – and after you told him straight to stay away. He's too big for his crocodile shoes that guy. Everyone's saying it. If I was him, I'd watch my back.' She picked up the car keys. 'Do you need anything else? Fags, Rizlas or anything?'

'No, you're alright. I'm not sure I'm hungry either.'

Her sister gave her a comforting pat on the back. 'Course you are. They do a lovely bit of fish.'

Dee gulped her drink. 'Did Nicky come back?'

Tiffany apologised for him. 'I don't think so. He was very upset and that bitch took him off.'

'Fair enough.'

'What about forty winks while I'm out?'

'Maybe.'

When Tiffany was gone, Dee trudged upstairs to try to take her sister's advice but there was no sleep in her body. She hissed aloud, 'You idiot John, you bloody fool, how could you? How could you? You promised me you were out and now I've got Uncle Frank and his psycho pal Carats on my case.' Since Uncle Frank had declined to tell her the name of the bloke who owned the gold she'd christened him – Twenty-four Carats. Carats for short.

'You're not here to look after things. How am I gonna handle these blokes without you?'

But there was no answer.

The silence of the house was unnerving. No John. No Nicky. It took all Dee's strength to lift herself up and make her slow way downstairs. The lounge had grown dark when she got back so she put on one of the sidelights near the fish tank and picked up a bottle of voddy.

As she did so, out of habit she asked aloud, 'Do you want something John?'

From John's old armchair, across the room, a voice answered, 'Don't mind if I do.'

The bottle slid out of Dee's hands and crashed on the floor. 'Kieran? What the hell are you doing here? And what are you doing on my John's throne?' No one, absolutely no one, sat in John's armchair.

Kieran leaned forward so the light caught his face. 'Sorry, I've shocked you. I should have knocked on the front door. But then you wouldn't have let me in, would ya?'

Her body was shaking, with rage or surprise she didn't know. 'How did you get in here?'

'You left the French windows open. Careless. There's a lot of crooks around, you know? Although with you being a grieving widow and that . . . understandable.'

'Alright Kieran, you've had your bit of fun. Why don't you piss off before I call the cops and have you arrested for breaking and entering?'

'I don't think you will, because then I'll have to tell them what the nature of my visit is and I don't think you'd like the consequences. For a start they'd have a JCB all over your lovely lawn, digging it up. After that, they'll be in the house with claw hammers having your floorboards over. And you know what the law are like – they don't tidy up after they've finished.'

Uncle Frank had been telling the truth down the graveyard. John and Kieran had done that gold job. She picked up a mobile lying on the mantelpiece and waved it at him. 'Perhaps you'd prefer it if I rang Uncle Frank and invited him over to have a word. As you saw at the cemetery, he's not best pleased with you. He thinks you've got something that belongs to a mate of his. It might be a good idea if you gave it back before the violence starts.'

Kieran shrugged. 'Good. I'm glad we've got straight to the point. I agree with you actually. It would be a good idea if I gave it back. But there's a problem. I ain't got it.'

Dee was horrified. 'Who has then?'

'I'm afraid John took the location to the grave. He wouldn't tell me. I think he was planning to rip me off actually. But I don't wanna speak ill of the dead so let's put that to one side. I can't deal with Uncle Frank and whoever he's working for until I've got the gold back. So you need to tell me where it is and you need to tell me fast.'

Dee felt her throat tightening. 'I don't know.'

He eased slowly to his feet and moved towards her. When he reached her he ran the tip of his finger softly down her cheek. He moved his head close to her ear. 'Remember how it used to be with us Dee?' She could hear the smile in his voice. 'How well we fit together.' He inhaled her scent. 'Makes me hard just thinking about it.'

Calmly, but with as much steel as she could muster, Dee put him straight. 'You better step away from me fella. If you don't you won't ever have the pleasure of getting hard again because I'm gonna make sure your nuts are yesterday's news.'

He turned the screws. 'What would John say if he knew?'

She gave him the once-over with contempt. '"Satan masquerades as an angel of light." That's what Aunty said about my dad. And that's you to a T Kieran.' She gazed at him with scorn. 'A man who would try and seduce the wife of his so-called good friend who's still warm in his grave.'

He stiffened as he stepped back. 'I didn't come here for a sermon . . .'

'Then use the French windows and close them behind you.'

'I'm warning you now, I need the gold back and if I have to apply a little pressure . . . You know me very well Dee and I won't hesitate. I'm sure you understand, the stakes are too high for me to let personal feelings cloud my judgement.'

The front door opened and Tiffany burst in on them, a smell of fish coming from the bag she was clutching. 'Dee, there's a motor outside, I'm sure it belongs to Kie—' She stopped short when she saw the man himself. Her hand twitched like she was about to decorate him with chips. 'Come to apologise for wrecking John's funeral, have ya? You're a disgrace.'

'Did you ever sort out a loan to cover your debts? They were getting a bit hefty, weren't they?'

'Mind your own business, you nosy sod.'

Kieran dismissed her like she was an annoying mutt and turned back to Dee. 'When you find out what I need to know, gimme a bell. Oh, and you might want to think about getting your burglar alarm serviced and window locks checked. You can't be too careful with your personal security these days.'

Once he was gone Tiff wanted chapter and verse.

'Remember that gold bullion job?' Dee started. 'Well, him and John pulled it off. Kieran did it and gave the gear to John to look after. Now he wants it back and he thinks I know where it is. I don't. Uncle Frank's trying to get it back for the bloke who it belonged to, any which way he can, you get me? This fella he's working for sounds like a proper nut job.'

Tiffany put their dinner on the table. 'He's a liar. And so is this Uncle Frank. Kieran's not important enough to get into something like that with John or anyone else. He's just an MC at a nightclub. He's scamming you.' When Dee said nothing, Tiffany begged, 'He is scamming you, ain't he?'

Dee didn't answer. She threw open the French windows. She stepped outside, looked up to the starry heavens and shouted, 'I've got a wagonload of bad geezers after me now, thanks to you John. Are you still fucking laughing?'

Forty-Five

Dee was fretting after the umpteenth phone call she'd made to John's close associates in an attempt to find out where he might've hidden the gold. Her theory was that whoever he was with last might be able to point her in the right direction. The problem was she couldn't just come out with, 'Do you know where my old man stashed some gold bars he thieved?' She'd had to tread so carefully that some people thought she was still off her head with grief.

Dee rubbed her tummy and looked at it with wonder. 'What are we gonna do little one, eh? You haven't even been born yet and there's a world of trouble waiting for you.'

The front door slammed. 'That you Nicky?'

He hadn't come home last night. A son leaving his mum during her hour of grief was bang out of order as far as she was concerned, but she could see that the boy was taking John's death hard.

The only reply she got was quick-moving footsteps on the stairs. Calling his name again she left the room and then hesitated at the bottom of the staircase. He'd better not have brought that woman with him, because so help me God . . .

She marched up the stairs with an energy she hadn't felt for ages. As she neared his closed door she heard bumping and groaning sounds. Bloody hell, him and that witch had better

not be having it away in her house. With indignation she
threw the door open but there was no sign of Flo or a love
nest. Instead his bed was covered with CDs and 12" records,
and he was rummaging around in his wardrobe. He didn't
seem to notice that Dee was in the room.

She sat down on the corner of his bed with relief. 'Going
back to college are you? That's welcome news.'

He turned and gazed at her with a wary expression. 'Oh
hello Mum – nah, I'm um, you know.'

'No. I don't know.'

He shrugged, not meeting her eyes. 'I'm moving in with Flo
– alright?' He raised his hand when her face contorted with
fury. 'Yeah, I know what you're gonna say . . .'

Dee rose to her full height. She was tired, grief-stricken
and shaken to the core by the events at the cemetery but she
had to try. 'And you think that the day after we put your dad
to rest would be a good time to move out and leave your old
mum on her own? How can you think of leaving me at a time
like this?'

'Don't you think I know that,' he shot at her. Suddenly his
breathing shuddered. 'I can't do it Mum.'

Hearing his voice become so small Dee realised something
was badly wrong. 'Do what?'

'Stay here. He's everywhere. In the bar, the gym, in his true
crime book collection in the lounge, in the garage munching junk
food behind your back.' His drawn eyes pleaded with her. 'John's
the second dad I've lost and I'm not even twenty years old.' He
inhaled deeply. 'All I want is some space to get my shit together.'

He started stuffing his belongings into the sports bag. Dee
shook with his revelation. When had her boy grown up and
become so wise? She didn't try to stop him. But still, going to
that bitch Flo's didn't sit well with her. 'Can't you go to one of
your mates'?'

He picked up his bag and turned back to her. 'I know you don't like her and I get why, but she's a laugh and I need a little laughter in my life now.'

Five minutes later she watched him load his gear into Flo's motor. Then he came back and sheepishly gave Dee a peck on her chilly cheek. 'I'm only a mobile away,' he tried to reassure her, 'and if you can't get me on it give Flo's granddad a call. I've written down his number and left it on the bed.'

Then he was off like a burglar. As soon as the door slammed, for the first time since John's death Dee felt totally alone.

Flo gritted her teeth. It was either that or deck Nicky one as as she drove them to her granddad's. He wouldn't shut up about his dad as he belched skunk smoke inside the car. How much he missed him, how close they were . . . It was almost sending her over the edge because it was bringing back sweet memories of her time with her own father. And it was breaking her heart all over again.

Suddenly she was no longer in the car with Nicky, her mind transported back to three years ago when her dad had taken her to see the houses in Mile End. *His* houses.

'*What do you think of your clever dad now, my little Florence?*' *he'd asked proudly as they stood in the first recep-tion room of number 10 Bancroft Square.*

She'd stared in wide-eyed awe around the room, not because it was a knockout – she was used to the splendour of her granddad's houses – but because Stanley was always giving her little surprises. He'd never breathed a word to her about this house.

'*Do these belong to you Pops?*'

He'd chomped on his cigar and smiled mischeviously. 'Now that would be telling.' He'd tapped a finger to the side of his nose. Then his expression had grown serious. 'Always hold your cards close to your chest. Never show your ace until you know for sure you're gonna be the winner . . .'

Nicky's aching, quiet voice intruded on her memories. 'There must be some bad luck about me to lose two dads in my life.'

Her mind screamed for him to stop. The tears were hot behind her eyes, threatening to spill any moment down her face. By the time they reached the plush Notting Hill villa, Flo's jaw was strained as she desperately held the pain back.

Nicky must've noticed how tightly her hands held the steering wheel. He asked, 'You alright babe?'

It took Flo a couple of seconds to answer as she swallowed and pushed her dad from her mind. Then she turned to him with a too-brilliant smile. 'I'm fine.' She took his hand in hers and squeezed and for the first time since she'd met Dee's son she really did want to give him comfort.

As soon as they got inside Flo introduced him to The Commander who was bent over his model of the *Titanic*. 'Commander – this is Nicky. He's gonna – oops, sorry – going to be staying with me.' She couldn't bring herself to say 'boyfriend' or resist adding 'for a while'.

The Commander looked up with a beaming smile. He got up so slowly Flo could almost hear his bones creaking. She hated to think of her granddad in pain. He approached Nicky and held out his hand. 'Nicky Black. Really wonderful to have you here son.'

She was surprised The Commander remembered Nicky's surname. A small smile played on her lips at that; her granddad might be getting on in years but his mind was as sharp as ever.

'That's a very distinctive aftershave you're wearing,' he noted, eyebrows lifting.

If it had been any other old man, Flo might have believed he really meant it. But she knew the Commander had been in just about every opium den and knocking shop in just about every port, on just about every continent. He knew herbal when he smelt it.

'I need a place to crash,' Nicky said. 'My old man just died and I need a bit of space.'

The Commander patted him on the shoulder sympathetically. 'Yes, it's never easy losing a loved one. Stay as long as you like.' He drifted back to his chair and got on with his model.

Grabbing Nicky's hand Flo drew him into the hallway. 'Great drum your grandpops has.' His gaze wandered around curiously.

'Don't ever call him grandpops. He likes everyone to call him The Commander.'

Nicky twisted at her words so quickly that he knocked into HMS *Grenada*'s bell and it pealed loudly. 'What the hell is that?' he asked.

'He's bonkers about ships. The bell belonged to the ship he commanded, hence the name Commander.'

When they got upstairs Jezebel was on the landing to greet them. Over the weeks, the cat and Flo had come to an understanding. Flo had to keep out of the cat's room unless she was out. When Jezebel came back, Flo was expected to leave immediately. In return, the Persian was allowed into Flo's room to sharpen her claws on the furniture but she too was expected to be about her business when Flo came back. A certain mutual respect had developed on the grounds that it took one to know one. Jezebel turned her head towards her and tilted it slightly. Of course she couldn't say 'Look what the cat's dragged in' but that was what her squinty look clearly meant.

'I didn't know you had a cat.' He smiled at it. 'Pretty thing.'

As if knowing she'd been complimented the cat prowled over to him and rubbed herself against his leg, purring.

You've got my room, now you want my man as well! Flo dragged Nicky sharply away and closed the door to her room. Nicky flopped down on the bed. 'I could sleep for ever,' he told her quietly. He reached out his hand. 'At least I've got you.'

But she didn't take it. Instead, Flo decided it was time to get down to business. Her voice was chilly. 'Yeah, but you won't have for long if we don't get some money together.'

'Money?' He sounded like it was the first time that he'd ever heard the word.

'Yeah, you know; pounds, shillings and pence, dough, bread, bunce, lolly.'

He had a think. 'Yeah, you're right. I'll get a job.'

Tempted as she was to say that there weren't many openings in the London job market for a dope-smoking, college dropout, Flo decided to keep the conversation business-like. 'No, that's not going to work. We can't stay here forever and do you know what it costs to rent a decent flat in this city and to afford the lifestyle I've become accustomed to? We aren't going to get that kind of cash with you putting on a paper hat and flogging burgers to chavs. No, we'll have to try something else, something a bit more ambitious.'

He leaned on his elbow and sighed heavily. 'Are you talking about me putting the screws on my mum to get a share of Nanna Babs' houses?'

That shook Flo up. Nicky was meant to be a lovesick teen she could bend to her will. 'Um . . . well . . .' she spluttered.

'I weren't born yesterday. When we started going out I always suspected you were after something—'

'I do like you.' And she did, that was the truth. But Nicky was also business and if there was one thing Stanley Miller had taught her it was never confuse the two.

'I like you too baby. You know how to have a laugh. But you've got to understand there's fuck all I can do to work on my mum. When it comes to Nanna Babs she's really protective and that includes anything that belongs to her.'

Flo slammed out, 'But those houses were my dad's. It's not fair that I'm cut out. I was his daughter too.'

She could feel her temper rising and rising. Those houses were the last piece of her dad she had. She couldn't lose them; it was the horror of losing Stan all over again.

'I'll go if you want me to,' Nicky offered.

Flo looked at him. Now he was of no use to her she should make him sling his hook.

'Florence dear,' The Commander called from downstairs, 'can you come down for a moment. My matchsticks have fallen on the floor and my old legs are rather tired.'

Her mind still on Nicky, she left the room. Ten minutes later she found him at the foot of the stairs with his belongings. Jezebel lurked behind him purring softly.

'Where do you think you're going?' Flo asked him furiously.

He gawped at her. 'I thought you wanted me to do one.'

She waltzed over to him and put on her winning smile. 'We're mates right?' He nodded, but still looked confused. 'And mates help each other out. I know you won't help me with the houses and that doesn't matter.' She wound her arms around his neck. 'But I'll help you out, so stay as long as you like.'

Forty-Six

Babs' eyes grew wide with alarm and her mouth formed a startled O. She managed to duck before the table tennis ball hit her bang in the face. It hurtled over her head and slammed into the wall behind. She peered up at Knox, her opponent on the other side of the table, and protested, 'Take it easy will ya. I don't know if you've noticed but I've got a broken finger.'

They were in the rec area, which hummed with the sound of women chatting, playing cards and chess and just taking it easy. It was most prisoners' favourite part of the day because there were no kangas standing over them telling them what to do.

Knox grinned, which looked more like a wolf getting ready to rip the flesh from its dead prey. 'It ain't my fault you've got two left hands Miller. Now straighten up and start playing.' Her feet almost danced from side to side like a boxer inside a ring, her bat pointed forward with the power of a shooter. 'I'm gonna take you down.'

Bloody hell's bells, Babs thought, deeply regretting ever saying she'd play a round with her personal bodyguard. Now she understood why the other women pretended to have something else to do when Knox asked if anyone fancied a game. All Babs had wanted to do was to keep herself busy, instead of worrying about the battle going on in her family. She still hadn't heard from the parole board, which was also doing her head in royally. Every day seemed to start with a slow tick-tock of the clock as she waited.

Babs located the ball, got back to the table. As she raised her bat Knox made a deep growling noise and cried, 'I'm gonna maul you Miller.'

Babs groaned inwardly as she hit the ball. The next fifteen minutes were gruelling and painful. So much for relaxing recreation! After being pinged painfully on her forehead she chucked the bat on the table and called it a day.

'You're a flippin' animal,' she shot at the other woman, who only started making squawking chicken noises as Babs walked away, shaking her head.

'Right, who's next?' Knox shouted menacingly as Babs took the metal stairs to her landing.

As soon as she reached her cell, she shut the door. Peace at last! She walked over to her TV, in the mood to watch some daytime telly, when her cell door opened again. Two prisoners she didn't know, but had seen around, waltzed inside and closed the cell door. They looked like a proper pair of toughs with large frames and stone cold faces.

Babs stammered, 'Can I help you two ladies?'

One answered in a surprisingly high, squeaky voice like a Munchkin, 'We've got a message for your girl Dee.'

'You mates of my daughter are ya?' Babs knew full well tthey weren't, but she planned to keep them talking until she found a way out of this.

Her plan went to pot. The one with large bug eyes rushed her, and before Babs knew it she was bashed into the wall, her head pulled so painfully back she thought her neck was going to snap.

'Fucking get off me,' she shouted.

Bug Eyes kneed her in the belly, making her gasp as the wind whooshed out of her. She clutched her middle.

Munchkin shoved her face so close to Babs she could see the tiny, red blood vessels in her eyes. 'Your girl has been trying to make a monkey of the wrong people.'

'Nah, that don't sound like my—'

'Shut the fuck up.' Babs whimpered as her hair was pulled harder until it felt like her scalp was coming away from her skull.

'What's the message you want me to give her?' she called out.

They both chuckled and Bug Eyes informed her in a steel voice, 'You're the message—'

'But I ain't done nuthin.'

'True,' Munchkin conceded, 'but that rank daughter of yours has.'

Babs continued to play for time. 'Whatever she's done I'll tell her to knock it on the head.'

'Too late for that. And orders is orders.'

She yelped as she was dragged towards her bathroom through the material that divided it from the main cell. Bugs twisted her head sideways over the sink.

'Now, I wouldn't want to make a mess,' said Munchkin as she pulled something out of her pocket. No, Babs cried mentally, they're gonna flippin' slit my throat and watch me bleed down the sink as I slowly die.

Then she noticed that what the woman had in her hand wasn't a homemade knife, but a bottle of baby oil. Babs was filled with horror because she knew that the clear liquid inside would be a mixture of urine and spit. The only reason it didn't include shit was because it turned the liquid another colour and the kangas would then suss what it was. Prisoners would leave the concoction to ferment until it was a rank, stinking mess. But that wasn't the only reason it was so feared – the bodily fluids meant it could carry some very deadly diseases. The last time Babs had seen Bug Eyes was when she was waiting to have her finger looked at and had overheard the quack talking to her tormentor about her HIV.

A fist came out of nowhere and slammed into the side of Babs' face. Her small world turned upside down as terrible pain ripped through her. Her jaw was grabbed and her mouth opened. No . . . No . . . They wouldn't . . .

'Time for some liquid refreshment,' Bugs' malicious voice rang around her head.

Babs willed herself to move but her body wasn't listening. The bottle was coming closer and closer. It reached her slack-jawed mouth. The evil woman started to press her thumbs against the plastic . . .

Then she was flying backwards along with the bottle. Babs slumped against the sink. And there she was, her hero, that animal Knox, grinding her teeth and flexing her fists.

'No one,' she ground out, 'No one touches my Babs.'

Bugs faced off, her voice dripping with scorn. 'No way you can take the two of us on Knox.'

In the following minutes Knox proved her wrong. She went at them with her fists, kicks and head butts and demolished both with her legendary one-two. The women lay in an unconscious, bloody heap on the concrete bathroom floor.

With a tenderness Babs would be eternally grateful for and didn't know she possessed, her saviour got her sat on her bed.

She inspected the injury to Babs' jaw. 'I've seen worse. It would be better if you don't see the quack.'

Babs knew what she wasn't saying; a visit to the doctor would raise questions she didn't want to answer. 'I'm alright.' She gazed fretfully towards the bathroom. 'What about them?'

Grim faced, Knox got up and dragged the still unconscious

women along the floor by their hair and dumped them, like rubbish, near the cell door. 'They'll understand which way the wind's blowing when they wake up.' She studied Babs closely. 'What the hell was all that about?'

Babs decided not to reveal what she'd been told. But as soon as it was lights-out she'd be on her mobile to Dee to find out what the fuck was going on.

Forty-Seven

Courtney's second session with Foxy was slightly different. They still met in the burger bar with some nosh – chicken burgers and shared coleslaw – but this time her counsellor asked her a question:

'Who's your favourite teacher?'

Courtney groaned. 'Do I have to have one?'

'It's up to you. My favourite teacher was Mrs Kendal, my history teacher.' Foxy smiled with memories. 'That woman knew how to make the past come alive.'

Courtney sucked on her mint-chocolate milkshake. 'Alright, I hate school, but Miss Patel is my P.E. teacher. She taught us all how to do a double back-flip.'

Foxy grinned. 'Why don't you show me how to do one?'

The straw popped out of Courtney's mouth with amazement. 'In here?'

'Why not? You can show everyone what a super talent you have.'

Courtney thought for a bit, but decided, 'Nah. I'd only make a show of myself.' She gazed shyly at her counsellor. ''Though I'm really good at it. Besides, you need to be safe and use a mat.'

Foxy stared shrewdly at her, but asked no more questions about school. They only talked about music and ate away. But at the end of the session Courtney couldn't help feeling she wasn't useless at everything. She was good at P.E.

'You gonna keep staring at it like it's an alien or you gonna open it up?' Kieran playfully asked Jen that night.

He watched Jen's eyes gleam with pleasure as she stared at the gold envelope he'd passed to her as they sat in The Lock having dinner. Usually he'd take his ladies to the private dining room, but he got the impression that Jen liked to be seen on his arm and he was happy to show her off. He felt bad that Babs wasn't too pleased about him wining and dining her girl, but this was business.

Jen beamed at him. There was no doubt about it, she was a stunning slice of womanhood. She was wearing a scarlet floaty Dior dress – off a warehouse job – that he'd gifted her last week. He smiled crookedly as he recalled how she'd tried it on, then lifted the hemline and climbed on his friend downstairs to show her gratitude.

She clutched the envelope. 'Are these the tickets to the Take That tour up in Manchester?' she trilled.

'Take That? Are you having a giggle bird? If anyone spotted me at a shindig for those teeny boppers my rep would be in the crapper.'

She laughed out loud, which made him smile. He liked hearing her laugh; it reminded him of Babs. 'Open the bloody thing and find out.'

With the delight of a kid in a sweetie shop Jen pulled out an elegant invitation card. She looked up at him, a glow of utter delight on her face. 'Oh Kieran babe, it's an all-expenses-paid trip to a spa.' Her voice choked up a bit. 'I've only ever been to a spa once, up at York Hall Swimming Baths.'

Kieran pushed his chest out, chuffed. 'You can forget about Bethnal Green, this is in Knightsbridge where they know how to treat a lady like a queen.'

'You total sweetheart.' She rushed around the table and dragged him into a deep hug.

'Steady on girl, I've still got to keep my reputation as a hard man.'

She let go with a little hiccup of a chuckle and sat down again. 'No one's ever done that for me before.'

He covered her hand with his, remembering all the times when he was growing up wild on The Devil and Babs had gone out of her way for him. Done things for him that no one had before. If it wasn't for her he wouldn't even be able to read the menu. Guilt took a seat at the table as he wondered what she would think about him using her daughter to find the gold. He couldn't deal with her thinking he had betrayed her. It tore him up to even think about it.

'Why don't we order some nosh,' he said quickly, to rid himself of guilty thoughts of his second mum. He raised a finger at one of the waiting staff and pointed to the bottle of almost empty Bolly on the table.

Kieran was a man who enjoyed simple food, so he ordered a plate of steak and chips and Jen settled on a fancy pasta dish on the menu.

Once they were tucking into their meal he got down to business. 'So, what's Dee's house like?'

'Fuck-off, as you would expect the home of John Black to be,' she answered, around a mouthful of penne. 'It's got all kinds of rooms with silly names. The Hollywood, Lover's Lane – if you can believe that.' She set her knife and fork down and stared wistfully into space. 'Mind you, I wouldn't say no to a gaff like that.'

'Does it have a basement or any outbuildings?'

She sent him a steely stare. 'Why all the interest in the nooks and crannies up at my sister's?'

'Oh, you know . . .'

'No I don't know. You wanna tell me?'

Jen was no fool. 'Dee – or rather John – has something that belongs to me. But your sister's giving me the old brush-off, swearing blind she knows nish.'

'What is it?'

'Nothing big. Just something personal I lent him a long time ago.'

A blush burned from her neck up to her cheeks. 'Is that why you're going out with me? To drill me for info?'

'I only go with the top sort of women Jen, that's why I'm seeing you.' And Jen was a pretty piece but there was something needy about her that put him in mind of his miserable childhood. He shook the feeling off as he reminded himself that she was a means to an end.

She glanced at him shyly from under lowered eyes. 'I ain't always had a great time of it.' Here we go – misery likes company! Kieran fixed his face into a fake smile 'You've got my full attention' as he indulged her. 'I tied the knot with a fella who used to beat me black and fucking blue and I've got the blood of Stanley Miller running through my veins. The days of me being scared shitless by anyone are long gone.' She sliced her finger twice in the air to emphasis the last two words. 'I fancy you something rotten Kieran, but I need to know whether you've had a chance to ask Mum about my girls' share of those houses.'

Kieran's thoughts turned sour. Frankly if he was in Babs' position he'd sell those houses, thumb his nose at the money-grabbing lot of 'em and take off on a jet set cruise round the world. But that's not what he told Jen. 'Of course your girls deserve a cut. Look, I didn't want to say nuthin to discourage you but Babs weren't best pleased when I had a word with her about it.' The truth was he hadn't mentioned it to her and had no intention of doing so. Jen might think she had him dangling from a bit of string, but the truth was he was the one who had her in limbo. As long as she thought he was going to put in a good word with Babs, he had time to suss out what she might know about Dee, John and the gold. He quickly added, 'But don't worry yourself about it. I'm gonna keep at your ol' mum until I wear her down.'

Her hand reached under the table and she cupped his cock. Squeezed. 'Thanks sweetheart . . .'

A shattering noise followed by a piercing scream came from the reception area. Kieran belted out of the restaurant. He crashed into one of the girls from reception who was running for her life. Her face was the picture of pure terror. He pushed past her and entered the front of the club. A window was broken and his bouncers and security were looking at something on the floor. The sound of a ticking clock filled the air.

He moved forward muttering, 'What the . . . Fuck!' On the floor was a bomb with a red digital clock ticking down.

60.

59.

58.

Kieran went into overdrive. He said urgently to his muscle, 'Get everyone out of here now.'

'But boss,' his head bouncer said, 'there won't be enough time.'

He roared, 'There won't be if you stand around like a fucking bunch of brainless mutts. Take 'em out the back. And not a word about what the problem was or I'll have your guts for garters.'

They ran, shouting at full volume for everyone to get out. Now.

Kieran nearly jumped out of his skin when a distressed Jen appeared by his side. 'What's going on?'

'Get the fuck outta here.' Seeing she was ready to argue he yelled, 'Now.'

Her gaze found the bomb and her mouth fell open. Her eyes jack-knifed to his. 'I ain't leaving you here with that. No way Kieran—'

'You don't get a fucking say in what I can and can't do with my life.' Her lips trembled at his harshness, but it needed saying. 'I'm not telling Babs one of her girls breathed her last on my watch. Now shift it.'

After one last frantic look at the bomb Jen scarpered back into the club. Kieran turned back to the device.

21.

20.

19.

No fucking way was he watching his beloved club get blasted to kingdom come. He'd spent years working his way up the criminal ladder and The Lock was his fuck-you statement that he'd made it. This was probably the stupidest thing he'd ever do in his life . . .

He ran forward, picked it up and sprinted outside. He headed across the road to lob it into the blackness of the Thames. He didn't know how long he had, but he kept going. And going. Almost there . . .

Then he tripped. Crashed to the ground and the bomb leapt from his hand. He could still see the clock.

4.

3.

He knew he was done for. When he was a kid, cops, teachers and social workers were all agreed he would come to a sticky end. Turned out they were right after all. At least he was going to go out with a bang; not many folk could say that. His only regret was that he hadn't got to kiss Babs ta-ra.

Kieran waited. And waited. Nothing happened. He gave it a couple more seconds. Still nothing. He almost crawled over to it but remembered he was the great Kieran Scott and it wouldn't do for anyone to see him on his knees. He got up and approached it. The clock had stopped ticking. Kieran jumped back as music started blaring – Spandau Ballet's 'Gold'.

The bomb was no bomb at all, but a dummy. Uncle Frank and the mysterious vault owner were turning the screws. This meant he had to pile on the pressure too – on Dee. She knew where the gold was and he wanted it back. He inhaled a blast of river air, then booted the bogus bomb with unleashed fury.

'Dee, what the effing hell is going on?' Babs asked her daughter quietly but firmly. She was sitting on the edge of her bed in her dark cell, the mobile held to the left side of her face because the other cheek was bruised from the earlier attack.

She compressed her lips when she noticed Dee's hesitation. 'I don't know what you mean. Everything's hunky dory.'

'Hunky dory my Aunty Nora.' She sucked in her breath as her face started to ache from the force of her words. 'I got jumped . . .'

'You what?'

'That's right. Two thugs tried to give me a good hiding, but someone sorted them out for me.' She hadn't told any of her girls about Knox. If they knew someone had to watch her back they'd only start to worry themselves silly.

Dee was beside herself with anger. 'No one puts their hands on my mum and gets away with it. You give me their names and I'll show them what it's like the next time I come up.'

'Funny thing was, the reason they were having a go was because they wanted to send a message to you.'

'What?' Her daughter sounded deflated instead of stunned.

'Said you'd made a monkey outta the wrong people. Now stop fobbing me off and give me the lowdown.'

Dee's breath galloped down the line. 'I'm really sorry Mum. I'd hoped that you'd never find out.'

'Find out what?'

'You know I loved John to bits, but the pillock only went and organised a robbery . . .'

'Are you talking about that gold?'

'How do you know about that?'

'We do have TVs in here you know. What was he thinking?'

She could almost feel Dee shake her head. 'And you know who his partner in crime was? Bloody Kieran Scott.'

'My Kieran?' Her eyes grew wide. She was about to say no way but then she remembered his line of business, the truth she'd always found hard to come to terms with. 'But how did he know John?'

'That don't matter. What does is Kieran and the owner of the gold think I know where it is, which I swear on my life I don't. Now Jen's thrown her lot in with him . . . I'm sorry Mum but as far as I'm concerned she's dead to me.' Babs could feel her heart breaking. Her family was falling apart. 'And, of course,' Dee raved on, 'she's after her share of the houses for her kids. This ain't a good situation Mum, not good at all.'

Those bloody houses again! Her instincts had been right when she'd first told the girls, anything that came via Stanley Miller could only be a bad luck charm. But she didn't mention that. 'Who's the gold's owner?'

'Not the foggiest. Uncle Frank says he's a not right and it's gonna be a one-way street of pure badness if he don't get it back.'

The alertness for sounds that Babs had developed since she'd been inside kicked in. She could hear distant footsteps on the wing landing. 'One of the kangas is on the prowl. You look after yourself.' Then she punched off.

Babs tucked her mobile under her pillow, snuggled into bed and quickly shut her eyes. The footsteps got closer and then, mercifully, kept going on their merry way. She gazed sadly at the ceiling. What was happening to her family? Jen and Dee against each other, Tiff against Jen, Nicky hand in glove with that bitch Flo. And Kieran smack bang in the middle of it. It was him she was most angry at. She'd told him point blank to stay away from her daughters. Babs almost called him up but decided against it; what she had to say to him had to be done face to face. She loved that boy but when she saw him there was going to be a reckoning.

Forty-Eight

'You ready then?' Tiffany asked Dee the following morning.

Impatiently she dangled the car keys in front of Dee, who was stretched out on her prized chaise longue. Dee had a couple of cucumber slices over her eyes and was resting, although she'd only been up a few hours. Tiffany had got alarmed when she'd seen Dee chucking up one morning and didn't understand why her sister wasn't on the blower to the doctor's. Tiff didn't understand why Dee kept insisting nothing was up so she'd taken matters into her own hands and booked an appointment.

'Oh that?' Dee didn't move. 'I told you I don't need to go.'

'Come on babe, move your arse or they'll give your booking away to some old dear and her on-going lumbago problem and then we'll have to sit there all day.'

Dee snatched the cucumber slices off her eyes and glared at her sister. 'I told you, I'm not going.' Her gaze zeroed in on something. 'Hold up a minute, has someone moved the fish food?' Tiff looked at the packet on the floor and shrugged. 'I always leave it right by the tank . . .'

'Stuff the tank, you're going to the doc's.'

'No can do. I've cancelled it.'

Tiff nearly jumped out of her skin. 'Cancelled it? Are you nuts?' She pulled out her mobile and called the private clinic.

'Yeah hello, my sister had an appointment this morning which she rang to blow out. Well, she's taken a turn—'

'I'm pregnant,' Dee cut over her softly. '*Fallen for a baby* as Aunty Cleo would say. I'm four months gone.'

'You're in the club?' Tiff terminated the call. 'After all these years? How is that even possible?'

Dee gazed at her with an arched brow. 'Don't you know how a girl gets pregnant? I know you bat for the other side but I'd have thought even you would have heard something about what happens along the way.'

'Poor John.' Tiff parked on the sofa opposite. 'And he never knew. Although that would have scotched the rumours anyway.'

Dee got furious on her dead husband's behalf. 'What rumours?'

'No disrespect sis but word on the street was that John was a Jaffa. Firing blanks. Although it was a very quiet word for obvious reasons.'

Dee collected herself. 'We always assumed he had a problem coz his previous wives never got up the spout. And in the end we thanked God for giving us Nicky and that was enough.' She laid her palm protectively over her tummy. 'This baby's a miracle for me and John.' Her voice became fierce. 'You hear anyone say anything to the contrary, they're a fucking liar.'

'What kind of lies?' Tiff enquired in a very different tone. 'Like you were diddling away from home with some other bloke?'

Dee's gaze appeared wild. 'I never said that . . .'

Tiff turned on her. 'Yes you fucking did, more or less. Who they saying you went with? Because . . .' Her voice dribbled away as she read her sister's guilty face. 'Oh Puhleeeeeeze – don't tell me the baby isn't John's? Don't tell me you really were playing away?'

Dee was defensive, ashamed and angry all at the same time. 'It was just once, right. I lost my head and was a tad tipsy. It didn't mean fuck all.'

'Fuck all indeed,' her sister blasted back. 'So who's the proud daddy?'

Dee turned nasty. 'Don't take the moral high ground with me little missy. You're one to talk. You've played enough dirty strokes in your time.'

'But I'm talking about you and John. You loved that man to bits. I used to look at you two sometimes and wish I could find my dream girl just like you'd found your dream fella.'

Dee did the one thing she rarely ever did – started sobbing. But Tiff remained in her seat offering no comfort, shell-shocked by her big sister's revelations. Finally, Dee looked at her as she sniffed the tears and the pain away. 'Truth is I . . .' She clammed up.

Although her tone was more forgiving, Tiff still let rip: 'You might as well spit it out. I'm gonna suss out soon enough who the bloke with the wandering dick is.'

Finally Dee broke her silence. 'Well, let's put it like this, who would be the worst possible father at this particular juncture?'

Tiffany's voice fell to a whisper again. 'Oh, please don't say Kieran, that would be too much.' It sounded like a joke but when she got no answer, Tiffany sat back in her seat and closed her eyes. 'For fuck's sake.'

The words tumbled out and Dee whined, 'It weren't my fault. He was hanging around with John and it just sorta happened. John obviously didn't want me to know who he was, he introduced him as a golfing partner and builder called Tom. The day we did the dirty he let slip what his real name was. I finished with him on the spot, banned him from the house and told John how much I hated the little bastard.' Her face crumbled. 'John guessed though . . .'

'You're joking.'

Dee shook her head. 'He said it didn't matter. That the baby's his.' She turned to her sister with a fierce gleam in her eyes. 'And that's how it is Tiff, you get me? If I hear anyone say different I know where it came from.'

Tiff's face softened. 'Get a load of bad boy Kieran. First he goes with you, now Jen. Fuck me, if I was straight I expect he'd be wanting a go at my vag too.'

They both laughed, breaking the tension in the room.

Dee lifted her head slightly as she heard a noise outside. Her face lit up. 'Maybe it's Nicky. Maybe he's driven her so mad she's chucked him out.'

On the drive outside, a motorbike could be heard ambling its way up the gravel. It pulled up but the motor was left idling. Dee went to the door to see who the visitor was.

But before she could open it, the house seemed to come down around their ears. There was a continuous roar while the windows upstairs crashed in one after the other, brickwork and walls were blasted and the interiors shattered. It took a few seconds before Dee realised what was happening – someone was machine gunning the house. She turned to Tiffany, whose face was contorted in terror, and grabbed her, pulling her to the floor.

She shouted, 'We need to get out back, downstairs will be next.' Hugging the floor, Dee dragged Tiff down the hallway to the kitchen.

She was right. After a long pause, the motorcyclist opened fire again, demolishing the downstairs windows and thudding bullets into the wooden door. There was another long pause before the motorbike revved again and made its escape down the drive.

They remained on the floor in silence.

Tiff gripped the tile as if she was afraid she might fall off it. She slowly switched her terror-stricken gaze to her sister. 'Someone just tried to kill us.'

Dee got slowly to her feet and Tiff was surprised that she didn't look particularly scared. 'Did you hear what I said?' Her voice rose in disbelief.

'I heard you.' She held her hand out and helped Tiff to her wobbly legs. 'Relax sis, the geezer wasn't here to kill anyone. It's a message.' She walked off to inspect the damage muttering. 'Three men want to give me a message – Uncle Frank, Carats or Kieran.'

Tiffany was white and shaking like a smoker who had just given up. 'What you gonna do?'

Dee pursed her lips. 'John taught me in this type of situation you need to be as patient as a cat creeping up on a bird. So I'm gonna call a glazier and a plasterer.' Dee surveyed the damage to her beloved house. 'Then I'm gonna let my feelings be known.'

'What the fuck do ya want?' Flo blasted out, reverting to her Cockney heritage, when the man appeared at her and Nicky's table.

They were in a trendy café in Portobello Market. It was the kind of place that dished up food to turn Nicky's stomach, like lentil and beetroot soup and spinach salad that looked like a bowl of leaves raked up from the garden. He'd said nothing because Flo liked the place. He was glad for the interruption because Flo was still asking him questions about his parents and those houses. She was starting to do his head right in.

Nicky had never seen the man before in his life. He looked slightly younger than his dad and had a small scar on the bridge of his nose. The man glared at Flo. 'What did you say to me bird?'

Nicky wasn't having that, even though Flo had enough nuts to fight her own battles. 'Watch your lip with my girl,' he warned.

Instead of fronting up the man grinned. 'I thought as much. You're just like your old dad.'

'You knew John?'

The man shook his head. 'Chris. You are Chris Keston's boy?'

Nicky's heartbeat did a strange little dance. 'You knew my dad?' Then he remembered, 'But everyone says I look like my mum.'

The stranger cocked his head to the side. 'She was a gorgeous, classy lady. Gentle and kind-hearted. You look like her alright, but Chris is staring right at me as well.'

Nicky got excited. 'Pull up a chair.'

As the newcomer did so Flo rose out of hers. 'I'll see you back at The Commander's when you and fuck face there have finished.' She chucked a filthy look at the man before she was gone.

'A bit of a livewire your girl,' the stranger said. 'My mum would give me a right clump for having such bad manners. The name's Mal.'

They shook hands. Nicky's eyes widened with delight as Mal explained how he'd met his blood father and some of the antics they'd got up to. He loved hearing these East End tales; it was a world he was desperate to get into. His mum would blow her stack, but he was a grown man and could make his own decisions.

Finally Mal said, 'Look son, great meeting you but I've gotta get off.' He tapped his nose. 'I'm in the middle of a deal, know what I mean?'

Nicky's excitement grew. 'What kind of deal?'

Mal leaned in close. 'First rule of the life is you don't ever give out that piece of info. But seeing as how you're Chris's lad . . . Let's just say I'm in the removal bizz. I've gotta move something from A to B.'

Nicky was spellbound. 'What?'

'Let's just say that if I get nabbed it will probably only be a fine and a slap on the wrist.'

Nicky was really into the 'Let's just say' way of talking about business. Made it sound secretive and daring.

'I like you kid,' Mal said, smiling, showing his crooked front teeth. 'Let's just say when the time is right I might need an extra pair of hands and give that person a bell.'

Nicky didn't hesitate. He nodded, knowing his mum would kill him if she ever found out.

Forty-Nine

At Courtney's third session with Foxy they decided to both go for the big burger meal, which was large fries with peri peri sauce, double cheeseburger and a soft drink of choice.

'I got taken to the cops for shoplifting when I was twelve,' Foxy said openly.

Courtney just stared and stared at her as if Foxy were in handcuffs. 'What did you nick?'

'A selection of pick-n-mix sweets from Woollies.'

Courtney bit her lip then asked with curiosity. 'Why did you do it?'

'My mother died and I missed her.'

The breath hissed in Courtney's chest. She didn't know what to say. Although her mum got right on her wick sometimes the thought of her dying when she was young made her throat clog up. She found the courage to ask, 'What did she die of?'

Foxy put her burger down. 'One day she had a cold and before I knew it she had pneumonia. Do you know what that is?' Courtney shook her head, feeling sad. 'It's when a bad cold gets in your lungs and chest. She was a fighter my mum.' She picked up her burger again and took a bite, then gently asked, 'Who's the fighter in your family? The one you look up to?'

Courtney didn't hesitate. 'My Nanna Babs. She ... She ...' She couldn't go on. The tears felt like they were bubbling all over her body.

Foxy touched a single finger against one of Courtney's hands. 'No matter. We can talk about Nanna Babs when you're ready.' She pulled her finger away and added, 'I'd like for us to meet tomorrow again if that's OK with you?'

This was the life! Jen let out an *Ahhhh* of pure delight as she enjoyed the luxurious spa massage. She was lying down, totally starkers, covered from head to toe in a thick layer of seaweed. A transparent material was wrapped tight around her body, securing her legs and arms and turning her into a green mummy. The masseuse had said that the plastic was needed to allow the 'positive energy and ions' from the seaweed to seep into the pores of Jen's skin; more like stop the seaweed from dribbling off, she thought. But nothing could dampen her dog with two dicks mood. She hadn't felt this cheery in aeons.

Kieran Scott knew how to treat a lady. He had dosh in spades to splash out. The spa was on the top floor of an exclusive hotel in Knightsbridge. Despite being a Londoner, Jen had never been to this part of town before. Back in the day she'd cruised up West with Bex, but usually to Oxford Street and Bond Street to check out the latest fashion. That prick of an ex of hers had only introduced her to Soho's nightlife. Knightsbridge had been for poshos and she wasn't one of them, so why would she go there? But as soon as she entered the hotel she knew she'd been missing out big time. It was all marble floors and huge mirrored walls. And the smell ... Mmmm! Jen's jaw had dropped when she looked at the cost of the treatments; nothing under two hundred nicker.

Kieran was the bloke she'd been looking for all her life. He showered her with bling, high-end clobber and had even sorted out the neighbour who played head-banging music at all hours. She felt like the young Jen again, the girl who had turned her nose up at the loser lads on The Devil and set her sights on a bloke with bigger ambitions. Except this time around she didn't mind if that drive was rooted in the world of dirty deeds. A man's got to make a living, right? Plus, he'd promised to have a word with her mum – who adored him – to nudge her in the right direction about the houses.

She let out a sigh of heavenly pleasure as the masseuse's fingertips rubbed her scalp with soothing, gentle strokes. Now that's what you called class. Ah yeah, this was the effing life. A delightful shiver went through her as the woman laid two sweet potato slices over her eyes.

'Relax. Rest,' the woman said in a soft, throaty voice. 'Let the chi take you on a journey.' Jen didn't have a clue what the chi was but if it was anything like the quality fizz they kept topping up she was more than happy for it to take her anywhere it wanted. 'I will leave you now and come back in twenty minutes.'

The woman put on some airy-fairy music that reminded Jen of a Jackie Chan movie she'd seen once and then left. She smiled and then drifted into sleep . . .

A noise woke her up. Blimey, had twenty minutes come and gone already? She heard the masseuse's footsteps around the room.

'I let myself go like you said. That chi thing was pure bliss.' Jen grinned. 'Can we do that coconut shell treatment now?'

'Oh, I've got a load of treatments lined up that you won't forget in a hurry babes.'

Jen's eyes pinged open in alarm, forgetting she'd covered them with potato slices. She tried to move but couldn't because her legs and arms were tightly bound by the plastic. The potato slices were ripped off to reveal Dee, her face hard and determined.

'What you doing here?' Jen asked, still trying to wriggle madly out of the plastic. It wouldn't budge.

'Last I heard it was a free country. When I showed my greenbacks at the door the owners of this very grand establishment were only too pleased to welcome me.' But her half-sister was completely dressed. Jen knew she was up to no good.

'I don't want no agg.'

'You, my girl, should've thought about that before that arse-wipe you're fucking pulled that cunt stunt at my gaff.'

'Someone sent a dummy bomb to his club. Was that you? All the guy wants is his property back.'

'I don't bloody have it. How many times have I got to say this?'

Jen twisted her mouth. 'If you agree to give my girls a share of Mum's houses maybe I can talk Kieran around for you.'

Disbelief clouded Dee's face. 'All you can think about is me, me, me. My yard got sprayed with lead. My boy could've got hurt. Bloody hell, Tiff was in the house as well.'

Jen cut her eye at Dee. 'Last I heard, Nicky's shacked up with Dad's slag of a daughter and as for Tiff, well, she could do with a bullet or two up her aris to keep her in her place.'

'Are you for real? You're chatting on about your family, your own flesh and blood.'

Jen scoffed. 'What? The same flesh and blood that are trying to diddle my girls outta their inheritance? The same flesh and blood who were happy for me to be a drudge and chuck pennies my way like I was a monkey in the zoo? My days of being played for a chimp are over.'

The stunned expression vanished from Dee's face. She pulled out a ciggy and lit up. She inhaled deeply, leaned forward and blew the smoke straight into Jen's face, making her start coughing and choking. 'You'll be sorry.' Cough. Cough. 'Kieran's here, so you wanna turn your shit around and fuck off back to Essexville.'

Dee straightened up, a small smile twisting the corner of her mouth. 'No he ain't. Know how I know? I've had someone following you for a couple of days. Like I said, it's funny what a few greenbacks can get you these days.'

'Piss. Off.'

Instead Dee started looking around the candle-lit room. 'Now, I'm thinking . . . what's the best treatment to remind you what happens to people who step outta line.' She muttered the words under her breath as if speaking to herself.

Jen started bricking it. Dee was a caring mum and wife but she was also known for being a complete nutter. 'You touch me . . .'

'And what sister dearest? You gonna pull my hair out? Duff me over?' She ran her eyes mockingly over the plastic around Jen's body. 'Looks to me like you're only in a position to run that poisonous mouth of yours.'

Jen thought about rolling off, but she might hurt herself when she landed on the hard floor. She stayed put and watched her eldest sister with a wary eye.

Dee used a large pair of tongs to pick up a hot stone from a machine that looked like a hair curler heater. She waved it at Jen. 'Now I could shove this down your gob to sort out that bitter tongue of yours.'

'Dee . . .'

'Nah.' Dee let the stone drop to the floor with a heavy bang. 'Let's see what else we've got here.' Jen's fretful and fearful gaze followed her until she stopped near a machine on wheels. She dragged it across the room to a twitching Jen. With glee Dee unhooked a large pen attachment and held it up. 'I hear one of these laser hair remover thingies hurts like a bitch.' She moved it close to Jen's face. 'They can also burn a nasty scar right into the skin. One of my mates went to an iffy salon to get hers done and ended up with a face that looked more like a piece of toast.'

Jen held her breath, her heart beating like the clappers as Dee moved it closer and closer to the skin under her right eye.

But Dee suddenly dropped it, leaving it swinging from its machine. 'Nah. Let's see what other beauty treatments us ladies torture ourselves with.'

'Dee, you're gonna regret this, you mad bitch.'

Her sister levelled a steady eye on her. 'Oh, I'm a mad bitch alright. You seem to have forgotten that.' A few seconds later she came back holding a jug with steam coming out of it. 'Do you know what this is?'

'Dee, you've made your point.'

Her sister ignored her. 'It's hot wax. I've decided that little Jen here needs a Brazilian she will never forget.'

Now Jen did start to try to roll off, but Dee gripped her legs effectively with one hand. With the other she held the wax above her sister's bush. 'Think about it, every time that polyester gangster gives you a portion you'll be hurting so much all you'll be thinking about is me.' A wide smile split her face.

'No!' Jen screamed.

Dee poured the hot wax all over the plastic covering Jen's vagina. Thank God it wasn't hot enough to melt through the plastic – the machine must be on a low setting.

Dee slung the jug into the corner. 'You wanna be giving this plastic some love, coz if it weren't there I would've poured wax up your family-betraying pussy.' She leaned over Jen again. 'I want you to give that cunt a message. Tell him to stop with the hard man routine or he's gonna be saying his prayers in hell a lot quicker than he thinks. I don't have no gold.'

Jen gazed at her, filled with confusion. 'What gold?'

Dee sneered. 'He'll know what I mean.'

Jen seethed with fury as Dee moved towards the door. Then her sister turned back. 'And I've got a P.S. for you. You should never, ever forget that family always comes first.'

Fifty

Satisfied with a job well done Dee got in her car. She turned the radio to a station pumping out some old style lovers' rock reggae, Susan Cadogan's 'Hurts So Good'. She was in the mood for something mellow after putting Jen back in her box. The bloody cheek of her! Dee pushed her disgraceful sister from her mind. She started shaking her shoulders to the tune and singing along with the chorus. She swung her motor into a side street where the traffic was slight and there was only one car behind her.

Her face creased up with confusion when she heard a popping sound. Suddenly the car swerved and she tried her best but she couldn't control it. Desperately she turned the steering wheel, but the car wouldn't play ball. There was another popping sound and the car skidded across the road and then flipped into the air.

A bewildered and aching Dee woke up to piercing fluorescent lights in the ceiling above her, which instantly made her snap her eyes shut again. Where am I? What am I doing here? Then it started coming back to her – tormenting Jen, getting in her motor . . . The pain hissed in her throat as she remembered.

A gentle hand touched her shoulder, making her eyes spring open again. A young, male nurse was looking at her. She was in the hospital.

Her hand clamped over her tummy with motherly protection. 'My baby?' Oh God! If anything had happened to John's unborn child . . . A few tears leaked from the corner of her eye.

'Your baby's fine.' Dee relaxed back with a relief she'd never felt in her life before. 'You were in a car accident.' The nurse smiled, a small one of reassurance. 'But you're fine. You've got some very minor cuts to your face but they should heal in no time without any scarring. We've put a neck brace on you as a precaution.'

An urgent voice shouted from the doorway, 'Dee? Bloody hell.' And then Tiffany was standing next to her. Her eyes were wild and her face chalk white. 'What happened? Is the baby . . .?' Her hand clapped over her mouth, stifling the rest of her words like they were too awful to give voice to.

'Little John's alright. I'm alright.' Dee glanced at the nurse. 'Can I go home?'

He nodded. 'But you have to take it easy. I'm going to give you some pain medication that you should take every four hours.'

After he had gone, with her sister's help Dee sat up and swung her legs over the bed. The neck brace made her move awkwardly. Her body felt sore, but she'd been in worse situations, far worse.

'What happened?' Tiff asked.

Dee got to her feet with Tiff supporting her on one side. 'One minute I'm driving and then all of a sudden I hear these popping noises. Then all hell breaks loose and I'm flying in the air like Mary Poppins.'

'Oh babe. Sounds like your tyres must've gone.' Tiff would know, with her years of experience working in a garage.

Dee gazed at her strangely. 'But my motor only had its MOT the other day. Everything, including the tyres, was bang on point.'

Tiff curved her arm round her as they walked carefully to the door. 'Don't you worry your head about nish,' Tiff soothed, 'we're taking you straight home for a proper chillout and rest.'

'No.' Dee would have shaken her head with firm determination if she wasn't wearing the neck brace.

'Whatcha mean "no"?'

'There's something we need to do first.'

If Tiffany had been watching her face she would've realised there was more bovver brewing.

'What the fuck do you mean you're gonna do eff all about it,' Jen blasted with disbelief at Kieran.

They stood on the balcony of his flat in Chelsea with its breathtaking view of the harbour. Courtney and Little Bea were watching a movie inside the main room. Jen had closed the door to make sure that her convo with Kieran was kept private.

'Just cool it, alright?' he told her.

'Cool it? Fucking cool it?' Jen's tone was hot and hard. 'Your girlfriend gets attacked by someone in a spa. A spa, I might add, you got her invited to.'

Kieran took a leisurely puff of his ciggy, which made Jen even madder. It was like he couldn't be arsed with what she was telling him.

'A woman? Jen, it was your sister, Dee.'

'Who would've, if she'd had time, shoved a hot stone down my throat.'

Kieran snickered. Jen saw red. She reared towards him. 'Oh, you think it's bloody funny do ya?'

'Come on Jen.' He didn't hold back his laughter this time. 'A hot stone? Not like she was gonna put you six foot under with that.'

'You don't know Dee.'

Kieran's laughter disappeared in a heartbeat. 'That's where you're wrong. I know Dee Black. Inside and out.'

Jen didn't like the sound of that. She couldn't put her finger on it but there was something in between his words that made her feel uncomfortable. Something he wasn't letting on about. Jen opened her mouth to find out what but quickly shut it. She didn't want to get his dander up, she wanted him to sort out that thug of a daughter of her mum's. That's what Dee was, after all: Babs' daughter. She'd only been in Jen's life for the last three years so she reasoned she was hardly a sister at all.

'Then you know what I'm going on about,' Jen started up again. 'She needs putting in her place. For fuck's sake, she threatened to do me – your bird – over and made a right plank outta you with that bomb stunt, despite swearing blind that she had eff all to do with it.'

He squinted at her. 'She said what?'

'You heard. That she never sent the bomb that never was.' Jen puffed her chest out. 'Course I don't believe her and told her the same to her lying face.'

Kieran gave her the eye. 'You just worry about looking pretty on my arm. Leave the rest to me.'

'The rest to you?' Jen sneered as she reared to her full height. 'I've been asking – begging – you, morning, noon and effing night to have a word in Mum's ears about the houses . . .'

'You know I've already done it and I've said I'm gonna give it another shot.' If Jen had known Kieran better she would've sussed by his tight tone that she was pushing him to the edge of letting rip.

She got in his face. 'When? Bloody hell, the second coming will be here before you finally tell Mum what's what.' Spit flew from her mouth. 'What are you scared of? That Babs will paddle her little boy Kieran's bum if he dares to ask her a question?'

His face turned purple at the insult. 'Jen . . .'

But Jen was in her own bitter world, too far gone to leave well alone. 'You need to start manning up. I want that money for my kids. Dee's pissing all over you—'

His hands gripped her arms like bands, so suddenly she didn't see it coming. He heaved her close to him until she was on her tiptoes. Froth bubbled at the corner of his mouth as he finally let rip. 'The last person who had the brass to tell me to man up ain't among the living anymore, know what I mean? I said I'd have a whisper in Babs' ear and I will. Same goes to your loud mouth cretin of a sister Dee. We'll have our day of reckoning – on my terms.' His hands tightened. 'You wanna be careful, Jennifer. You're living it up at a great height now, so you wanna be careful of tripping up. It's a long way down.'

Instead of being scared witless her eyes blazed back. 'Is that what you wanna do? Belt me one?'

His hands abruptly fell from her like they'd been burnt. 'I never said—'

'Go ahead,' she goaded him, her breathing harsh. 'Do your worst. I've been beaten from one end of Mile End to the next and I ain't just talking about my ex-arsehole of an old man. That's how my family have been treating me for yonks, like something that needs kicking to the kerb.' She shook her hair back. 'Well, I ain't putting up with it no more. I'll say it again, Kieran – and you can shout the odds as much as you like – if you're a man, start behaving like you've got a dick and a pair between those thighs of yours. Dee's rubbing your face royally in the crap to the max. Do something the fuck about it.'

Courtney hid by the balcony doors on the floor listening to her mum and that Kieran talking. She didn't like her mum's new fella, not one bit. Alright, so he bought her and Little Bea lots of prezzies and flashed the cash, but she didn't like the way her mum behaved all desperate around him. She didn't like her mum's new hairdo either; made her look like a flippin' skin-head. She did have to admit that Kieran never laid a hand on her mum. Her dad had treated her like a personal punch bag. She wanted them to have more money so she could buy clothes her mates would envy but she didn't want Kieran to be the one supplying it.

'Can I turn the film off? It's boring,' Little Bea called out.

Her younger sister was curled up on the sofa, book tucked close to her, one hand already reaching for the remote.

'Do what you want,' Courtney threw back sulkily. 'I don't even wanna be in his crummy flat.'

Little Bea turned the telly to one of the satellite crime chan-nels and her face gleamed as she watched a programme called *Snapped: Women Who Kill.* The show took Courtney storming back to the terrible memories of the day her grandfather had died. Her tummy clenched and she started sweating. She quickly picked up the glass next to her, filled with coke but also brandy she'd swiped from Kieran's drinks cabinet, after him and her mum had gone on the balcony.

Desperately she guzzled the drink down as her ears pricked up at her mum and Kieran's conversation. Aunty Dee? Bomb? Gold? Share of the houses? What houses? Her mum and wonderful Aunty Dee had had a barney and weren't talking to each other. Courtney knew all these problems were down to her. If she'd told her mum about her secret maybe none of this would've happened. She hated watching her family fall apart. Finishing her drink, Courtney decided she had to do some-thing about it.

Then she rose to her feet as her mum and him came back in the room.

Mum stared at the TV in horror. 'What the hell's this you're watching?' Her face grew outraged when a very grisly crime scene came on the screen. She got the remote, snapped the telly off and then rounded on her youngest. 'This is your doing, ain't it?'

Courtney watched her mum march over to her little sister. She snatched up Bea's book, a hardback of the latest Harry Potter, and flicked it open to find the real book she was reading.

Courtney caught her baby sister's skittish gaze. *You're done for now.*

Their mum flicked to the front cover. 'Christ almighty, *Lady Killers*!' She pierced her youngest with a disapproving gaze. 'Don't think I don't know what you've been reading all this time. I only let you because it's helped get you such blindin' grades.'

Little Bea looked at her and whispered, 'Did you know that they never caught Jack the Ripper?'

As her mum started kicking off again, Courtney stiffened her resolve. Her family was really cracking up and she knew what she had to do.

Fifty-One

Tiff had pleaded with Dee but she wouldn't see reason and go home. Instead she'd made her drive to the garage in Bethnal Green where Tiff had once earned a crust as a mechanic. Tiff would always be grateful to the former owner, Richie Watson, for taking her under his wing and making a woman out of a tearaway. Now his two sons were in charge, a right pair of chancers who'd steadily run the old place down. Well, that's how Tiff saw it.

When they drove into the garage Tiff noticed that it was deserted except for one man; clearly Dee didn't want recorded whatever they were doing here by more than one set of ears. The man was one of Richie's sons, Big Ron. There was nothing big about him except that gob he liked to run. He was standing next to a covered vehicle.

As soon as they got out of the car he was all over Dee. 'Mrs Black, my heart nearly broke when I heard about Mister Black.' Tiffany rolled her eyes. What a drama queen!

Dee went up to him. 'My John said that you're a man who knows when to keep that,' she touched her mouth, 'shut.'

He puffed his chest out. 'He got that right. My mouth can sometimes let me down, but not when it came to John's business.'

Dee eyed him shrewdly. 'Now that wouldn't happen to be coz my old man knew a secret or two that you wouldn't want broadcast in the *East London Advertiser*?'

He blanched. 'Mrs Black, I'm sure I don't know what you're talking about.' Clearly trying to distract her, he acknowledged Tiff for the first time. 'So how's my little Tiff doing?'

She folded her arms and stared him out, stubbornly keeping her mouth zipped. Since when had she been his little anything? As soon as Richie had passed the business on, his sons had treated her like she was a pack donkey, working her from dusk until dawn. Little shit!

Dee stared at the covered car. 'Did you have any trouble getting it?'

He chuckled away. 'I know everyone Mrs Black. A few choice words in the right ear and it's in the palm of my hand.'

He grabbed the edge of the cover and pulled. Tiff's mouth dropped when she saw Dee's car. Fucking hell, it was a total write-off. The top was crushed and the windows smashed to pieces. Good grief, how had Dee survived this crash with only a few cuts and bruises?

Tiff frowned. 'I don't get it. What are we doing here?'

Big Ron gave her a scathing look. 'I see not much has changed. You never got it then and you don't get it now.' He finished with a sniff.

Tiffany opened her mouth to give him what for but her sister got there before her. 'So what's your verdict?'

Big Ron hunkered down near the tyres. He might be a knob-head but Tiffany had to concede he was an expert on cars. He pointed to the tyre. 'To the untrained eye it looks like you've got a flat, but someone who's been in the business as long as me knows that—'

With dread, Tiffany finally understood what was going on. She could see the evidence herself. She completed his sentence in a daze. 'Someone shot out the wheels of your car.'

As soon as they got indoors Dee yanked off the neck brace and threw it across the hallway.

'Dee, I don't think you should be doing that,' Tiff warned.

But her sister took not a blind bit of notice as she stalked up the stairs. Alarmed, Tiff followed her. Dee had refused to answer her questions on the way home. She'd set her face into a chilling mask that could only mean trouble.

'This is getting out of hand Dee,' she said quickly. 'Someone's gonna get hurt, maybe the baby. Tell Kieran where his fucking gold is.'

Dee snapped round so forcefully that Tiff stumbled back. 'I don't know where it is. But believe me, if I did Kieran would be the last person I'd get on the blower to.'

'How do you know it was him that did that to your motor?'

Dee screwed her mouth up, which wasn't a pretty sight. 'Believe me, I know.' She pointed to a framed photo of her, John and a young Nicky on the wall. 'Do you see that?'

Tiff was puzzled. 'What?'

'It's wonky. I've got a thing about all the pictures being hung straight.' She walked over and put it right.

'Maybe it got like that after that guy shot up the place. Mind you, there's been so much toing and froing around here, a picture out of place is the least of it.'

Dee made no comment as she took herself into her bedroom. She went to her dressing table and opened up a beautiful, satin green jewellery box. She took out four chunky rings and placed them on top of the dressing table.

'I used to wear these back in the day. If anyone gave me any jip I'd clobber them and these beauties here would cut their face.' She picked them up. 'When I married John I put them away. You know, a sign that my punching-people-out days were over.'

Setting her mouth into a determined line she placed each ring on a finger of her right hand and vowed, 'If Kieran comes after me again, it's game on.'

Fifty-Two

'Will you friggin' listen to me . . .' Babs tried to get a word in edgeways as she spoke to Pearl Hennessy the following day.

She had the volume on *Loose Women* hiked up to mask the forbidden conversation she was having. She was taking a real chance doing it during the daytime.

'Will you give it a break for a minute,' she slammed out. She looked heavenward as Pearl was finally mercifully silent. 'Now listen—' But she got no further because C Wing Queen Knox Benson abruptly swung into her cell and closed the door. Startled, Babs tried to shove the phone out of view and cut the call at the same time, but her splinted finger made her clumsy and it clattered onto the floor.

'I've warned you to be watchful with that,' Knox said. 'You could get the lot of us in deep shit.'

Babs leaned down but the other woman got there first and covered it with her foot. 'That belongs to me now.'

'Eh? I thought you said our mutual friend gave it to me for my exclusive use?'

Knox scooped it up. 'Get you, exclusive use. Where do you think you are? In the VIP lounge at some *ex-clu-siff* club in Benidorm?' She rolled her eyes like Babs was the stupidest person alive. 'That was then and this is now. Word is that the kangas have got some fancy machine to monitor if anyone is making calls from a mobile and jamming signals. So unless you want another couple of years added to your stretch you'll let me do a vanishing trick.'

Babs chewed her bottom lip. The mobile had been her lifeline to the world outside – although her daughters were currently giving her calls the bum's rush – and after the battle lines had been drawn around John's deathbed she needed to know what was going on. And, of course, there was the gold.

The door opened. Knox spun to face Babs and shoved the mobile down her bra.

'Alright Miss,' Babs greeted Mrs Morris, one of the nicer POs on the wing. She was new to the job, an eager beaver who believed much more in rehabilitation than punishment.

She looked suspiciously between Babs and Knox. 'Benson, you're not giving Babs here a hard time?'

'Me Miss?' she answered sweetly, her eyes widening innocently. 'We were just watching *Loose Women* together. That Gloria Hunniford has got a right lovely voice.' She shifted her gaze to Babs. 'Be seeing ya Miller.'

Mrs Morris moved closer. 'Are you sure everything's fine?'

Babs nodded. As much as she liked the occasional natter with this kanga she didn't fancy a one-to-one now. But the PO said, 'You're needed upstairs. The Governor wants a word.'

Mrs Field was smiling. The treat she was giving her poodle looked much tastier than the muck they served the girls in the dining room, Babs thought.

'Ah, Miller,' she said once they were alone. To Babs' surprise she waved her hand at the chair on the opposite side of the desk. She'd never been seated in the presence of the Number One and didn't know if this was good or bad. She parked her bum on the edge of the chair.

'This came for you today.' The other woman pulled an envelope from the top of a pile of paperwork and passed it to her.

Babs held it gingerly. 'What is it Miss?'

No emotion showed on Mrs Field's face. 'Best thing to do, in my experience, is to open it and see.'

Babs nervously fumbled with her broken finger before getting it open. Inside was a piece of paper, which she took out and opened up. Her heartbeat went into overdrive as she realised what she was reading.

Her head jerked up. 'Miss, it says here that I've got my jam roll . . . I mean parole. They're gonna let me out in two weeks' time.'

For the first time ever the Governor smiled at her, making the hard lines of her face much softer. 'You've always admitted to the crime and conducted yourself well in prison.' Babs thought about the mobile phone and thanked God for sending her a nut job like Knox who kept her ear to the ground. 'The board feel that you have made very good progress and, above all else, that the time is right for you to rejoin the world outside and make a go of your life.'

The tears gathered in her eyes. 'But I thought after you stopped me going to work outside there was no way you'd vouch for me.'

The other woman gave her a penetrating stare. 'I've been in this job a long time and that day you came back with a broken finger . . . well, let's just say that my fishy tale radar was on high alert. But on the whole your record shows you've kept your head down and your fingernails clean.' Then she chuckled. 'Except at the memorial gardens, of course.' Babs didn't feel much like laughing but let out a trilling hehehe to keep the Number One buttered up. 'And you've got a lot to thank Margaret Sparks for. She wrote a stellar letter of support to the parole board.'

Good ol Mags! What a mate! When she got settled she was taking Mags for a slap-up girls' night out. Babs wiped the tears from her eyes. 'Thank you Miss. Can I give my family the good news?' She quickly added, 'From the phone in the hall that is.' Stupid. Dumbo. What did you go and say that for. Now she's gonna think what other phone could you be chatting on about.

Babs was rescued from her slip-up by the opening of the door. One of the POs, looking slightly harassed, said, 'Sorry Mrs Field, we've got a bit of a situation in the reception.'

The Governor beckoned her forward and the other woman whispered in her ear, so that Babs couldn't hear. Not that she was taking a blind bit of notice. All she could think about was one word. Free. Fucking, bloody, bollocks free. She'd be back in the bosom of her family. Wake up and go to bed anytime she wanted. Go down to The Roman and Whitechapel Market. Have a natter with her mates down The Knackered Swan.

'Miller.' Babs snapped out of her wonderful thoughts. The smiling woman of a minute ago was gone. 'Miss, is something up?'

'It seems your wish to inform your family has come true much sooner than any one of us would've anticipated.'

Fifty-Three

Nicky was on his way home to drop off his dirty washing, listening to his fave CD – 2Pac's *Greatest Hits* – when he got the call from his new pal Mal.

'Alright matey.'

Nicky's heart started beating like crazy. 'Are we on?'

'It's a definite.'

Mal gave him a time and a place. Nicky knew he was cutting it fine but he needed to get a new set of clothes so he continued on his way home. Flo had gone postal, so he'd told her straight, she could always do his laundry for him. He thought that would shut her up. He'd heard The Commander chuckling away at their row. He liked Flo's granddad; he was kinda cool in an old man style.

He stopped at a zebra crossing to let a pretty girl cross, clocking her soft brown skin, thin, braided extensions swinging down her back and a perky, curved bum. He was feeling so high about finally getting a taste of London's underworld he called out, 'Alright baby girl. Need a lift somewhere? I'm going your way.'

She kissed her teeth long and hard at him. 'Piss off, you cocky little toerag.'

Charming! He tooted his horn merrily. Nothing could dim his day. But underneath he knew he was faking it, smiling on the outside but grieving deep inside. He missed his dad something terrible. John had meant the world to him. His blood father had entrusted him into John's care and he had done a bang-up job of bringing him up. He knew his mum was bitterly disappointed in his decision to scarper – although she hadn't needled him, which he was grateful for – but he couldn't stand it at home one moment longer. He liked Flo. She was a good laugh when she wasn't having a go.

He banged on his horn at a van in his way. Slowly the van moved round and let him be about his business. When he passed, Nicky leaned out of the window and shouted, 'Wanker!' but he got no response. He turned up Tupac's 'Me Against The World' and sneered, 'Sunday afternoon driver' at the van in his rear view mirror. Nicky started shaking his shoulders as he got into the groove. It was only a few minutes later, when he checked his rear view again, that he realised that the van was following him. Then he remembered that this part of Essex was the wrong place to be calling a bloke a wanker.

He grew alarmed as the van kept pace in his rear view. The driver looked like a typical Essex van man with a baseball cap pulled down and he had a mate in the passenger seat, a geezer who looked like an Essex van man's sidekick. Their vehicle was big and hogged pretty much all the narrow road.

Nicky picked up as much speed as he could and sighed with relief when he saw the sign saying he was only two miles from home. As he rose over a slight bump in the road, he could see all the traffic in the distance. He was even more relieved when he saw that the van had pulled over to the verge behind him to let a saloon pass. They weren't after him. He was being paranoid.

The saloon drew up close and began flashing its lights. The driver waved his hand indicating he wanted to pass. Nicky didn't fancy it but having already pissed off one other driver, he didn't want to do it a second time.

He slowed and ran up on the verge to let the saloon go by. As he went, the guy honked in thanks and Nicky moved off. No sooner had he done so when the car's brake lights flashed full on and it ground to a halt in front of him. Shocked, Nicky managed to judder to a halt just as he was about to shunt the bumper in front. In the mirror, he could see the van had driven up a couple of inches behind him. He was sandwiched between the two vehicles. The doors of both were flying open and men were jumping out. Panic stricken, Nicky reversed the Jag into the van but there wasn't enough weight or power in it to shove the tailgater backwards. He crashed into the car in front and managed to jolt it forwards, reversed and went forward again to squeeze through the gap onto the verge. As the metal scraped and buckled, he managed to mount the grass, wheels spinning before he hit the hedge.

It seemed men were all around him, pulling the doors open.

His seat belt was unbuckled and he was dragged out. Mal's leering face looked at him and that's when Nicky twigged – he'd been set up.

'Courtney?' Babs was stunned to see her granddaughter through the Perspex panel in the door of the Visitors' Centre. When Mrs Field had told her that someone had turned up at the prison claiming to be her daughter, demanding to see her without a V.O. and then creating when they wouldn't allow her in, Babs figured it was either Dee or Tiff. Only those two had the bare-faced audacity to give that level of front. No way would it be Jen; she'd always played it by the book, even though at the hospital her middle girl had developed some claws. But Courtney? Never.

Mrs Morris, standing next to her, said, 'From the look on your face I can assume that this isn't your daughter.'

Babs shook her head. 'It's my granddaughter.'

'How old is she?'

Courtney had obviously gone to some effort to give the appearance she was much older. My poor girl has gone a bit overboard with the slap, Babs thought. And Babs had no idea how she was able to walk in the heels she had on. 'Thirteen,' she said softly.

'We thought she was underage but she had papers claiming to be twenty-year-old Susie Cane.'

Babs tightened her lips. Anyone could pick up fake ID on The Devil if they had the right readies.

She turned to stare beseechingly at Mrs Morris. 'I can see her, can't I?'

'The Governor shouldn't really permit this, but she's going to let you as a favour. But only ten minutes mind. She'll need to be picked up. Can I have her mother's details?'

When they walked into the room, Courtney catapulted out of her chair and rushed into Babs' waiting arms with such strength she staggered back slightly. Emotion choked her as she hugged her granddaughter tight. It had been three long years since she'd seen her beautiful little princess. When she'd gone down she'd made it clear to Jen her girls were not to visit her. She didn't want them growing up remembering her as some pathetic case inside the bleak walls of a prison. Especially Courtney.

'We haven't got long.' Babs quickly eased away, catching Mrs Morris's warning gaze reminding her about no physical contact. Her little baby had grown up so much. 'Let's go and get comfy.'

When they sat down opposite each other Babs started worrying again about why Courtney had come. 'You haven't told —?'

'Nah Nan.' Courtney shook her head. 'I'd never do that. You told me to keep our secret here,' she patted her heart, 'and this . . .' She made a closed-zip motion across her lips.

'So what are you doing here lovey?' Babs put her stern grandmother hat on. 'And what are you doing telling porkies about your age and who you are? You must've gone to some dodgy people on the estate to sort that bogus ID out. I never brought you up like that nor did your mum.'

'How else was I gonna see you?' Babs heard the rebellious-ness in Courtney's voice. Oh yeah, her little girl was growing up. 'I needed to talk to you Nan. How else was I gonna do it? You won't let me come see you.' Tears glistened in her blue eyes.

Babs reached across to hold her hands, but forced them back. 'You know why. I don't want you to see me here.'

Her granddaughter burst out, 'It should've been—'

'Don't say it.' Babs was back to being stern, although her heart ached at the terrible expression on Courtney's face. 'Remember, we agreed, we don't ever chat about it. What's done is done and there's no going back. In this life the best way to live is looking forward. And don't you forget it.'

Courtney crumbled. 'But Nan, sometimes I can't sleep coz it's all in my head. I keep whispering "go away, go away, go away", but it won't leave me alone. I can't talk to anyone . . .' The words dried up as agonising sobs broke free.

Fuck this! Babs took her granddaughter in her arms. She stared warily at the prison officer, waiting for the reminder about the rules. Instead Mrs Morris mouthed, 'ten seconds.' Babs rocked Courtney. She felt so bad that their secret was tearing her granddaughter apart. But Babs toughened her heart. That was how it had to be; there was no other way. She'd make the same decision in a heartbeat.

'Babs . . .' Mrs Morris reminded her, so she gently loosened her hold. With a reassuring smile she used her fingertips to mop up the tears.

'Look at you, all gorgeous and so grown up,' Babs said proudly, desperate for them not to dwell on the past. Then it occurred to her that Courtney could tell her what was what on the home front. 'It gladdened my heart that your Uncle John had a peaceful send-off.'

Courtney huffed. 'Peaceful? There was a right punch up.'

'You what?' The girls hadn't mentioned a word of this.

'That sleaze ball Kieran, who's going out with Mum, got into it with some of Aunty Dee's mates. And then she sent him a bomb.' Babs' mouth flapped open but she was so flabbergasted she couldn't utter a word, 'coz he says she's got his gold or silver or something. And he says he's gonna sort her out. Mum ain't talking to Aunty Dee, especially after she nearly bashed Mum up in that spa place. Mum's acting all weird since Kieran came along. I don't like him.'

Babs was stunned, her world rocking back and forth. She knew it, just knew it that things were going to the dogs outside.

'But your mum's so soft-hearted. She wouldn't say boo to a fly.'

Courtney had scorn written all over her. 'She's putting herself about like she's Paris Hilton on crack. She's always shooting her mouth off. And the clobber that creep Kieran buys her makes her look like a right slapper.'

'I've got to get outta here.' She didn't even realise she'd mumbled it under her breath. 'My family's turned into a horror story.'

'What did you say Nan?' Courtney looked at her curiously.

'Nuthin.' Babs beamed, although she felt sick. 'Don't worry your pretty head about a thing.'

*   *   *

But Courtney couldn't get it out of her head as she sat in the cab. Arse face Kieran had paid for it and Mum had been going on and on at her since she'd arrived to collect her, jabbing her finger and blowing her stack. What a show. Courtney turned her ears off and bit her lip. This was all her fault. Her mum, Aunty Dee and Aunty Tiff wouldn't be trying to rip each other's heads off if it wasn't for what she'd done.

Fifty-Four

Although he was shitting himself, Nicky tried to think what his two dads would've done in this situation.

Mal and another geezer had blindfolded him and dumped him into the boot of their car. He'd tried to keep track of time as he bounced in the dark. The motor had stopped at his calculations after well over an hour, so he thought he was somewhere in London. He'd fought hard when they'd taken him out, receiving a major league slap across his mouth for his troubles. Then he'd been dragged unceremoniously down a set of steps, tied to a chair and left in a place that smelt musty. The blindfold kept him in the dark.

He knew exactly what Chris and John would've tried – to get free of the plastic cuffs that tied his wrists to the back of the chair. He stretched his fingers, trying to get to the cuffs' centre, but couldn't reach it. He gritted his teeth the second time, sweat coating his forehead. With an almighty effort he did it again and this time the chair toppled over on its side. He crashed to the floor.

Someone slow-clapped behind him, putting him on high alert.

'I'm not scared of you,' he screamed, noticing that his words echoed off the walls.

Footsteps. 'No one has to be scared here. All you've got to

do is tell me the truth.' It wasn't Mal. The man's voice was soft and slight as if he was trying to disguise it.

His captor lifted the chair and got Nicky in an upright position again.

'You can go home.'

'But?' Nicky said tightly.

'It's simple really. All you've got to do is answer one question.'

Nicky said nothing, just waited.

'Where did your dad hide the gold?'

'What gold?'

Footsteps around his chair. 'Don't play silly buggers with me kid. I want to know now.'

Nicky started shouting with all his might, which made the man laugh. He stopped, his throat hurting.

'Scream blue murder all you want boy. No one's going to hear you. The walls are soundproof, plus you're in the bowels of hell. Tell me where my gold is.'

His hands were like rings of steel around Nicky's throat. 'Tell me.'

'I don't know.' Nicky's voice was hoarse.

The hands dropped away and the man stepped back. 'I didn't want to do this but you leave me no choice.'

There was a moment of silence before Nicky heard them. He started bricking it. The vicious barks and snarls of dogs entering the room.

Babs found Knox doing what she loved doing best – beating the shit out of one of the other girls. She was kneeling on a terrified and tearful younger prisoner while her two goons looked on laughing. They were round the back of the kitchen, Knox's favourite spot to dispense her brand of justice because it was a security camera blindspot.

When Babs coughed to get her attention she received a growled 'knob off,' in response. Usually she'd be on her way, but what she wanted was urgent. If there was any way she could do it without involving mad girl she would, but there wasn't.

'Knox, can I have a word?' Babs stood her ground.

Knox viciously kneed her victim in the chest and turned round, cursing beneath her breath. Her face scrunched up when she spotted Babs. 'This better be life and death Miller.'

'A private word.'

Knox rolled her eyes. 'Private she says.' But she got up. 'Whatcha want?' She surprised Babs when her face fell, revealing a human layer under her usual scowl. 'Nuthin's happened to my Kieran?'

Babs' mouth opened. Her Kieran? She wasn't his girlfriend or something? Perish the thought. As if reading her mind Knox lowered her voice. 'He's my brother, you twat.'

'Your brother?' She was speechless. Of course she knew that Kieran had sisters, as well as brothers, but Crazy here being one of them had never crossed her mind.

'What are you? Some friggin' parrot? That's what I said, didn't I. I'm the one who had the brains to do a runner when I was fourteen. Got married to Bob Benson when I was sixteen. He was twenty-five years older than me and had the good grace to cock his toes up when I was twenty.' She leaned in closer. 'Course his kids said I hastened him on his way. They couldn't prove nish.'

Babs could only gawk. A shiver broke out like cold sweat at the final part of Knox's story. Mind you, who was she to point the finger? She was doing bird for offing her old man. 'I need your help.'

The other woman got sarky again. 'Well, I didn't think you wanted a chinwag coz you like the colour of my eyes. Now gob it out.'

'You know this prison inside out? The comings and goings?'

Knox puffed her chest out. 'Like the back of my hand,' she smiled maliciously at Babs, 'which you'll get if you don't get to the point sharpish.'

Babs held the words back, playing with them inside her head and then she spat them out. 'I need to get outta here.'

'Join the queue.'

She grabbed Knox's arm desperately, her fingers digging tight. 'No, I need to escape.'

'Are you off it or what?'

Babs pulled her close. Not many people would dare do that to Knox Benson. 'I've got to get outta here pronto.'

'Your jam's only two weeks away.'

'How do you know about my parole?'

'Like we've established, I know all the comings and goings. Put your head down for a couple of weeks and then you're out.'

Babs almost wept, 'I can't. I can feel it in my bones. Something terrible's gonna happen if I don't get to my family.'

Fifty-Five

'Have you heard a word I've said Babs?' the inmate next to Babs asked at lunchtime the next day.

'Wh ... What?' Babs faltered. She flicked her gaze away from the food in the dining area or, as the women nicknamed it, Noshers' Yard. The room was noisy, as per usual, which didn't help her already cracking nerves, although she'd taken her last remaining Benzo. She was keeping an eagle eye on the counter because Knox was going to pop her head from the back of the kitchen to give her the nod. The other woman hadn't been happy to aid Babs' escape, but after she promised her a nice drink when Knox got out she'd been all grim sunshine and smiles. Knox was keeping the escape plan close to her chest until the last minute, which Babs hadn't been best pleased about, but what could she do? Her anxiety was hitting the stratosphere because Knox still hadn't put in an appearance.

'Babs you're a million miles away,' said Lucy Warren-Jones, a very posh and pretty inmate who'd been done for cooking the books at her City job to finance her increasing coke habit. 'Is there something wrong?'

'Nah, nuthin's up.' Everything's up. Where the bloody hell is Knox?

'Like I was saying, my fiancé has given me the elbow. The

creep. After all I did for him. He won't find another girl who enjoys being tied up . . .'

Babs wasn't listening. All she could think about was getting shot of this place. She needed to bang some heads together. But doing a bunk less than two weeks away from her parole was crazy . . . Maybe she should bottle it, tell Knox to forget it, do the rest of her time and hope her family kept themselves quiet. No, she knew her daughters. If things were already bad they were only going to get worse.

She drew in a deep breath when she saw Knox at last. The other woman nodded. Babs got up, picking up her tray.

'You haven't finished your rice pud,' Lucy noticed.

'Not hungry,' she threw back and started moving. Here we go. She added her tray to the other empties and secretly checked out the kangas monitoring the hall. She breathed easy when she saw they weren't looking her way. She moved cautiously towards the end of the counter. Took a step around it to the door, which Knox said would be open. Reached for the handle . . .

An alarm tore through the air. She stumbled back as a bunch of kangas flooded the hall.

Bully kanga Bradley took control. 'Right, you lot, everyone back to their cells. It's a lockdown ladies.' A lockdown meant something serious had gone on or the prison wanted to ship someone out with minimal fuss.

A huge moan filled the room. Shit. Had they found out what she was about to do? But the POs shepherded her into line with the others and didn't single her out. She twisted around to see if she could catch Knox but the other woman was long gone. There was no way she was going to be able to do a flit now.

Five minutes later she was banged up in her cell.

She moved to the wall and shouted to the woman in the cell next door. 'Why's there a lockdown?'

'Someone must've been making pigeon pie coz they found two dead birds in her cell, every drug known to man stuffed inside.'

'Who was it?'

'Knox. She's being shipped out.'

Babs slumped against the wall. Her escape route had just become a dead end.

Tiffany inhaled deeply, a dreamy expression on her face as she passed the spliff to Dee. They were reclining near the indoor pool at the back of Dee's house. Mel and Kim's 'Respectable' played on Tiff's mobile, hooked up to a mini speaker.

The smoke left her with a hugely satisfied grin. 'Now that's what you call a tote. Not like that shit skunk,' she arched her brow at her sister, 'which I hope you don't indulge in. I hear it's sending people doolally.'

'Maybe we should let Kieran have a tote, it might send him over the edge.'

Tiff chuckled as the spliff was passed back. 'You can tell me where John hid the gold. I won't tell a dickie bird.'

There was a violent banging at the front door, but both women ignored it. Dee stared hard at her sister. 'Like I've said from the off, John never told me bollocks about no gold.'

Whoever was banging at the door was making a right racket. Dee yelled, 'Go. Away,' knowing full well whoever it was wouldn't hear her. She wasn't in the mood to deal with people. The truth was she was knackered. Tired of this nonsense with Kieran. She just wanted it to stop, so she could get on with trying to make a life for herself, the baby and Nicky without John. She did miss him so.

Her palm gently covered her tummy where her baby lay. Her baby. She still couldn't get over it. She was going to be a mum. After all these years she was finally going to hold a little one in the crook of her arm. Nothing could happen to this kid. She waved the spliff away when Tiff offered it to her again.

The banging had stopped, but Tiff's mouth hadn't. 'Come on, you can trust me.'

'Last time I looked you had a pair of ears, so hear me again—'

Dee never finished. A violent thumping on the closed French doors startled her. When she saw Flo glaring at her through the glass she was fit to do murder.

She leapt up and marched over. 'You're looking for your death little miss. You'd never come near me otherwise. Now fuck off my property.'

Flo sounded fit to be tied. 'Where is he?' she yelled like a banshee. She looked like she hadn't slept in an age, her hair all over the place and her slap half sliding off her face.

Tiffany had got up to stand next to her sister. 'Take it easy Dee. Don't forget about the next generation of hard girls you're carrying.'

Dee carried on as if she hadn't heard, all her attention focused on the woman outside. 'He?' She kissed her teeth long and hard, looking Flo up and down with disdain. 'Like I'd know any wanker who's matey with you.'

'Try a wanker called Nicky.'

If there wasn't glass between them Dee would've gone for her. Just hearing her son's name on that cunning slut's lips made her see red. 'Done a bunk, has he? Finally seen through your posho tramp-stamp moves, has he? I brought my lad up to use his noodle.'

Tiff took a warning step towards the door. 'Go on, sling your hook.'

'Nicky,' Flo bellowed, 'what's she effing well done with ya? I'm here babe. I ain't moving an inch until the old crow lets you out.' The Cockney patter Flo had learned from her dad

Stanley Miller set Dee even more on edge. It wasn't natural for a body to shift from uptown chatter to East End lingo, as far as she was concerned. But then there was nothing normal about Flo Miller.

'What are you going on about?' Dee shouted back. 'Nicky's not here.'

Flo fixed a fiery gaze on her. 'I. Don't. Believe. You.'

Tiffany started opening the French doors. 'What are you doing?' Dee blasted.

Her sister shrugged. 'You don't want the whole bloody neighbourhood to know your business.'

An agitated Flo stepped inside. Dee and Nicky's unwanted girlfriend glared at each other like gunslingers ready to draw. Dee broke the silence. 'What makes you think Nicky's here?'

Flo was red with anger. 'Yesterday, he went back here to get . . . some clobber . . .' She switched back to her girl from a well-to-do family voice, 'Clothes. And then he was coming right back.' She smirked, 'Into my loving embrace.'

Dee started going for her, but Tiff pulled her back. 'This is one of her tricks.'

Dee stalked over to Flo and stabbed one of her ringed fingers into her face. 'I don't know what you're playing at, but if you've touched one hair on my boy's head . . .'

Flo wriggled her shoulders defiantly and went back to being Stan Miller's daughter. 'You'll what? Try to batter me? Bring it on, you wig-wearing witch.'

If there was one thing likely to send a black woman over the edge it was a statement that rubbished her hair. Dee grabbed the front of her blouse. 'By the time I'm done with you, you won't need to be worrying about hair. You'll be leaving here as bald as your arse.'

Flo went for her arm and they began grappling furiously, twisting around the pool.

'Ease off, the both of ya.' Tiff tried desperately to intervene, but neither woman was up for being reasoned with.

Crack! The sound echoed around the room as Flo managed to slap Dee a hard one across the face.

'I'm gonna rip your head off,' Dee roared.

'Watch out,' Tiff screamed in alarm.

But her sister was in hurricane Dee mode and the only thing that mattered was putting this tart in her place. She raised her hand, her four rings glinting in the air, balled her fingers tight...

'Flippin hell,' came out of her as the weight of her sudden move upset her balance. She dragged a stunned Flo with her, splashing into the pool. Dee fought frantically to come up for air. She spluttered as Tiffany clutched her belly, laughing the place down.

'I'll give you something to giggle about when I get out,' Dee growled at her.

The laughter vanished as quickly as it came when Tiff remembered the baby. 'Bollocks Dee, you alright?'

'Help! Help!' They both looked over to Flo, flapping her arms furiously and kicking her legs madly. 'I can't swim ...' Her head went under. Came back up again spitting water. 'Can't swim.'

'What do they teach you at those posh schools for fuck's sake?' It did cross Dee's mind to let the cradle-grabbing bitch drown, but she swam over to her. She started to pull her out of the pool, but Tiff quickly reminded her, 'You shouldn't be doing no heavy lifting.'

Tiff hauled Flo out. She pulled in air at an alarming rate, the vision of a drowned rat.

Tiff pointed a finger at both women. 'Right, enough of the *Baywatch* palaver. We've got a big problem. If Nicky's not at Flo's and he's not here, where is he?'

*   *   *

For the next twenty minutes they cruised around the countryside near the house, but found no sign of Nicky. If the situation weren't so serious, Tiff would've smirked her head off. Dee had given Flo some dry clothes to put on, but had maliciously taken them from the charity bag she was sending to Oxfam. A fluorescent pink, shrunk crop top and Sporty Spice style baggy joggers that Flo had to roll up at the bottom. But there was no time for laughter; Tiff had a bad feeling in her gut.

'I think this is a waste of time,' Flo said.

'Keep driving,' Dee and Tiff ordered.

They went on for another fifteen minutes.

'This is getting us no—' Flo started, but Tiff cut her off.

'What's that?' She couldn't make out what it was but it wasn't on the road.

Flo pushed her foot against the accelerator.

'It's deffo a car,' Dee confirmed as they got closer. Then she wailed, 'That's my Nicky's motor.'

Dee was the first to jump out of the car, Tiff and Flo following close behind. Nicky's car was at an angle in the grass and the driver's door was wide open.

Dee looked at the empty car in a daze. 'What's happened here?'

If there was one thing Tiff knew about it was cars. She pointed at the ground. 'There's another set of tyre treads here. And the back of his car is smashed up.'

'But . . .' Dee fought to find the words. 'I don't understand. Where's my boy?'

It was Flo who supplied the answer. 'Looks to me like someone has taken him.'

'Someone?' Dee's features scrunched into an expression of absolute thunder. The fingers of her left hand ran over the rings on her right. 'I'm gonna kill that fucker.'

*   *   *

Go on, do it, Babs ordered herself. She stared at the prison gate in the distance. It's an open prison, for crying out loud, all you've gotta to do is walk out. Simple. The tabloids were right to some degree; HMP Hillsworth was run in a more informal way. It didn't really have a gate as such, just two poles acting as a barrier over an open driveway. The women inside were usually nearing the end of their sentence or serving two years or less, so it would be daft to try to bolt. Except if your name was Babs Miller of course.

Despite Knox being shipped out she was still determined to escape. All she had to do was walk.

She'd chosen her time well; the kangas were busy across the prison. After Mrs Field had put a stop to her work outside she'd been assigned ground duty, taking care of the flowers and plants with a crew of three other women. The PO meant to watch them wasn't, having gone off to have a ciggy somewhere. Babs knew she wasn't going to get a second chance.

'Just off to get permission to go to the Ladies,' she told the woman next to her.

She started walking towards the open gate. The sweat was popping on her forehead and running like a razor down her back. But she kept going. And going. She was less than a half inch from the pole . . .

'Babs Miller,' a voice called out.

Bollocks. She turned to find Mrs Morris looking at her. Usually the woman's face was soft and serene. Now it was stone cold.

Fifty-Six

Uncle Frank threw his head back as laughter gushed out of him. He was sitting in a boozer in Brick Lane with a group of pals from back in the day. Ah, he loved a tickle about the good old days, although he wouldn't give up his cushy siesta life in Spain.

'You've made me nearly piss myself,' he told them. 'I've gotta take a leak. Next round's on me.'

He wobbled slightly as he got to his feet; one too many Bacardis. His security, sitting at a table nearby, instantly rose on autopilot. He waved them back down impatiently. He might not be living here anymore but his name still commanded maximum respect. Anyone trying to take a pop at him on his old stomping ground was a fool.

He bypassed the bar and entered the Gents. He started whistling, 'Daisy, Daisy,' as he did his business. The door opened behind him but he took no notice . . . that was until he felt the barrel of a gun in his back. His whistling halted abruptly. Apparently there were fools still out there.

'Where is he?' the person behind him growled.

'Is that you Dee?'

Dee watched Uncle Frank twist towards her. She kept the gun trained on him. He must have realised that his dinkle was hanging out, as he snapped back around.

'A bird shouldn't be in the Gents. What's the world coming to,' he said, miffed. Typical Uncle Frank, no sense of danger, more concerned with the traditional roles of men and women.

'I'll blow your bloody whizz off if you don't tell me where my Nicky's at.'

He zipped up and turned back to her, wearing a stunned expression. 'Your Nicky? Why the heck would I know where the nipper is?'

She pressed the barrel into his chest with the force of her raging anger. 'You've either got him or your mate Carats has.'

'Who the fuck is Carats?'

She jabbed him. 'Your mate who owns the gold. I don't know his name so I'm calling him Carats—'

'Oh, I get it.' Uncle Frank chuckled. 'Twenty-four Carats. Nice one.'

She was losing her rag. 'This ain't no laughing matter.' Emotion shook her voice. 'I just want my boy back. He don't have nuthin to do with this.'

He became serious. 'That lad's like a grandson to me. I'd never touch a hair on his head.'

She eyed him, weighing up his sincerity and, with a tightening of her lips, finally put John's shooter away. 'This Carats has taken him then.'

'Nah.' Uncle Frank shook his head and went to the sink to wash his hands.

The door burst open and his two henchwomen stormed inside. They clocked Dee and reached for their weapons. But Frank stopped them. 'No need for that me lovelies. Be with you in a jiffy.'

They gave Dee one last sweep with their lethal eyes and then left. It was clear from the lack of footsteps they remained on guard outside.

'What makes you so sure that Carats hasn't got him?'

'Believe me, he wouldn't hurt Nicky. He could have used him anytime against John or you, but he hasn't.' He tore off a piece of paper towel and wiped his hands. 'You wanna be looking closer to home.'

She knew exactly who he meant. Dee turned and left, thoughts of revenge heating her blood.

On their fourth session Courtney wouldn't talk about her Nanna Babs and she was grateful that Foxy didn't get in her face about it. They ate sweet potato fries and a salsa burger with a major league spicy dip.

Foxy asked, 'What's drinking booze like?'

Courtney stiffened and sputtered, 'How would I know? I ain't never taken a drop in my life. I swear on my heart.'

It was as if Foxy hadn't heard her. 'Soon after my mother passed away, I started stealing from my dad's drinks cabinet. You know what I would do?' Courtney shook her head, all ears. 'I'd take some Bacardi – I liked that best of all – then pour some water into the bottle so he wouldn't notice. I kept drinking and drinking until I was twenty.'

'What happened?'

Foxy popped a long chip in her mouth and chewed before answering. 'I was so drunk one day I fell down the stairs and broke my arm.' Courtney gasped. Foxy rolled up her sleeve to display her arm. 'See, I can't bend it properly. That's the problem with alcohol – it can really mess you up.'

'Did you have nightmares?'

'About my mum?' Courtney nodded, her gaze fixed on the other woman. 'Yeah. Sometimes I'd wake up screaming because in my dream it was happening all over again.'

'It's the same for me.' Courtney made herself say it. It felt good to finally admit it.

'What do you have nightmares about?'

Courtney hesitated and then she couldn't stop the words; they'd been desperate to find a way out. 'Dead people. Blood. It's everywhere.'

She was surprised when, instead of taking advantage, all Foxy said was, 'Next time, tell me about your Nanna Babs.'

Fifty-Seven

'I'm afraid I'm going to have you refuse you admittance, madam,' the doorman at The Lock informed Dee firmly.

'I beg your pardon?' Dee made herself sound wide-eyed with shock even though she'd prepared herself for this first hurdle.

The doorman was apologetic. 'I'm afraid you're barred for causing a disturbance in the restaurant the last time you were here.'

Dee took a step closer to him, her most killer smile in place. 'Tell Kieran that Dee Black is here and wants to talk business with him.'

'I'm sorry madam but Mr Scott isn't on the—'

Dee leaned right into him and watched his eyes bug out at the feel of the gun barrel she had pressed into his side. 'There's no call for any drama. And if you think coz I'm a lady I won't plug you full of holes you don't know who you're dealing with.' Her tone hardened. 'Where's your boss?'

The man gulped. 'In his office.'

'Lead the way. And get a smile on your chops; we wouldn't want anyone to think that you're having a bad time.' He popped a stupefied grin on.

And with that Dee waltzed into the club. She nodded pleasantly at the reception staff as they made their way to the stairs.

When they reached Kieran's office she kicked the door in and levelled her gun at the stunned occupants. Kieran and – surprise, surprise – Jen. She moved quickly into the room.

'Boss–' the doorman started.

But Kieran cut him off. 'It's alright. I'll deal with this. And keep your mouth shut. I don't wanna be disturbed.' After the doorman left he added sarcastically, 'Hello Dee, I'm hoping you've got my bag of golden goodies.'

Dee only had eyes for her sister, sitting in Kieran's big chair behind his desk, so blinged up she'd give the Bank of England a run for its money.

Dee tutted in disgust. 'My, my, you've gone up in the world. From a crap flat on The Devil to muggins here's right-hand squeeze? Are you the brains behind the operation these days? Given the pickle your guy's got himself into, he could use some.'

'I don't want no more trouble–'

'Is that why you're going out with fuck face here? Did you know he had the tyres of my car shot out?' Jen gasped. 'The car went flying and the next thing I know I'm in the ozzie.'

Jen turned sharply to Kieran, who'd got to his feet. 'She's lying, ain't she? You wouldn't do that?' Horror coated her every word.

'Course she is,' he told her softly.

'Don't believe a bollocks word that comes out of his cake hole,' Dee shot back hotly. 'And now he's gone and taken Nicky.'

Jen's head swung so quickly towards Kieran it was a blur. She couldn't get the words past her lips, she was so shocked by Dee's accusation.

Kieran made a very nasty noise at the back of his throat. 'As if! I told you Jen, you don't know this woman. She's making it up. She should be writing for *EastEnders*.'

'He's right,' Jen decided, her lip curled. 'You'd do anything to get your way.'

Dee's finger tightened on the trigger. 'You wanna be careful, sister dearest, coz I'm just itching to blow your fake, hard bird arse to kingdom come.' She turned to Kieran. 'Where's my boy?'

'Don't answer her,' Jen snapped. 'Everyone knows that he's with that slag Flo.'

'That's where you're wrong,' Dee informed her with relish. 'She came knocking at mine to tell me she hadn't seen him.' Her voice cracked slightly. 'We found his abandoned car.'

Jen looked slightly more worried. She glanced at her boyfriend again.

Dee could barely contain herself. 'Cut the crap Kieran. You've got my boy and I want him back. Pronto. And if I don't, I swear to God . . .' The gun hiked up, aiming squarely at his heart.

'So where's my gold?' he jumped in viciously.

Dee's jaw tightened. 'Where's my son?'

The room rang with his hollow laugh. 'Your kid's probably just left town for a couple of days. Or the battery on his mobile has conked out. Or maybe he's out on the lash with a new girlfriend. Kids of his age are always disappearing. I know, I used to do it myself.' Then he added, 'Of course, if he is in a spot of bother, I might be able to help with that. I could put the word out. I'm sure I could get any trouble resolved. But I'd expect some help in return. After all, I'm a big-hearted Arthur but I'm not a charity. And you know what I'd want in—'

Kieran made his move. He flew at her in a whirl and chopped the edge of her hand. Hot pain shot up her arm and the gun tumbled to the floor. He quickly kicked it away.

She gave him the evil eye. 'You bastard.'

Through clenched teeth he said, 'What the fuck are you playing at in your condition?'

Dee reared back. 'What do you mean, my condition?'

Jen's quiet voice got between them. 'Dee, are you pregnant?'

They were interrupted by a hammering on the door. An anxious voice shouted, 'Boss, you need to come quickly.'

Kieran screamed. 'Fuck off, I'm busy.'

The door burst open. 'You need to get out guv. The place is on fire.'

Kieran looked stunned for a few moments. 'What do you mean on fire? Go and put it out!'

Instead of waiting for an answer, he pushed the guy out the way and hurried to the door. He stood on the landing peering down. A wisp of smoke blew around his head, bringing an acrid tang with it. He turned to Dee and Jen, standing close behind him.

He forgot all about Dee's delicate condition and grabbed her by her blouse. 'If you've fucking–'

She wrenched out of his grasp. 'Set your club on fire? What, with me in it? Do I look like I've got a death wish?' she ended on a sarky note.

'If you've done this Dee it ain't your death you've got to worry about, it's the one you've placed on your son's head.'

'You bastard.' Dee fought with Kieran to get out of his grip. 'You fucking bastard. I knew you had my kid here.' He still wouldn't let go.

'Knock it off Dee,' Jen ordered. Sternly, 'Carry on like this and you'll hurt your baby.' She gave Kieran her full attention. 'Are you saying you've had Nicky all this time?' The flaring of his nostrils was all she needed to know the truth. 'Why?' she couldn't help crying.

'We don't have time to ask why! We've got to get out of here.'

Dee lunged forward but he yanked her back. 'I've got to get Nicky.'

'Look.' He shook her slightly. 'My men will have made sure he's out. He's got a guard. What we need to worry about is how *we're* gonna get out of here.'

Kieran herded them back into his office and slammed the door. He rushed over to the drinks cabinet and pulled out silk napkins from a drawer. He tore open a bottle of tonic water and upended it on the cloth. He held them out. 'Put these over your mouths.'

He stood by the door and opened it. It had only been seconds but smoke gushed into the room and began to gather like thunder clouds. Choking and spluttering, the three of them ran out onto the landing. There were no flames but grey and black fumes everywhere.

Kieran warned them. 'Not the lift! You'll suffocate. Wait here.'

He bolted down the stairs, two at a time, into the darkness. He was gone a long time. First Dee and then Jen began shouting his name. There was no answer. Dee went down a few steps and saw Kieran struggling back up the stairs carrying a sports bag. She took him by the arm and dragged him back onto the landing. The two women held him up while he croaked, 'The office, get back in the office.'

They rushed back inside and he booted the door shut and leaned against it. Already, the floor beneath their feet was growing warm. Wheezing he told them, 'Get me the Scotch from the cabinet.' He took a gulp, gargled and spat it out. 'There's no way out downwards. We're gonna have to escape ourselves.'

Dee said furiously, 'Shouldn't we wait for the fire brigade?'

'We'll be dead by then. These old warehouses are like tinder boxes.'

He struggled to his feet, went over to the window and peered out. On the street far below, members and staff had gathered while neighbours and gawkers were being kept back by the cops. The sound of sirens tore through the air. Kieran knew they couldn't afford to wait. Breathing deeply, he put his sports bag on the desk. He pulled out an Uzi, loaded a magazine in the breech, put some spares into his pockets.

'Follow me; we're going up into the eaves. And for fuck's sake,' he gave them a little smile, 'cheer up. I'll get us out.'

They rushed out as the fire licked at the top of the stairs. Jen twisted back yelling, 'I've left my mobile.'

Dee snapped her around. 'Don't be daft girl. We need to get out of here now.'

Kieran pulled down a metal ladder leading up to the loft space above. A century earlier, it had been used to store bales before they were loaded onto boats. Now it was empty except for a pile of boxes along one wall.

'There's a door here, but I don't have the key on me.' He pushed the boxes out of the way. 'OK ladies, get down on the floor. Keep your fingers crossed none of us get hit by ricochets.'

When Dee and Jen had curled up in a corner he took the safety catch off the gun, crouched and opened fire in steady bursts. The shooting shook the loft like thunder and splinters went in all directions. He lowered the Uzi and kicked at the door until there was space enough to climb through.

Dee squeezed through first. Then Jen and finally Kieran. Both women looked round with fascination as they took in the whips, chains and manacles on the wall.

Dee said snidely, 'I didn't know you were a kinky bandit Kieran.' She leered. 'Who would've thought?'

Kieran cut his eye at her. 'We need to go.'

They hurried down a flight of stairs towards the flat's front door. It was only when they reached it that Jen shouted, 'Kieran! Your shooter.'

Kieran realised he had the machine gun slung over his shoulder. 'I'll go back and hide it.'

'Just chuck it, we ain't got time,' Jen screamed.

'Both of you get out and wait for me.'

He heard both of their cries of warning but he legged it back up the stairs and through the hole into the loft of his beloved club. The floor was shaking from the pressure of the smoke and flames below. He knew it was only a matter of time before it collapsed into the inferno. He trod gingerly on the baking floorboards and made his way over to the door. He gripped the gun in one hand, used his jacket to take the handle in the other and pulled it open. He was blown backwards by heat, smoke and flames and hot air, which began to engulf the loft. With one final effort, he threw the gun and magazines into the office below. As he crawled back to the flat next door, he could hear bullets being ignited in the heat and firing off in all directions. It was like the blaze itself was shooting at him.

Kieran ran down the stairs and out on the street. He found Dee and Jen standing by the police lines, gazing upwards in horror as cinders and scraps of paper floated down around them. He noticed the two women were holding hands. 'Are you alright?'

It was Dee who said 'Yeah, we're alright. Pretty tasty with a machine gun, aren't ya?'

'Yeah. John used to take me into Epping Forest for target practice.' He was unable to look behind him at the burning building or ask the cops if there were any casualties. He stared Dee straight in the eye. 'I'm asking again. Was this down to you?'

Dee whispered. 'Me? Oh yeah, I was in your office while my mini-me set the fire. Use your effing noodle.' Then she became distracted as she checked the crowd. 'Where's Nicky?'

Kieran called one of his men over. He pulled him to the side so they could talk without the women hearing. When he turned back to them the colour behind the soot and sweat had drained away.

'Where's Nicky?' Dee cried out in dread.

Kieran ran towards the burning building.

Fifty-Eight

Dee made to run, but Jen grabbed her arm. 'Leave it to Kieran.'

Dee violently shook her off. A cop blocked Dee's way. 'Sorry madam, you'll have to stand back.'

'My son's in there.' Nicky might be choking this very minute! Or, God no, dead.

'I can't let you through, sorry.'

Dee let her head drop. When he relaxed she shoved him out of the way and legged it to where Kieran was arguing with the firemen.

One was explaining, 'Don't worry about it mate, the fire's under control and we've checked everywhere inside. No one's trapped, OK? Now leave us to get on with our job, owner or not. Otherwise, you can talk to the police.'

Kieran was backing away when Dee joined him. She slapped his face. 'How could you?'

He grabbed her wrists and hissed, 'Calm the heck down. He'll be alright. I just need to get in there. Instead of fighting, why don't you help? Eh? Fires go upwards and the kid's in the basement. He'll be alright if I can get in there.'

He went around the back of a fire engine where he found a heavy-duty axe and big torch. Someone shouted, 'Oi,' as he ran past but he kept on until he was back in the club.

'So, where is he?'

Cursing his head off Kieran turned to find Dee next to him. She was soaked in the water being hosed over the burning club. 'What the fuck are you doing? You're carrying a baby. Get back.'

'Not on your life. That's my son in there. The longer you keep up the patter the less time Nicky has.'

Kieran prised the door open and the former lovers went down the stairs. The corridor at the bottom was awash with water; the torchlight swam back and forth. At the end of the hall, through a mist of blue-tinged smoke, was a heavy oak door. They sloshed their way to it. Dee held the torch while Kieran set to work with his axe. The door didn't come down easily but when it finally did, they rushed inside to find an unconscious Nicky tied to a chair lying sideways on the ground.

Dee screamed and wailed and desperately tried to shake her son awake. She twisted round to Kieran like a mad woman. 'You fucking cunt. You tied my son up, how the fuck could he get out?'

Kieran quickly untied his wrists. Nicky groaned as Kieran heaved him into a fireman's lift. Dee almost collapsed with elation when she heard him. 'You're going to be alright babes, you're gonna be alright.'

Then she prayed like she was a child back in church with Aunty Cleo.

Jen, Dee and Kieran stood in the cold night while Nicky got checked over by a paramedic. The tension between them was electric.

Dee broke it, speaking with all the disgust she could muster. 'Nicky said you threatened to set dogs on him. You let one chew at his shoe to put the frighteners on him. You are a despicable human being. You need putting down.'

'Is this true?' Jen asked tightly.

He turned on her. 'I was – am – in a jam and needed to think of a way out of it. I had no choice—'

'No choice?' It was Jen who slammed out at him. 'Nicky's a child. A young boy. How could you do it?' She walloped him a good one. 'That's what Mum would've done.'

His face stilled with awful pain. 'There's no need to tell Babs about any of this. It was a misunderstanding.'

Both women remained silent. Then Dee said, 'I've got a plan to end all this.' As she looked at the burning building she explained her idea. After she'd finished she took Jen's hand. 'Now it's time for me to see to my son.'

'Me and you need a word,' Kieran stalled her.

'Go on Jen,' she told her sister. 'I'll be with you and Nicky in a mo.' She turned to Kieran. 'What?'

Kieran looked pointedly at her belly. 'How's my kid doing?'

'It's not yours.'

'Course it is, everyone knew John was firing blanks.'

'Well, John finally hit the mark. Me and you were a one-time booty thing. I don't want to ever clap eyes on you again.'

As she walked towards her son the tears fell. She'd already lost John. What would she have done if she'd lost Nicky as well?

Tiff jumped off Dee's chaise longue when she heard the front door slam.

'Dee, that you?' She'd been worrying herself silly when her half-sister went after Kieran with a shooter and refused to take her along. 'Have you got Nicky?' Stuff was getting well out of hand . . .

A grim-looking Dee strode in with her son. Tiff couldn't help gasping. They both looked like they'd been to hell and back. Then Jen came into view. Jen and Tiff snapped their eyes at each other.

'I'll take Nicky upstairs,' Jen offered.

When they were gone, Tiff fumed, 'I can't believe that Kieran really nabbed him.' She didn't like the expression on her sister's face. She knew it all too well; Dee was ready to blow her stack. 'Bloody hell, Kieran didn't hurt him, did he?'

Dee stalked over to the drinks cabinet and got herself a rum and Coke. Tiff couldn't understand why she was staying schtum. What was going on here?

Dee casually leaned against the cabinet, facing her. She rested her beady gaze on Tiff. 'How long have I known you?'

Tiff didn't like how quiet and controlled her voice sounded. A quiet Dee could be as deadly as a slithering snake.

'Longer than most folk know.' Their meeting years back when Tiff was still a yob up to no good was their secret still. 'Why are you going on all funny?'

'Funny!' Dee burst out laughing, but there was zero laughter in her eyes. She took a hard slog of her drink. 'There I am up at Kieran's natty club, which I might add burned down to the ground tonight–'

'Oh my God, you never–'

'I would've done anything on this earth to get my boy back.' Dee's voice was hardening by the minute. 'But it weren't me who lit the flame. There won't be any more bovver between us.'

'That's a relief –'

'Except one little wrinkle that needs ironing out.' She slammed her glass down and advanced on her sister. Tiff stood her ground; she was never one to back away from a ruck, even from a hard girl like Dee. 'Kieran starts chatting on about my pregnancy. And I start asking myself, how does wannabe bad boy know about my impending arrival.'

Tiff swallowed and heat piled high on her cheeks. 'Dee . . .'

'Is that what's been going on here?' Dee was foaming at the mouth. 'You been getting on the blower all this time, behind my trusting back, and whispering my bizz in that bastard's earhole?'

Tiff fronted it out. 'Come off it. Can you imagine me doing that?'

'See, that's the problem – *sister* – I can.'

Tiff rolled her eyes. 'You're seeing stuff that ain't there. Plus, you're being a touch ungrateful, ain't ya? I've had my arms around you since John passed. No one else has been here to give you a shoulder to cry on.'

Dee raised her hand violently. It remained in mid-air, shaking with fury, before she dropped it. 'Stop with the fucking lies. There's only three people, outside of the quack's, who know about me carrying John's kid. Me, the baby, and – surprise, surprise – you.' Dee tapped the side of her head. 'Then I got to thinking about all that fuss you made when I cancelled the quack's appointment. You knew he was sending some shit to play gunslinger with my house. I wasn't meant to be there, was I?' She took a step closer again. 'And it's you who's been searching my house.' Tiff blanched. 'As soon as I saw the fish food and wonky picture I knew someone had been nosing around. But my own flesh and blood?'

Tiff knew the game was up. 'I had to do it. He made me.'

Dee went ballistic. 'Get your gear and get outta my house.'

But she didn't move, instead pleading, 'I was in a sticky situation with my dosh and Kieran bailed me out.'

Dee advanced on her. 'I don't wanna know. You better get out before you need a face transplant.'

Tiff shook her head. 'You've got to hear me out. I told him about the baby coz I thought he would put a kybosh on the whole thing. After the car crash I told him point blank I wasn't doing no more.'

Dee had had enough. She grabbed her sister's arm and started marching her towards the door. Tiff didn't fight back like she usually would. Or give any ducking and diving patter to try to wriggle out of it. She was in the wrong. She'd betrayed her own sister.

Dee threw the door wide and flung Tiff outside with glee.

'See, that's the prob with you Tiff. You think you can sweet talk the bees off their honey. Well, this queen bee ain't having it.' Dee stabbed her finger as Tiff stumbled back. 'Don't you ever, *ever* darken my yard again.' She slammed the door so hard it reverberated against its frame.

Shattered, Tiff stared up at the house. She was the first to admit that she could be a sneaky, cunning sort. But when Kieran had agreed to pay off her debts if she spied on Dee to find out where the gold was, even she had not been happy about it. But he'd had her over a barrel. If she didn't do what he asked those two no-marks she owed would've found her. So she'd pushed her dodgy conscience aside and gone along with the plan. Until Dee had announced she was expecting and she'd felt rotten inside.

Something hit her head and tangled over her face. Frantically she fought until it fell on the floor. She recognised one of her T-shirts. She looked up to find Dee and that bloody Jen at the window.

'And take this shit with ya,' Dee shouted and proceeded to throw the rest of her clothes out into the night.

Fifty-Nine

'When do you want to drop our story about the gold?' Jen asked Dee as they sat with a brew each.

'Tomorrow will have to be soon enough. I'm properly washed out.'

They looked at each other. Before they knew it they were on their feet hugging each other and shedding tears.

'Mum,' Nicky said sleepily at the entrance to the kitchen.

'What are you doing up? The ambulance guy told you to rest up.'

'I'm bored.' Dee almost laughed. Her Nicky was deffo back to being himself. 'I'm going to watch some telly.'

When he'd left Jen got back down to business. 'But do you think he's gonna believe us?'

Dee shrugged. 'If Kieran does his part then this is a closed case.' She looked the picture of exhaustion. 'I just want this all done with so that—'

Nicky shouted from the lounge, 'Mum, you're going to wanna watch this!'

Dee and Jen filed into the front room and sat down. Nicky gestured at the screen with his thumb. 'It's that TV show *Inside Information*, where the law appeal for help solving crimes.'

'And?'

'They're asking viewers for help with Kieran's bullion job.'

There was a moment's stunned silence before Dee picked up the remote and turned up the volume.

A presenter did a spiel outside the private vault and there was a reconstruction of the robbery. All three of them agreed that the actor playing the leader of the gang was nothing like Kieran. The show then went to the studio where another TV bod interviewed the senior officer leading the investigation. In Dee's house, they were all hoping that he had no leads and wasn't closing in on the thieves. Thankfully, the cop didn't look like he was about to make any arrests any time soon. 'So this might have been an inside job?' the presenter asked him.

'We're confident that none of the staff were involved in this robbery.'

'Is there anything unique about this robbery that might jog the public's memory?'

The detective had a prop. He produced a crate and put it on the desk in front of him. 'The bullion was packed in crates, like this. Typically, the gang would have disposed of them and it's likely that they were destroyed. However, it's possible that if the thieves were disturbed or were careless, they might have dumped them somewhere. If they did that would be of real interest to us.'

'And I understand they have distinctive markings?'

The cop turned to a screen on which the markings were displayed. 'That's right. We understand they're army surplus and were originally bought second hand in the 1960s or '70s. As you can see in the photo they were stencilled, "Property of—"'

Dee and Jen didn't hear the rest because Nicky was on his feet. 'I've seen that before.'

'What?'

For once in his life he looked deadly serious. 'I think I know who the gold might belong to.'

* * *

Shoulders slumped, head down, Tiff walked across The Devil's Estate like a wounded animal. Shame dogged her every step. How could she have done that to Dee? She should've fessed up from the off about what Kieran wanted her to do. Might've even been able to come up with a plan to double cross him.

Tiff didn't feel like going to hers; she'd only have more 'we want our money back now' letters piling up against her front door. Instead, she was off to her mum's to lie down in the comfort of her old room.

'Alright Tiff.' Her head shot up to find Stacey coming towards her. Her one-time bestie was pushing her mum in a wheelchair.

The great Mel Ingram didn't look so great anymore. She was shrunken, head leaning slightly to the side, her rheumy eyes staring into space. Only her small finger moved in a hand curled like a claw in her lap. The finger stroked the blanket covering her legs, which was made of a furry material. She'd been such a tough old bird in her day, a woman Tiff had done her best to steer clear of. Now look at her. How the mighty had fallen. Tiff knew that feeling all too well.

'Wotcha Stace,' she said and out of respect to her mate added, 'Mrs Ingram,' but there was no flicker of response.

'You get that problem with those two goons sorted?' Stacey asked.

Tiff shuffled her feet. 'Yeah, but I did something stupid to get out of it.'

'Bad piling up on top of bad.' Stacey smiled wistfully. 'Yeah, I know all about that. Then I turned a corner. You ready to do that?'

Tiff cocked her head to the side. 'Let's just say that one of my sisters shoved me around one. Dunno if it's good or bad yet.'

Suddenly Mel Ingram pinned her watery eyes on Tiff. Her tongue was thick as she announced, 'Stan ... effing ... cunt ... of the year.' Then her head slumped to the side and she stared into nowhere again.

'You got that right,' Tiff whispered. Her dad had left his brand of badness on every life he'd touched, like an untrained tom spraying all over the gaff.

'Maybe we can go for a bevvy sometime,' Stacey asked tentatively.

Tiff grinned for the first time that day. 'Yeah. Yeah, let's do it.'

'Right, better be off.' Stacey stared down at her mum. 'Don't want you to catch cold, do we.' She looked back up at Tiff. 'Be seeing ya.'

Tiffany perked up slightly as she watched her friend walk away.

The Devil was still on its worst behaviour – music blasting from blocks, hard-faced kids up to no good at the entrance to Bridge House, a couple having a barney outside the offy – but some of the flats were privately owned with plants and flowers growing outside and bamboo blinds instead of curtains at the windows. Maybe it wasn't such a bad world after all, Tiff thought.

She climbed wearily to her mum's flat and used her key to go inside. Then went on high alert when she noticed the light coming from beneath the closed bathroom door. Probably squatters. That's all she needed. The council had allowed Babs to hold on to her home while she was banged up on the understanding that the rent was paid, which Dee had sorted out. On tiptoes Tiff crept into the sitting room, picked up a three-year-old bottle of gin by the neck and moved to the bathroom. She booted the door in. And staggered back.

'What the fuck you doing here Mum?'

Sixty

'Last I heard, this was still my home,' Babs answered irritably as she heaved herself out of the bath. First thing most inmates did when they got out of prison was have sex or eat their favourite meal or head to the nearest boozer to get liquored up. Not her. All she'd wanted to do was have a bath. She hadn't had one in three, long years. It had been heaven to scrub away the prison grime.

'Don't stand there gawking. Let me get a towel round meself.'

Her youngest turned away so she could sort herself out.

Tiff asked, 'You ain't gone over the wall?'

'If I have, you gonna shop me to the cops?' She heard Tiff suck in her breath. 'Make me a brew and I'll be with you in a mo.'

Tiff sniggered, 'Escape from Alcatraz,' as she went off to do her mum's bidding.

Babs got herself dry and in a dressing gown and slippers then went into the sitting room. She plonked herself next to Tiff on the settee and picked up her cuppa. She took a sip and let out a long sigh. 'Now that's what you call a cup of Rosie Lee. Inside the stuff was like ground earth.'

'Mum, can you stop with the tea commercial,' Tiff sharply cut in, 'and tell me what's bloody going on.'

Babs thought back to earlier that day. She thought she was done for when Mrs Morris had summoned her just as she'd been ready to step past the gate. How they'd known what she was about she didn't know. Maybe Knox had fingered her before she'd been shipped out.

'Miss, I'm sorry,' she'd pleaded with Mrs Morris. 'I didn't mean to—'

'The Governor wants you in her office.'

Babs had followed her, cursing herself from one side to the next. Trying to scarper by walking out of the gate – had she been off her flamin' trolley? Now Mrs Field was going to revoke her parole, and worse, probably top up her sentence for her shite escape attempt.

The Number One had peered over her glasses with a serious stare.

The words of regret had tumbled out of Babs' mouth. 'Miss, I know that—'

'Barbara, please take a seat.' That got her on her guard immediately. The Governor had never used her first name before.

She'd seated herself nervously. Her heart dropped as something occurred to her. What if this was sod all to do with her escape attempt and about one of her girls? Desperately, she'd leaned forward, breathless with worry. 'Has something happened to one of my girls? Oh God.' Her hand covered her mouth.

'No. It's nothing like that.' The governor had swallowed hard and for the first time Babs realised she was nervous as well. Why, she couldn't say. 'Your parole date has been brought forward.'

'What?'

Mrs Field linked her fingers together. 'You can leave today if that works for you? I know you've got a family waiting for you so we don't have the problem of finding you somewhere to stay . . .'

Babs had almost wept with joy. Finally, the day had arrived – she was going home.

Tiff stared at her with open confusion. 'Just like that,' she clicked her fingers, 'they let you waltz outta the door?'

Babs nursed her cuppa in her palms. 'Just like that. I was rolling out on my jam. I was out and about this afternoon. I've gotta wear a Peckham Rolex.' She pointed to her ankle to show her bulky electronic tag.

Tiff grinned. 'Mum, that looks the business. Can you take it off so I can send my mates a snap of me wearing it? It'll go really well with my skinny jeans.' She peered hard at her mum. 'Hold up, you said you ain't been in long, so where have you been all today?'

'Oh, nowhere,' Babs said breezily. 'I just walked around breathing in fresh air.'

'And how did you get back?'

Babs slammed her cup down. 'Never you mind about none of that. I wanna know what's been going on. From what I've been hearing, my girls have been at each others' throats like a pack of vampires. There's something going on and I wanna know what it is.'

Tiff looked everywhere other than at her mum. 'Like what? You got gate fever or something? The only thing on your mind should be that you're as free as a London pigeon breathing the same clean air as the rest of us.'

Babs shuddered. She never wanted to hear the word pigeon again.

The front door knocker went. Mother and daughter stared at each other.

Babs said, 'If it's any of my mates who think they spotted

me tell them they need an optician's appointment coz it weren't me, alright?'

Babs fretted as Tiff got up to answer the door. She was still gobsmacked about what had happened earlier, especially the sauce of planning to leg it just as they were going to release her.

Tiff reappeared in the doorway, her face chalk white. 'It's the plod . . .'

Before she could finish two female officers appeared behind her. Tiff stepped into the room to give them space. Babs got anxiously to her feet.

'Barbara Miller?' She nodded, the feeling in her belly getting worse. 'You need to accompany us to West End Central Police Station.'

Sixty-One

Nicky stuck his key into the door. When it opened he let his mum and his Aunty Jen in. The hallway was dark. He whispered, 'Let me get the light on so you can see.'

He found the switch and flicked it on. It bathed the hall in light. The Commander was standing on the third stair from the bottom. He wore an old silk dressing gown and slippers.

'Nicky my boy,' he hailed them. 'I'm so pleased that you're back. Flo was getting very upset. She's just stepped out to see some friends.' He moved down the stairs into the hallway. 'And who are these charming young ladies?'

But none of them were looking at him. They were staring at the large ship's bell.

A solemn Nicky pointed at it. 'See. That's what that crime show said was written on the crates. HMS *Grenada*.' They all looked at The Commander. Nicky carried on, 'And he was the commander of a ship with that name.'

An awful silence descended. Dee stepped forward. 'Did you own the gold that was robbed?'

The Commander seemed to grow taller as if steel had been inserted into his spine. His usual hunched appearance was gone. 'Did Frank McGuire let his mouth run away with him?'

Dee, Nicky and Jen froze. He fixed his steely blue eyes on

Dee. 'My condolences madam on the passing of your husband. Interesting character was John.'

The breath shuddered in Dee's body. 'Did you know him well?' She found the idea that this English gentleman of the old school had travelled in the same circles as her husband inconceivable. John's Alley Club had always been more of a hangout for celebs, footie stars and their WAGs. Nothing about this man fit. It terrified her and there wasn't much that made Dee Black want to run the other way.

'At one time, yes. I frequented his club in Soho and lost a lot of money to him at cards. That was a long time ago.' He paused for a moment.

'I don't understand,' she said. 'Nicky's been living here all the time, right under your nose. You never used him against me as leverage for the gold – which I'll say now I never had.'

His gaze darkened. 'I couldn't do that. He was a friend of my darling Flo and he made her laugh. If I'd done anything to Nicky she might have become sad again.'

Dee gulped. She had a very dangerous man on her hands. The only reason he hadn't made a move against Nicky was because he saw him as a puppy to keep his granddaughter cheery. It chilled her to the bone. No wonder Uncle Frank had told her that Carats wouldn't touch Nicky even though he could've anytime he wanted to.

'Would you like a drink? I've got some lovely white tea imported from Sri Lanka.'

This man was giving her the willies. 'Nah, thanks very much, we won't be stopping for long.'

His voice hardened. 'Then I think you need to state your business.' It was like he was back in command of HMS *Grenada*.

'Your gold's gone.'

'Has it now?'

'Kieran decided to hide it in his club, The Lock – the club Uncle Frank burned it down to the ground tonight in an effort to persuade Kieran to give it back. It all got melted in the inferno. Bit of a show-up for you really, don't you think?'

The Commander pursed his lips. 'I see.'

'You knew Uncle Frank back in the day as well, didn't you.' It wasn't a question but a statement of fact. 'No doubt a man in your position would insist on the best when it came to recovering his gold. And whatever his other faults, there's no doubt that Uncle Frank is the best man for a job like that.'

Finally the Commander fessed up. 'You'd have thought so wouldn't you? I should have known better than to trust a Cockney wide boy like that with such a sensitive task.'

'The gold's gone. Are you going to tell Uncle Frank to call his dogs off?'

The Commander was lost in thought. 'I want some evidence. I'm not a fool.'

'It's difficult to provide evidence of something that doesn't exist. Of course you're welcome to go over to The Lock and search through the ruins. No doubt you'll find melted gold in it. Or you can speak to Kieran. He'll tell you.'

'Where did the gold come from?' It was Nicky who asked, sounding mesmerised.

Dee didn't wait to hear the answer. The less they knew the better. She grabbed Nicky's hand. 'I hope that's the end of it,' she told The Commander.

She dragged her son and her sister out of a house she hoped never to set foot inside again.

Dee's mobile went off. She took the call and handed it to Jen with a confused look. 'It's for you.' Then she remembered that Jen had lost her mobile in the fire.

Dee got very concerned at how white Jen went as she listened.

When the call was over Dee asked, 'Who was that?'

'The Bill. They want me to come over. It's something to do with Courtney.'

As they rushed down the road they heard the bell of HMS *Grenada* tolling behind them.

The Commander stilled his hand against the bell to stop it ringing. His face didn't show it but he was raging inside. That gold had been his legacy for his darling Flo. He wasn't a poor man so there was still plenty to leave her but it was his special treat. The loss of it galled him. He grabbed the bell in anger, ripped it off the wall and with his whole might threw it on the beautifully tiled floor. The sound was deafening.

'Commander?' He looked up to find his cherished Flo on the stairs, Jezebel in her arms. 'I think you might need one of your pills.'

She was right. When he got like this it was not a pretty sight.

Flo and Jezebel joined him. 'It doesn't matter about the gold. I did try my hardest to find out if Nicky knew where it was.'

'I know you did my angel.' He cupped his hand around her cheek. When John's son had first arrived and it looked like he was going to leave, he'd called Flo downstairs. He'd told her all about the gold and that it was her job to see what the lad knew. She'd put on the charm and asked him to stay.

'Do you believe them?' she asked. 'Or do you think they're filling their boots up with it?'

'I don't know. If the gold's still out there we just have to wait. Someone will make a false move. It might be tomorrow, next year, the year after that. Whenever it happens we both need to be ready. And you, my precious, are going to worm your way into the hearts of the Miller family.'

His granddaughter started seething. 'Those Millers have got a lot to answer for. First my houses and now your gold—'

He kissed her on the cheek, halting her spitting words. 'Haven't I taught you that there's no point fussing and kicking up a storm when all you've got to do is keep your eyes on the prize and strike when the time is right?'

Flo let The Commander's words wash over her. Usually they would've soothed her, but not tonight. The Millers had made mugs out of her and the one man she still loved in this world. She relaxed against her granddad, making him believe all the anger had left her.

Flo kissed him on the cheek. 'I forgot, one of my mates has got something for me.' And before he could question her more she quickly grabbed her jacket and left the house.

Sixty-Two

The last, and only, time Babs had been in West End Central was back in '93 trying to save her fifteen-year-old daughter Tiffany from a life of crime. Now here they were again, this time the roles reversed.

'Come on fellas,' Babs begged the two officers who had escorted her and Tiff there, 'tell me why I'm here.'

One gave her the eye, but no answer, just like all the other times she'd asked on the way. She wasn't daft, she knew it had something to do with why she'd been released early, but what that something was . . . It was cracking her up inside not knowing.

They finally stopped walking down the station corridor. One of the cops opened a door. Behind it wasn't the small interrogation room Babs had been expecting, but a larger one with soft chairs. Part of one wall was a long mirror and in front of it was a cabinet with refreshments. Now she was even more curious. 'If you could please wait here,' the cop said.

Babs and Tiff walked inside, but Babs immediately turned back to the door. 'Look, you've gotta—' The door closed firmly in her face.

She almost banged her fists against it with pent-up frustration, but then remembered her broken finger. It was throbbing for the first time in days. Babs was scared. Very scared. Although she told herself things were on the up, there was something going on here that she didn't like; not one bit. Babs desperately wanted one of her pills to steady her frayed nerves.

She turned to Tiff. 'You ain't got some gear on ya?'

Her daughter's mouth fell open. 'Gear? Are you having a senior moment?' She lowered her voice as her eyes darted suspiciously around the room. 'Anyone could be listening. They might have them secret cameras. Plus, you know, I don't do that type of shit any—'

'Not even a bit of weed?' Babs butted in. If she didn't get some chemical assistance soon she was going to start screaming. 'I'm tearing me hair out here. My nerves are climbing the walls. I'm . . . I'm . . .' She couldn't finish; emotion clogged up her throat. She looked at her youngest with beseeching eyes. 'I'm fifty-three years old. All I want is a bit of peace and quiet to get on with my life.'

Tiffany took her mum's arm and got her sat down in a cosy chair facing the mirrored wall. She made two brews and joined her. 'If it were anything funny they would've arrested you at the flat,' she reasoned. 'Or here, as soon as you walked through the door.'

Babs cried, 'But why all the cloak and dagger then? Why won't they just spit it out and tell me what the heck I'm doing here?'

Tiff looked at her with a glint in her eye. 'Maybe they're gonna give you some compo for your broken finger. I had this mate once who got scratched by a rusty nail inside. She put in for some compo and left the big house with two large.'

'Don't be silly,' Babs snapped, her cold hands starting to warm up around the cup she held. 'I never put in—'

She jumped up, sloshing tea over her hand as the door began to open. Her heartbeat started galloping as three people were escorted into the room. 'What are you lot doing here?' she asked Jen, Dee and Nicky.

*　　*　　*

Next door, the man watched the tense family gathering through the two-way mirror. Now they were all here he thought of making his entrance. Instead he jammed his hands into his pockets and kept watching and listening, especially to Babs.

'Mum? What the hell's going on?'

'What you doing outta prison?'

Dee and Jen threw their questions in quick succession. 'They let me out early.' She sucked in her breath. 'Has someone got a nut tab, my head is bustin' something chronic.'

Dee sorted out her mum with a Paracetamol and they all sat down. Babs carried on, 'I don't understand why I'm here. Did the Bill tell ya?'

Jen's face fell. 'Courtney's here.' Her eyes grew wide. 'All they would say was they needed to talk confidentially. Mum I'm shitting myself, scared to death what it might be.'

Babs' feeling of hopelessness was replaced by anger. 'And where were you when she did a flit, eh? She's been telling me all about how your attention is taken up with Kieran. If he were here I'd give him a piece of my mind.'

Dee lowered her voice. 'When we get out of here I'll tell you chapter and verse about what's been going on.' She looked around the room. 'Walls have ears and all that, especially in a cop shop.'

'Hang on,' Tiff joined in, staring hard at Babs, 'when did you chat with Court? I thought you put the brakes on her coming up to see you?'

All eyes turned to Babs. She shuffled uncomfortably in her seat. 'Yeah, well, if you'd been keeping an eagle eye on her, she wouldn't have been able to visit me the other day using fake ID.' Babs struggled to her feet and cast an accusing eye at her gathered family. 'I don't know the full story of what's been going down these last few months, but Courtney gave me the headlines. And when what's happening here is done and dusted we're gonna have a family sit-down,' she jabbed her broken finger at them. 'The lot of–'

The door opened and all the words dried up in Babs' mouth when she saw the tall, distinguished man standing there. Nah, it can't be. She blinked a couple of times. *My eyes must be getting dodgy* . . . But there he was. All the years floated away.

'Tricky Dickie?' Her tone was dreamy. She couldn't get her head around this.

'Babs.'

She moved towards him as if they were the only two people in the room. Richard Smith, that's what she'd known him as, even though that wasn't his real name. The first time she'd seen him back in '78 he'd been a dead ringer for that fella who played Poldark on the telly. He was still a looker, but now with grey strands in his black hair and lifelines creasing his face. And those grey eyes of his were still intent with a soft centre. She'd only seen him once since then. The day she was arrested for murdering Stan. He'd visited her in the holding cell and given her the wise advice to keep her mouth shut until her brief got there. She swallowed and folded her arms tight. Was this something to do with her very dead ex? Was Stanley Miller going to keep haunting her from his rotting grave?

'Richard, I don't understand what's going on.'

Tiff jumped in with, 'Who's this geezer then?' She sniffed the air. 'I can smell a cop a mile off.'

Richard peered at Tiffany. 'You must be Tiffany. You were always screaming your head off as a kid.'

She went red. 'What business is it of yours what I do with my mouth?' With a flash of her eyes she dismissed him and turned to her mum. 'Who's this jester?'

Babs shifted to stand sideways, so she could keep an eye on the man from her past as well as her family. 'This is Richard

Smith ... I mean Patrick Johnson. We knew each other donkeys ago.' She couldn't help the blush that leaked across her cheeks. Oh, she'd known Tricky Dickie alright. 'He's a policeman—'

'Was,' he cut in. 'I've been retired for the best part of a year now.'

Dee stood up and, as usual, was the one who said it as it was. 'Let's cut through all the bullshit, mister ex-police officer. Just tell us why a top cop needs to see Babs and what this has to do with our Courtney.'

Patrick's gaze roamed over her face with wonder. 'You're Desiree. I was glad to hear that you and your mum reunited.' His gaze fixed on Babs' middle child. 'You must be Jennifer. Courtney's mother?' She got to her feet and nodded, her face very grave. 'I need to speak to you and your mum in private.'

Babs made up her mind that the time for secrets was over. She shook her head. 'Whatever you've got to say you'll say it to all of us.' Her gaze ran over the others. 'We're a family and whatever needs sorting we'll do it together.'

For the first time in three, long years Babs took her place as the head of the family.

Patrick took a seat facing Babs as Dee and Jen also sat back down. 'I'm here because my former colleagues know that I have a history with this family, in particular Babs and Stanley Miller.' Some in the room drew in their breaths sharply, but no one interrupted him. 'The last time I saw Babs was just after her arrest.' He switched his gaze onto Babs, his look filling her body with the coldness of winter. 'Babs, someone has stepped forward to say they murdered Stanley.'

Babs cringed as Dee called out, 'You what?'

A startled Tiffany added, 'What you going on about?'

'No, no, no,' a dazed Jen repeated over and over, sensing and dreading what was to come.

He carried on without emotion. 'Courtney contacted her counsellor and told her that she was ready to tell her about Nanna Babs. She told her that she killed her grandfather not Babs.'

Cries of dismay filled the room. Jen's face crumbled as she turned to confront her mum. 'Is this true?'

Babs didn't realise it but she was shaking her head again and again. 'Jen . . .'

'I want the truth Mum.' Jen's voice made an ugly, strangling sound in her throat. 'Now.'

Everyone's attention drilled into Babs. She felt like an animal that had been cornered. For a split second she thought about denying it, telling them all that Courtney was playing a joke on the lot of them. But she realised that if her family had any chance of knitting itself back together she was going to have to put the truth plainly on the table.

She licked her dry bottom lip. Then she spoke. Her mind rewound to the events of that awful day. 'It was my birthday. I'd just finished getting ready and was having a happy bop around the house to "Leader of the Pack", you know by the Shangri-las.' Eyes unseeing, she burst into song, her voice croaking. She was halfway through when she figured out which line she was singing – the one about feeling so helpless, what could she do. The strangest thing was everyone remained silent while her rusty voice filled the room, almost as if they recognised that this was the way the story had to be told.

Babs' mouth moved, but she couldn't sing the next line. 'I was singing it you see. Then someone knocks at the door and I think to myself, Oh my girls are here to take me out.' Her face clouded over. 'But when I opened the door it was Satan himself. Before I knew it Stan had pushed his way inside. He wanted me to sign those documents – you know the ones.' Her lip curled. 'He was such a greedy, selfish bloke. It took me years to realise that. I didn't know at the time but he was broke and those papers were his only chance to get his mitts on some quick cash.'

She forced herself to look at each of her daughters in turn, even though it made her tummy clench and burn. 'Those houses I'm selling belonged to him. Well, they did until he used that Stan trickery to sign them over to me. I didn't know it though. For years he had me down on my knees, cleaning his insurance policy. Now he wanted them back and all I had to do was sign his papers.'

She heaved in a deep punch of air, feeling like she was going to collapse. 'Do you want some water?' Richard asked quietly.

She waved a dismissive hand at him. She had to tell this all now; if she stopped she didn't think she would make it to the end. 'Anyway, one thing led to another and we started going at it. Before I knew what was what he had me on the floor with his hands around my throat—'

'Oh God, Mum.' That was Dee, but she ploughed on.

'He was squeezing the life outta me. He kept squeezing and squeezing . . . then all I felt was blood in my face. He topples over and . . . and . . .' she focused on Jen, 'and there was my beautiful Courtney, so brave, so scared, with my iron in her hand.'

Babs shot to her feet and pleaded with Patrick. 'She didn't mean to kill him. All she saw was this man she didn't know from Adam, choking me. What was she meant to do? Just let him go on with it?'

Now it was Jen's turn to stand, trembling, her eyes filled with unshed tears. 'You should've told me. She ain't been right since you got banged up and now I know why.' Her voice rose. 'She has nightmares all the time. What she must see when she closes her eyes. I could've helped her if you'd just told me. No wonder her mouth always turned down when she saw me ironing. It must've reminded her. '

Babs toughened her spine. 'Don't you get it? Stanley Miller was my grief to bear. That's why I kept him well away from you and Tiff. Dee as well. God if you knew what he'd done to me and Dee. It was best everyone believed it was me that did him in. If I let on about what really had gone on Courtney would've been locked up in one of those places for naughty girls. My little princess hasn't got one bad bone in her body. So we made a pact. It was our secret. And I'd make the same decision again in a heartbeat.' She desperately switched her attention to Patrick. 'She won't get into trouble will she?'

Patrick sighed. 'Now the truth's out, that isn't going to be my decision to make. But I'll say this with my cop cap on, it's a good thing that she stepped forward. I know you did what you did with the best of intentions but it was eating that little girl alive Babs. She's got a drinking habit because of it; she thinks it helps her sleep. Children shouldn't have to deal with such horrible things on their own.'

The door opened. Another policeman stepped inside and called Patrick over. They left the room and a terrible silence descended over everyone. Babs couldn't meet Jen's eyes as guilt ate into her.

When Patrick came back inside Babs could tell by the strain and paleness of his face that something was wrong. She got to her feet. 'What's going on?'

Jen stood up too. 'Can I see my daughter?'

Patrick addressed the room like he was back in his commander brass and stripes. 'My colleague has just taken a call from social services. Two social workers were driving her to a temporary foster home when she did a runner.' Jen gasped. 'No one can find her.'

Sixty-Three

'Trouble is, where would a thirteen-year-old girl on the run go?' an exhausted Tiffany asked.

It was almost one in the morning and she was sitting with her equally shattered sisters and mum in Babs' sitting room. The atmosphere was filled with desperation. They couldn't find Courtney. They'd called her mates – no joy. Trawled every nook and cranny on The Devil – no joy there either. They'd even gone down the dreaded Bridge House but no one knew nish. She'd vanished into thin air.

To say Jen was wrung out was putting it mildly. She was living every parent's nightmare of their child going missing. All she kept seeing in her head were the terrible things that might be happening to her girl, dragged off the street by a group of pervy men and ... Jen quickly covered her mouth, frightened that she was going to chuck up.

'Lovey, you alright?' her mum asked, her face filled with worry.

Jen looked at each member of her family and for the first time in forever she felt grateful for them. Grateful that she had them to lean on as she went through the worst ordeal a mum could ever face. She knew that they were expecting her to crack and crumble, bless 'em. The old Jen certainly would've by now, but not this new, reborn Jen. Her emotions were tearing her apart, but she made sure she didn't let it show. When she had Court safe and secure in her arms again, that would be the time to break down and cry. And she would find her daughter. She silently prayed that when that happened she wouldn't be looking at her girl's dead body.

Jen swept that last dreaded thought aside. 'You should know where a thirteen-year-old on the run would go Tiff; you were one often enough.'

Tiffany gave a wry grin. 'Most times it was down the ol' cemetery. I told Court all about the naughties I got up to but the young ones don't really hang there since that education centre was built.'

Dee stood up in frustration. 'She's got to be somewhere.'

Babs gazed at them sadly. 'This is all my fault, ain't it? I should have told the truth from the off . . .'

Dee cut her off. 'This is no time for a wander down a street called *What If*. We can all do that trip when we've got Courtney safely home—'

'There's one place we haven't thought of looking,' Nicky piped up.

The darkness enveloped Flo as she stood outside the houses in Mile End. She had what looked like a doctor's bag gripped between her fingers and a holdall over her shoulder. Her knuckles were white with fury. She looked at her dad's properties, which she'd set out to win back in her old man's honour. It was a matter of principle. She'd lost and the Millers had won. But that battle was over. Now it was time for revenge.

She walked up the steps of 9 Bancroft Square and ran a finger over the door lock. She had no key but she had something just as good. From her holdall, she pulled out a sledgehammer and with an evil grin she let fly at the door with savage blows. The freshly painted wood splintered, cracked and warped before finally giving way. The door swung open and Flo stepped into the hall with the sledgehammer resting on her shoulder. She put on the lights and wandered up and down, wondering where to start. The banister, carefully restored to its original glory, wound her up for a start. She took the sledgehammer to it, knocking out its supports until it collapsed under its own weight.

'I'll teach those people to fuck around with Stanley Miller's girl.'

She'd considered burning the houses down but that ran the risk that the Millers might think it was accidental. There was going to be nothing accidental about the scene when they turned up to check out their winnings. The whole place was going to be trashed. She fished around in her doctor's bag and found a claw hammer and machete. She went from room to room, slashing furniture and fittings with her blade and digging lumps out of the plaster with her hammer. She paid particular attention to the period features. Around the fireplaces were the original Georgian tiles. They'd been painted over during the joint's spell as a knocking shop but the builders had carefully restored them so they looked as they must have done when the place was first built. With careful aim, Flo shattered or cracked each one in turn. When she'd done she stood back and admired her handiwork. 'What do you think, Dad? I think they'll need a trip down Homebase, don't you?'

But even as she whacked her hammer for the final blow, she felt the power in her arm weakening. What was the point of this? The Millers were selling the house, not the features. The kind of tosser who bought a place like this would soon fix the repairs with the change they lost out of their trouser pockets and didn't notice.

She remembered the final words of her old dad on the phone before he'd gone to his death at the hands of his 'wife'.

'Don't worry babe, I'm going to have a word with Babs about the houses. I'll make her see reason. She ain't a bad person. We'll get 'em back.'

Flo had had a bad feeling about this visit. 'Be careful Dad.'

He'd laughed. 'Oi! This is your ol' man talking! Take more than some ol' East End slapper to get the better of me! Don't worry about it, I'll call you later.'

But he never had called her later. The next time she'd seen him was at the morgue. And then his killer had got off, or five years which amounted to the same thing.

Flo felt her fists clenching around the hammer. She looked around. 'Right. Let's have these carpets up. They'll cut into nice strips.'

She pulled the high-end carpets up from their fittings in the back reception room. Flo reared back when she found a trap door under the carpet in one corner. She yanked it up by the iron ring in the middle. She tugged on it and when it opened she saw there was a flight of steps leading down to a room below. After switching on a light, she peered inside to see a collection of old furniture scattered around. The coverings had been torn. 'What the fuck?'

Then she looked up with a start. Through the open front door, she heard a set of panicking voices. She'd only chosen to do this now was because no one would be around.

Shit! She wasn't going to be able to make her escape now. On tiptoes she eased into the underground room and closed the door. She looked upwards as she heard footsteps above. And then they started coming closer and closer. The footsteps hit the stairs leading to her. Torchlight flashed down towards her. She saw legs and then faces. She shielded her eyes with her hand as the torchlight was deliberately beamed into her face.

'Well, well, well,' a familiar voice said. 'Given up on scamming people and cradle snatching and taken to smashing up houses instead?'

A furious Babs stepped ahead of Dee and looked with murder in her eyes at her dead former husband's daughter. 'What the fuck are you doing in my house? Did you do all that damage upstairs? Coz if you have I'm gonna—'

'Your house?' Flo spat. 'I think you mean my dad's houses.'

Babs bristled back, 'Legal paperwork says different—'

'You conned me out of my dad's property and the way you've been carrying on since would make the Corleone family look like a boy band. Why the hell aren't you in prison?' Her eyes grew wild. 'They should've locked you up for the rest of your life and thrown away the key.'

Tiff wasn't having that. 'You hold up a minute. You fancy-talking turd, *our* dad tried to strangle *my* mum and she should've never been doing bird in the first place. They should've pinned a medal on her.'

Dee was the only one who didn't let the rising temperature get to her. 'Even if you think the houses are yours by rights, what are you doing trying to destroy them?'

The younger woman clamped her mouth shut. Dee moved closer. 'It's all starting to fall into place. Did your granddad send you here looking for gold?' Her eyes roamed around the space near Flo. 'Looks like you've come up empty.' She folded her arms. 'Or did you come here with malicious intent to trash the houses?'

'It's just one more thing you Millers have stolen from my family.' Her raging gaze swept her sisters. 'I deserved *something*. My whole life I've had to live knowing my dad had a first family. How did you think that made me feel? Flo Miller, always second best. Even though he cut out on you when you were young he was always saying, I wonder what my Tiffany or Jennifer are doing. Those girls are going to make me dead proud one day. Anything he wanted me to do, I did it. Came and stayed with him in Spain so he had a hostess for his business meetings. Begged and stole from my mother so he didn't have to go without when he had cash flow problems. Went along with his plans when he came back for the houses.' Her voice cracked, hot tears shimmering in her eyes. 'And not once, not once did he ever say he was proud of me. I was the daughter that stayed with him, made sure he was looked after ...' She started shaking. Her body bent double and Florence Miller, for one of the first times in her life, lost control and started sobbing.

The sound was so wrenching that the others couldn't help but feel their hearts breaking for her. Even Tiff, who had zero respect for con artists in general and Flo in particular, was moved. As an on-off scam merchant herself she knew when someone was faking and Flo wasn't. The agonising sound she made could only come from someone whose very heart was being ripped open. But what to do? She was still Stan Miller's wrong-side-of-the-blanket daughter.

And maybe because Dee understood all about growing up that way, she was the one who gingerly approached the crying Flo. She reached out to touch her, but then her hand fell away. 'Look girl.' Flo raised her tear stained face to her. 'I know you don't want to think your old man was a wrong'un – who does, eh? – but that's exactly what Stanley Miller was. He might've been giving it the big 'un about being well chuffed about Tiff and Jen, but the geezer was lying out of his back hole. How would he know the first thing about 'em? He didn't bring 'em up, weren't around when they had to go through the ups and downs of life.' She put her hand on Flo's shoulder, waiting for her to shrug it off, but she didn't. 'They haven't had it easy, but you know what, I think they caught a lucky break. It sounds like you're the one who got the crap end of the stick, having to put up with his demands and yeah, I'm gonna say it, evil.

'I think he deliberately poisoned you against Babs. I know you feel shitty towards her, but I swear on the baby I'm carrying that she killed him in self-defence.' The story of what Courtney had done was going to stay in the family, no one else had to know. 'Think, what would you have done if you'd gone home to find his hands around your mum's throat? The Commander's neck?'

Flo gazed at her and stepped back. She wiped the tears from her eyes. 'I did love him.' Her voice sounded so alone in a room filled with people.

'I know,' Babs conceded. 'I loved him too. Once. But there comes a time in your life when you have to see a person as they really are, not what you want them to be.'

'Mum?' Jen said softly. 'We still need to find Courtney.'

Flo looked concerned. 'Has something happened to your daughter?'

Jen caught her lip, still unsure about Flo, but she finally admitted, 'She's done a runner. We came to see if she's hiding here.'

'I've been here for ages and not heard anything, but then I've been buried down here.'

'Right.' Tiff got back onto their main business. 'Let's check the rest of the house.'

'Can I help too?' Flo asked shyly.

Dee, Tiff and Jen all looked uncertainly at their mum. She was head of the family and they were going to leave the decision to her. Babs smiled at Flo, something she never thought she'd do. She finally figured out that it wasn't this young woman she hated, but what she represented – Stan's bigamous marriage. Every time she saw Flo or heard her name she suffered through the pain and shame it had caused her all over again. Stan had used Flo for his own gain, just like he'd done to Babs. 'Come on then love.'

As they set off, Babs pulled Dee aside. 'That below stairs room never used to be there. What did your husband have his workmen doing?'

Dee came clean with her. 'I think he was planning on hiding the gold here. I don't know where it is now and I don't want to know.' She placed her palm on her mum's arm. 'And truth be told, Mum, I'm glad. All that gold ever did was bring misery to our doors. And, I suspect, it cost my John his life.'

Sixty-Four

For ten minutes, the house rocked to the sound of doors being banged and rooms being searched. Then Babs called out from the attic. The other women hurried upstairs. They found it empty but Babs gestured through a door leading onto a roof balcony. There were tubs of plants there but no sign of the missing girl.

Until finally, like a child playing hide and seek, a face appeared over the top of one of the tubs. At last they'd found Courtney.

Back in Babs' sitting room, Jen and Courtney wept hard tears as they clung onto each other for dear life. Dee and Babs were tearful too; Tiff's raw emotions were only evident in the wobble of her mouth. The one member of the search party who wasn't present was Flo. As much as Babs understood why Flo had acted the way she'd done, allowing her into her home was a step she hadn't been willing to take. Not yet anyway. After they'd discovered Courtney, a solemn Flo had gone back to The Commander's home. It turned out that Courtney had used a stanley knife to cut out a window pane in the back of the house. Her nan shook her head; she was only thirteen and already knew how to break into a house!

'We need to go,' Patrick Johnson said softly. Babs had called him as soon as they'd got back to The Devil.

Jen pulled her wet face away from her daughter, and pleaded, 'But she's just a child. She only did it because he was hurting Mum. Why do you have to take her away?' Courtney clung tighter.

'I wish I didn't have to take her,' he admitted, 'but we need to clear this business up, once and for all.'

'Is Courtney going to get locked up?' Babs asked, fear changing her face into a mask of horror.

Patrick looked her in the eye. 'Let's not make any assumptions. Let's stick with what we have to do and that's get Courtney back for another chat.'

Jen collected her and her daughter's coat. Courtney flew into her Nanna Babs' arms.

'Nan I'm sorry, I couldn't keep our secret any longer.'

Babs caressed her beautiful hair. 'I know pet, I know. It was wrong of me to ask you to. Now you tell the whole truth and you'll be back home before you know it.'

A minute later the door closed behind Jen, Courtney and Patrick Johnson. A shattered Babs had her arms locked around the waists of her other daughters for support. God she was so afraid, so afraid that what she'd promised her brave Courtney wasn't true – that she wouldn't be coming home soon.

The following afternoon, a bone-weary Babs was relaxing on the settee having a G&T. She didn't want to get up when she heard the knock at her door. She put her glass down, slipped her feet into her slippers.

She opened up and didn't smile at the person outside. 'I thought you'd come around sooner or later,' she told Kieran.

He was excited and eager. 'Get your coat. I told you that I was gonna take you for a bit of nosh. I've booked a table at this floating Chinese restaurant near Canary Wharf. You won't believe it, but they do a bang-up . . .'

She let him rabbit on as she ran her gaze over him, desperately searching for the boy she'd known all those years ago. Her heart flipped; there was no trace of her little Kieran left.

Babs held up her palm wearily and his words froze on his tongue. 'Kieran, that ain't gonna happen.'

His brows met in confusion. 'Whatcha chatting on about? We agreed to do this.'

'And we agreed that you would leave my girls alone.'

'Ah, come on Babs.' He inched forward like he was trying to get inside but she blocked his path. Stunned, he moved back.

'You know why I didn't want them to get to know you. And I was right. As soon as you opened the door to that wicked world you live in there's danger on every one of their doorsteps.' He opened his mouth, but she raised her finger to stop him. 'All that badness is down to you. I know John didn't behave like no saint—'

'You got that right,' he punched in, showing some rebellion.

'I admit that my girls were already at each other's throats, but you took advantage of that for your own selfish reasons. Dee could've died in that accident. You preyed on Jen's desperation to get money for her kids' future. You had Tiff spying on her own sister. And what you did to Nicky . . .' She shook her head sadly. 'The truth is I don't know you anymore.'

He pleaded, 'Of course you know me. I might not be wearing a plaster to correct my lazy eye now but it's still the same ol' me.'

She shook her head sorrowfully. 'But I don't know you. You tried to get me roughed up inside.'

He looked outraged. 'Are you losing your marbles or what? I wouldn't touch you in a million years. That weren't down to me, probably Frank McGuire's way of putting pressure on Dee.'

'I'm glad that wasn't you.' Babs' next words hurt her chest. 'You'll be my boy no matter what, but my girls will always come first. It took me a long time to realise that I can't have all of you.' The pain she saw in his face almost made her cry but she held it back. 'I'll always love you, but I can no longer be there for you. The sad thing is, Kieran, you've started to remind me of Stan.'

Babs took a step back and closed the door in his face. She leaned her forehead against it. Daggers of agonising pain pierced her heart.

EPILOGUE: 2007

'All this bad blood that Stan left has got to end.'

Sixty-Five

'Nan, Mum says get a move on! We're gonna be late.'

Babs scrambled to get her foot into her shoe as she heard her granddaughter's voice through the open letterbox. 'I'll be there in a mo,' she shouted back. She walked over to the mirror and checked her appearance. She was wearing a gorgeous rich-purple knot dress with diamantes round the neckline. Babs wasn't one for going to the hairdressers too often but for this occasion she'd got her hair specially done.

She picked up her handbag and walked past Tiff's room. Her youngest was back living with her again. She wouldn't tell Babs what had happened, but she figured her youngest hadn't kept up with the rent. Mind you, she'd always thought there was something fishy about Tiff's gaff in the first place. Whatever the story, her girls were welcome to come home anytime. Babs picked up speed. When she opened the front door she found a smiling Courtney waiting for her.

'You look lovely Nanna,' Courtney beamed.

Babs' heart lurched when a dreadful *been here, done that* feeling hit her. Jen sending Courtney to fetch her was how her innocent granddaughter had got caught up in the net of all that terrible business. Babs wasn't a praying woman but she thanked God every day that the law hadn't pressed any charges against Courtney. 'Not in the public interest,' was the outcome.

It hadn't been so sweet and easy though. Courtney had been kept in a girls' care home for a week before the decision had been made. That had been a really trying time. Jen and Little Bea had stopped at Babs' because Jen had been such a wreck. Babs knew that they would've never had this result if it weren't for Tricky Dickie. He wouldn't admit that he'd spoken up for Courtney, but she knew he'd done it.

After Courtney was back home, Patrick had come knocking with a bunch of gorgeous flowers and had, to her gobsmacking surprise, asked her out. Yeah, Poldark had asked her out. Alright, a Poldark with a touch more grey hair and creased skin. He was the type of man Babs felt she deserved after all these years of despair and turmoil. Kind, loving, a good laugh and, most importantly of all, he'd gone out of his way for her in times of trouble. But she'd turned him down flat. The reason was simple – he was a cop. He might be retired, but once a cop always a cop. Living on The Devil and having a policeman as your fella just wasn't going to cut it. So she'd let the best man she'd ever known go and her heart was still trying to mend.

Babs banished the past as she ran her eyes over Courtney. 'You look a picture lovey.'

Still grinning, Courtney caught her hand and they made their way downstairs, across the estate, over Mile End Road and towards number 9 Bancroft Square. Rihanna's 'Umbrella' pumped out of the open windows. The christening party to celebrate the newest member of the Miller clan was in full swing. Babs and Courtney shared a smile full of sunshine and happiness and then started dancing up the stairs to the rhythm of the music.

'Nanna you can really bust some moves,' Courtney said with disbelieving appreciation.

'I've got a pair of legs ain't I?' Babs threw back and did a little spin at the door that had her granddaughter giggling like crazy. It was so good to hear Courtney laugh. Even though she hadn't got done for Stan's murder, there was still something about her that troubled Babs. That light of innocence in her eyes seemed to have blown away for ever. Babs prayed for the day it would come back. All her wonderful granddaughter needed was time, Babs reassured herself.

Jen opened the door. 'You took your sweet time Mum.' Her daughter still wore the cropped hairdo Babs wasn't sure about. It gave her once gentle girl an edge of hardness she didn't care for. But at least Jen seemed to have more money these days, although where that was coming from Babs didn't know. Jen had jacked in her job at the supermarket.

The main room was packed with well-wishers including Tiff and Nicky, who was doing his DJ routine at the music system he'd hired. Babs was surprised to see Cleo dancing away; she usually disapproved of anything that wasn't God's music. And she was really going for it, even though she clutched a small Bible in her hand. Shaking her head with amusement Babs turned away with eyes for just two people – her Dee cuddling her newest grandchild. She made a beeline straight for them.

'Mum,' Dee let out, her voice catching with emotion. It was an emotional moment for the both of them. That Dee was sitting here was a miracle twice over. Firstly because she had the baby she never thought she'd hold to her breast. And mother and daughter had been separated for most of their lives. Now look at them, three generations together.

Babs leaned down to kiss Dee on the cheek and her eyes lit up as they turned to baby Nathan – who, in typical East End tradition, people had already shortened to Natty. Babs took him into her arms with the gentlest care and looked down at him with reverence and pure joy. He was much lighter than Dee and had mostly straight wisps of brown hair with a slight flick at the end. Everyone kept telling Dee he was a dead ringer for John, Babs suspected out of respect to him, but she just couldn't see it. When Natty's green-brown eyes were open her breath stilled in her throat. He reminded her so of her father George.

Babs looked at Dee. 'He's the most beautiful person I've ever seen. So precious.'

Dee's puffed up proudly. 'He's the spit of John.'

Babs frowned. There was something about the way her eldest spoke that didn't feel right. She was about to ask her about it when she heard Tiff angrily call out, 'What the heck are you doing here?'

Jen spat out, 'Turn around and go back the way you came. The cheek of it.'

Silence fell in the room and every eye turned to the newcomer. When she clocked who it was Babs could've slapped her forehead; she'd forgotten to tell Dee.

Babs quickly handed Natty back to his mum, as Dee asked, 'Mum, what's going on?'

Babs left her and walked over to the unwelcome visitor – Flo Miller. Babs took her arm and guided her to the middle of the room. She knew that some in the room weren't going to take this well, but she was head of this family and had made a decision. And what she had to say needed to be said public-ally so everyone got it into their noodle. She coughed and started. 'Right, as everyone knows, Florence here was my ex-husband's daughter from another relationship.' She heard Tiff bristle, but wasn't deterred. 'Now whatever Stanley may have done wasn't this girl's fault. He pulled her strings just like he did the rest of us. Me and Flo here have met a few times and all she wants is a chance to get to know her other family—'

'She ain't getting to know me,' Tiffany protested and stalked over to the drinks table.

Babs took not a blind bit of notice. Her youngest had been giving the two-finger salute to anything she didn't get her way about since she could remember.

She continued, 'All this bad blood that Stan left has got to end. Anyone who don't like it can hit the door.' She waited. No one moved. 'Good.' She gave Flo her full attention. 'Now, come and meet my baby Natty.'

Ten minutes later Babs hushed the party, her beloved grandchild nestled in her arms. Nicky cut the music as everyone's attention turned to her. Babs stood up and addressed the room again.

'I want to thank everyone for making this such a great turnout and welcoming my grandson to the family. But his family isn't just his mum, aunts and me; it's all of you in this room. Family are the people you can turn to when you need a little help, a shoulder to cry on, a supporting hand.' There was a murmur of agreement around the room. 'That's how we've always done it in the East End. It's one of the things that makes us special. We might not have a lot of dosh but our community spirit is priceless.'

Aunty Cleo cried out like she was in church, 'You tell it Sister Babs.'

And she did. 'I came to Mile End when I was a teenager expecting Natty's mum.' Her loving eyes found Dee. 'I'm not gonna lie – life weren't easy. I lost a lot but I gained a lot of mates. And without them I don't know how I would've got through the tough times.' She looked down at her grandson adoringly. 'And that's what our Natty's going to need, people around him to get him through the tough times . . .'

Suddenly there was the screech of car wheels outside. Nicky peeped out of the window and turned back with a shocked face. 'It's the cops.'

*　　*　　*

'You've got the nerve of the Devil bursting in here like this,' Dee seethed at the lead cop in the doorway of the main room.

There had been uproar when a van load of plod had arrived. Despite their warrant, Dee was barring their entrance into the room.

'Are you Mrs Barbara Miller?' the officer asked.

'Dee,' Babs said quietly, 'stand aside and let me find out what all the fuss is about.'

Her daughter threw daggers at the detective before kissing her teeth and getting out of his way. Babs took her place. 'What can I do for you officer?'

'Are you the owner of number 9 and number 10 Bancroft Square?'

'Course she is, you Muppet in blue,' Flo called out. 'What do you think, she's in the habit of breaking into other people's houses and having a shindig?'

'Florence,' Babs pleaded. She turned her attention back to the policeman. 'I'm Barbara Miller and I own this house and the one next door.'

He handed her a piece of paper and announced for all to hear, 'We have evidence to show that both houses were purchased with monies obtained from illegal activities by your former husband, one Stanley Miller. The houses are being seized under the Proceeds Act of 2002.'

She stared at him gobsmacked. 'What do you mean?'

'Both properties no longer belong to you. They are now assets in the hands of the Metropolitan Police.'

The party turned into a gathering of very angry people.

Babs let out a very heavy sigh as she finally kicked off her shoes at midnight. The party had almost turned into an open brawl as people turned against the cops. The girls and Flo had been outraged and were at the centre of the disturbance. Only

Babs' calling order and giving the police the keys had put a stop to it. She knew that her daughters had been hurt that she'd thrown in the towel, no doubt watching their inheritance going down the pan.

She listened to make sure there was no sound coming from Tiff's room before she pulled her mobile out and made the call.

'Tricky Dickie,' she said quietly, 'thanks big time.'

There was a pause before he said, 'Are you sure about this?'

She said with steely determination. 'This is the right thing to do. Those houses have only brought trouble and division and I need the girls and Stan's daughter to think they're gone for ever.'

'What are you going to do if your kids ever find out you got me to get the ball rolling on this criminal assets seizure?'

'They won't find out, unless you blab.'

'I'll do the paperwork.'

The raid had been real but not real. She'd asked Richard – that's how she'd always think of him – to organise the seizure but sort the paperwork so they remained in her hands. What she was going to do with them she didn't know. But they'd only brought misery to her daughters' lives. And with them out of the way Flo could really get to know her new family. 'We could go on a cruise together if you sold those houses.' Richard kept telling her to go out with him and to use the houses to change her life.

And strangely she told him, 'I might just do that. Watch this space.'

For the first time in years Babs felt the control Stanley Miller still held over her slipping away.

Sixty-Six

The next day Babs got off the Number 25 bus at its final stop in Ilford and spent the next five minutes looking for the block of flats she was after. This wasn't a part of town she was familiar with but Jen had taken her out there for a day of retail therapy at the shopping centre.

In the end she had to ask a stranger, who was happy to point her in the right direction. The block was single storey, small and white with gleaming windows. It looked like a nursing home, which it was in a way. The council had built it to house some of their older residents.

Babs pressed the intercom. There was a buzzing sound and a female voice asked, 'Can I help you?'

When she gave the name of the person she'd come to visit there was another buzzing sound and a click as the door came away from its automatic lock. Babs entered a clean reception area that smelt as if it had just been cleaned, a vase of gorgeous flowers on a tall table.

A middle-aged woman appeared with a cheery expression on her face. 'She's in flat six, along the corridor.' She pointed the way.

Babs knocked at the door and her one-time prison neighbour Pearl opened the door. 'Babsie girl, my old eyes are glad to see you.'

Pearl had on a dressing gown and her silver bangles jangled together. As Babs stepped forward the other woman stopped her.

'What are you doing?' Babs asked.

'I've got to run some energy over you, just in case you're bringing evil spirits along for the ride.' Pearl huffed, 'Them evil spirits can be really sneaky. Once they're in they're like squatters and it's hard to move them out.'

As Pearl raised her hands Babs batted them away and pushed inside. 'We don't have time for none of that clap trap. Show me where it is.'

Muttering under her breath Pearl closed the door and took Babs into a cosy, compact sitting room. They moved to the battered looking beige settee and started pulling off cushions and peeling back the lining. Babs couldn't help gasping as she stared at the piles of gold bars.

Her mind shot back to the call she'd received from Pearl in her cell.

'Have you cleaned Stan Miller outta my houses?' she asked.

'Well kind of.'

Why couldn't anything be easy peasy with this woman? 'What did you find? The Devil's firstborn living in the attic?'

Pearl's voice hushed. 'Much more valuable than that. I found gold.'

The old bird really was losing the plot. 'Pearl, you been on the Jamaican Woodbines again?'

'Listen.' Her voice became more urgent. 'I cleansed upstairs and then went downstairs. As soon as the builders saw me they got on with their work elsewhere. Although I don't mind telling you that they were really going off for a quiet drink . . .'

'Get on with it. I'm on the clock here.'

'That's when I noticed there was something strange about the reception room, you know the one near the kitchen.' She wheezed, then added triumphantly, 'The carpet in the corner was a bit rumpled so I bent to straighten it and Babsie, you wouldn't believe it, there was this door. So I says to myself, Babs told me to cleanse the whole place, top to bottom, so I pulled it back and found some stairs. There was another room. Strange thing was there was all this banged-up furniture inside.'

'I never told the workmen to build another room.'

'I don't know about that Babsie. Anyhow, seeing as it was so peaceful I decided to put my legs up on the settee. My varicose veins were giving me hell. As soon as I sat down I knew something was wrong. I took off one of the cushions and noticed some of the stuffing was missing. When I peered inside there it was – gold . . .'

To say Babs was shocked was the understatement of the year. She'd known immediately that the gold came from the robbery Dee told her John and Kieran had pulled. She'd wanted to get rid of it, but Pearl had other ideas.

'I'm an old lady with a crap pension,' Pearl had said, her voice very hard indeed, reminding Babs she was dealing with a woman who knew a thing or two about the underworld. 'I want a slice of the action. I've always dreamed of building a house back in Jamaica.'

Babs had been outraged. 'No way.'

'Suit yourself. I'll get someone else to do it and spread it around that you knew where it was all the time.'

The crafty old bitch. If word got out that would put her girls in the frame. So she'd agreed and when she'd come out on parole, instead of going straight home she'd had Pearl pick her up in a removals van with two of her sons. They'd gone to the house and removed the settee. When Pearl's sons had complained about the weight she'd hoodwinked them with some BS about keeping her Madam Pearl knickknacks inside for safe keeping.

They'd decided to wait six months, until there was less heat out there before discussing what to do next.

'So what we going to do with it?' Pearl asked, bringing Babs back to the present.

'Dunno. I'm going to need to think.'

Pearl straightened up in a way that had Babs' mouth falling open. She hadn't realised the other woman could do that. She squinted. There was so much about Pearl she didn't know.

'Well we need to get our skates on,' Pearl said firmly. 'We can't keep it here much longer. You don't know Frank McGuire and The Commander the way I do.'

Babs was shocked. 'You know them?'

Pearl twisted her mouth. 'The stories I could tell you about Uncle Frank. And as for Jimmy Fullerton-Green . . .'

'Jimmy who?'

'The Commander. That's his real name . . .' She let it hang suggestively in the air. 'So, Babsie girl, what are you going to do with that gold?'

Babs shook her head. 'The truth, Pearl? I don't know.'

acknowledgements

Mega thanks as ever to my fabulous agent Amanda, editor Ruth and all the Hodder crew.

In the best books, the ending often comes as a shock.
Not just because of that one last twist in the tale,
but because you have been so absorbed in their world,
that coming back to the harsh light of reality is a jolt.

If that describes you now, then perhaps you should track down
some new leads, and find new suspense in other worlds.

Join us at www.hodder.co.uk, or follow us on
Twitter @hodderbooks, and you can tap in to a
community of fellow thrill-seekers.

Whether you want to find out more about this book,
or a particular author, watch trailers and interviews, have
the chance to win early limited editions, or simply browse
our expert readers' selection of the very best books,
we think you'll find what you're looking for.

And if you don't, that's the place to tell us what's missing.

We love what we do, and we'd love you to be part of it.

www.hodder.co.uk

@hodderbooks

HodderBooks

HodderBooks